D0812716

Can You Keep A Secret?

KAREN PERRY

LIBRARIES N
WITHDRAWN FROM STOCK

PENGUIN BOOKS

PENGUIN BOOKS

UK | USA | Canada | Ireland | Australia
India | New Zealand | South Africa

Penguin Books is part of the Penguin Random House group of companies
whose addresses can be found at global.penguinrandomhouse.com.

First published in Great Britain in Penguin Books 2017

001

Text copyright © Karen Perry, 2017

The moral right of the author has been asserted

Set in 13.6/16.9 pt Garamond MT Std
Typeset by Jouve (UK), Milton Keynes
Printed in Great Britain by Clays Ltd, St Ives plc

A CIP catalogue record for this book is available from the British Library

ISBN: 978–1–405–92033–9
TPB ISBN: 978–1–405–92035–3

www.greenpenguin.co.uk

Penguin Random House is committed to a
sustainable future for our business, our readers
and our planet. This book is made from Forest
Stewardship Council® certified paper.

Prologue

Night has entered the house. Crept in like an intruder.

Outside, crows gather in the trees. Sharp beaks jab at unseen feathers.

Beyond the window, the black outline of the avenue beckons. You feel your way in the dark. The floorboards creak. The surfaces of the room are blindly unfamiliar. The house around you feels vast, empty. Where are the others?

Your hands reach out and find the door, fumbling for the handle. You realize that you are trembling. That's when you hear it again – a sharp crack echoing through the silence, a shot fired in the rooms below. This time you are sure. Your breathing snags in your chest. Blood pounds in your ears. You try to be still, struggling to listen.

The dark pushes up against you, thick and oppressive. The crows in the trees cease their flutter and call.

Someone is on the stairs.

Panic grips you by the throat. You take a step backwards. On the floor about your feet, the pictures lie scattered. The footfall is drawing closer.

You stare hard at the door as it opens, straining for a chink of light, but there is no familiar silhouette. Night has crept into the hallway.

You say a name, but there is no answer.

You hear the shallow breathing approach and the knowledge plunges through you like a dead weight. You know – you are sure of it: you should not have come back to this house. A reckless decision. Ill conceived, ill-judged, and – you are certain of it now – fatal.

PART ONE

I

Three months before the killings I returned to Thornbury. Chance took me back, a set of unpremeditated
circumstances, although in many ways it felt inevitable.
It had been over twenty years since I had last set foot in
the place, but in all that time, the house and the grounds
around it had occupied a singular space in my memory,
a bright pocket filled with summer grass and lofty ceilings, laughter, music and self-discovery. Despite all that
happened there, I still retained the sense that I owed
something of myself, of the person that I had become,
to that house, and those who lived there.

We had been called down to cover a scene in a farmhouse outside Borris – a quaint village near the Carlow–
Kilkenny border. It appeared to be a murder-suicide
attempt, and the poor bastard had made a hash of it. By
the time the team got there, he and his wife were already
in Waterford Regional Hospital, fighting for their lives
or whatever was left of them. The local sergeant, a
Roman-nosed depressive who looked as much like a
farmer as he did a representative of the law, was a man
named Savage, and he stood to one side, watching,

while I and the others tiptoed over the scene in the small hours of the morning, fingerprinting, taking samples, documenting the whole sorry mess. One of my colleagues recorded what he saw with a drawling monotone into a Dictaphone, while I struggled with the light and remounted one flash after another in my search for the right exposure and a maximum depth of field.

Both victims had been at the kitchen table when the gun was fired. The blood had mostly seeped into the woodwork by the time we arrived, but there was still a slow drip on to the floor beneath. Sheets of newspaper were inexplicably covering the ground and it was the pat-pat of blood meeting paper – not the suicide attempt – which made me think of Thornbury and what had happened that summer all those years ago. I remembered we had gone hunting and two of us – Rachel and Marcus – had killed rabbits. They had hung the rabbits from a hook in the scullery. There was paper on the counter beneath, and that same pat-pat of blood dripping down came to me now as it did when I was fifteen years old.

'We're not far from Thornbury, are we?' I asked Savage as we were packing up our things. It was still early, not yet nine, but the sun had broken clear of the clouds and it felt warm for a morning in April.

Savage's mouth puckered with consideration. 'Thornbury,' he said, glancing down at the scuffed surface of his old brogues, enunciating the estate's name as if it were one he had not heard in some time. 'You know it, do you?'

'I used to know people who lived there.'

'The Bagenals?' he said, his interest piqued now.

'I went to school with Rachel and Patrick,' I said, before asking breezily: 'Do you know if anyone's still living there?'

'The son is still running the place, so I believe. Don't know about the sister. Mrs Bagenal died some years back. Nice woman. Brain tumour, God love her.'

'Yes, I had heard that.'

'And then the father . . . Well.' He looked at me then, an up-and-down assessment, so that I couldn't help but feel that he was judging me, fitting me into whatever it was he knew of the Bagenals' troubled history. 'He died a long time ago.'

Neither of us spoke for a minute, Savage leaning down to rub a crumb of muck from his shoe with a stick he had picked up off the ground.

'You could drop in on your way back to Dublin,' he remarked. 'It wouldn't be much of a detour,' and proceeded with a detailed itinerary of the minor roads that led to the estate. I didn't comment, and if he saw the sudden change in my demeanour – nerves rushing to the surface – he didn't comment.

His farewell to me was delivered in a deadpan tone: 'Mind yourself,' he said.

I did not intend going back. To this day, I'm not sure why I did. A seed of curiosity planted by Savage's suggestion, perhaps, but that alone could not have been enough to drive me back to a place I had once sworn off for ever. The challenge of it rose in my mind as I drove alone through roads flanked with cow parsley and gorse, one eye on the satnav, nervy at the knowledge that the house was close by; niggled by the sense that I should test myself by just taking a quick look, to see if it still held the same power over me that I remembered as a girl. It had been so long. Rachel and I had lost touch years ago. I'd heard she was living in London. It wasn't difficult for me to picture her married to a stockbroker – a rich divorcé – living in Kensington or Primrose Hill, childless from what I had heard. Patrick, I knew, had taken over the running of the estate while the rest of his peers were at university, and even though our paths hadn't crossed since leaving school, I was still curious about him and Rachel, about the house.

The estate, though large, was well off the beaten track, and by the time I found the old granite pillars that marked the entrance it was getting on in the day, and I needed to get back to HQ. Still, I had come too close not to take a quick look. The memory of the warm yellow stone crawling with ancient wisteria and roses, those gracious rooms beyond, lured me nervously through the gateless pillars against my better judgement, along the curving road, tussocky grass growing in a furrow along the centre.

My first clue all was not well was the sight of a car that appeared to have been driven off the avenue and into a shallow ditch. It was an old VW Golf whose registration plates and wheels had been removed. The bonnet was buckled and twisted where it met with the wide solid trunk of an old beech tree. Weeds grew within the car's interior, visible through the passenger door, which was slightly ajar. The windows remained intact but were smudged with moss and sap and the littered seed from overhanging branches. I slowed to survey the scene, before continuing past the overgrown rhododendrons to where the avenue rounded on to the front garden leading up to the house.

What I remembered of the front lawn was a clipped expanse of grass rolling down to the driveway, and a striped marquee pinned to the ground in front of the house for Patrick's party. What a shock it was now to turn the corner and find the grass grown coarse and long, balding in places. An ugly fence had been erected around the perimeter as if at one stage livestock had been grazing here. But worse than that was the state of the house beyond. The sash windows with their bevelled-glass panes twinkling in the sun were sagging and cracked, paint peeling off their frames. In some cases, the glass had been removed and the gaps patched up with plywood. Ivy had grown thick and wild across one side of the house, hanging low over the windows or shorn back sharply over others, as if someone had made an effort to clip it back but then lost interest and given up. There was still beauty in the tangled rose that was just coming into bloom over the south-west corner of the house, and the contours of the building retained something of their former majesty and grandeur. And yet it felt, as I pulled the car up in front of the main entrance, that the house was slowly surrendering to decay. I had a flash of Mrs Bagenal – Rachel and Patrick's mother – her elegant hands and neatly set hair, standing proudly at the door to welcome her guests, and wondered how she might have felt had she lived to see its fallen state.

For a moment I sat there, prevaricating, a voice in the back of my mind instructing me to turn the car around and drive out of there. But instead I got out, an ache of tiredness in my legs and across my back, squinted up at the house, and thought I saw movement at one of the upper windows. For one loopy moment, I was sure the window was leaning precariously down from the frame, poised to drop and smash on the gravel below. But then my vision cleared, and the house righted itself as I blinked up at it. I told myself not to worry, that it was the result of too little sleep, and too much work, the drive down in the early hours conspiring to summon up strange images.

The front door opened, and a dog came bounding towards me – a red setter, ears flying back – a voice shouting after to heel. I leaned down to stroke the dog's head, and it flopped back on to the ground, displaying its tummy.

'Don't mind Jinny,' Patrick said, stepping over the threshold. 'She's a dreadful slut.' He was coming towards me now. I could tell he had not recognized me yet, and it wasn't until I held out my hand for him to shake that his face cleared in recognition.

'Lindsey?' he asked, taking my hand, and half smiling. 'Is that really you?'

'Hello, Patrick,' I replied, nerves prickling all over my body, regretting my decision to come this far.

Patrick shook his head, as if he couldn't quite believe it. 'My God,' he said, and there it was again, the rush of the familiar as he stepped back and took me in, asking with a kind of muted but polite astonishment, 'What brings you back here?'

'I was in the area, on a job. I had some time to kill, so . . .'

He blinked and stood back: 'It's been years since you've been here, an absolute age.'

'More than twenty years.'

'Yes, it would be that long, wouldn't it? I'm looking down the barrel of fifty now.'

This was hardly true – he couldn't be much past forty. I myself had let that significant birthday pass uncelebrated just a few weeks before. Patrick kept his gaze on me as he spoke, the same lively grey eyes that I remembered, although the face had changed somewhat. Lines around the eyes and a sprinkling of grey in the growth of stubble. His hair, too, although still thick and curly and, for the most part, the same coppery red, was threaded with silver, and he was wearing it a little longer than I remembered. With his faded jeans and a navy fleece that had seen better days, he added to the careworn impression I had of the house.

'Well, well. Lindsey Morgan on my very doorstep. Who would have believed it?'

For a moment, I'm not sure either of us knew what to say. In an effort, I'm sure, to dispel the awkwardness between us, Patrick invited me inside.

'You'll have breakfast?' he asked.

I declined at first, tried to make my excuses, but he waved away my protestations and ushered me inside.

After the brightness of the morning, the hall, once the door was closed, seemed gloomy and cold.

'You said you were on a job?' he asked over his shoulder, as he led me past the staircase with its ancient tiger skin pinned to the wall – a hunting trophy shot by an ancestor in the days of the Raj.

'Yes. I was called to a crime scene in the area.'

'You're with the guards?' he said with unveiled surprise.

'Forensics.'

'Really. So what's the case? Or can't you say?'

'An attempted murder-suicide.'

At first, he said nothing. I wondered if I should have lied, or said something more sensitive. It seemed as though, with those words, I had summoned up the ghosts of both his parents. Neither of us commented on it. The dog's claws clicked over the floorboards as we followed her down the chilly corridor.

'There seems to be so much of that about nowadays,' he said finally as we reached the back of the house, where the rooms were smaller, and the ceilings low. 'The suicide part, at any rate. You can't turn on the news nowadays without hearing about it . . .'

The radio was playing in the background in the kitchen, Patrick's half-finished breakfast on the table, and I wondered whether he was thinking of his own father as he spoke those words. I felt a stab of regret and wondered why I had come at all. Hardly in the door, and I had put my foot in it. But Patrick welcomed me, nonetheless.

'Sit, sit,' he commanded, clearing away some newspapers and files that cluttered the table. 'Let me cook you up some eggs,' he said convivially, as if I were a chum he had not seen in a few weeks, and not an old school friend of his sister's.

'No, really, Patrick. A cup of tea is fine.'

But he wouldn't hear of it.

'By now, I'm a dab hand at whipping up a breakfast fry,' he said, clattering about with pans on the old Aga. 'Did you know I ran this place as a guest house for a while?'

'Really?'

With the smell of frying butter filling the room, he chattered above the spit and crackle of the eggs in the pan, explaining how he had given the hospitality thing a go for a year or so before chucking it in.

'Too many complaints,' he explained. '*The bed's too hard. The room's too cold. The house too spooky.*'

'Too spooky?' I asked cheerfully.

'It's a house with a lot of history, as you know,' Patrick said, sliding the eggs on to a plate and setting them before me with a flourish. 'Not to mention what they thought of the food.'

'Looks good to me,' I answered, suddenly famished, and while I ate, he poured tea and filled me in on the other money-making ventures he had tried: farming, leasing the land to a local farmer, advertising the property as a location for film and television projects, airbnb.

'The trouble is,' he explained, 'there's barely enough money to be earned from those ventures to keep me going, let alone the house. As you can see, it needs a serious injection of capital.'

I looked around the room – the scuffed wooden countertops, the Victorian tiled floor, the Aga filling the room with heat. There was a fireplace with a little wood-burning stove inset, and a chaise longue had been drawn up next to it. The dog had settled herself on a folded blanket on the floor. The chaise longue I recognized as one that had stood in front of the drawing-room window all those years ago. I had slept on it the night of Peter Bagenal's death. It had grown shabby with the years, the upholstery worn to the weave. A pillow and blanket were slung in one corner along with a paperback novel, and I wondered did Patrick sleep down here? My mind wandered back to the abandoned car driven into a tree, and I couldn't help but question the way he was living. The whole expanse of this grand house and how enthralled I had been with the Bagenal family, all of it reduced to a fortyish bachelor son eking out an existence within the confines of a kitchen. It seemed wrong, somehow.

'Why don't you sell it?' I asked, and he shot me a look of amusement.

'What? Sell the family home? Don't you understand anything of my tribe?'

This was an old joke from school. I remember the day Rachel gleefully whispered to me that she 'kicked with the other foot'. I had stared at her, clueless. Our school was predominantly Catholic with only a handful of Church of Ireland pupils. The domain of rich landowners' children, the sons and daughters of lawyers and bankers, I was the only one in the school to claim a publican as my father.

'What does Rachel think?'

'Rachel!' he spluttered, but his amusement was thin. 'I'm sure she couldn't give a hoot what I do with the place. I could put the old pile up on Done Deal and she wouldn't bat an eyelid. So long as her life in London can carry on uninterrupted.'

I suggested he might parcel off some of the land that surrounded the house and try to sell that. It was in the commuter belt, within driving distance of Dublin. Surely he could find a developer who might be interested.

'Ten years ago, perhaps,' he answered. 'Not now, not since the collapse. Developers don't have the funds and the banks aren't lending.'

He didn't appear depressed or gloomy about it, more matter-of-fact, like it was something he had accepted a long time ago.

'Perhaps I should find myself a wife,' he said, brightening with amusement at the prospect. 'That's what my mother used to advise. A helpmeet to bring this place back to the way it ought to be.'

'You'd better find a rich wife,' I remarked, and he laughed and asked me had I any cash?

'Publican's daughter? Come on, how about it? You and me,' he joked, laughter lines wrinkling the sides of his face, and I remembered how I had always enjoyed his flirtatiousness, his easy charm.

'Do you remember the groomsman's cottage?' he asked, changing the subject. 'I've been trying to make it habitable. You wouldn't believe the state it's been in – the ceiling was nearly collapsing.'

'What will you do with it?' I asked, pushing my empty plate aside. 'Rent it out?' I couldn't imagine he'd want to live in it, not after what had happened in the stables next door.

'Perhaps,' he said.

I pressed him a little more on the subject, but I could feel his reluctance. We talked some more about some of the others from school, about Marcus and Niall and Hilary. I had lost touch with them all. Rachel had been my only real link and, once that had broken, I fell out of contact with the whole gang.

As our conversation petered out, I became aware of the brooding silence of the house around us, and the feeling began nudging at me that I was somehow trespassing. The truth was I was disappointed, even a little sad, at the state of the house. It seemed a lonely place now, neglected, and mired in financial difficulties, not the glittering social hub it had remained in my memory. I looked over again at the unmade couch by the fire, and Patrick followed the movement of my eyes and laughed self-consciously.

'The place isn't quite how you remember it, I'm sure.'

Although I made some noises of protest, there was sadness in his smile as he got to his feet. We walked in silence back out to the front door. Rain had begun to fall – a slight drizzle dusting my car as we went outside, the dog lingering on the step.

'She hates the rain,' Patrick explained. 'Not much of a hunting dog, eh?' He laughed, nudging her with the toe of his boot.

That put me in mind of our weekends again, teenagers hunting rabbits, and I asked him if he still went shooting.

'Not much.' He shrugged. 'Although I'll have to do something about these crows.'

He looked past me to the trees that lined the avenue and spread around the back of the house. The whole time I was there, I had been aware of a distant blur of noise, and now it crystallized in my consciousness. It was the loud cawing of crows. Looking around, I saw the trees were full of them. The dark shadows I had taken for foliage were actually birds among the branches. There must have been hundreds of them – thousands, maybe. I stood there staring, mesmerized.

'I might try airbnb again,' he said with determination. 'I just think I need some decent photos of the house and the grounds. Market it a bit better, you know?'

I thought of the cheerless rooms we had just left, the abandoned car in the ditch, the pervasive suggestion of the past in every groove of Thornbury's masonry, the echo of history whispering through its corridors.

He was fishing. I could tell he was, in the same way I could tell his sunny chitchat was really a cover for something far closer to loneliness.

'I'll take some photographs for you, if you like. Free of charge,' I said, looking in my bag for my card, conscious of the colour rising to my cheeks: it's not, after all, the kind of offer a guard makes. We don't do nixers. Besides, I wasn't completely sure I did want to return, and yet the suggestion was mine.

'You're very kind, but I couldn't ask you to.'

'The offer stands,' I said, trying to stifle the conflict of emotion within me.

'If you think you could spare the time, well, then, maybe later in the month, once I've cleared things up a little?'

'Absolutely,' I said.

He kissed me on the cheek and stood watching as I got back in the car and drove down the avenue. Out through the pillars, I wondered briefly what had happened to the gates, before finding the road and heading back to the office.

For part of the journey back to Dublin, as fresh air rushed in through the open windows filling up my senses, I allowed myself to fantasize about Patrick and me, running Thornbury together, straightening it out, making it come alive again. A foolish notion, I know. I couldn't even account for why I had gone back there this morning. It was because of the suicide attempt – they always make me a little down and inward-looking, sending me off into brief but searching examinations of my life and all the things I do not have: a partner, a family of my own, a place to call home.

2

1991

I am constantly watching her. *Rachel.*

Her head is in a book – *Jane Eyre.* Her expression is alert, inquisitive, rapt. The train rocks gently from side to side, and it's hot here in the carriage, despite the open windows. She doesn't slouch like the rest of us. Not like me, or Hilary who sits beside me in a slump, flicking through *Just Seventeen* with an air of boredom. Rachel is still wearing her school uniform – only the boys bothered to change. But unlike me and Hilary, she hasn't loosened her school tie, her collar.

Across from us, Patrick has balled up his jumper and slotted it between his head and the window. Marcus is listening to music – The Cure, most likely – his CD Walkman whirring on the little table. His eyes, smudged with black kohl, are closed, a scattering of pale chest hair showing between the gap in his black denim shirt. Niall drinks from a litre bottle of Cidona, looks around, bored. He's a sixth-year student – all three of them are. Man-boys, Rachel calls them, with their rugby shoulders. In school, we have little to do with them, being fourth-years.

Niall's eyes alight on Rachel, her dark brown hair pushed back with a black velvet hairband. He puts the lid of the bottle near the edge of the table then flicks it across the aisle towards her. It pings off her book, and she looks up slowly. Her face is open and clean-looking, as if she's just scrubbed it with a hot flannel.

'Stop it,' she tells him, cool and authoritative.

'What?' he asks, all innocent.

'You're such a child,' she breathes, and returns to her book.

I have known her a month and already I am in awe of her.

At the station, a man is there to meet us. A tall, brownish man, leaning against a Nissan Bluebird, arms folded over his chest. Rachel breaks from my side and runs across the road to greet him. She kisses him on the cheek and his arms unfold just long enough for one hand to touch her face. She says something to him, then turns and gestures to me, but I feel shy suddenly, hanging back as the boys and Hilary charge across the road, bags slung over their shoulders. It's not until they've all shaken hands and are flinging their luggage into the boot of the car that I come forward.

'You must be Lindsey,' he says, taking my hand. His voice bears no trace of this midland town but is sharp with the same crisp clarity as his daughter's. The handshake is firm, the skin paper-dry, and for those few seconds he holds me in his gaze. Like Rachel and

Patrick, he is tall, imposing. I break his gaze and look down at the asphalt, my 'Hello, Mr Bagenal' addressed to the ground.

'You must call me Peter,' he says firmly. I think that I will never be able to call him that. But Hilary does.

'Hello, Peter!' she calls out, and he wraps an arm around her and kisses the top of her head. But Hilary is Rachel's cousin, which makes it different for her.

'Can I drive?' Patrick asks, and his father throws him the keys.

Peter Bagenal takes the front passenger seat, while the rest of us clamber into the back. Rachel sits between the two boys, and one of us must sit on her lap. As I am the smaller and lighter, Rachel chooses me. Privately, she has joked to me about Hilary's weight, expressing surprise that a vegetarian could be so fat. Hilary squeezes herself between Marcus and the car door, while I perch on Rachel's knee.

'You're so light!' she exclaims, and I feel her hands on my hips, the firm strength of her legs beneath me. 'I wish I were as light as you.'

The car draws away from the kerb and out on to the street, Peter Bagenal issuing instructions to his son in low, steady tones – *easy with the clutch, check your mirrors, indicate.* The instructions dwindle then cease as we leave the town behind us and the car travels along country roads bound on either side by cow parsley in full bloom, honeysuckle in the hedgerows.

I wonder how long it will take us to get to the house.

Thornbury. I haven't been here before. It's uncomfortable on Rachel's knees, my head jammed against the ceiling. I feel too close to Patrick and Peter, bracing myself against the backs of their chairs. I'm worried that the sweat I can feel on my back and under my arms will grow visible through my blouse. Peter reaches forward, takes the cigarette lighter from the dashboard. Cigar smoke fills the car. The skin around Patrick's neck is mottled, either from heat or nerves. His hair is reddish-brown, a long fringe falling over his eyes, which are fixed on the road ahead. Freckled hands clutch the steering wheel.

Hilary hums to herself, and someone behind me rolls down the window. Marcus. Pale-faced. Boney wrists. Curehead. Clever. One of his parents is German. He was there in Berlin when the wall came down. Rachel says he has a chunk of it in his dorm – a bit of concrete with blue spray-paint on one side. Not that she has seen it. It's one of the strictest rules of St Alban's – girls cannot visit the boys' dorms, and vice versa. The penalty is expulsion.

Peter Bagenal blows smoke towards the windscreen.

'Sorry,' I say to Rachel, shifting my weight on her lap. I'm sure her legs must be numb. She squeezes my hips to reassure me. I try to turn back to smile at her, but there isn't enough room. I catch a glimpse of Niall's hand clasped around her calf, rubbing. He has worked her sock down to her ankle. I cannot see Rachel's expression, but her hands remain on my hips while his hand continues to stroke and massage her leg. I catch sight of my face in the rear-view mirror, red with confusion. I feel the squeeze of her hands again, and I know that she is reassuring me about something else this time. About Niall, his hand. It's another one of Rachel's jokes. I feel better.

The car slows, then turns through a pair of white wrought-iron gates, and we are suddenly thrown into shade. The coolness of the trees that line the route is a relief, and I find myself looking out eagerly for the house. It takes so long for it to come into view and, when it does, I feel something move in my chest. The house stands clear above a smooth green lawn. It is larger and grander than I had imagined. Warm yellow stone basks in direct sunlight, so many windows glittering. Even high in the roof, I can see circles of glass like a row of eyes peering down from above, and there are statues at intervals along the top of the high wall. An image comes into my head of what it must be like up there – the view over the gardens and trees beyond, how tiny this car must appear as it speeds over the gravel driveway.

A dog has emerged from the house and comes bounding towards us, ears flapping, tongue hanging out, and Peter Bagenal rolls down his window and gives a low chuckle. Patrick slows the car and the dog runs alongside, making occasional leaps towards Peter's outstretched hand.

Up at the house, the front door opens.

'There she is,' Peter says, and he waves: 'My current wife.'

The boys laugh, and Hilary says, 'He's been calling her that for as long as I can remember.'

The gold band he wears on his little finger catches the light.

Heather Bagenal stands in the shadow of the doorway, one hand raised to shield her eyes from the sun. I cannot see her face, only the long yellow sundress, brown slender arms, a scarf wrapped around her hair.

As the car draws to a halt and we all come tumbling out, two things occur to me: first, that I can never ever invite Rachel to my own home, and second, that this house is more beautiful than I had expected. My heart fills up as I take it all in, the house, the yellow sundress, the knotted vines of wisteria twisting around the door, the boys' laughter, the dog leaping madly. Rachel comes and tucks her arm in mine, and smiles at me in that conspiratorial way she has.

'Come on,' she says, and leads me in.

3

Something happens to me when I visit a crime scene. It starts the moment I step in. A feeling or sensation that I can best describe as a quieting of the senses. Not that I have ever described it like that to anyone. People think you're weird enough when they find out that your line of work is photographing dead bodies, blood-splatter patterns, knives on floors. God forbid you might get a sensual pleasure from it. But ever since my first crime scene, I have had the same experience every time. It's as though all the buzz and noise and chatter that occupies our waking lives falls away as soon as I cross the threshold to the place where violence has been done. Everything grows still. My heart beats slower and quieter, my nerves become calm and I feel a kind of peace. A clarity. Like I can experience the world, in that place, for that brief pocket of time, with fresh eyes. I smell things as if for the first time – the metallic odour of blood, the sulphuric smell of gunfire, even the cloying stench of a rotting corpse. And I get the faintest tingling at the back of my neck, just there where a nub of bone nears the top of my spine – a sensation akin to being touched by a new lover.

It scared me to remember how calm I was, how peaceful I had felt in the face of that carnage. But back then I had a lot to be frightened about. Over the years, with experience, I have come to accept these feelings as part of the job. Outwardly, I appear professionally dispassionate. My inner feelings I keep to myself.

When I visited Thornbury that day, I think some residue of those feelings remained – that clarity I had experienced when picking over the crime scene in the early morning at that farmhouse near Borris. Perhaps that is why the occasion of going back to the house, seeing Patrick again after all those years, felt so vivid. But by the time I got back to Dublin, the feeling had faded, and other things – my ordinary life – kicked in.

April was a busy month – a double murder in the midlands, a gangland shooting in west Dublin – the kind of work I relish. I was happy to put in overtime. I was in a good place workwise, and the feeling spilled over into my personal life. After a bet with another member of my team, I had signed up to run the Dublin marathon later that year. Taking the challenge seriously, I had joined a running club and found myself looking forward to the training sessions and to my solo runs around the Phoenix Park as the evenings grew longer and the weather warmer. Feeling good about my improved fitness, I had reconnected on Facebook with an old boyfriend from my university days and was enjoying an online flirtation. It was, all things considered, a good time in my life.

The only blot on the horizon was some trouble I had begun to experience with my peripheral vision. The leaping window at Thornbury had just been the start. Since then, there had been a number of occasions where I could have sworn I'd seen something jumping from the shadows – the sudden movement of a parked car, or a door in my apartment opening without warning. Every time, it turned out to be nothing. I had been putting it down to tiredness, too much overtime, a side-effect of my new exercise regime, but when these episodes were joined by headaches – the sensation of pressure behind my left eye – I decided to get it checked out. A referral from my GP led me to a consultant in the Eye and Ear Hospital, blood tests, scans, tests and procedures, all of it combining to suck me down corridors I was reluctant to travel. I tried to tell myself that it was nothing – a blip – that everything would be all right, my health restored. But the anxiety remained, like a low hum in the background.

With all that was happening, I had almost forgotten about Patrick and my offer to take photographs of Thornbury. So when, a few weeks later, I received a phone call from him asking if I was free to meet for lunch, I was pleasantly surprised. As it happened, I had taken the day off work. An appointment with my consultant in the Eye and Ear Hospital on Adelaide Road was scheduled for that morning, and I had taken the day as a precaution in case the diagnosis was not good. I suggested to Patrick that we meet somewhere close by, along the canal, listing a few sandwich bars and cafés in the vicinity.

'Fuck that!' he declared with an erratic but good humour. 'Let's go someplace fancy. My treat!'

And so we ended up in House on Leeson Street, among the black walls and chandeliers and plush velvet chesterfields, dining on walnut-crusted halibut and gorgonzola ravioli, a bottle of their finest Sancerre sweating in a bucket between us.

I was jittery with nerves. My consultation at the hospital had not gone as expected. That, combined with the complicated feelings that arose within me whenever I thought about Thornbury or the Bagenals, made me feel skittish and unsure. Patrick seemed to share my unease, his nerves revealing themselves in his indecision – labouring over the menu, agonizing over what wine to choose. For my part, I sat still in my chair and chose quickly, kept my voice steady, my gaze and smile direct, while inside, emotion wheeled around like a flock of birds.

'I'll come straight to the point,' he said, once the wine had been poured and our orders taken. 'I'm selling Thornbury.'

I couldn't hide my surprise.

'But I thought you said you'd never sell it? All that talk about your tribe—'

'I know, I know. But maybe it's crazy holding on to the old ways, the old traditions, preserving the family estate, and for what? It's not like I have any children to pass it on to. Rachel neither.'

'You're still young. There's time enough for that.'

He shook his head, leaning forward with his elbows on the table, his wine glass in one hand. 'Even so. It's time for a change. Time to start living my life properly, not trapped in that mausoleum.'

I must have looked stunned, maybe even a little affronted, enough for him to remark, 'Oh, come on, Lins. Don't look at me like that. You know, it's partly your fault I'm selling it.'

'My fault?'

'Yes. When you turned up out of the blue that morning, I saw the way you were looking at the house—'

'Oh, Patrick—'

'No, no! I'm not trying to make you feel bad, believe me! I'm grateful that you did. It made me start looking at the house through your eyes, the eyes of someone who hadn't been there in twenty years. Because even though I'd been living in the place all that time, doing battle daily, it seemed, with the myriad problems of the house, I was still blinkered to how truly dire the situation had become. You coming back to Thornbury changed that. When I watched you get into your car and drive away that morning, do you know what I felt? Envy. There you were, driving off to your exciting career, your life in the city, while I was trapped there

30

in that sinking house trying desperately to keep it afloat.'

'My life's not that exciting. Trust me.'

'But it's not just you,' he went on, undeterred. 'I started thinking about everyone else – Marcus, Hilary, Niall, even my sister. All of you have a kind of freedom that I don't have. Every time I talk to Marcus, he's just come back from Amsterdam or New York or Madrid. Either that, or he's planning a trip. And Niall – okay, so he doesn't have quite the same freedom as Marcus, but his responsibilities seem different to mine. He has a wife, kids. He's making money. His efforts are all about building a future, whereas mine just seem to be about preserving the past. I feel trapped by this responsibility towards previous generations, like I have this bunch of dead relatives breathing down my neck every time the boiler fails or a hole appears in the roof!' He laughed then with self-mockery, and took a long sip of wine, before continuing: 'Even Rachel managed to escape the place.'

'What about Rachel?' I asked, trying to keep my voice light, casual. 'What does she think of your idea to sell?'

'I didn't think she'd give a hoot what I did with the place. Turns out I was wrong about that. It's prompted her to come home again.'

'Rachel's back at Thornbury?' I felt a small jolt at the news, but he didn't seem to notice.

'Yes. She's been there almost a month. Ironic, isn't it? She hardly sets foot in the place for twenty-odd years, and then, as soon as I make noises about selling up, she decides to move back in.'

'But what about London?'

'I imagine she'll go back once everything is finalized and the sale has gone through. Or maybe she won't. She's being pretty cagey about it all. I get the feeling all's not well between her and Graham.'

I chewed my ravioli carefully, but swallowing proved difficult. The very mention of her name caused my throat to constrict. Every word he spoke about her – about the difficulties he perceived within her marriage, about how she refused to open up to him about it – made the sensation of tightness within me worsen. Strange as it was, I didn't like the feeling that she had returned.

Rachel and I lost touch as soon as I left St Alban's. Too much had happened for any semblance of real friendship to have survived. It sat inside me, the unease over how things had turned out between us. In fact, the difficulty of our parting had come back to me when I saw her again four, or maybe five years ago. I was going through Heathrow with some time to kill before a connecting flight, browsing in W. H. Smith's, when I looked up and saw a woman in a grey cashmere scarf and designer glasses examining the cover of a paperback novel. The glasses were new, and her hair was shorter, cut into an angular bob, the ends skimming her jawline. Still, I would have known her anywhere. The set of her shoulders gave her away. So square and perfectly thrown back. Her posture had always been terrific. She held herself like a model, moved like one, too. I studied her over the rim of my magazine, summoning up the courage to approach her, and when she looked up and caught my eye I felt a brief stab of recognition. It lasted but a split second, before she broke my gaze, returned the book to the shelf and walked coolly and elegantly out of the shop.

I was stunned by the rejection. She had known who I was, after all. Looking down at the magazine in my hands, I saw I was trembling, and my thoughts travelled instantly to that day in the long grass beyond the avenue, sunlight bringing out the threads of copper in her otherwise dark hair, the house looming some distance behind us, the way she sat up suddenly, looked at me so intently, and said, 'I can trust you, can't I? You're not to tell anyone. Ever.'

Old secrets. Old promises. Still she sailed past me, unwilling for our lives to become entangled once more.

The waitress took our plates away and Patrick poured out the last of the wine. We talked some more about his plans, gossiped a little about mutual friends and acquaintances, and then he paid the bill and we both stood up to leave.

Outside, the sun had come out, a warm breeze whisking pleasurably down Leeson Street, and when Patrick suggested a stroll by the canal to walk off our lunch, I was happy to agree.

'When you turned up at the house that morning,' he said as we walked, 'it threw me.'

'Did it? You hid it well.'

His mood, now that we were out in the open air, became less jokey, more serious. We stopped to watch a pair of swans gliding towards the locks by Charlemont Bridge, their quiet poise juxtaposed against the blaring traffic that was building along Canal Road.

'When I heard the tyres crunch over the gravel that morning, I felt a wash of relief. That there was some-one there. Someone to talk to. And then I opened the door and saw you and it was like . . .'

'Like what?' I asked gently.

'Like seeing a ghost.'

He held my gaze, then laughed with embarrassment.

'Stupid, right?'

I shrugged. 'We hadn't seen each other in such a long time. And there was no reason for you to expect to find me there.'

'I know, it's just that the house . . . sometimes, it feels . . . Not just you coming, but, oh, I don't know. Those bloody crows. They make such a racket, morn-ing, noon and night. Sometimes, even when I've left the place, it's like I can still hear them cackling . . .'

He stopped talking then, ran his hand quickly through his hair – a gesture of irritation. He seemed angry and embarrassed, regretful of what he had said, although it was so jumbled and confused I wasn't sure what he was trying to tell me. But it seemed connected with the complicated feelings he had over his decision to part with the house. I knew it had not been easy for

34

him. I reached out and touched his sleeve, felt the rough weave of it beneath my fingertips.

'I'm glad it was you, Lindsey. At my door that morning. It's changed things for me.' He said these words with a quiet seriousness, keeping his eyes on the ground, before making a quick smile as if to mark an end to that line of conversation, and then we began walking again.

A hush had fallen over us, and maybe it was because of his admission, because for a fleeting moment his vulnerability reminded me of my own predicament, that I felt compelled to say: 'Can I tell you something? Something that I haven't told any one else?'

'Of course.' His eyes were on mine, interested, concerned.

'I have a tumour. It's growing behind my eye, leaning on the optic nerve. I was just diagnosed this morning.'

'*What?*'

He stared at me, aghast, and as I explained to him calmly and evenly about my symptoms, about the discovery of my illness, I noticed that the colour which had come into his cheeks from the fresh air and exercise seemed to drain away. There was no disguising the horror in his expression.

'But is it malignant?' he asked. We had stopped again, and this time he was the one to put his hand out, to take hold of my wrist.

'I'm afraid so.'

'Dear God.'

'But it's treatable.'

'Well, yes, of course.'

'I'm told that it's relatively small.'

'So what's the plan? Surgery? Chemotherapy?'

I recounted to him what I had been told that day by my consultant – about his plan to shrink the tumour a little before operating – and as I spoke, the memory of my morning's appointment with Professor Puri snaked its way into my thoughts. I remembered him writing out my prescription, then capping his silver pen and returning it to the little wooden tray on the desk, the groove where the pen slid in. A neat man. Fastidious. I remembered his hands, the short digits and square pink nails, and imagined those hands gloved in latex, fingers creeping around inside my skull. And as I thought about it, I found that I was crying. Tears rolled down my face, and I stifled the sob that rose from my throat.

Then Patrick did something that endeared him to me more than any other gesture he had made. His hand moved from my wrist and went to touch my temple next to the afflicted eye. I felt the tenderness of his fingertips, read the depth of his concern in the fear-filled expression he fixed me with, and then he leaned down and I closed my eyes and he kissed me very gently on my eyelid.

'There,' he said softly, his head still bent to mine, our foreheads touching. 'All better now.'

He kissed me again, this time on my lips, and it was a long, slow kiss that seemed to contain layers – passion, old friendship, the longings of an adolescence well past. Hope, too. The promise of better days ahead.

Hope for a future that felt uncertain for both of us. Right then, it felt like nourishment. It was a long time before either of us broke away.

Not the most hopeful way to start a romance. But it was our way, and perhaps because of the portentousness of that opening moment, our relationship quickly grew serious.

Change swept into my life swiftly and with hardly any warning. Professor Puri had advised me that the bouts of disorientation would most likely continue, along with fatigue from the treatment drugs. Driving was no longer possible and, given that accurate and incisive observation was a crucial part of my job, I was obliged to inform my boss straight away. His response was sympathetic, and he put me on desk duty with the caveat that I would return to the field as soon as I was well again. Outside of work, I cut back on my exercise regime, under doctor's orders. I couldn't risk accident or injury, he said, and while fitness was an advantage when fighting my disease, I needed to conserve my energy. I still ran a few times a week, but shorter, less taxing runs. On the weekends when Patrick was with me, we often went running together in the Phoenix Park, stopping for coffee and cake at the tea rooms near Farmleigh afterwards – 'We've earned it,' he would joke, as we tucked into a slice of chocolate cake.

Patrick was the one big change that stopped my life from slipping into a minor key. His arrival every Friday evening became something I not only looked forward to but came to depend upon. Our weekends together were quiet but comforting. We went for long walks, visited galleries and museums, dined in local restaurants. We were tourists in our own capital city. It felt new and fresh and, at the same time, like uncovering a memory of something old and long-loved.

At that point, the fatigue I had been warned about had not yet surfaced. Every second week, I spent a day in the hospital, receiving my medication intravenously, my mother or father by my side. They took it in turns to come up and attend to me, despite my protestations that I didn't need assistance. I didn't tell them about Patrick, although I knew I would have to, eventually. Our feelings for each other were growing deeper, so that when one evening, as the two of us prepared dinner in the galley kitchen of my apartment, he told me softly – almost casually – that he loved me, and I said those words back to him, it felt like the most natural thing in the world. Any misgivings I had – about opening up old wounds or uncovering secrets best left buried – I managed to ignore, so caught up was I in this love affair.

But there were things that niggled away, no matter how much I tried to ignore them. Like the fact that Patrick always came to Dublin and stayed with me. He never invited me down to Thornbury. It was an unspoken arrangement between us that I think suited us both. I had no desire to see Rachel, and even the prospect of returning to the house filled me with doubt, unwilling as I was to relive what had happened there. For his part, I believe Patrick was happy to escape on those occasions. The responsibilities of the estate bore heavily upon him, and his time spent in Dublin with me was part of the process of removing himself from Thornbury and all that it meant to him.

In June, a buyer for the estate emerged and, as the sales process got underway, I noticed a lightness entering his behaviour. He began to envisage what his life might be like once freed from the yoke of the estate. We talked about what we would do together once Thornbury had been sold, once my tumour was gone. The date for my surgery had been set for the end of the month, and I welcomed the distraction of these fanciful conversations from the creeping fear I had over the operation. We talked about sabbaticals and foreign travel. I would take a six-month leave of absence and rent out my apartment, and the two of us would fly off to South America, followed by a tour of Asia. These wild flights of fancy carried me through the anxiety and the fear. Somehow, I managed to convince myself that I could overcome the past. That it no longer had the power to hurt us. Foolish thoughts. For even I was aware that if things between Patrick and I were to solidify into a real commitment, as I hoped they would, then that would mean facing Rachel. The time arrived sooner than I expected.

'How would you feel about going back to Thornbury?' he said to me one day. We were sitting outside a café off Grafton Street, not really talking about anything of note, marvelling in the opportunity to take a coffee outdoors in Ireland, when he brought it up.

'What for?' I asked, taking my sunglasses from my head and placing them carefully over my eyes. Inside, I felt a dizzying sense of trepidation.

'I want to have a party – a kind of send-off to the house. The sale will be finalized soon and I just thought it would be fitting to have a get-together there. One last hurrah. What do you think?'

In truth, I felt a little nauseous at the prospect. For several weeks now, we had existed in our own little bubble. The thought of spending an evening among a throng of old acquaintances, with some of whom I shared a troubled history, filled me with dread. The prospect of returning to Thornbury would not have been so daunting if it was just the two of us alone. No Rachel, and no one else. What I wanted was to be sitting with him on the chaise longue in his kitchen, the deep silence of the country night outside the house. I had the most pressing desire for it – the fire purring in the little stove – the two of us making plans, the dog lolling at our feet.

'It won't be a big crowd,' he went on, perhaps seeing my resistance. 'Just the old gang from St Alban's. Marcus and Niall. Hilary.'

'And Rachel.'

'Well, of course. I can hardly leave her out!' He laughed.

'How much does she know about us?'

'She knows enough, Lins,' he assured me gently.

'I can't imagine she's impressed.'

He reached out and took my hand, held it loosely in his lap. 'Don't worry about Rachel. She'll come around.'

He spoke with confidence, but the doubt continued to niggle.

'There'll be partners, of course,' he continued. 'Everyone arrives down on Friday night for drinks and supper. Then, on Saturday morning, I thought we might have a bit of a crow shoot – to liven things up, get everyone outdoors for a few hours. Then dinner that night in the dining room – ladies in dresses, lads in tuxes, candlelight, music, the works.'

'Sounds formal.'

'It will be! Let's get dressed up, for a change. I want to see you in some sexy, slinky number.'

'I'm not sure I have anything suitable.'

But he dismissed this and carried on with his plans. Over the course of the weekend, he returned to the idea again and again, his vision of a reunion of sorts gathering force so that I had to focus on setting aside the doubts and fears I had about being in the house with those people again, particularly Rachel, and think instead about returning to a place that had once meant a great deal to me. I tried to force myself to forget all the pain that had been inflicted there, the danger that house had held for me, reasoning that nothing terrible had happened when I called into Thornbury some months ago out of the blue. For a while, I managed to quell my fear, and the rooms rose in memory, smartly elegant, the forlorn look of them I had witnessed those weeks ago shrugged off now, replaced by the golden light of nostalgia. Was it possible to go back? I wondered. Could we shrug off the weight of the years and return to a place and time that had shone brightly, though briefly?

Later in the week, on my lunchbreak, I went out and spent money I could ill-afford on an exorbitantly expensive dress. I took it home that night and hung it on my wardrobe door. Then I lay on my bed, hands behind my head, and stared hard at it, trying to summon from memory an image of the dining room, the long table spread with the delph and silverware of generations. Alabaster vases holding flowers cut from the woods and gardens surrounding the house. The arms of the candelabra stretching out across the mahogany surface. I saw myself at one end of the table, smiling in my new silk dress, a changed person, so different from the girl with the scuffed shoes and grave face.

'So serious,' Mr Bagenal used to say, kindly admonishing.

I could hear his voice echoing down the halls of time as I was sucked into the vortex of that house once more. How much had really changed? I asked myself. Even with my new, expensive dress, I was still, in many ways, the same fifteen-year-old girl, worried and watchful, frightened of being found out.

4

I follow Rachel up the stairs, watching the sweep of her hand along the polished bannister. Behind me, Hilary's footsteps fall heavily. An assortment of antlers occupy the petrol-blue walls at various intervals, growing cob-webby and dusty the higher up we go. At the top of the stairs, leaning over the balustrade, I see the glass-bead eyes of the various stuffed animals below twinkling in the light.

'It's a taxidermist's dream,' I say in wonder at the foxes and otters, badgers and stoats, all trapped in vary-ing poses in their glass cages below.

'It's revolting,' Hilary remarks. 'Using dead animals for ornamentation.' As a vegetarian, she is particularly offended.

There are so many doors up here – I try to calculate the number of rooms but lose track.

'This is us,' Rachel tells me, opening a door into a bright space with ochre walls and a black slate fireplace. A large window with a cushioned seat gives on to trees and sky.

I cannot imagine growing up here. The fireplace in

this bedroom is bigger and far more impressive than the stone-clad offering in our sitting room at home. I stand there, taking it all in: the dark wood floors, the heavy-looking furniture, the giant raft of a bed adrift in the middle of it all.

'You're in the spare room, Hils. Just by the bathroom. You don't mind, do you?'

Hilary glances at me, and I can see a brief calculation going on behind her eyes.

'No. Not at all.'

But she makes no move to go and find her room, simply stands there with her bag slung from one hand and watches as Rachel throws herself on to her bed, letting out a long, slow breath.

'Thank God,' she says, looking up at the distant ceiling. 'A moment's peace from those boys.'

She loosens her collar and kicks off her shoes, then hooks one toe under the rim of the sock on the opposite foot, pushing it down until it falls on to the floor. She does the same with its twin, her bare feet stretching. 'We'll have to share the bed, Lins. But I promise I don't snore.'

She reaches across to her bedside locker, fumbling inside the top drawer until she finds what she is looking for: cigarettes and a lighter.

'You're sure you don't mind sharing? Because now's the time to say it if you do. I can always kick up a fuss about you needing your own room. Get Niall or Marcus to bunk in with Patrick.'

'I'm sure Niall would rather bunk in with you,' Hilary says quietly. The image of Niall's hand on Rachel's leg comes into my head again. Hilary must have seen it, too. Rachel leans into the flame of her lighter and, above her cupped hands, her eyes wrinkle with humour.

'Yes, I'm sure he would.' She leans back on the pillows, one arm behind her head.

'Do you like him?' I ask.

She shrugs. 'He's all right. A child, of course, but then, they're all children,' she says, tapping ash into a scallop shell.

'She's kissed him, you know,' Hilary announces, her eyes flaring with amusement.

A shadow passes over Rachel's face, but then she brightens and gives Hilary her sweetest smile.

'Do you want to go have the first shower, Hils?'

'I wasn't going to . . .'

'That train was so hot, and in the car . . . Well, I didn't like to say anything to you in front of the boys.'

She picks a fleck of tobacco from her lip, then pauses to examine it.

Hilary drills her with a hot stare, before turning and slamming the door behind her. The noise reverberates through the room and, as her footsteps charge away from us down the hall, the corners of Rachel's mouth twitch into a grin.

'You're wicked,' I tell her and we both laugh, and I fall on to the bed next to her and reach for the cigarette in her hand. Taking a drag, I say: 'When?'

'When what?'

'You and Niall. When did you kiss him?'

'Over mid-term. Before you came to St Alban's.'

'What was it like?'

'Like someone shoved a stick in my mouth and had a good poke around.'

I make a face and she grimaces.

'Does Patrick know?'

'I expect so. I expect everyone knows.'

I pass back the cigarette and sit up again. It is not the first time I have felt on the edge of things at St Alban's. There is so much I have missed. For all Rachel's kind attention to me since I started a few weeks ago, I remain the new girl, unsure of myself and those around me.

'Hey,' she says. I know that she has sensed my prickling feeling of exclusion. She rewards me with a smile, that familiar flash of mischief in her eyes. 'Can you keep a secret?'

Warm feelings flood through me. I nod my answer.

'He did more than just kiss me.' Her voice drops a notch, and I wait for it. 'I let him dry-hump me.' Her eyes flare again and shock makes my mouth fall open, but there is no chance to react as the door opens and Heather Bagenal walks in.

'Hello, girls,' she says breezily, casting her gaze over us and around the room, her eyes resting briefly on the cigarette in Rachel's hand. I feel the breath catch in my throat, but she says nothing. The only sign of her disapproval is when she goes to the window and pulls it open a fraction. From outside in the garden, I can hear the boys — their voices raised in laughter. Heather looks down on them briefly.

In a way, she is very much what I had expected — tall and slender, blonde, rather beautiful, with the same grace and ease as her daughter. Yet there is something vague about her, too — a dreaminess that surprises me. She smiles when she speaks, but every so often the smile slips and then her face looks blank and a little plain.

'How do you like St Alban's, Lindsey?'

'Good, thank you.'

'It must be tricky joining halfway through the school year. How are you managing to settle in?'

I mumble something about everyone being very kind, and again I feel the slipperiness of her gaze.

'I'm not sure I'd take my child out of school in the middle of term and pop them into another school. Still, I'm sure your parents had their reasons.'

Her tone is perfectly polite, but I feel confused by her remarks. There is a reprimand in there somewhere.

Rachel laughs. 'Don't mind her, Lins. She's just prodding to see if you were expelled from your old school, aren't you, Heather?'

'I am not.'

I watch Rachel carefully. Smoking openly in front of her mother, addressing her by her first name. *I let him dry-hump me.* I am way out of my depth.

'Although it's a reasonable assumption,' Heather asserts. 'If a girl or boy arrives during the year, it's normally because they've done something terrible at their old school. Either that, or their parents are getting divorced.' She stops and gives me a misty look. 'Your parents aren't getting divorced, are they, dear?'

'No.'

'Well, thank heavens for that.'

'Heather thinks divorce is vulgar,' Rachel explains, and her mother admits to it without fear or hesitation. She doesn't seem to notice the mocking tone in Rachel's voice.

'Dinner at eight, girls, all right?' She glides towards the door and I notice the length of silk scarf running down her back beneath her neatly cut hair. 'And change out of those dreary uniforms.'

The door closes behind her and the air settles. Rachel swings her legs down and goes to her dressing table. It is littered with cosmetics, hairbands and trinkets; another ashtray contains a few crushed stubs.

'Sorry about that. She's a nosey old stick.' She stabs out her cigarette butt, then picks up a hairbrush.

'Come over here,' she says, and I do as she instructs.

Submissively, I sit, facing the mirror.

'Hold still,' she says, gathering up my hair in one hand and drawing the brush across my scalp. I feel it crackling with electricity.

'You could tell her if you wanted, you know. She's very understanding.'

'That's okay,' I say. I don't want it to be a big thing. It's enough for me to have shared it with Rachel.

I had told her almost as soon as I arrived at St Alban's – an intimacy she had forced with her direct and persistent manner, but I was glad of it afterwards. I explained in a sheepish way about a problem I had been having with another girl in my old school, a persistent bully whom I hadn't the courage to stand up to. For months, I had struggled in silence with my tormentor, and the ones I had reached out to for aid – my parents and teachers – had been reluctant, hand-tied. It got to the point where I felt like a nuisance. Every time I brought home a new bleeding scrape on my leg or a ring of bruises around my upper arm, it seemed to exacerbate the problem. The bully's father is considered a 'big man' in our town. To alienate him is to alienate the whole clan, and a family like that have ways of making their grievances felt. Ours is not the only pub in town. My father said I could either stay where I was and put up with the bullying, or I could move schools. As there is only one secondary school in our parish, that meant moving away.

Rachel has worked the brush over my whole head, and now her hand slows, then stops. Tentatively, she hooks a finger under the back of my collar and lifts it free of my skin so that the back of my neck is exposed. She says nothing at first, but I can feel her finger touching the ridged surface of the burn. I have told her about it but never shown her. I feel the tenderness of her touch. I can hear her breathing gently. I want desperately for her not to ask me about it. About the way they held me down. About how something so small can hurt so much.

'Well, I'm sure your parents know best,' she says quietly, yet still in that grown-up voice of hers, 'but were it my father, he'd have taken out his shotgun.'

She presses the collar back against my neck, and resumes brushing.

'You've got gorgeous hair,' she tells me. 'So sleek and shiny. I wish my hair were like yours. Tell me, what was she called, the bitch that did that to you?'

'Antoinette,' I tell her, and she snorts with derision.

'Fucking Antoinette,' she says primly. 'Off with her head, say I.'

Her voice – the certainty and humour within it – makes it fade away. The burn, the cuts, the humiliations, all of it pushed aside by these waves of relief and gratitude.

Down the hall, we hear the door to the bathroom open and close. Rachel moves to the window, and I watch her open it wider until she can lean out and observe the boys taking turns to drive the car across the sweep of gravel in front of the house. Her amusement is palpable.

'What idiots,' she says warmly, sitting to watch them, taking the brush to her own hair.

My heart flies open.

5

2017

Marcus drove with the same casual yet sharp-eyed concentration that I remembered of him when we were in school. Pale, bespectacled, his hair neatly combed, wearing a light blue sweater and jeans, the gaucheness of his teenage self had disappeared, and he seemed both relaxed and urbane.

It was Patrick who had arranged the lift for me. I had protested that I could easily catch the train, but he was adamant.

'It will be fun,' he insisted, 'you and Marcus catching up on the journey down.'

Privately, I baulked at the idea of two hours alone in a car with Marcus, envisaging conversation that could only be stiff and contrived. The years that had passed made strangers of us; old connections, if not already broken, would certainly have thinned. Even back when we were teenagers, there was always something slightly stand-offish about him. Not that he was aloof or snooty – far from it. But his bookishness had been offputting – that sense that he was steeped in knowledge that none of the rest of us possessed. I always had the fear whenever I opened my mouth of saying something to him that would sound stupid or naïve, unworldly.

Much of my reluctance proved unfounded. When he pulled the car up outside Garda HQ, where I waited with my weekend bag on the steps next to me, I watched him hop out, a grin on his face as he approached.

'Hello, stranger,' he said, and there was a moment of physical awkwardness, neither of us sure of how best to greet each other after the long years apart. Catching ourselves out at our foolishness, we both laughed and Marcus leaned in to kiss me on the cheek and the awkwardness dispersed.

'It's been so long!' he exclaimed. 'I often wondered what had happened to you. Why you had slipped off the radar like that.'

'Well,' I said brightly, not wanting to get into the real reasons. 'Here I am again.'

The journey down proved more relaxed than I had foreseen. We chatted about our lives while Bach's 'Goldberg Variations' played on the in-car stereo. Glenn Gould had replaced Robert Smith in the intervening years and while Marcus was still clever, the coldness had disappeared. A lot of what he told me about himself I knew already from Patrick – that he was a partner in a successful architectural firm; that after years of fiercely guarding his privacy, he had come out some time ago and had had a few boyfriends since, none serious. He had started seeing someone recently, a TV executive he'd met through a mutual friend.

'I hear you've been keeping Patrick busy,' he remarked. 'I've hardly seen or heard from him these past few months – not since you reappeared on the scene.'

I wasn't sure how much Patrick had explained to the others about me and him, our nascent romance, and reading my hesitation, Marcus reached across and gave my thigh a quick pinch.

'What a dark horse you are! Stealing our Patrick's heart.'

The forwardness of the gesture surprised me as much as what was uttered. Marcus had always seemed so reserved, eschewing tactile communication. But the words he used, the warmth and humour with which he said them, made my own heart soar, and I couldn't suppress the grin that came to my face.

'It's as much a surprise to me as to anyone else,' I told him.

'A whirlwind romance.'

'Yes, I suppose so.'

'Although he always did like you.'

'Did he?'

'Oh yes, of course. Had circumstances been different, I'm sure you two might have got together years ago. But then, who's to say, if you had, whether it would have lasted. It's all about timing, don't you think?'

I agreed.

Traffic was building on the M50: we weren't the only ones looking to get a head-start on the weekend. Not that I minded. My feelings of trepidation about this weekend began to fade. I had doubted the wisdom of attending this reunion. Fear announced itself in my dreams, which had grown troubled the closer the weekend drew. I was never prone to nightmares. The violence I spent my professional life analysing and recording never made its way home with me. But in the nights that led up to my return to Thornbury, some of those crime scenes paid visits, bodies submerged in my subconscious began to find the surface and float: one victim after another. But the more Marcus talked, the more convinced I became that everything was going to be all right, that the past could remain the past and this weekend would seal the end to all those dark memories, and Patrick and I could face into a bright future together.

'I'm glad for you both,' Marcus said. 'He needs something hopeful in his life.'

It was a curious statement to make, one that hinted at something deeper. I knew that, of all his friends, Patrick had always been closest to Marcus, and I wondered what private thoughts or fears he might have shared with him.

'Why do you say that?' I asked, and he made a sort of pouting expression as he concentrated on the road, as if trying to summon from memory exactly what had prompted the statement.

'I always thought it was hardest for him, Peter dying like that. It wasn't just the shock of it, but the sudden transfer of responsibility to Patrick of that whole estate. He was so young – barely eighteen. It was unfair, in a way. All the plans he had – university, travel, just the freedom to be young – all of that was swept away in an instant. I'm not saying it wasn't hard for the rest of the family. But Rachel got to escape – she hightailed it to London at the first possible opportunity. And as for Heather . . . You'll have heard the rumours that circulated about her?'

'Yes,' I said calmly.

'Not that I ever believed them. She loved Peter, despite their differences. And violence just wasn't in her nature. Rachel believed it, though.'

I felt the push of some dark emotion threatening to surface. 'Did she?'

'She never returned to Thornbury – not until after Heather died. Never spoke to her mother again – so Patrick says.' He shakes his head in sad reproach. 'Poor Heather. You couldn't really blame her for taking refuge inside a bottle, not with all that to contend with.'

He said this gloomily, and I thought of Heather, how the sparkling hostess could wilt once the party was over and all the guests had left. I remembered those large, watery eyes, her late-night rasp.

'To tell you the truth, I'm glad he's selling the place. Cutting himself free. He's been shut away there for too long. It's not healthy.'

'When's the last time you were down there?' I asked.

'At Thornbury? Two years ago was the last time. I was there for Heather's funeral. Awful occasion.'

'I can imagine.'

'In some ways, it was worse than Peter's. But of course,' he went on, stealing a glance at me, 'you weren't there for either.'

I kept my eyes on the road. 'How was it worse?'

'Heather's funeral? I don't know, really. I mean, his death was obviously far more shocking. But she had survived so much. The scandal of Peter's death, the dip in that family's fortunes. Not to mention the whispered rumours that circulated about her involvement in his passing. Most people there could still remember what she had been like before Peter died – in her heyday. By the time she died, she was virtually a recluse. This aging alcoholic living alone with her bachelor son in a crumbling old pile falling down about their ears.'

'Was Thornbury in a bad state then?' I asked, thinking again of the windows with their plywood covers, the overgrown avenue, the gloomy, shut-up rooms of the house. I didn't like to admit to Marcus that I hadn't been there myself in all the time Patrick and I had been seeing each other.

'After the funeral, the mourners were invited back to the house for something to eat. There was a decent crowd and Patrick had set out buffet tables in the dining room, drinks in the drawing room. All very elegant and restrained, but you could tell those rooms hadn't been used in years. I knew just by looking around that Patrick and Heather had taken to living in the back of the house, where the rooms are smaller and cosier. He admitted as much himself. But the thing is, people don't realize that houses need to be lived in to keep them alive. Shutting up parts of a house for years like that, well, it's like cutting off the blood supply to a limb. Sooner or later, the house will start to wither and fade. It will go into decline. It's a shame,' Marcus said, as we exited the motorway, the hedgerows springing up along the edges of the road, yellow fields of rapeseed showing luridly between the gaps. 'I told Patrick at the time that he ought to sell the place. Get shot of it before it fell apart completely. He refused, of course. Couldn't shake off the burden of his responsibilities as the only son and heir. The steward of Thornbury.' He said this with mock-bombast, but I felt his frustration, nonetheless.

'I do think he tried, Marcus, to be fair.'

'You're right. And I'm not being fair,' he said, relenting. 'The poor guy was in a state. Shocked, mourning. You know, I think he never really got a chance to properly grieve for his father. Too bewildered by everything – the suddenness of it all, grappling with the running of the estate, not to mention the shame.'

'The shame?'

'Of course it was shameful. A death like that? A man's brains blown out while his son's eighteenth birthday party was in full swing? Come on, Lindsey. You were at the party that night. You must realize that a scandal like that would attract the wrong kind of attention to the family – to those left behind. The obvious question being: Why? What led him to commit such an act? He wasn't sick. There was no mental illness. The man was in the prime of his life.'

I stared out the window, my eyes straining on the corners that sprang up before us, the roads growing narrow and twisty.

'There must have been a reason,' I said quietly. 'Otherwise, the guards would have followed it up.'

'I imagine so. Although what that reason was we may never know. A closely guarded family secret, perhaps.'

I didn't comment, and soon enough our conversation turned to other, happier subjects. Still, I felt the tension in my body had returned.

Much of the rest of the journey was spent in idle chitchat, snippets of gossip about various people we both knew, sprinkled with some political talk, Marcus quizzing me on some of the recent scandals within the ranks of the Gardai that had been making headlines. It was all fairly safe, mundane conversation.

It was not until we were almost at Thornbury that Marcus said:

'Can I ask you a question? Why is Patrick doing this?'

For a moment, I misunderstood and thought he meant the sale. It was only as I began to rattle through the shopping list of reasons for selling the place that he corrected me. 'No, I mean this reunion. Gathering us all in again – the old crew.'

'It's like he said: a send-off to the house before he sells it.'

'Yes, I know that's what he said, but I just wondered if there was anything else behind it. Anything he hasn't told us.'

'I don't know what you're getting at.'

He winced slightly, drummed his fingers on the steering wheel – a small gesture of irritation. 'It just feels odd, that's all. I don't know why. Just a feeling I get,' he said, before falling silent.

I glanced at the clock on the dashboard and saw that it was after five. Sunlight was weakening, casting the trees around in a lovely orange glow. It felt like we had driven much further than the actual distance travelled. We had reached the entrance and, as Marcus turned the car into the avenue, both of us fell silent. The tussocky grass running along the centre of the road had been given a haircut, and I could see that some effort had been made to rein in the rogue rhododendron. The abandoned car had been removed from the ditch. All that remained of the crash was a gash across the trunk of the tree – a single scar that would soon be covered by ivy and moss. Auspicious signs, and as the car came around the curve of the bend and the house came into view, it seemed to me a brighter, cheerier prospect than I remembered from that April morning.

The grass of the front lawn had been mown and that awful fencing removed. The yellow stone of the house glowed in the late-afternoon sunlight. The windows shone brightly among the clipped-back ivy. Over the high arch of the front door was a magnificent sweep of dripping wisteria, its knotted and twisted trunk rising proudly from the ground. Long lines of bunting had been draped from window to window of the upper storey, lending a festive air to the place. And high up above, the statues that stood guard along the perimeter of the roof had all been decked out with ties fluttering around their thick stone necks, a murder of crows flying above their heads, cawing loudly.

'Look – there are the girls,' Marcus said, glancing past me through the passenger-door window, and following the direction of his gaze, I saw two figures walking together, one taller than the other, both slender, both turning their heads towards the car, the smaller one raising her hand in greeting, then breaking away and half running towards us. Hilary. Even from a distance, I could see how much she had changed. The dramatic weight loss, the long, curly hair, the diaphanous fabric of her dress. In my mind's eye, the dumpy schoolgirl with the frizzy hair had grown into a plumpish woman with some kind of safe, sedentary job in the civil service. It was like seeing a stranger coming towards us now.

She was laughing and calling to us as I drew down my window.

'Oh, you lovely people!' Hilary exclaimed, as she leaned in the window to kiss me on the cheek, almost climbing into the car to reach Marcus, who laughingly stretched across to embrace her. She brought with her the scent of flowers and cut grass, and as she brushed past me, I saw a tattoo on the inside of her lower arm – some kind of Arabic writing. 'Isn't this just wild? All of us back here again! Look at you!' she said to me. 'God, you've hardly changed a bit. And don't you dare say the same to me,' her eyes flaring briefly with mock-indignation before she collapsed into giggles, displaying teeth that had been straightened and whitened in the years since we'd met. Underneath the gaiety and self-mockery, there was something watchful about her. Despite all the laughter and teasing, her eyes flickered over me, taking me in.

'Are the others here?' Marcus asked.

'Niall's just arrived. Look.' She gestured towards the house, where a white Range Rover gleamed in the sun, three figures standing next to it. 'We were just coming over to say hello.'

As the two of them chatted, my attention was drawn to Rachel, still standing some way off. That erect posture that I remembered so well, dressed darkly, her hair wrapped loosely in a scarf – just like her mother. Her arms were wrapped around a bucket containing a sheaf of flowers – wild flowers, I guessed, that they had just gathered from the fields and woods around the house. She had stopped where she was, watching after Hilary, making no effort to join her. Even though her face was in shadow and I could not make it out, I knew somehow that it was unsmiling.

'Can we give you a lift?' Marcus asked, but Hilary just laughed. It was a very short distance to the house – and as we drove away from her, I watched through the wing mirror as she ran back to join Rachel, hair and skirts flying, like an ad for shampoo or vitamins – something healthful. For all the warmth of Hilary's welcome, it was Rachel's lack of engagement that held my thoughts. If she had only approached the car, even raising a hand in greeting, it would have gone some way towards allaying my fears. A hard feeling formed inside my tummy – the sense that this weekend was going to be difficult.

Marcus drew the car up alongside Niall's and Patrick came towards us, his arms held wide and a broad smile of welcome waiting as he hugged Marcus first and then rounded the car to take me in his arms and kiss me full on the mouth. I heard Niall wolf-whistling and the woman next to him giggling and, despite my shyness at their attention, I felt happy, too.

'Get a room!' Niall yelled before Patrick released me and told his friend good-naturedly to shut up. He held my hand as we walked over to the others, Niall coming forward to plant a kiss on both my cheeks, saying, 'Well, well. We meet again.'

He had put on weight in the years since we had met, grown portly. Out of all of us, he seemed to have aged the most, or perhaps it was the evidence of his straining against the advancing years – the wrap-around shades, the trendy jeans, the sports shirt with the collar raised in the same manner as he had worn it back in school – that brought into sharp relief the changes in him.

I didn't hold his interest for long, and he looked past me to the two women approaching over the lawn.

'Girls!' he shouted, marching towards them, Hilary squealing with delight and breaking into a run again, Rachel waving at him, and this time, I could see her smiling. We watched as he embraced each of them, Hilary lifting her feet as he swung her around, and Rachel wrapping a slender arm around his neck and kissing him long and slow on his cheek. There was something more than flirtatious about the kiss – something seductive – which brought to mind the history between them. I glanced across at his wife. Like Niall, she was wearing shades, although hers were more of the Jackie Onassis variety, the kind that covered most of her face. Apart from that, she was all hair and legs. A miniskirt in a nude colour like the high heels she was wearing, dark hair in long, wavy tresses. I stepped towards her and held out my hand.

'I'm Lindsey. You must be Claire.'

She accepted my hand, a startled look coming over her face.

'No, actually, I'm Liv.'

'Oh! I'm sorry, I misunderstood . . .' I stammered, mortified at my mistake, and coming upon us, Niall picked up the thread of the conversation and laughed.

'Yes, there's been a change of plan,' he announced, putting his arm around Liv and pulling her close to his side. 'A bit of a Cabinet reshuffle in my life.' I could tell from Patrick's and Marcus's expressions that this was news to them, too. Oblivious, Niall smiled broadly and kissed Liv while the rest of us stood around, unsure of what to say.

Hilary and Rachel had joined us, and thinking it was best that I approach her now, I said, 'Rachel.' Licking my lips, finding that my mouth and throat were dry, my confidence wavering, I went on: 'It's so good to see you,' and reached across to kiss her hello, the same way I would greet any old friend, and to my relief she did not rear back in astonished disgust. Her response was gracious, if a little cool.

'Good to see you, too,' she said, her voice calm, the slightly lower register that I remembered having deepened with age and perhaps two decades of smoking.

Conscious of Hilary and Marcus, who were both observing this tentative reunion, I went on: 'You look wonderful.' She was perfectly groomed in a long, casual dress that showed off the elegant lines of her figure, her hair cropped into a short, silky bob. Her feet, I noticed, were slender and lightly tanned, dressed in flat woven-leather sandals that looked expensive. Her toenails were polished brown.

She didn't respond to my compliment, alighting instead on something Patrick was saying to Niall.

'What's all this I hear? What about a shoot?'

'He's making us work for our board,' Niall joked. 'No such thing as a free lunch, eh?'

Patrick laughed and said, 'I just thought it would be

fun if we all went out with the guns. Tomorrow morning, after breakfast.'

Rachel looked unconvinced. 'To blast away the hangovers?'

'What are we hunting?' Niall asked. 'Pheasant? Deer?'

'Nothing quite that exciting. I thought we might try and clear these crows from the land.'

'Crows?' Niall's nose wrinkled with disgust. 'For fuck's sake, man. You got us down here to clear the vermin off your land?'

Patrick laughed it off, telling Niall that it was rats or crows, he could take his pick, while Hilary pulled a face and said she'd sit that one out.

'So where are these feckers?' Niall asked, and we were all following the sweep of Patrick's arm towards the fields when a noise I can only describe as a deep groan seemed to come from the house. I didn't actually see what happened next. Instead, what I felt was a whoosh – a sudden displacement of air behind us – and then Niall shouted: 'Get down!', all of us ducking as an almighty crash sent a spray of gravel and dust into the air, and I realized with nerves jangling that I was on my knees. I was not the only one. All around me, people were crouching and cowering, blinking in confusion, and as the dust cleared we slowly got to our feet, shock turning to disbelief. On its side outside the window of the study lay the stone remains of a Bagenal ancestor, the statue of which had served until a moment before as one of the sentinels along the perimeter of the roof far up above.

Niall was the first to find his voice.

'Jesus Christ!' he exclaimed, a shrill note entering his voice. 'That could have killed one of us!'

'Is everyone all right?' Patrick asked, getting to his feet and looking around at the rest of us. 'Is anyone hurt?'

'Fucking hell, Patrick! I know you said the house was crumbling a bit, but I didn't think you actually meant there'd be flying masonry.'

'It must have been when I went up there earlier,' Patrick was saying, trying to keep his voice reasonable, although he was clearly shaken. 'When I was putting the ties on the statues up there. I must have dislodged something.'

'Dislodged something? Look at the size of that thing! Another couple of metres – that's all it would have taken – and we'd have been toast! My car could have been written off entirely.'

Marcus, having taken a step towards the statue, was standing staring upwards, one hand shielding his eyes from the sun as he gazed up at the space along the top of the wall it had vacated. I followed Patrick as he went to it now – so much larger than a lifesize man – and put a tentative hand to the place where it had broken free from the wall. He touched it with a kind of reverence, as if he couldn't quite believe what had happened. The statue in front of him still bore its pose, one hip thrust forward into a stance of power or defiance, facial features chiselled into a blank severity, eyes staring out blindly up at the sky above. I noticed with a pang that there was a St Alban's tie knotted around its neck.

'Are you all right?' I asked Patrick softly, but he shrugged off my concern with a muttered 'I'm fine,' before joining Marcus, who continued to stand some way off, his arms folded, peering up at the roof.

Hilary was asking Liv the same question, having noticed that she had turned away towards the car and was leaning over slightly.

'Something in my eye,' she said. 'Probably just dust.'

'Let's have a look,' Hilary said, tilting the other woman's chin upwards, and Liv blinked into the light.

Patrick and Marcus, having deliberated quietly together, turned and marched purposefully back into the house.

'Oh, that's fucking great,' Niall remarked, watching them go.

Rachel, I noticed, hadn't moved. Her bucket of flowers had toppled over on its side, a tumble of montbretia and cowslips and wild garlic spilling on to the gravel. She, however, appeared unfazed.

I decided to follow Patrick and Marcus. The statue lay almost in front of the entrance to the house, and I had to round it to reach the front door. Once inside the hall, I could hear noise from far up in the house, and I took the stairs two at a time, crossing the landing to the open door that led to the attic stairs. It was not as dark up there as I had imagined. A grainy light was coming in through the cloudy glass of the *oeil-de-boeuf* windows, and the narrow doors that led on to the roof itself were thrown open.

'Be careful,' I heard Patrick say, and as I stepped outside I saw him leaning against the balustrade, peering across at Marcus, who had climbed up, the better to examine the gash in the stonework where the statue had until recently stood.

'Should he be up there?' I asked, and Patrick turned, only noticing my arrival at the sound of my voice.

'No, he shouldn't,' he agreed, before shouting to Marcus, 'Look, come down off the ledge, Marcus, unless you want to follow him to the driveway below.'

Marcus climbed down and I felt the drumming in my chest ease a little. The breeze was stronger up here, and it whipped his carefully combed hair up above his head, lending him a kind of rakish air. He rubbed his hands together to clear them of dust and came towards us.

'There's some evidence of cracking near the base,' he explained. 'But I can't see any real disturbance to the stone – not significant enough to cause it to fall.'

'If only I hadn't put those fucking ties around their necks,' Patrick said, berating himself, and all three of us looked at the remaining statues, the neckties flapping about as if to make a mockery of him.

'It's windy up here,' I said. 'Perhaps, if a strong gust came up . . .'

'These statues have stood here for almost three hundred years, Lindsey,' he replied. 'They've survived storms. and even a hurricane back in 1973. I don't think a stiff breeze toppled him.'

'We should check the bases of all the other statues,' Marcus suggested. 'Make sure the fault line was limited to just the one.'

'Right,' Patrick replied, but in a half-hearted way. He was already turning back towards the entrance to the house. 'But let's do it tomorrow, shall we? It will be dusk soon, and better to do it in the light, don't you think?'

But Marcus was reluctant. 'I don't know. What if another were to fall?'

'Let's be optimistic, shall we? And hope that the rest of these stone fuckers have the decency to wait until this weekend has passed before they all go crashing to their doom. Now, if you don't mind, I'd better see to my other guests.'

He stepped past me into the attic. Marcus shot me a look, and we stood together in silence, taking one last glance around the parapet, before we followed Patrick inside, Marcus silently closing the doors on the sky and roof, the row of stone ancestors bereft of their leader.

6

It is Rachel's father who tells us about the costumes in the attic.

'They're somewhere up there,' he says, without looking up from his paper. 'At least they used to be, when I was a boy.'

There is a loud crunch as he bites into his toast.

It is my third weekend at Thornbury since mid-term, and I am growing accustomed to certain things – Peter Bagenal's taciturn silence over breakfast, Heather Bagenal's leniency towards her children, the constant stream of people through the house.

'Look at the hair on that one,' Hilary sniggers, jabbing a finger at the photograph in Rachel's hand.

'Careful,' Rachel says. 'These are old.'

There are other photographs scattered on the breakfast table – sepia prints of boys and girls our own age. Peter has unearthed them from one of the drawers in his study and has brought them in here for our amusement. While the boys show little interest in them, both Rachel and I pick through them. Hilary, too, is mildly interested in the Victorian ancestors with strong jaws and puffy hair, wearing elaborate costumes as if dressed up to perform some kind of play. A Greek tragedy with gods and heroes. Dresses falling in drapes, velvet cloaks, toga-like things. The boys wearing laurel crowns, sandals on their feet. The girls in heavy eye make-up.

'Strange to think they're all dead now,' Hilary remarks, and there is a collective groan.

'You're always so gloomy,' Rachel observes, until her father addresses her sharply.

'Be nice,' he says.

'You know, this isn't bad,' Patrick says, glancing up from the sheaf of handwritten documents spread out on the table amid the toast and the marmalade and the half-drunk tea. 'Some of it's illegible, but there's some funny stuff, too. *Ye cursed knaves of treachery*,' he reads, laughing to himself.

Along with the photographs, Peter has found the text of a play which he believes to be that depicted by the costumed folk in the pictures.

'You should rehearse it yourselves, the lot of you,' Peter declares, casting his dry gaze around the room at us all. 'Something to occupy yourselves.'

Marcus groans, and Niall mutters, 'I don't fucking think so.' He is surly this morning, maintaining he's not fully human until he's had three coffees inside him and it's midday. This weekend, he has taken to borrowing Peter's *Financial Times*. The previous evening, over dinner, he announced to us all his ambition of making a million before he is thirty. He reaches for the news-paper now, flattening its pages, and slurps his coffee.

Rachel tugs at my wrist.

'Come on, Lins. Let's go hunt in the attic.'

'Don't make a mess!' Peter shouts after us. 'We have guests arriving later!'

We close the door on the others, and I follow Rachel through the north passage and up the back stairs. Our feet clatter on the wooden treads, and the boards upstairs on the landing creak. We can still hear the boys below, their voices raised, shouts of laughter, but as we hasten towards the attic stairs, the silence around us thickens. I feel only the tiniest bit guilty about leaving Hilary alone with them. I glance back to see have we been followed, but there is no sign of her.

'Thank God,' Rachel says, as if finishing my thoughts. Her ability to do this is uncanny. 'She's such a leech. The way she clings to me. Ugh!'

She affects a sigh of exhaustion, tramping up the narrow stairs to the attic. I see the flash of her bare legs beneath a denim miniskirt, the skin on the backs of her calves pale and dusted with sandy-coloured freckles.

'And I know what you're thinking,' she continues, 'why on earth did I invite her? The answer is: Daddy made me. Gave me a big lecture on not leaving her out. How she's family, and all that.'

Everyone at St Alban's knows that Rachel and Hilary are cousins of some sort, although it's a fact that Rachel does not advertise. Even though they're the same age and have known each other all their lives, their differing natures hold them apart. They are chalk and cheese. While Hilary seeks out her cousin's approval, Rachel is loath to give it.

'When I asked if I could just have you to stay this weekend, Heather said no, spouting some crap about the importance of fostering lots of friendships rather than focusing on just the one. God forbid I might have a best friend. It's unhealthy, in her opinion. Dangerous.'

'Did she actually say that? *Dangerous*?'

'Mm-hmm.'

She pushes open the door to the attic, and dusky light falls through the gloom. I follow her, feeling the sting of her mother's words, which seem directed at me. As if she has sought to have Hilary here to somehow dilute my presence. Until this moment, I thought that Heather Bagenal liked me.

'Poo! This place reeks,' she says, and it is true that there is a sour, uriney smell rising up off the floorboards with the dust.

Milky light falls through the small round windows on to an array of chests and boxes and abandoned-looking pieces of furniture. It's hot up here, despite the gloom, the roof warmed by the unseen sun rising in the sky. An ancient cot stands alongside some rickety bedsteads. Rolled-up carpets are propped against the far wall. It's a long space full of shadows. A doorway opens on to another neglected room with discarded chairs and boxes, dustsheets concealing bulky objects.

'That room was the maids' bedroom when my dad was growing up,' Rachel tells me. 'When he was little, one of them died up here.'

'How?'

'Not sure. Pneumonia or TB or something. You can't imagine how cold this place is in winter. Pity the other poor girl who shared the room. There was just the one bed between them. She would have woken up in the morning to find her friend stone-cold dead next to her.'

She shivers theatrically, then starts poking around the clutter, looking for the costumes. Dust rises off the scuffed lids of chests as she throws them open. I move towards the maids' bedroom and peek inside. Rosebud-print wallpaper is coming away at the corners, a large brown stain spreading from the eaves.

'We used to dare each other to come up here when we were younger – me and Patrick,' Rachel tells me. 'We used to scare ourselves that the attics were haunted by the ghost of that dead maid. Once, when I was six or seven, Patrick locked me in here on my own for over an hour. I was hysterical when they found me.'

I don't know Patrick all that well, and yet this account of his cruelty surprises me. He has struck me as being fair and decent.

'He got the beating of his life afterwards. Served him right, too,' she concludes. 'Ah! Here they are!'

She holds up a dark-coloured garment. It looks heavy

and stiff. Setting it aside, she pulls out another, squealing with delight at each new find.

'Oh, we will have to put on a play now!' she cries with glee. 'What do you think?'

'What's the matter?' she asks, the delight on her face falling as she notices my despondency.

I don't know how to say it. The thought of Heather Bagenal having a quiet word to her daughter about me. Her whispered disapproval. It makes me feel depressed, strangely tearful.

'All that talk of dead maids. Ghosts.' I give her a watery smile, and my effort is rewarded by her bright laughter.

'Oh God! I'm sorry! Spooking you out like that. You'll never want to come here again!'

She couldn't be further from the truth. When I think about the rooms below – the grandeur of the hallway, the sweeping stairs and vaulted ceilings, furniture that has been passed down through the generations, everything bearing the patina of age – I feel some kind of pull inside me. A longing. But it is the Bagenals themselves that engage me the most. I think I'm a little in love with all of them. I want to be one of them. And the thought of this makes me feel instantly guilty, for I have my own parents, my own brothers, who all love me in their own ways. And yet, it is not enough.

'Here!' she declares, getting to her feet clumsily, folds of heavy fabric in her arms. 'You must wear this!'

She holds it up for me to see and, even though it is worn and nibbled by moths in places, there is beauty in the heavy brocade, the embroidered detail along the bodice, the scalloped edges of the sleeves.

'No, I couldn't.'

'Why not?'

'Because you should wear it.'

I feel too mousy and slight for such a dress. Not elegant or regal enough to carry it off. She swings me around so that I am facing my own reflection in the foxed glass of a mirror I had not noticed. Holding the dress up in front of me, she sweeps my hair over my shoulder, and I can feel her behind me, her hands firmly against my waist, keeping the dress in place, while my own hands go up to grasp it to my shoulders.

'There, you see?' she says, her voice close to my ear. A gold thread mingling with the darker fabric catches the light. I watch my reflection, unsure, afraid of appearing foolish.

'I look like Lady Macbeth.'

'No.' In the mirror, her gaze is kind, generous. Sometimes, I think, she sees things in me that I don't see. 'Desdemona, perhaps. Or Ophelia.' Her voice has dropped to almost a whisper. She touches my hair. Whatever ghosts I have imagined are whisked away. 'Lindsey,' she says, 'you can be anyone you want.'

7

I came upon her outside the house, half sitting on the fallen statue, alone and smoking a cigarette. Perhaps that is not completely true. Rather than coming upon her, I had sought her out. Best confront this thing head on, I thought. Get it over with quickly so that we could all move on. I had spied her out here alone, no witnesses to our first real encounter in twenty years, and while one part of me turned away from it, another part of me thought: *Fuck you, Rachel – do your worst.*

She regarded me cautiously as I approached, before saying slowly, 'So. Here we are again.'

'Yes.'

'Although the circumstances are rather different now, don't you think?'

I admired her poise – her sangfroid. For my part, I had my hands in my pockets to hide my nerves, a warm smile on my face as I rounded the statue and came towards her. I watched her peel an illusory fleck of tobacco from her lip. Strange how even the smallest gesture or tic can be a touchstone to the past. We could be fifteen again, but for the gulf in feeling between us.

'So where's my brother got to, hmm? Fretting over the guests, is he?'

'He's showing the others to their rooms.'

Disconcerted by the incident of the falling statue, Patrick had struggled to regain his composure and sought to hurry his guests to their rooms so this weekend could get back on track. I felt for him, his obvious distress over the incident, and his desperate desire for the weekend to pass off peacefully – joyfully, even. Despite all his nonchalance, I couldn't help but feel that this reunion was heavily invested with too much meaning.

'It's hardly going according to plan, is it?' she remarked, with a trace of gleeful wickedness I remembered of old. With her free hand, she gave two firm pats to the stone ancestor beneath her. 'The Earl of Baldonnell,' she told me then, by way of explanation, or even introduction. 'The patriarch of the dynasty. Did you know that?'

I said that I didn't.

'My father made us learn by heart the names of all of them, all those hulks of chiselled stone up there. It meant nothing really, at the time. It was just like learning tables, or spelling lists. It was not until later that we began to grasp what it meant, and even then . . .' She stopped, her gaze held by the statue upon which she perched. The corrosion of his features, several digits disappeared from his hands, the attrition of years passed on the roof, abused by the elements. 'I've had

the feeling ever since that if he had lived a little longer –
if he had been afforded that opportunity – there was so
much more he wanted to teach us about our past, about
where we came from. So much more he needed us to
know.' She dropped the cigarette on the gravel, ground
out the embers with her heel. Any dreaminess in her
voice disappeared, replaced by a harder tone as she
went on: 'God knows what he'd make of this. The state
the house is in.'

'There's no point thinking that way,' I said quietly,
hoping the thump of my nerves did not make me sound
querulous. I couldn't escape the feelings of disgust at
my own fraudulence – saying those things while she
invoked her father's memory.

'Patrick's let the place fall apart. Literally. I was
shocked when I came back home from London and
saw the house. I couldn't believe he'd let it slip quite so
badly into disrepair. Surely you must feel the same.' She
looked at me hard, in a challenging way, and while
there was no denying the truth in her words, still I felt
compelled to defend him and the efforts he had made.

'He tried his best to make it work,' I said firmly, reasonably. 'Anyway, what does it matter now?'

But Rachel, in her own inimitable way, did not hear
my question, or pretended not to, and had already
started to say:

'It was different when he had that one living here
with him. What was her name? Oh, Louise,' she said,
enunciating the name clearly, and I felt myself grow

still. 'Louise, yes. She kept the place in some kind of order. Gold-digger, of course. Like the one before her. They all are – all the women who go for Patrick. Still. Shame they fell out. She was good for him.'

Rachel returned her attentive gaze upon me. I felt every cell in my body prickling.

'My brother, I'm afraid, is the type of man who is helpless against women like Louise. Women who see this house in its state of neglect and whose eyes light up at the prospect of sweeping in here and transforming it, becoming lady of the manor. Transforming Patrick, too. But it never works out. Pretty soon they realize the size of the task they have taken on is not worth the reward. They all think that Patrick is the easy bit – that the house is the Herculean task. It's only when he has them safely installed that they begin to realize the real problem is him. Not that any of that matters now. It's goodbye to Thornbury, and poor Patrick will have to find something else to occupy his worrisome mind.'

She stopped then, somewhat abruptly, and I wondered if she realized she'd gone too far, regretted the candour of her words.

Old feelings of rage suppressed came rushing back at me, along with the memories of how easily she could stick the knife in, the pleasure she used to take in twisting it. Rage was alive within me, but I wouldn't give vent to it. I refused to give her the satisfaction of seeing me lose my temper. I would not play this game with her.

'I have no desire to be lady of the manor,' I told her

calmly. 'Nor do I want any hand, act or part in what happens to this place.'

'No, but you want something, don't you? You always have. Trouble is, I've never been quite sure what it is you want?'

'All I want is for Patrick to be happy.' She made a small huffing noise, but still I went on. 'Whatever happened here, whatever you think of me now, I'll always look fondly on our friendship, Rachel. It was something I cherished. And I understand that we cannot return to the past. Those days are long gone. But Patrick . . . He means a great deal to me. I don't know if you realize just how much. All I want is to try and help him. To be there for him.'

'And you think that's possible, do you?' she asked, her eyes swarming over my face as if seeking the answer there, and for an instant I was duped enough to believe she was sincere in her question. But then her face changed, a sneer drawing down over those fine features. 'God, how deluded,' she remarked with disgust, before moving away from the statue. Without a backward glance, she walked away from me and into the house. I watched her go, one part of me wanting to run after her and try to make her my friend again, try to persuade her to forgive me, to say that all was forgotten, that she was happy for me and Patrick. But I was a grown-up now and well used to living in the real world. I would never win back her approval – I knew that for sure. Nor did I need it. It was only a corner of my consciousness – a pocket of guilt made large by the shock of being back here – that made me crave the warmth of a friendship that had once meant more to me than almost anything else.

I stayed where I was, waiting until I was sure she was gone. In the dark foliage of the trees beyond, I heard the occasional guttural squawk, the sudden flap of wings, as if the crows had been witness to our conversation and, like an audience at the interval, were stretching their limbs, clearing their windpipes.

Once it was safe to do so, I went back into the house, letting out a long breath that I hadn't been aware I was holding. A hard feeling had started in my tummy, an old tension returning. It irked me how easily she could get under my skin. Despite myself, petty feelings of jealousy were stirring – the name Louise circling my thoughts. Why hadn't he mentioned this woman before? From upstairs, I heard a door closing, but looking up to where the staircase rose to a balustraded landing, I couldn't see anyone. Jinny was barking somewhere deep in the recesses of the house, and I heard Patrick calling to her to be quiet. His footsteps were growing louder now, and I waited at the foot of the stairs until he rounded the corner. His face filled with a smile at the sight of me, and I was happy and grateful to feel his arms around me again, his kiss somehow warmer – more sincere – now there was no one around to witness it.

He drew back and looked at me, playfulness in his regard.

'Is everything all right?' I asked. 'The statue on the ground – have you decided what to—'

'Oh, screw the statue! So the house is falling down around our ears – so what? Let's not allow it to spoil our time together, hmm?'

'Agreed.'

'So, mademoiselle, let me take you to your room,' he intoned, in a stab at a seductive voice.

Taking my bag in one hand, he led me upstairs to the wide landing, pausing briefly to let go of my hand as he reached for the brass doorknob. Pushing through the door, he led me into our room, where the early-evening sunlight was falling through the dual-aspect windows.

Having set my bag down on a low bench, he turned to look at me.

'Well, what do you think?'

'It's lovely, Patrick. Such a pretty room,' I said, although that seemed too small a word for what was a substantial space with high ceilings and an open fireplace of generous proportions. It had a feminine feel to it, with walls in pink distemper, the colour of the calamine lotion I remember being daubed all over my body when I was ten years old with chickenpox. A comforter with a rosebud print overlaid the bed.

'I thought you might like the view,' he said, gesturing towards the window, and we both went to stand there for a moment, looking out on one side to the kitchen garden at the back of the house and on the other over the copse of trees, beyond which lay the old stables. I knew that this room had once been his mother's bed-room, and the knowledge of that made me feel wary.

'Is this your room now?' I asked, noticing as I looked around that there was little evidence of him here.

'No, but I thought you'd prefer to be in the main house.'

'But what about you?'

'I'm not in the house any more,' he answered, then, seeing my surprise, he went on: 'The groomsman's cot-tage, by the stables – do you remember I said I'd been working on it? Making it habitable again?' I nodded. 'Well, I moved into it a couple of weeks ago.'

'Oh.'

'But I thought we'd be better off in this room for the weekend,' he said, to my relief. 'The place in the stables is a bit of a mess – and the bathroom's not fully plumbed in yet. Besides, here, we're closer to the action.'

'It feels strange, us sleeping together in your mother's room.'

His eyes lit up with sudden mischief as he pulled me to him and began kissing my neck. 'I've an idea. Let's pretend we're teenagers. Let's imagine that you're fif-teen again and I'm seventeen, sneaking to your room in the middle of the night to seduce you.'

'Your mother's room,' I reminded him, but he was undeterred.

'Yes,' he murmured, his kisses working down towards my collarbone, and I felt myself being drawn in. 'Let's hope she doesn't catch us at it.'

I giggled, and he speculated on the likelihood of Rachel's old school uniform being around the house somewhere. 'You could put it on for me – I'm sure it would fit you.'

'Perv,' I murmured.

His arms tight around me, holding me against the length of his body, his mouth found mine and I let myself relax into his embrace. After a moment or two, I felt him stepping back, drawing me with him towards the bed, and as my eyes opened, a shadow moved across the front of the wardrobe, so suddenly it made me look. With the sharp turn of my head, a little pop of light came into the field of my vision. I blinked and instinctively reached to touch my temple.

'What is it?' he asked, and I heard his concern but didn't see it, as I'd put both hands to my face, small stars bursting against the inside of my eyelids.

'Lins? Are you all right?'

'I'm fine,' I said, forcing my eyes open. 'I just thought I saw something. It's nothing.' The burst of light had dissipated now, but there was still an odd sensation, as if particles of the light remained, like gleaming dust motes travelling through the air. 'It's nothing,' I repeated.

But for a moment I could feel it: the throb of that foreign body settling against the bones of my face, squeezing the jelly of my eye, corroding the nerve.

'It scares me when you do that,' Patrick said quietly.

He was standing very still, his anxiety evident.

'I know. But I'm all right. It's just something that happens sometimes. I think I see things out of the corner of my eye, things that aren't there. It's weird when it happens – disconcerting. But at least I know what it is – what's causing it. At least I know I'm not going mad!'

'I thought my mother was going mad,' he said then, 'when it happened to her.'

He sat down on the bed, put his finger to his eye as if to rub away a stray eyelash or crumb of dirt. I felt the need in him to talk about her – Heather – and it surprised me, such was his caginess when it came to discussing her illness. Her death was still relatively recent – hardly even two years had passed. Taking a seat next to him, I reached for his hand and waited.

'Funny how it's only afterwards you realize the signs were there all along. I just hadn't understood them. Small things at first – slipping out of her routine, you know? She used to walk into Borris every day to get the papers, but then some days I'd find her still in her dressing-gown at lunchtime, wandering about the house like she'd forgotten something. Other things, too, erratic behaviour like getting into her car to go for a drive in the middle of the night. She started saying she could hear noises in the house, from up in the attic, or in the study, even though there was no one there. I dunno – probably a mouse in the walls, or a bird trapped in the eaves, some simple explanation.'

I waited.

'And then, one evening, we're sitting in the kitchen having supper, just the two of us, when all these cars start coming up the drive. People getting out and coming to the door, friends of Mum and Dad's who hadn't been to the house in years, all dressed up, thinking they'd been invited to dinner, even though my mother hadn't thrown a dinner party since my father died.'

'Did she realize she'd invited them?'

'No. She hadn't a clue. Some of the guests who turned up were people Mum wouldn't have dreamed of inviting – people we knew had been spreading false rumours about her and about Dad's death . . . Anyway, it was at that point I brought her to the GP. Honestly, I thought she was having some kind of breakdown. When the doctor suggested a brain scan, I was shocked. As it happened, by the time she had the scan, she was already in a coma. The night before her appointment, she drove her car into a tree. She never regained consciousness.'

'The wrecked car in the avenue,' I said, remembering my visit here three months ago – the old VW Golf twisted and buckled and sticky with dirt, wrapped around the trunk of a beech tree. It made sense to me now.

'Her diagnosis came too late,' he went on, but he was looking at me intently now. 'That's why I'm so grateful they've caught this early.'

His hand went to my temple, stroked my cheek with the backs of his fingers.

'Are you worried?' he asked, and it was not the first time he'd put this question to me. It had become a bit of a refrain and, like the other times, I answered the same way:

'A little.'

'You'll be fine,' he said, with conviction. 'I know you will be.'

I took his hand from my face, kissed his palm. The thought crossed my mind about the strangeness of life. The last time I had been in this room – twenty years ago, when it was Heather's domain – I would never have guessed that one day Patrick and I would be sitting here as lovers, that I would have such strong feelings for him, and have them reciprocated. It seemed almost miraculous.

Down the hall, a door banged, footsteps following towards the stairs. His eyes went to the door.

'You'd better see to your guests,' I told him gently.

'Are you sure you'll be all right?' he asked. 'Is there anything I can do? You have your medication?'

I told him not to worry, that I would be fine. And as I watched him stand, his posture slightly stooped, pausing to run a hand through his hair, the auburn colour of it appearing blond under the low-hanging light, a thought occurred to me.

'You know, right now, you look just like your father,' I said.

I don't know what made me voice my thought aloud. The past pushing up strongly at that moment, maybe, but it was true. His air, his manner, how his body had changed in the years since I'd seen him, his father's genes coming through, moulding the son into that familiar shape.

'Is that a good thing or a bad thing?' he asked.

'A good thing.'

He grinned. The gravity of the moment had passed, and I felt a lightness come into the space between us, a kind of optimism filling the room.

'Get yourself settled in,' he told me. 'Then come downstairs and join us for a drink.'

I sat on the bed for a moment after he'd gone, listening to his voice and footsteps retreating towards the back of the house before silence crept slowly in. How odd it was, being in a room I had only ever glimpsed through the doorway while Rachel was attending to some wish of her mother's. I had a distinct memory of staring at Mrs Bagenal's back while she sat at her dressing table, fixing her make-up. In my mind's eye, I could still see clearly her pale white-blonde hair above a silk paisley dress, bangles jangling along the stretch of her slender arm as she reached to tap the ash from her cigarette into a little brass dish in the shape of an upturned turtle-shell. There was no sign of the ashtray now. Gone were the brightly coloured clothes on their hangers hooked over the doors of the old wardrobe. Indeed, the room bore little evidence of the previous inhabitant, but it seemed to me that it still held her familiar scent – rosewater mingling with cigarettes.

In a bid to banish it, I sought to fill the room with activity, opening my suitcase and setting about finding temporary homes for my belongings, laying my cosmetics bag on the dressing table next to Patrick's shaving kit, hanging my evening gown in the wardrobe alongside his tuxedo. I noticed with surprise that some of Heather's clothes continued to hang there. Dresses of chiffon and silk in faded colours, covered in the crêpe paper and plastic of the dry cleaners, hanging there like ghostly presences.

I shut the door quickly and firmly, surprised at how unnerved they made me feel. Then I sat at the heavy antique dressing table in the corner, where someone had laid out hairbrushes and combs with mother-of-pearl insets, the grooming devices of a long-dead relative. As I examined my reflection in the mirror, my hair looked shiny, with a lustre that seemed new. My face was flushed with excitement, my eyes bright, my skin luminous and tanned. I looked well, healthy. I did not look like a woman with a tumour nudging her optic nerve. I picked up the brush, felt the weight of it in my hand, the bristles still soft, and for a moment I sat there, brushing my hair.

Downstairs, I heard Patrick calling to the dog to follow him, then the clipping of her nails over the flagstone hall. I put the hairbrush down and leaned closer to my reflection, my attention snagged by something gleaming within my hair. I put my hand up and retrieved the strand from my head and looked at it. White-blonde, with a dryness to it suggestive of age. I looked at the hair and then again at the head of the brush, and saw the other hairs that were hidden there, camouflaged by the pale bristles. Heather Bagenal had been dead for two years but, as I sat there at her dressing table, holding her hairbrush, the dry fibres of her hair caught in the pinch of my left hand, for a moment I felt her presence, a sweep of air behind me as though she had only just moved away.

8

Heather Bagenal is at her dressing table when we enter the room. From my place by the door behind Rachel, I can see her long, straight back beneath a floral silk dressing-gown. The gown itself seems exotic, like a kimono, and above it, her white-blonde hair is combed and free of ornament. She likes to wear scarves in her hair – loosely wrapped around like a hairband and, on one occasion, worn like a turban, diamond earrings flashing beneath. It is mid-morning, and yet something of the night lingers in this room. It's there in the half-drawn curtains, the bedclothes in disarray. Heather's reflection in the mirror appears tired and pale. She reaches for a powder puff and begins dabbing at her cheeks, her neck. Among the assorted cosmetics, a cigarette rests in an ashtray, sending a thin line of smoke up into the air.

'Mummy,' Rachel says, leaning against the dressing table. 'Can we raid your wardrobe?'

'Whatever for?' Heather asks. Bracelets jangle along the stretch of her slender arm as she reaches for her cigarette.

'For the play we're putting on. The costumes in the attic are falling apart.'

'Whatever are you talking about, darling?'

'The play that Daddy found. Remember?'

Heather winces, the hand holding her cigarette going to her forehead to press the skin between her eyebrows.

'So can we?'

'Yes. Yes, of course,' she agrees, but I can tell she is saying this to get us out of the room. There is a pained and delicate air about her.

Rachel opens the wardrobe, revealing an array of brightly coloured garments. She works quickly, finding what she wants, handing me a couple of dresses on hangers while she takes some for herself.

'You look pretty today, Lindsey,' Heather says, and I turn, surprised at her attention. Her smile is weak, but her eyes look sharp. 'Is that a new blouse you're wearing?'

I look down at the white crêpe top that I have put on over my jeans. It's one of Rachel's that she has allowed me to borrow. I can tell from the way she is looking at me that Heather knows this already. There is something mean about her this morning. I feel pinned down by her words, and I think back to what Rachel had said, repeating her mother's words about our friendship. *Unhealthy. Dangerous.*

She stubs out her cigarette in the little ashtray, looks down at her cosmetics, and selects a lipstick.

'You'll include Hilary in this play of yours, I hope,' she says.

'Course,' Rachel answers, and we leave Heather to her face and hurry out of the room.

Downstairs, the boys are hauling the Persian rug from the hall out into the driveway.

'It's too nice to be indoors,' Patrick explains, as the three of them drag it towards the grass and the leafy shade of the giant sycamore. Hilary is there already, with the costumes heaped at her feet. It seems the boys have been persuaded, in our absence, to participate in our play.

'Won't your parents mind?' I ask Rachel, but she just laughs and runs after the boys.

It's still a shock to me, the irreverent way they treat their home and the lovely things that fill it. Heather Bagenal had hardly looked up to see which of her clothes Rachel was taking. None of them appear to attach value to their possessions – even Rachel, by the casual manner in which she had flung open her own wardrobe and told me to help myself, like she couldn't care less what I took.

Niall has found a long, sharp stick and is wielding it like a sword. At St Alban's, he fancies himself a fencing champion. Hilary slips one of Heather's dresses over her head. It's a long, silky garment in a bright pea-green colour. I can imagine its elegance on Heather's slender frame, but on Hilary, dumpy and small, it looks plain and ill-fitting. Rachel sees this, too, and we smile at each other behind Hilary's back.

Patrick has the script and takes charge of assigning the roles.

'I'll be the narrator. Marcus, you can be the evil count—'

'Lindsey is to be the princess,' Rachel informs him, and instantly Niall protests. He has already claimed the role of avenging hero, and has his sights set on a love scene with Rachel. The prospect of wooing me instead horrifies him.

'I don't even want to be the princess,' I tell them. 'Rachel, you can be her. I don't mind, really.'

Rachel is having none of it. She declares herself in the role of wicked sorceress.

'No offence, Lindsey,' Niall says, 'but I hardly even know you.'

'It's just a bit of fun,' Patrick interjects reasonably. 'No one's asking you to marry her.'

'C'mon, Rach,' Niall says.

She turns from him. 'My mind's made up.'

'Fine. Then find someone else.' He throws down his sword and sits cross-legged on the rug beside Marcus.

The argument persists. I move away, embarrassed, and pick my way through some of the other costumes. Beyond the garden, Peter Bagenal is peering out of the library window, a faint look of dry amusement on his face.

'You should try on this one,' Hilary says, and she offers me the green dress that she has changed out of. 'I'm too pudgy. It will look better on you.'

'Thanks,' I say, unsure of how to respond. I don't know Hilary very well.

'She loves doing that to him,' Hilary says, meaning, I assume, Rachel and Niall. 'Getting him wound up like that. It works every time.'

Something about the way she says it makes me angry. The knowingness of her remark. Revealing, too: for all her wide-eyed innocence, she's a kitten with claws.

'It's rude to stare,' I tell her, my voice cold enough to make her notice. I take the green dress and go back to the others, leaving Hilary where she is.

The argument is settled by an intervention from Marcus. He volunteers to play the avenging hero to my damsel in distress. Niall is to play the scheming count and Rachel the wicked sorceress, so he gets his desired pairing after all, just not in the way he had thought. Patrick is the narrator, and Hilary a handmaiden, and so the roles are filled.

Once the order of play has been established, the air lightens and there is laughter and slagging as we dress in our costumes and get into character. Someone suggests make-up, and Heather comes out on to the lawn — dressed now, having shaken off her earlier fatigue — and surrenders her bag of cosmetics to us.

We rehearse for hours, pausing for lunch in the coolness of the kitchen. Even then, we speak to each other in the manner of our characters. 'Pass the bread basket, wench,' Niall demands, and Rachel gives him a dig in the ribs.

Late in the afternoon, cars begin to arrive – friends of Peter and Heather who have come for dinner, some to stay the night. The men all wear dinner jackets; the women are beautifully dressed. We watch them from our spot beneath the tree, before breaking away to rehearse our individual scenes down by the river or over by the stables. The shadow of the tree lengthens, the sunlight grows soft and golden.

It has been decided that we will put on our play in the folly – a mock-Gothic old ruin built by the first Bagenal ancestor to settle at Thornbury. Eroded and neglected over the years, all that remains of it is a cluster of old plinths and columns around a sort of stage. Roman statues in varying states of undress. Stone benches, urns. All of it hidden away within a shelter of yew trees and holly bushes.

The light has faded, a bluish glow along the path as we troop down – the cast of six. The adults are waiting – Heather and Peter and their friends, occupying seats we had carried down earlier in the day. Later, there will be a formal dinner for the grown-ups in the dining room, supper for the actors in the kitchen. For now, they are drinking champagne, bottles stowed in an urn, Peter taking photographs and filming with his cine camera. We can hear the clink of their glasses, the talking and laughter before we emerge on to the folly, our stage lit with candles in jars, some old kerosene lamps propped up at the sides. It is as we are coming out to perform that Hilary tears her robe, a white tunic edged with gold and tied loosely at the waist with a length of cord that had previously been used to hold back the curtains in the drawing room.

'Shit!' she cries, and Rachel bends down to examine the gash in the seam. 'What should I do?' Hilary asks, crestfallen. Rachel has done her make-up, eyes heavily outlined in charcoal black, lashes lengthened with mascara. Around her head, she wears a corona of tinsel to match the gilded edging of her Victorian costume. It shines among the frizz of red hair. In the dusky half-light, she looks curiously beautiful.

Peter Bagenal is reclining in his seat, one arm slung about his wife's shoulders. She is cheerful tonight, bright-eyed and smiling, enlivened by her guests – they both are. It is Peter who comes to Hilary's aid. Getting up from his seat, he says, 'One of my dress shirts ought to do just as well. Come along, young lady.'

He leads Hilary back to the house, his camera dangling from its leather strap slung over his shoulder. The adults loll about on the chairs, refilling their champagne flutes, and Rachel begs a glass from her mother.

'Oh, all right.' Heather laughs, and she pours a drink for me and Rachel to share. The boys are allowed a glass each. They are seventeen, while we are only fifteen. Heather has draped herself over a couple of chairs. Her mood has improved since this morning, her manner is loose-limbed and casual, a hazy amusement in her beautiful face.

We withdraw to a spot under the shade of the yew trees. Patrick wants us to run through our lines. I see Niall put his hand around Rachel's waist; he whispers something to her and she throws her head back and laughs. Our glasses are empty now, and Marcus gathers up the flutes. Hilary returns, wearing a white shirt, ruched across the chest, little dress buttons in onyx blinking in the candlelight.

'That looks nice on you,' I say to Hilary of her new shirt. She seems embarrassed by the attention, and I feel a touch of remorse for snapping at her earlier. She mumbles, 'Thanks,' but doesn't meet my eye, her mouth downturned.

The play is a riot, unintentionally so. Rachel and I, giddy on champagne, giggle throughout. Niall relishes his role of evil count, all twitching eyebrows and wicked grins. Marcus and Hilary try their best to fade into the background, while Patrick grows red-faced with exasperation as his production falls apart.

The adults enjoy it, and afterwards Peter Bagenal rewards us with an almost full bottle of champagne to share. We stay up late in the kitchen, polishing it off. And then Niall produces a bottle of peach schnapps and the boys mix Fuzzy Navels, and we all retire to the TV room to watch *Betty Blue* until Heather Bagenal switches it off and urges us to go to bed.

Rachel falls asleep quickly beside me. From the fold-out bed near the window, I can hear Hilary's gentle breathing and assume she is asleep, too.

As I close my eyes, and turn on to my side, I think of the maids in the attic all those years ago. I imagine I see them lying side by side, moonlight coming through the small, round window, their day's work done as sleep comes for them at last.

9

'Right, then! Drinks!' Niall said, clapping his hands together, as I entered the room. 'Patrick's gone off to poke around the kitchen, so I'll do the honours.'

'God, I need a drink after that,' Hilary said in a hushed tone. She was standing by Niall's side, rubbing the backs of her bare arms as if she were cold, even though there is a fire puttering away in the grate. 'I don't know about the rest of you, but that really freaked me out.'

'It's a fucking disaster,' Niall agreed, swiftly and sloppily assembling G&Ts before passing them to Hilary, who handed one to Marcus and one to me before taking one for herself and raising it to her lips.

'You wouldn't believe what I told Liv about this place to get her to come down here with me,' Niall went on. 'Waxing on about five-star luxury and old-world charm. Jesus! She's upstairs now, doing her nut.' He knocked his drink back with some haste, adding: 'Calm the nerves, eh?'

After the high-pitched sociability of our initial reunion, both Niall and Hilary seemed subdued, the wind taken out of their sails.

I looked about the room: much of it was as I remembered – the same butter-yellow walls, the hectic patterns on the mouldings and cornicing, the wide planks of the floorboards darkly stained. I sat down next to the dog on the sagging sofa, and she looked up briefly as I stroked her flank.

Niall stalked the room, the ice in his glass clinking.

'I don't know what he's planning to do with that statue,' he said, keeping his voice low enough not to be overheard. 'Is it even worth shifting it? The thing must weigh a ton.'

'He'll need to get help,' Marcus replied.

'He must have insurance of some sort. What do you reckon?'

'I'm not sure if it will cover something like this.'

'Hmm. An act of God?'

'Perhaps.' Marcus sipped his drink, tight-lipped and thoughtful.

'What do you think he'll do with it?' Hilary asked absent-mindedly. 'He'll hardly stick it back up on the roof, will he?'

'It will look strange if it doesn't go back up,' I remarked. 'Like a missing tooth.'

Niall glanced across at me. 'I think that's the least of his worries – what it looks like.' He stopped prowling around the room, and nodded his head towards the crack running up through the wall. 'Christ, would you look at this? The whole fucking place is falling apart.'

Marcus glanced at the crack, before looking back at Niall.

'What about Claire?' he asked quietly.

Niall examined the contents of his glass, as if considering a refill. 'What about her?'

'Where is she?'

'I buried her in the garden,' he answered darkly, before giving a brief wheeze of a laugh and turning back to the drinks tray. 'She's at home, in Dublin.'

'Does she know you're here with Liv?'

'It's none of Claire's fucking business where I am or who I'm with. We're separated.'

He splashed some more gin into his glass, foregoing the tonic, then straightened up and gave Marcus a challenging look.

'I'm sorry to hear that, Niall.'

'Gee, thanks, Marcus.'

'Since when?' Marcus asked softly.

Niall shrugged. 'Recently enough. But it's been coming for ages. Both of us knew it.' He took a slug of gin before adding: 'Should never have gotten married. I think we both realized that within a year of the wedding. But then Sammy came along, and Jake, so what could we do?'

'How're the boys taking it?'

'They're absolutely fine. I have them every other weekend, take them to football every Wednesday. They're young enough. Kids adapt. Far quicker than adults, that's for sure.'

He trotted out these phrases in a defensive manner, and I couldn't tell whom he was trying to convince.

'And Liv?' Marcus pressed gently. 'Where does she fit into all this?'

'Liv's my little gift to myself,' Niall said smugly. 'My reward for the shit-storm I had to go through to get out of that marriage.'

His voice was hard and flat, two feet planted firmly on the thin carpet, one hand in his pocket, tension running across his shoulders and chest.

'How long do you think that's been there?' Hilary asked, bringing the conversation back to the crack in the wall. It shot up through the masonry into the ceiling.

'Who knows?' Marcus said, at last turning his attention towards it.

'What does it matter now?' Niall remarked. 'Cracks or no cracks, it will be someone else's headache soon.'

I looked around at all the lovely objects, the antique furniture, the heirloom paintings. 'Everything in here seems to fit so perfectly,' I said. 'I hope the new owners won't take it all out and replace everything.'

'Replace it?' Niall scoffed. 'What planet are you on, Lindsey? This place is going to be demolished.'

I felt the jolt of his words, a shock of sadness coming at me at the thought of the destruction of the house. Cracks in the masonry, broken windows, falling statues – these rooms were still lovely.

'I wonder if it continues into the bedroom above,'

Marcus said, ignoring him, his eyes fixed on the ceiling, where the crack disappeared into the cornice.

'That's Rachel's bedroom,' I said.

'She's probably in Heather's room now, though, right?' Niall asked, and Hilary took the opportunity to tease him, asking 'Why? Are you going to go knocking on her door in the middle of the night?'

'Maybe I will.'

'Why should tonight be any different, hmm?'

'Or maybe I'll come knocking on your door instead,' he told her, sidling up to where she was standing, putting a meaty hand around her waist. It brought into sharp relief her dramatic weight loss. She was almost concave, her bare arms sinewy and stalk-thin.

'Besides,' she added, 'I believe Patrick and Lindsey are in Heather's room.'

'Really?' Marcus asked, and I heard the surprise in his voice, read in it his realization of the seriousness of my relationship with Patrick.

'That's right,' I said.

'Poor Heather,' Hilary said. 'It's still hard to think that she's gone. She was a sweetheart.'

'She was a lush!' Niall barked.

'Niall!'

'Oh, come on, it's true. You know it, I know it. It was bloody obvious to one and all.'

'Well, so what if she liked a drink or two. It's hardly a crime.'

A spark of mischief entered his expression as he said

to all of us, 'Can I let you in on a little secret?' Pausing for a moment to ensure he had all our attention, he said: 'She hit on me once. Heather.'

'What?' The word shot out of Hilary's mouth like a bullet.

'Honest to God. In this very room. Back when we were in school. I had left something in here – my Walkman or something – and was nipping in here to get it when she grabbed me by the wrist and asked me would I call on her later, in her bedroom.'

'No way!' Hilary squealed, laughing now at the deliciousness of the gossip.

'I was only sixteen or seventeen at the time, a bit gormless, and I said to her, "What for?" and she just looked at me, then took a step closer so that she's right up close to my face. And all she does is puts a finger to my lips, gives me this meaningful look, and then walks out of the room.'

'I don't remember that,' Marcus said quietly.

'I'm not sure I told anyone.'

'And did you go to her room?' Hilary asked.

'Course I didn't! I mean, I liked her and all, but she was no Mrs Robinson.'

'She was a good-looking woman,' Marcus countered.

'Yeah, but up close you could see all the make-up clogging in the cracks of her face. And her breath smelled of stale booze.' He shook his head, a trace of something close to pity coming into his voice. 'And there was something desperate about it—'

'Desperate to resort to sex with you,' Hilary joked, but he continued on, still serious:

'No, I mean it. There was just something sad about her. Even if she hadn't been my best mate's mum, I still wouldn't have gone near her. There's no joy in fucking someone who's depressed.'

There was a sudden spit and hiss from the fire that roused the dog to a sitting position. Liv put her head round the door, her phone in one hand.

'Babe. Everything all right?' Niall asked, all attentive. 'Sit yourself down and I'll fix you a drink.'

'I can't get any mobile reception.'

'Oh, you can't in the house,' Hilary told her. 'It's a bit of a black hole.'

'Still?' This from Niall, as he unscrewed the cap of the gin. 'Un-fucking-believable. I said to Patrick two years ago that he needed to sort that out – ring the mobile network, put some pressure on his local politician. And it's still not working?'

'I'm afraid not,' Hilary confirmed, before telling Liv: 'Patrick says it's fine for us to use the landline in the hall if we need to. Otherwise, you'll have to walk back down the avenue – the reception kicks in after the second bend.'

'That's just fucking great,' Niall said, before Marcus interjected:

'You should make sure Claire has the landline number. Just in case.'

'She's got it,' Niall said, without looking at him, but his voice dipped as he said it, and I could tell he wasn't happy.

Liv accepted a drink and sat down on the couch on the other side of Jinny, patting her head, and saying, 'Beautiful dog, isn't she?'

Marcus and Hilary had moved towards the window, and I heard Marcus ask: 'How does Rachel feel about the decision to sell?' but I had no opportunity to hear her answer, as Liv had leaned towards me, saying:

'I hear you're a photographer?'

'Sorry?'

'A portrait photographer – that's what Niall said.'

'He's winding you up. I work in forensics. My subjects are frequently the victims of violent crime.'

'Oh.'

'I don't know how you do it, Lins,' Niall said, oblivious to his girlfriend's embarrassment. 'Really I don't. Would you not prefer to take nice black-and-white portrait shots of new babies, and kids in bare feet, and have a nice little studio and shop in some posh village, and make your living that way?'

It was not the first time someone had made that suggestion to me – not least my own parents, who would far rather I spent my time photographing weddings or bar mitzvahs than capturing images of the dead lying in their own blood. It's a difficult thing to explain to strangers – how preserving the scene through pictures is a particular skill, one that I have an inherent gift for. How it takes a certain kind of person who can hold their nerve and tiptoe through the aftermath of violence while remaining dispassionate, casting a cold eye around them.

I didn't say anything of this to Niall. Instead, I said: 'Someone has to do it.'

'You must see awful things,' Liv said, her voice dropping low. 'How did you get into it? I mean, did you become a guard first and then realize you wanted to get into forensics?'

'It was photography that got me there. I was always into it, and I realized at some point that my gift was for detail – for capturing the accuracy of a scene, rather than finding an imaginative way of framing it. I discovered that I was more clinical in my approach than artistic. One thing led to another and, after a degree in science, I went to the UK to do my masters in forensics, and that was my route in. So you could say that my camera led me to my profession.'

'I remember you and your camera well,' Niall said. 'Back in the day.'

Something in the way he said it made me sit up straighter. I could feel it now, the undercurrent of danger in his voice, his air.

An uncomfortable silence had fallen over us. Hilary, looking to break it, said, 'Wasn't it Heather who gave you your first camera?'

'No,' Rachel said loudly. Until that point, none of us had been aware of her standing at the open door, listening to our conversation. 'No, it was my father who gave it to you, wasn't it?'

She was looking at me in a direct way, and it occurred to me that, for the first time since we'd been thrown together here again, she was addressing me in front of the others, and looking me clear in the face.

'That's right,' I said softly. 'A Leica.'

A Leicaflex SL2, in fact. Made in 1975. I loved that camera – love it still. I might have told her that, at that moment, it was upstairs in my camera bag, waiting to be used. I don't know why I packed it – a last-minute nudge of nostalgia that made me pluck it from the shelf and check for film before throwing it in with my Nikon and lenses. But I didn't tell her. The spikiness of her address had everyone's attention.

'Patrick and I weren't allowed to touch that camera,' she went on. 'It was one of Dad's treasured possessions. Until you came along.'

She put her cigarette to her mouth and softly inhaled, never once breaking her gaze. And even though she was standing a good ten feet away from me, I felt her looming over me, imperious, a quiet anger burning behind the cool exterior, the softly spoken words. A pulse was beating in my head. The smoke was making me nauseous. A log slipped in the fire, sending a storm of lit embers up the chimney.

'Dinner is served,' she announced coolly, before turning on her heel and leaving the room.

10

1991

Rachel is gone when I wake up, the space in the bed next to me abandoned. The fold-up bed by the window is also empty. I sit up, bleary-eyed and confused as to the time. From below come sounds of industry – doors opening and closing, the clatter of crockery. Pipes gurgle down the hall – someone is running a bath. I get out of bed and squint at my watch. It is almost ten.

Padding downstairs, barefoot and still in my pyjamas, I follow the sounds of voices until I reach the kitchen. Marcus is reading the paper, while Niall and Rachel are deep in conversation. There is no sign of the adults. All three look up as I come in.

'Look who's up!' Rachel says, beaming at me. She is always bright-eyed in the mornings. I have known her to stay up half the night, reading, and still she is first up, dressed in her uniform, hair neatly combed, before my feet have even touched the ground.

'Sorry. I overslept.'

'Tea?'

'Yes, please.' I approach the table as she pours,

conscious that the others are all dressed. Rachel's hair is still wet from her shower.

'Where's Hilary?' I ask.

'She wasn't feeling well. She's gotten a lift home.'

'Is she all right?'

'Tummy bug or something.'

'Hangover more like,' Niall remarks.

I take the mug of tea she offers, noting the way Niall's eyes glance down at my nightwear – white flannel pajamas with a love-heart print, the words *Sweet Dreams* emblazoned across the chest.

'I'd better get dressed,' I say, backing away from them.

'We'll leave the breakfast things out for you,' Rachel tells me.

Her voice sings out as I close the door behind me: 'And help yourself to my clothes!'

I linger a moment in the corridor, the mug in my hands, listening. It is dark and cool out here, and their words, though spoken quietly, still reach me.

From Niall: 'Christ. That was a sight I could live without seeing.'

'What?'

'Those pyjamas. Talk about a passion-killer.'

In the corridor, I feel a deep flush of shame.

Rachel must have hit him for I heard him cry out: 'Ouch!'

'Contrary to whatever you might think, Niall, we don't all sleep in flimsy little nighties or sexy lingerie.'

'Oh now, don't do that! Spoiling my fantasies . . .'

From Marcus: 'Is there any more tea in that pot?'

'I know she's your friend, but let's face it. She hasn't got much taste, has she? I mean, why else would you lend her your clothes? Admit it.'

'So what? I still like her. She's my best friend, for God's sake!'

'Limpet, more like.'

'You're an arse, Niall,' I heard Patrick say, before adding fondly, 'but you're my arse,' and they all laughed.

'Everything all right, dear?'

I turn quickly, tea slopping over the rim of my mug. It runs over my hand on to the floor.

Heather Bagenal stands beneath the low arch that leads to the back stairs. She is a few feet away from me, her face in shadow, but there is a hard note to her voice.

'Fine,' I say, turning away and hurrying back towards the hall and the staircase, aware of her eyes on me the whole time, watching, judging.

I dress quickly, in my own clothes, screwing my pyjamas into a tight ball and stuffing them deep inside my rucksack. *She hasn't got much taste, has she?* His words claw around inside my skin, until I cannot stand it.

Hurrying down the stairs, I go outside into the garden, running across the front of the house, hurrying towards the river. I don't want to be near any of the others – not even Rachel. Her defence of me seems flimsy and insufficient. I know how she can change her behaviour to fit whoever she is talking to. I am well aware how she can alter her tone, her form of address, when looking to get what she wants. The way she calls Heather 'Mummy', for instance, when seeking to get on her good side. The way she sidles up to teachers at school, the perkiness of her manner when addressing them. It occurs to me as I charge through the long grass of the meadow how there is a shift in her manner whenever Niall is around. Had anyone else voiced the opinion he had just offered about my lack of taste – about my being a limpet – Rachel would have snarled at them, defending me fiercely. I'm sure of it. But with him, she just simpers and smiles, mildly berating him in that flirtatious manner that she only uses when he's around. It's infuriating. Baffling, too. Niall is a boor, a mindless brute, with no subtlety or even humour. A snob, too. I think again of his gaze passing down over my body and squeeze my hands into fists, queasy with humiliation.

In the field to the west of the house where the grass grows long, Peter Bagenal has set up his tripod and camera. He is bent over it, peering through the view-finder, his back to me. I can see a long, dark strip in his shirt where the sweat has broken through. It's not yet eleven, but already the day is a scorcher. My jeans feel hot and itchy around my legs, my scalp burning beneath the sun. I pick a stem of long grass and whisk it above the heads of the others as I move across the field towards him.

'Hello, Mr Bagenal,' I say, and instantly he straightens up and whisks around to see who's addressing him.

'Lindsey,' he remarks, the surprise leaving his voice as he says: 'Call me Peter,' and we both smile, because he has said the same thing to me on each of my visits.

'No Rachel?' he enquires, and I shake my head no and look away.

'Had a falling-out, have you?'

I shrug and whisk my grass stem back and forth against the side of my leg. I'm not inclined to say why, and he doesn't ask. Instead, he invites me to come and look at his camera.

'My latest toy,' he says, enunciating the words in a particular way. The previous evening, Heather Bagenal had referred to his new camera using those same words. I cannot tell if a sharpness should be read into his tone or not.

'I'm trying to capture the sunlight on the house,' he explains, gesturing towards the building, then looking through the viewfinder again.

He has to stoop to press his eye against it, even though I can see the tripod is fully extended. 'Well, come along,' he urges, his impatience rising, and I step forward to the camera, waiting while he adjusts the tripod to my height.

I feel shy of him, although I have been coming to his house for a few months now. His terse manner can be intimidating. He is a tall man, taller than my own father, and on the lean side, with the same brownish colouring as Rachel. His skin is darker than hers, though, ruddier, as if he spends his days outdoors. I watch his hands as they adjust the lens. They look like farmer's hands, large-fingered, dirt gathering around the nails.

'Now, then,' he says briskly. 'Try it out.'

'I hardly dare to touch it,' I tell him, laughing with nerves.

'Well, it was terribly expensive,' he remarks. He is not a man given to smiling, but there is a dryness about him that hints at humour. 'You buy cheap, you get tat,' he adds, a phrase I have heard him trotting out before.

I put my eye to the camera and listen while he tells me how to adjust the focus. Tentatively, I give it a go.

The air is dry and dusty, the sunlight catching tiny insects on the wing.

'Hasn't your father ever let you use his camera?' he asks.

'He isn't really into photography.'

'What is he into? Sport?'

'I guess. Watching it, not playing it.' I think of the bar with the TV on in one corner at all times, the notices put up in the window of the pub whenever a match is being shown.

'Rachel says you don't let her use your camera,' I remark.

When I step away, I see the twitch of a smile at the corner of his mouth.

'Perhaps I should,' he concedes. 'Come now, don't

be afraid of the thing,' and he gestures impatiently to it, encouraging me to adjust the lens, to reposition it to better capture the house.

I press down on the shutter. The thrill of it is breath-taking. Not just the simple act of pleasure involving the use of something I could never afford myself, but the feeling of responsibility conferred on me in that moment. By allowing me to use his camera, he seems to convey a sense of trust in me that he doesn't have in his own children. As if I am older, more mature than they are.

'You must cast a loving eye over it,' he tells me, in his brisk, instructional tone. 'Look for what you love about the subject. The picture you take will reflect that.'

I cannot imagine my own father talking this way. Even though the strangeness of it registers with me, it is only fleeting, for I am taken by a new thrill. The feel of the camera in my hands, the press of it against my face. I click and click again, allowing myself to be drawn in, wanting to explore and discover.

My coolness towards Rachel fades. I say nothing to her of my conversation with her father, of his camera, and the rest of the weekend passes peaceably, without incident. Heather drives us to the station on Sunday evening, and we all slump in our seats as the train pulls away, the gentle rocking motion drawing us back towards St Alban's.

Later, back in our dorm room as I unpack my bag, I find one of my photographs of the house. It is in an envelope in the front pocket of my rucksack. Mr Baganel must have slipped it in as we said our goodbyes and prepared to return to school. My first real photograph. It shines with newness, the chemical smell of the developing agent still noticeable. I could stick it to the wall above my bed or use it as a bookmarker. But I am wary of the attention it would draw, the questions Rachel would ask. Instinctively, I know it is something best kept to myself.

11

We ate in the kitchen that night. A less formal arrangement than what was planned for Saturday night, as Patrick assured us.

'Sit anywhere you like,' he instructed as we filed in, general noises of appreciation greeting thc food, the wine, the conviviality of the room.

'Here,' Niall said to me as I approached the table. 'Have a glass of wine. You look like you need it.'

I accepted his gesture of appeasement and sat down alongside him.

Over spaghetti bolognese and Chilean Merlot we discussed the points which our lives had reached, each one of us offering up a sort of snapshot of our careers. Niall had made a fortune in hedge funds and now operated as an angel investor for various tech start-ups in the city. Rachel worked on and off for a gallery in London owned by a friend that specialized in mid-twentieth-century design. Hilary had her own business – something to do with lifestyle consulting. Niall teased her, calling her a 'wellness guru', which didn't bother her in the least. She gave a short account of an epiphany she'd had as a first-year arts student at Trinity. She had been standing waiting for a friend one day outside the dining hall when she heard a tourist asking another student for directions to the Buttery. 'Just over there,' she had heard the student saying, pointing to where Hilary was standing, adding: 'The entrance is right behind that fat girl.' That one crass remark changed her life completely. Assiduously, she had set about changing her body, her diet, her lifestyle. It disgusted her now to think how careless she had once been about her own flesh, the disregard she had shown for it.

The French doors to the patio were thrown open, the evening sunlight falling on to the chequered tile floor, warming it, and we ate in the glow of candlelight, with the occasional sounds of birds and insects outside filling the pauses in conversation. The wine was consumed with alacrity, glasses chiming as we toasted and toasted again, and before long Patrick made the trip to the scullery to fetch another couple of bottles.

For my part, I didn't drink much. The wine tasted strange. I felt it coating the roof of my mouth like a bitter skin. No one else seemed to mind, which made me wonder whether it was a side effect of my medication. I had been warned to expect changes to my taste buds, along with other sensory distortions. It made me uneasy. But if I remained quiet, the others grew increasingly chatty and garrulous. Hilary kept them entertained with a string of anecdotes which all seemed designed to draw attention to her hopelessness when it came to financial matters. Rachel gently admonished her, saying that it was only because she was such a soft-hearted person that she wound up in these messes. Niall, who was quite drunk, argued that soft-heartedness in business amounted to commercial negligence, and that if the recession had done one good thing, it was the introduction of some hard-hearted realism to all those socially minded amateur entrepreneurs who publicly berated capitalism while privately crying over their lack of return on investment. He was sick to death, he went on, of listening to these whingers and moaners who'd lost their homes or their businesses and now expected the state to swoop in and be the instrument of social justice. If they couldn't keep up their mortgage repayments or hang on to their businesses, then tough fucking luck. He said all this without hesitation, oblivious to the meaningful looks being cast his way by the rest of us as Patrick stared down at his plate, his arms folded over his chest, keeping his thoughts to himself.

'It must have been amazing,' Liv remarked, changing the subject, 'growing up in a house like this.' She glanced past us to the doorway beyond with its fine architraves and the ancient dresser laden with china, before adding with a half-embarrassed laugh: 'It certainly beats a three-bed semi in Artane!'

'We had the run of the place,' Rachel acknowledged, grateful to run with the changed topic. 'In the summer, my mother would let us wander out into the woods and fields beyond and she wouldn't see us until dinnertime. We had such freedom, didn't we, Patrick?'

He nodded his head, but remained quiet. Having finished eating, he was leaning his elbows on the armrests of his chair, his hands clasped under his chin, a thoughtful look on his face. I could see he was not relaxed. Rachel seemed bright and loquacious – happy to hold court – and in Liv she had an appreciative audience. But I knew this much about Rachel: it was the moment when she was at her most dazzling that she was likely to jump up and sting you.

'Of course, this house is much changed from how it was in my parents' time,' she added sinuously. 'Back then, we had a whole legion of people running the house and the farm.'

Patrick took a sip from his glass but said nothing. He was no longer looking at Rachel but staring down at his empty plate. The rest of us had fallen silent. Marcus was thoughtful, Niall drunk and morose. Hilary had taken out her vaporizer and occasionally put it to her mouth, delicately drawing on it, her eyes downcast as smoke came from her mouth.

'My parents loved to entertain,' Rachel went on. 'There were always parties in this house – big ones and small. Patrick and I were encouraged to bring our friends. That dining room,' she said, waving a hand back towards the formal rooms at the front of the house, 'was always in use. My father would have died rather than entertain people here in the kitchen!'

'Most people entertain in their kitchens,' Marcus interjected. 'Dining rooms have become passé.'

'We'll be in the dining room tomorrow evening,' Patrick said, ignoring Marcus's kindly intervention. Two red spots had appeared high on his cheeks.

'Oh, Patrick, I wasn't criticizing, darling,' she said. 'I was just trying to draw a picture for Liv of how this house used to be.'

'I think you've made your point, Rach.'

Family members have their own verbal shorthand and, while I may not have been fluent in theirs, we could all read the signs.

'That bolognese was delicious,' I said. 'Did you make it from scratch, Patrick, or was there a jar of Dolmio in there somewhere?'

'Definitely Dolmio,' Marcus joked, and Patrick shot me a grateful look.

Back on safer ground, the volume of our talk rose with tentative and giddy exchanges: Hilary telling us about her bread-making, for example; Marcus sharing a story about a food co-op he had been a member of when living in London. Throughout all this, Niall looked restless. Liv tried to nudge her way into the conversation by asking a lot of questions, and I couldn't help wondering why nobody was talking about the obvious. It was as if none of us wanted to be the first to say anything about Patrick's relinquishment of the house. In the end, it was Niall who brought it up.

'We need a toast,' he said, refilling his glass and raising it to the gathering around the table. 'And it appears as if it's left up to me to do it.'

'Why should today be any different?' Patrick quipped.

'To this lovely, crumbly old pile,' Niall went on, 'Literally crumbling,' he added, gesturing with his wine glass to the front of the house, and beyond it to the driveway, where the Earl of Baldonnell still lay on his side, pitched into the gravel, the St Alban's tie knotted around his neck adding insult to injury. I glanced across at Patrick, but he seemed to take it well, smiling up at Niall as he concluded his toast.

He drank from his glass, and we all followed suit, but we did so uneasily. His words had brought a sombre note to proceedings, and the ambiguity of his tone added to the uncertainty.

'They'll hardly have much to demolish, the rate this place is collapsing,' he added, laughing as he took his seat.

'Enough of that,' Patrick said, but it seemed there was no stopping Niall.

'To the highest bidder, then.'

This last comment seemed to have touched a nerve. 'There's a lot more to it,' Patrick said stiffly, before standing to collect the finished plates, 'than simply cutting our losses and selling to the highest bidder.'

'I just can't believe that this is the last time we'll be here, in Thornbury,' Hilary opined. 'It just seems wrong.'

'We tried hard to find a buyer who would care for the house in the way it deserves. It just wasn't possible,' Patrick said quietly.

'What are you saying?' Niall interjected, returning to the thread of his argument with Patrick. 'You would rather have sold to the under-bidder so long as he agreed to restore her to the grandeur and beauty she once demonstrated?' He laughed again derisively, disdainfully. 'No wonder you didn't make a good job of running it as a business.'

'There's history here,' Rachel cut in, jumping to her brother's defence. 'Heritage. This is more than a ruin in a field. We wanted to know the place would be taken care of . . .'

'Because you couldn't,' Niall interrupted her.

Patrick had already turned away from the table, so I couldn't see his expression, but I heard the sharp crash as he dumped the stack of plates on the countertop.

'I tried everything I could to keep this place going.'

There was a brief pause before Niall reacted, nodding his head in understanding.

'Oh, I see. You're pissed at me because I wouldn't lend you the money?'

'No, I'm not.'

'Look, I explained to you at the time – it just wasn't feasible. I couldn't make the numbers work. For fuck's sake! Marcus said the place was practically falling down!'

A dark look had come over Patrick's face, a furious expression which he now directed at Marcus.

'I never said that,' Marcus protested.

'You fucking did!' Niall exclaimed.

'Thanks a lot, mate,' Patrick said to Marcus, coolness in his tone.

I reached out a hand to his arm, seeking to steady him. The situation was getting out of control. But he lifted his hand to his brow, shaking off my touch, and rubbed at a wrinkle of tiredness or stress, before taking his hand away and saying in a quiet voice:

'This hasn't been easy for me – coming to this decision, then having to break the news to you all. You say it doesn't feel right, Hilary, well, just how do you think it feels for me? Marcus, you say the place is falling down, but when I went to you to ask for help with plans for this place, you shrugged me off because you were too busy. The same way you were all too busy. You talk about this house in wistful tones of nostalgia and longing, but none of you has even bothered to call down here – not once since my mother died. And I don't blame you, Niall, for not investing in this place, but I do think you could have been a better friend. If any of you had taken the time to visit, even just once in a while, then you could at least have seen what I was going through, talked a bit about it, and then the idea of me selling the place mightn't have come as such a shock.'

Hilary was the first to apologize. 'I'm so sorry, Patrick. I've been wrapped up in myself – we all have.'

Marcus agreed. 'And for the record, I think it's a good thing you're selling this place. Freeing yourself from the stress of it – I think it will be the making of you. And if I can help in any way—'

'Thanks, Marcus.'

'I'm an arse,' Niall admitted self-pityingly. 'Ignore everything I just said.'

'I know you're an arse, but you're my arse,' Patrick joked, and we all laughed, even Liv, who can't have been aware that this was an old joke between the rest of us. 'This is our last weekend here,' Patrick went on, more serious now. 'All of us together. Let's not waste it feeling angry or disappointed.'

'Hear, hear,' Marcus said, and all of us clinked glasses and drank to that.

'Dessert,' Rachel announced, and went out to the scullery, returning with two tubs of Ben & Jerry's.

'What will you do?' Liv enquired of Patrick as Rachel began scooping out the ice cream. 'Will you stay in the area? Or travel, perhaps?'

'I'd like to travel,' he said. 'Lindsey and I have talked about it, haven't we? A six-month tour – South America, Asia. We could both do with a holiday. But Thornbury will always be home. And you know, I'm not selling off the entire estate.'

'No?'

'Only this house and the parklands surrounding it. The stables I will keep, along with the land to the west of the house that's currently used for agriculture.'

'So you're going to be a farmer,' Niall said, sounding unimpressed as he tucked into his dessert. It was evident that, despite admitting to being an arse, he was still bristling.

'Why not? It's an honest living.'

'If you say so.'

'I have some ideas I'd like to try out.'

Patrick proceeded to talk us through his plans for producing organic lamb, as well as his intention to plant several acres of wildflower meadows and establish an apiary.

'It's almost impossible to buy pure Irish honey,' he told us, his voice taken with passion for his idea. 'That stuff you buy in supermarkets is only packaged in Ireland, not produced. It all comes from Eastern Europe or South America.'

'What about that Manuka honey?' Liv asked.

'That's from New Zealand. And for all its health properties, you'd be better off consuming real Irish honey from Irish flowers, indigenous to this country.'

Patrick continued talking us through his notions of producing beeswax candles and other goods. He talked of converting the other stables into workshops, developing a cottage industry, providing some employment for the local people. I had heard it before and, even though it sounded fair-minded, even idyllic, my mind went to that stable and I had a sudden blinding flash, imagining blood spattered over the whitewashed wall, fragments of bone and other matter mingling with the straw on the stone ground. All of that had been washed away now, and yet I couldn't help but feel that the place was contaminated by what had happened there, polluted, its poison lurking in the corners, waiting for a chance to grow. An unexpected feeling of nausea came over me. My eye was at me again, the feeling like it was swelling in the socket, as if someone had jammed their thumb into it. I put my hand to my face, pressing gently on the temple.

'How much will it take to get this business off the ground?' Niall asked, getting down to brass tacks.

'I haven't quite worked that out yet,' Patrick admitted.

'Still, seed funding's not going to be a problem,' Niall commented. 'I imagine you'll have a whack of cash after selling this place.' He waved his fork in the air to indicate the house, the land that surrounded it.

'Less than you'd imagine,' Patrick said in a regretful tone. 'After all the debts have been paid off, you'd be surprised at how little is left.'

'I would be surprised. Come on. Seriously. How much are you getting for this place? Several million, I'm guessing. Right?'

'I'd really rather not get into that,' Patrick said, sounding uncomfortable. 'It's complicated.'

'A tidy package should uncomplicate things, I would think,' Niall said, putting his fork down and wiping his mouth with his napkin.

'Look, why don't you just drop it?' Marcus interjected. 'It's clear he doesn't want to discuss it.'

'I was only asking,' Niall said, his voice growing cold. 'Just trying to make conversation.'

'Well, don't,' Marcus said, coming to Patrick's defence. 'It's vulgar to discuss money at the table.'

'Come on, guys. Let's be nice to each other, remember?' Hilary said, trying to calm the situation, but Marcus ignored her.

'And I never said anything to you about Thornbury falling down. Where do you get off spouting such bullshit?'

'Not in so many words maybe—'

I had taken my hand away from my eye, and saw Patrick sitting back in his chair, staring hard at the table in front of him, a strange look coming over his face.

'It's so fucking like you,' Marcus went on. 'Prodding a man about how much he earns or what he made on the sale of his house. Unless he volunteers the information, you don't go there.'

'Christ, a lesson in etiquette from you . . .'

Patrick tried to placate the two:

'I didn't ask you all here so we could argue about the past. Nor do I want to talk about money. I asked you here because of how close we once were. We shared something in this house – all of us – and I wanted you to be here with me for one last weekend before I let this place go. So could we please just stop bickering and actually enjoy ourselves.'

But it was too late for that. The bickering had become something else. It had been simmering between the two men from almost the moment we had arrived.

'I am enjoying myself,' Niall said, his words laced with sarcasm. 'I'm having an excellent time.'

Then, under his breath, Marcus uttered the word 'Prick.'

There was a sudden rush of air and movement as Niall lunged across the table, toppling candles and sending glasses crashing, grabbing for Marcus.

We all jumped to our feet, each of us pulling at one man or the other, trying to separate them as they clawed at each other, struggling to gain some kind of purchase in a desperate scramble to thrash the daylights out of their opponent. Everyone was shouting. I suppose, in all, it only lasted two or three minutes, until Liv, assisted by Patrick, managed to pull Niall back. She continued holding on to his arm, even after the two men had been broken apart. And it was in this pause that the real damage happened.

The table was ruined. A couple of glasses had smashed, a jug had toppled over spilling flowers across the tabletop, two of the candles had been snuffed out. Hilary had come forward and begun mopping up the spilt wine and water, while Rachel and I were picking slivers of glass from the table and putting them on to a plate. The French doors remained open but a breeze had picked up now, causing a curtain to billow. The awareness of it was bothering me somewhat, jarring as it did with the pulse in my eye. I was turning to look at it when the blow came.

Throughout the meal, I had been sitting with Niall to my right. He was still standing at this point, Liv holding on to his arms and remonstrating with him, while he attempted to extricate himself from her grip. At the moment of my turning, he must have snapped, violently wrenching his arm free of her grasp, the recoil sending his elbow straight at my face. Instantly, I went down.

I can't say for how long I was out. But I do remember a narrow hissing sound coming into my ears, like the noise of something deflating. And then the pain abruptly announced itself, throbbing and vital, waves of it like some kind of convulsion. I could hear their voices now, Patrick's rising above all the others, shouting, 'Give her room! For God's sake, stand back!' A faintness of light as I tried to open my eyes, and then someone's arms beneath me, hauling me to my feet. I clutched at the table for support, muttering the insane protestation that I was fine, really.

'What's the matter with her?' I heard someone ask. Patrick's hand went around my waist, and I felt my arm being placed around his shoulder, my weight leaning into his body.

'Out of the way,' he said, steering me towards the open doors, and it was only when we were outside in the coolness of the kitchen garden, away from the others, that the fear came rushing in.

'My eye. Oh God,' I said, feeling the pain coming at me, the thrum of it alongside the doctor's warning: no

undue pressure, no hard impacts, under no circumstances. The pain wormed through my eye to my brain
and I felt the damage seeping out.

'Hang on,' Patrick said, and I felt his body holding
me up as he steered me towards a bench. 'It's okay,
Lins. I've got you.'

12

1991

Rachel and I are studying in her bedroom. There will be exams all next week before we break for Hallowe'en. She has plans to visit cousins in the south of England. I will go home and help out in the pub. INXS plays on the new stereo – a present from her parents for her sixteenth birthday. Above her bed hangs a new poster of Michael Hutchence. Rachel thinks he's a god.

I sit cross-legged on the window seat, my history notes spread next to me. Rachel is lying on her front on the bed, smoking, her legs, crossed at the ankles, swinging lazily back and forth.

'God, this is tedious,' she says, flipping the page of her textbook. 'What's the difference between the Federal Republic and the Weimar Republic?'

'Hilary would know,' I remark carelessly.

Hilary had not come to Thornbury this time. *I'd rather give it a miss* were her words. Rachel had hardly reacted. 'Suit yourself,' was all the response she gave.

'Pity she's not here,' I say, testing. When Rachel doesn't reply, I add: 'I wonder why she didn't come.'

'Haven't the foggiest,' she says, disinterested.

A low fire putters in the grate. Our socks hang from the mantle above, still damp from the shoot this morning. Shortly after seven we had gathered on the lawn, all four of us still bleary with sleep. Me and Rachel. Patrick and Marcus. The mist hanging thick over the grass and the trees beyond.

Rachel has been quiet all weekend, moody. The shoot had lifted her spirits. For a brief while afterwards, she remained cheerful and upbeat. The fresh morning air, the thrill of stalking the land while everything around us was still waking. She shot a rabbit. Marcus did, too. Patrick's attempts were unsuccessful, and I didn't fire my gun once.

We had all returned, tousled, happy, full of talk of our shoot. In stockinged feet, we padded about the kitchen, searching out food, before sitting at the table, drinking mugs of tea while reliving the experience, talking back through the woods and trees, the early haze over the lake, the sudden rush of a drake stretching its wings in the rushes. I had watched the way Rachel's eyes had widened when telling of the flash of a rabbit's tail, the snap of the barrel slotting into place and the jolt of the gun against her shoulder as the first shot rang out. All the while, out in the pantry, the pat-pat-pat of blood hitting paper as their kill dripped from scullery hooks.

'Perhaps we should take a break,' I suggest now.

Sitting at the window, the panes of glass cloudy and dripping with condensation, I feel the heaviness in the air between us.

She doesn't look up from her textbook, stubs out her cigarette in the shell ashtray.

'And do what?'

'Go for a walk, maybe? We could see if the boys want to come.'

'No, thanks.'

'I bet you'd go if Niall were here.'

I say this softly and I mean it kindly. But her eyes flash at me with sudden anger.

'I don't know what you mean.'

'Don't you?'

Niall is spending the weekend with his new girlfriend. Her name is Thea. He met her at a party in Blackrock. She goes to Alexandra College, and her parents have a massive house on Shrewsbury Road. Niall was quite specific about that.

'You're not yourself. You seem down. And I just thought . . .'

'You thought I was mourning the loss of Niall? Please. I'm not that desperate.'

'I know you like him,' I try tentatively.

'He amuses me, that's all.'

She pushes herself up off the bed, goes to the bureau where she has left a magazine.

'The Waterboys are playing McGonagle's next month. Any interest in going?'

I drain the last of my coffee. It's cold against the back of my throat.

'We'd never get permission.'

'We'll just say we're going home for the weekend.'

'Where would we stay?'

'A hostel. Patrick's done it loads of times. How else do you think he got to see The Pixies?'

She flicks quickly through the pages of the magazine, as though searching for something she cannot find.

'Anyway,' she continues, returning to our previous conversation, 'I have my eye on someone else.'

I look up. 'Who?'

'I can't tell you.'

'Why not?' I cannot keep the sting of hurt from my voice.

'It's too soon,' she answers loftily. 'But I will say this: he's not an infant like Niall. I'm done with playing nursemaid to children.' She puts down the magazine, stretches and yawns. She picks up a loop earring and slots it into her earlobe. I watch her carefully as she examines her reflection in the mirror, tucks her hair behind her ear. 'I need someone older. More mature. Someone I can learn from.'

'Learn what?'

She rolls her eyes angrily. 'Sex, of course. Duh!''

'Oh, go on – tell me. I promise I won't tell.' Still she won't budge, so I say: 'I'd tell you.'

'Really? Tell me, then – who do you fancy?'

Patrick's face flits across my mind and I look down at my notes, studying them.

'Not Patrick?' she says. Her ability to read my thoughts is uncanny. Or perhaps my interest has been obvious to all.

Rachel is laughing now, clapping her hands with delight. 'Oh, Lins – no! You can't, you just can't!'

'I don't really,' I protest, embarrassed at her reaction.

'You do! I can see it. Holy shit – you're lusting after my big brother.'

'I'm not lusting! I just think he's nice, that's all.'

'He's nice all right. Perfectly nice and perfectly dull. And I say that with a lifetime's experience of him. No, no. You're far too interesting for my boring older brother. We shall have to find you someone with more spark, more sex appeal.'

'Like your mystery man.'

She returns to her bed, picking up a vial of purple nail polish on the way. The chemical smell of it enters the air, and she smiles to herself as she dabs at her nails with the little brush, a private, inward kind of smile, as if she's remembering a joke I'm not in on.

'You won't tell Patrick, will you?' I ask.

She blows on her nails. 'Don't worry. Your secret's safe with me.'

'I'm going to make some more coffee,' I say carelessly, taking my cup and hers. I let the door swing shut behind me.

The house feels different now that the weather has changed. Autumn has come on suddenly, and I can feel it in the draughty coolness of the landing. All the doors are closed. I get the feeling that everyone has retreated to their various corners. Small creaks and groans accompany me as I take my time descending the sweeping staircase in my bare feet. Even on a dull day like this, the chandelier shines with majesty. Through the bevelled glass of the windows that flank the front door I see the gardener – Henry – astride the lawnmower, cutting the grass that sweeps down to the line of trees along the avenue.

The noise of the mower fades as I move past the hall, back towards the kitchens. I feel a little down. Remembering Rachel's laughter, the gleefully incredulous look on her face as she said: 'Not Patrick?' All right for her, I think bitterly, and not for the first time I envy her her confidence. Niall is not the only guy she has wrapped around her little finger. She and I are best friends – a fact firmly established over the past year since we've been thrown together at school. I spend more of my home leave at Thornbury than I do with my own family. And yet, at times like this, I feel the wide gulf in experience and understanding between us. Apart from a few shifts at school discos, and one awful occasion at a rugby-club disco where I endured groping and fumbling under my T-shirt at the hands of some spotty fifth-year from Terenure College, I have nothing to bridge the gap between us in terms of our sexual experience. At times, I worry she'll leave me behind.

The kitchen is empty. I fill the kettle and plug it in. A sudden noise from the corridor alerts me to someone's presence. I look out the door but there is no one there.

'Hello?' I say, and when there is no reply I think of

Rachel's story about the dead maid. And even though I don't believe in ghosts, a whisper of fear passes through me.

Dismissing it, I follow the noise, feeling the coolness of the flagstones coming through the soles of my feet. I find Peter Bagenal in the scullery, taking photographs of the dead rabbits.

'I thought you were meant to be studying,' he says, barely glancing up. 'Can't have you failing class tests now, can we? Your parents will blame us – say we distracted you from your work.'

'I am studying. I just came down to make more coffee.'

The blood is no longer dripping. The newspaper has been cleared away. With the dull autumnal light coming through the small window, the rabbits appear long dead, like the taxidermy animals in the hall with their glass eyes.

'It's a strange choice,' I say. 'Those rabbits.'

'You don't see beauty there?'

'No, it's not that. It's just that you always take photographs of the house.'

'The house is not my only subject. Nature and people draw my interest, too.' He sounds almost affronted, but I am more relaxed around him now. His terseness no longer bothers me.

'Rachel says you're to have an exhibition.'

'Indeed. My first foray into that scene.'

'Are you nervous?'

He answers simply: 'Yes.'

In the kitchen, the little bell in the kettle pings to announce it has boiled. I am still standing in the doorway of the scullery, and as I start backing away, making noises about returning to my study, he says: 'Wait. Come here a moment, won't you? I want you to do something for me.'

I feel the strangeness of his request but curiosity gets the better of me. I step forward into the room.

'Stand here,' he says, indicating the space in front of the counter above which the rabbits hang from their hooks.

He takes two steps back and shifts to the side so that the light, paltry though it is, can fall through the window towards me.

'Try to keep still,' he instructs in a flat voice as he raises the camera to his face.

'Put your hand on the counter. No, the other hand.'

I do as he says. He issues more instructions: turn your head towards the door but keep your body facing forward, look at the rabbits, tuck your hair behind your ear, untuck it, look back at me, keep your eyes open, don't smile.

All the time, I am acutely conscious of my own appearance. I know he is just installing me in the frame to create a more interesting picture, but still my vanity nudges to the fore. I feel myself pushing my shoulders back, my chest a little forward. I dip my head and look up into the camera, as I've heard this is the most flattering way to be photographed, but he tells me not to do that.

'That's not the kind of picture I'm after,' he says. There is a reprimand in his tone, and I can't help but feel ashamed. 'That's it!' He is excited now. 'Hold that look. That's exactly it.'

His attention sharpens, and I feel his intensity as he rapidly captures the image again and again, and I am so pleased to have found what he is looking for and presented it to him that I don't even notice Heather Bagenal until she is at the doorway, one hand on the architrave as if to steady herself.

'What is this?' she asks. 'What is going on here?'

'Nothing,' I answer quickly.

Peter stops what he is doing and looks at his wife.

'Heather,' he says.

'What is going on here?' she repeats, louder now, more insistent.

The vagueness of her expression looks more like confusion, but there is something spiky there. Something dangerous.

'I'm just indulging my hobby,' he says calmly, slowly fixing the lens cap back into place.

She is about to say something to that, but stops herself suddenly, the words disappearing into a little burst of air from her mouth. Her lips look thin, her face twitchy. She looks at me again, and then at the rabbits above me, and her face becomes a mask of bitterness.

'It's disgusting,' she says under her breath, before

turning and leaving the room, and from out in the corridor I can hear her repeat this, the words hissed into the cool air.

The atmosphere in the room has changed. It's as if her misinterpretation of the scene has somehow sullied it. From the slump that has entered his frame, I can tell Peter feels it, too. He looks sadly at the Leica in his hand, then holds it out to me.

'Here,' he says gently. 'Why don't you borrow this for a while.'

'Oh, no, I couldn't,' I say quickly, knowing already that it was one of his possessions deemed out of bounds.

'Go on,' he urges, a weary expression taking over his face. 'I need to see to my wife, and it's probably best if I don't . . . Well. Just take the camera. Take it with you outside around the park, or further into the woods and fields. Take some pictures. Then bring it back to me and I'll show you how to develop them.'

I put out a tentative hand and accept it from him.

'I have a feeling you may turn out to have an eye for this,' he says, and the kindness in his voice makes my cheeks grow hot so I look away.

I do as he suggests. For the rest of that weekend, in the intervals between study, I take the camera outside. It is something I must do secretively. Something I don't want to have to explain to Rachel or the others. Heather Bagenal remains in her room that night and Peter has made arrangements to meet friends in Kilkenny, so the four of us dine alone. Patrick steals two bottles of wine from the cellar and we get drunk and stay up late telling ghost stories. I feel warm and happy and don't even mind too much when Rachel drops a heavy hint about my feelings for Patrick.

Peter doesn't show me how to develop the pictures. When I deliver the Leica to him the next morning, in the hallway, he looks mildly confused, almost as if he has forgotten that he had lent it to me. 'Very good,' he says, accepting it briskly, and then he goes into the library without another word and closes the door behind him.

Heather does not appear to see us off. Rachel and Patrick say goodbye to her in her bedroom while Marcus and I wait downstairs. Shortly afterwards, a taxi comes and takes us to the station.

13

2017

Everything narrowed to the point of pain. The world around me, the house, the others, all of it shrank to the fear that had jumped alive inside me. Dimly, I was aware of Patrick's voice and Rachel's, but I couldn't latch on to any words, I was more aware of their physical presence as they led me out into the darkening evening light, the taut strength of Patrick's body against mine, holding me up and half dragging me towards a bench.

He sat me down, and I felt my body weaken, so much so that I would have liked to lay down my head, but at that moment I was conscious only of holding it still, as if that might limit the damage, stop the rot from spreading. Something cold pressed against it, and I reared back suddenly, Rachel saying; 'Calm down, Lindsey,' in that clipped no-nonsense tone that I found oddly reassuring. Her hand was cupping the back of my head, the other hand holding the ice pack against it, and I sat like that for a few minutes, feeling her firm but gentle grip about my head as the fluttering in my heart came under control, my breathing became less shallow, the throbbing in my head diminished.

'No, not now,' I heard Rachel snap with irritation to someone at the door. 'Make yourself useful and fetch a brandy. Hold still.' This last command directed at me.

I did as I was told, and gently she peeled away the ice pack, Patrick saying: 'Careful,' in a sharp voice. I felt his fear and her cold, examining gaze.

'Does it look bad?' I asked, my heart stirring with nerves again.

'You're going to have one hell of a shiner, that's for sure.' Her face was close to mine as she continued to look at the planes of my face. I was aware of her perfume, something smoky and dark that called to mind late nights and cocktails.

'How does it feel?' Patrick asked.

'There's a sort of throbbing sensation.'

'Where?'

'Behind my eye.'

'Look at my finger,' Rachel instructed, and I stared at the pointed index finger as she drew it to the left and then to the right, carefully following the movement of my eyes. Satisfied, she said: 'You seem all right to me.'

Patrick was unimpressed, and just as he began stressing the need for a professional opinion, we heard a noise from behind and Niall came forward with a brandy cradled in his hands, an anxious look of enquiry on his face.

'You've got some nerve,' Patrick said, as Niall stepped past him and offered me the drink. Another alcoholic peace-offering.

'Lins, I'm so sorry. I'm a fucking arse, all jokes aside. Are you okay?'

'Well, of course she's not okay,' Rachel answered for me, taking the glass from his hand and putting it into mine with an instruction to drink. I lowered my head and took a dutiful sip, feeling the burn at the back of my throat like a small but instant comfort.

'If it's any consolation, I feel awful.'

'So you should,' she replied indignantly. 'And Marcus is just as bad. What were you thinking?' As she led Niall back indoors, continuing to berate him about grown men acting like children, Patrick hunkered down beside me and took the opportunity to speak to me privately.

'He gave you a fair old whack. You went down pretty hard.'

I put my hand to my temple again, and following the movement with his gaze, he asked:

'Is that where the tumour is?'

I nodded, not trusting myself to speak. Emotion was clawing its way up my throat, questions filling my head: What if the blow had caused the tumour to rupture? What if it had dislodged it? Could the optic nerve have been damaged?

'Tumour?'

I looked up. Rachel was standing there, having ushered Niall back inside. Neither of us had heard her come out. Patrick stood up, half turning towards her, his voice lowered as he explained the location of the growth, the estimated size of it, the proximity to my brain. I could see her taking it all in coolly, attentively, but I could see she was trying to mask her horror.

'I'll be fine. This is helping.' I indicated to the brandy.

She thought about this for a moment. Then, addressing her brother, she said: 'The others are talking about walking to Borris, for a couple of pints in Lynch's. What do you think?'

He was happy for his guests to leave, but declared no interest in joining them, telling her: 'I'll stay with Lindsey.' Then, looking back at me, he said: 'I'd best go see to them. Be back in a sec.'

Rachel lingered by the door for a moment, her eyes on me.

'Your eyelid looks swollen,' she said.

The night had come on dark and close, but the light thrown from the windows was sufficient for me to see her face, her assessing gaze. She took a cigarette from the pack she was holding, then offered it to me. It had been years since I had smoked, but I wanted one now, and I don't know if that was the fright I'd just had, or if it was the effect of being in Rachel's orbit once again.

'You've had quite a shock, haven't you?' she said, handing me the Zippo, and my hand trembled as I took it. Rachel noticed, and said: 'Keep sipping that brandy.' I did as she instructed, while she watched me through eyes narrowed against the cigarette smoke. 'You sure you don't want to go to the hospital?'

'Thanks, but I'm okay. Besides, I'm sick of being ruled by this thing.' I gestured towards my head and her eyes flicked to a point past my hairline, as if she were imagining the angry little knot of gristle growing in there, my unwelcome guest.

'Can you feel it?' she asked, her eyes fixed on that point of my head with a sort of morbid interest. 'Can you feel it growing?'

'Not really. I get headaches. And occasionally it interferes with my peripheral vision.'

'How?'

I explained to her about the sudden movements spied out of the corner of my eye, movements that were imagined. She was a good listener, Rachel – I had forgotten that – prodding me in all the right places with her candid questions.

'Are you frightened?'

'Yes.' And it was true. But I was also angry that this was happening to me at all, angry at the attempts this tumour was making to derail my life. I was sick of having to monitor my body's reactions, every ache or rush of blood to the head requiring analysis and assessment. Sick of worrying about it, about whether it was growing, at what rate, of the possible side effects, real or imagined. Would I no longer be able to do my job? A job that required clarity of thought and vision, where a mistake could mean the difference between a conviction and allowing a guilty person to walk free. These were the things that kept me awake at night. I said as much to Rachel and she nodded in agreement as she stared down at the fish pond, the occasional flash of orange within the murky depths.

'It consumes you, doesn't it?' she remarked. 'It takes over your life.'

Her tone was flat, but there was a wistful undercurrent, a sort of sad droop to her now as she stabbed out the end of her cigarette on a broken flagstone, flicking the butt aside. We had been talking about me, but I knew from her inward stare that she was referring to something deeply personal. Whatever it was, she wasn't anywhere near ready to share it with me. Instead, she gave herself a little shake, looping a stray lock of hair with her little finger and flicking it back.

From inside the house, someone was calling her name. Affecting a heavy sigh, she straightened up and brushed down the creases in her dress. 'Best get going before they leave without me,' she said.

I made no move to join her. It was peaceful out here, my nerves calming, and all I wanted was to sit for a while, smoke my cigarette, drink my brandy and gaze at the flicker of fish in the water below. The others were welcome to Lynch's. I didn't envy them.

It was only as Rachel stepped back into the house that she paused at the door, turning to look back at me, her expression changing to one of enquiry: 'Do you really have a tumour?'

The question startled me.

'Why would I make up something like that?'

She held me there in her gaze, any hint of closeness we had achieved disintegrating in that stare. 'I don't know,' she replied. 'You've done worse.'

With the others gone, the house took on a new depth of silence. Patrick and I sat outside together, watching the night draw down upon us, both of us recovering from the shock of the incident. From high up in the trees that bordered the kitchen garden there came the rustling of wings. A low cawing broke out among the branches, the sound carried from tree to tree until the chorus grew in voice – a harsh, grating call. Patrick shifted in the seat, and stared up at them, his shoulders held high with tension. I could see how much they bothered him and, now that my attention was drawn to it, they seemed a dark and sinister presence. The house behind us no longer appeared to be a refuge, but rather a building under siege, and I was struck by the notion that their presence outside was an echo of another unsettled presence hiding in the shadows within the house. A foolish thought, born no doubt of the fright I had taken at the blow to my head. Whatever dark introspection I was tending to, Patrick must have been tending to his own.

'Let's get out of here, shall we?' he suggested. 'I know somewhere that may feel more welcoming.'

He took me by the hand and led me through the kitchen garden, the white jasmine ghostly and sweet as we brushed against it.

The air felt cool in the shadow of the house. A gentle wind was blowing through the fringe of long grass and it was a relief to hear the diminishing call of those crows as we left them behind. The dog trailed in our wake, the gentle pad of her feet audible on the gravel as we veered off along the path that led to the outbuildings surrounded by a crumbling brick wall.

Patrick stopped in front of one of the doors in the horseshoe of buildings that enclosed the central yard. 'It's a work in progress,' he warned as he unlocked the door and pushed it open. 'So just bear that in mind before you pass judgement.'

It was a lovely space. Small, clean, spartan – so different from the big house beyond. He turned on lamps and the dog went straight to hop up on the chaise longue, which I saw had been moved down here from the house and now took up its place in front of the narrow stairs. Like the kitchen of the big house, the floor here was covered with old chequered tiles in black and red, softened with rugs. A blackened stove stood in the alcove of the fireplace, a basket of turf next to it, and indeed I could smell recently burned sods in the air. Exposed beams in honeyed wood held the roof aloft, and there was a sort of mezzanine area where I could just glimpse the edge of a double bed.

It was weird being back there, but not in the way I had imagined. All this time, the prospect of this space had intimidated me. I had expected to feel fear or anxiety – the cold prod of memory best forgotten. How strange, then, to feel nothing other than immense calm, as if the place itself was completely untouched by the past.

'It's beautiful, Patrick.'

'Ah, but you haven't seen the best bit yet. Here, come

this way.' And he began clattering up the narrow stairs, and I followed him.

Up on the mezzanine, the roof was low and I could just about stand without having to duck, unlike Patrick, who stooped a little as he led me past the low bed to a square window beneath the apex of the roof.

'Look,' he said, and I came forward, understanding at once what he meant. It was the most perfect view of the west side of the big house.

I stood there, gazing at the darkened stone of the house, itself a silhouette now as night fell. Bats flew into the eaves, their wings fluttering, and above the high slate roof and the chimneystacks the sky had taken on a purplish hue. You could just make out the dark humps of the hills of Kilkenny beyond.

'You'd hardly think anything was wrong with it, would you?' Patrick said quietly, his voice very near.

And it was true. From this distance, the house looked perfect, its glory from the old days recaptured. I understood why he had chosen this house to live in, but at the same time there was something about it that did not feel quite right. I suppose I thought it might be difficult watching from this view while other people took over his ancestral home, the place he had fought so hard to keep and yet, ultimately, lost.

I was musing on this as I gazed out of the window when, suddenly, to the left of my vision, the low roof seemed to swing down sharply. I jumped back with a swift intake of breath and then his arms were around me, and I felt his body pressed against my back, his head leaning down to mine, his chin brushing against my hair, my heart hammering away in my chest.

'I'm so glad you're here,' he told me softly, before drawing me with him to the bed.

Up there under the eaves, there was only the dimness of moonlight falling through the bare window, and we didn't say a word to each other as we hurriedly undressed beneath the sheets before coming together again. All language fled, the only sounds the parting of lips, the brush of skin on skin, the sharp inward breath.

I don't know how long we slept. When I woke, it was still dark, still silent, no early-morning birdsong, no lavender-blue dawn. My head was pounding, and the events of the previous evening came rushing back through the pulse that was beating in my eye. I needed water, so with Patrick still asleep beside me, I felt around for my clothes and dressed silently in the dark. Downstairs, Jinny lay curled up on a chair, and in the little kitchen I filled a glass with water. As I leaned against the countertop and drank deeply, I felt the discomfort around my eye grow more intense, a tightness in the muscles beneath my skin. I needed to sleep properly. I needed pain relief. I had left the wad of my pills back in the big house and felt a stab of guilt now at having forgotten to take them the night before.

The twitter and call of the dawn chorus was just beginning as I let myself out and hastened back towards the house. I could see the outline of the roof, the proud chimneystacks darkly silhouetted against the sky. All the lights were turned out, the occupants having retreated to their rooms to sleep. It was as I neared the house that my eye was caught by the flare of a tiny red light in an upper window. The glow of burning embers in a cigarette when seen from a distance. It was so small and far away that at first I thought I was imagining it. But as I paused on the path and stared up, the light briefly flared again, then disappeared. As my eyes grew accustomed to the half-light, I could make out the figure of a person standing in the window looking down at me. Half hidden by the curtain, I couldn't make out their face. The window was directly above the drawing room. Realization came to me like a cold, hard shock. Someone was there, in my room.

I ran. My feet hitting the gravel hard, I pelted around to the kitchen door and flung it open. Any concern I had for the sleeping occupants was lost as I hastened through the house and up the stairs, feeling the breath dragging in my lungs as I ran along the landing, flung open the door and switched on the light, fired up to confront this intruder, only to find nothing. The room was empty.

The curtains were drawn back, exposing the swathe of darkness beyond. I stood at the window and stared across at the stables, seeking out the window beneath the eaves beyond which I had left Patrick sleeping. I found it easily, and imagined my own ghostly face peering back at me through the darkness.

Enough, I thought, pushing myself away from the window and hastily drawing the curtains. Had there been someone in my room? It seemed unlikely, and I told myself I'd imagined it. After all, how reliable was my vision after what had happened?

I sat on my bed, exhausted, perplexed. I was aware of a smell. The odour of cigarette smoke lingering in the air. Beneath it the sweeter – almost sugary – scent of rosewater.

I needed to sleep. Slipping off my shoes with irritation, I kicked one of the them across the room, and it chimed against something hard and glassy. A picture leaning against the wall. I got up and went over to it. This picture, I am sure, had not been there when I arrived yesterday, when I settled in. But there it was, and even before I crouched down next to it, even before I took it in my hands and held it up to the half-light falling thinly from the dusty overhead bulb, I knew somehow what it would be.

Round eyes staring into the camera, a question in them. Bare feet, dead rabbits hanging from above, and that naked stare.

I looked at it for only a moment, then I put it back, placed it turned away from me towards the wall.

I switched off the light and lay on my bed, but the image remained in my head. My own face, twenty years younger, staring right back at me. Turning over, I felt the lift of the mattress, as if some ghostly figure had only just left. I closed my eyes in the darkness, cigarettes and rosewater troubling my sleep.

14

The exhibition is taking place in the Arts Club on Fitzwilliam Square. A lively throng fills the stairwell when we arrive and we have to push through to make our way up to the exhibition space. Hilary goes ahead after the boys but Rachel holds me back.

'Loos,' she says.

It was her idea to bring a change of clothes. She insists we get out of our uniforms immediately before entering the crowd. I have brought with me a purple top and black jeans. Rachel squeezes herself into a clinging black dress with a plunging neckline.

By the sinks, she takes out a tube of red lipstick and applies it carefully. Her lips, naturally full, swell now with the vivid shade. Passing me the lipstick, she insists I use it: 'Colour yourself in a bit,' as she puts it. But it looks garish on me. My lips are too thin. I rub most of it away with tissue so that only a smudge of colour remains.

Standing back to survey her appearance, she asks: 'Too much?' and I tell her no, that she looks beautiful. Which she does. Beautiful and grown-up. Older than

157

sixteen. Older than me. And it's not just the clothes or her figure that make her look older. It is in the way she conducts herself. The way she moves. She oozes confidence.

The exhibition is taking place in two large rooms already heaving with people. It is bright, hot, crowded, so that the photographs lining the walls are obscured. Heads turn in Rachel's direction and I watch as she pretends not to notice the stares, the occasional wide-eyed leer.

Her parents are in the middle of the throng in the first room, and we push our way towards them. It's been a while since I've been invited to Thornbury and I've worried that I have somehow offended them, over-stepped the mark. I am a little nervous as I approach.

'Ray-Ray! My little ray of light!' her father says. He makes no comment on her appearance, just draws her into a fatherly hug. Then he turns and hugs me, too. The gesture catches me off guard. So often with the Bagenals, I feel on uncertain ground, but his embrace seems an acceptance of some sort, like I am part of the family.

'Look at you two girls,' Heather says, kissing both of us to the side of each cheek. 'I'm quite sure this isn't school regulation,' she remarks, tweaking the short skirt of Rachel's tight-fitting dress, but her expression is warmly complicit, and I have the sudden insight that this is exactly the way she herself would have behaved when she was sixteen. 'Isn't this wonderful? Such a good show!' I think she means the photographs, but it is only as she looks around the room, her face animated as she identifies various friends within the crowd, that I realize she means it's a good turnout. 'Make sure you go and talk to the Brennans, Rachel dear. They were asking about you earlier. Look, there's Maureen Quinn – go over and say hello.' In response to Rachel's groan, she says, 'Take note of your brother over there.' Patrick stands chatting to an elderly couple in front of a large framed shot of the granite pillars and white wrought-iron gates that lead to the avenue at Thornbury. It is the first time in this crowded room that I get a true glimpse of one of the exhibits. The picture is black and white and there is an ethereal quality to the light falling on to the dust road and the shadiness of the trees beyond.

'If I must,' Rachel says, and drifts away from us through the crowd to talk to 'the oldies', as she puts it.

I expect Heather to turn back to her husband, who is deep in conversation with a group of peers, but instead she reaches out and takes a gentle but firm hold of my upper arm. 'So good of you to come, Lindsey,' she says.

'Oh, it's nothing. I'm happy to be invited,' I say, a little confused. She is like a different person tonight. It's as if the incident in the scullery never happened. As if I just dreamed it. She even looks different. Her hair appears shorter than usual, more chic. Long earrings the colour of jade hang low underneath the wings of her newly cut hair, and her face is brightly made up.

When she reaches to smooth back a stray lock of my hair, the batwing sleeve of her green silken dress spreads and shimmers. I am reminded of a butterfly.

'You're such a good friend to our Rachel,' she tells me, with warmth and sincerity. 'Such a comfort to me to know she has someone to rely on. Someone to look out for her.'

'She's my best friend.' I sound foolish to myself, but it's all I can think of to say.

'Watch her for me tonight, will you? Make sure she doesn't go too crazy with the wine. I'd say it to her myself, only I fear she would react by doing the exact opposite. We can't have her returning to school drunk and getting expelled now, can we?' She gives her little tinkly laugh, and her dress shimmers as she touches my hair again with affection. Dazzled by her, I murmur my agreement.

Once she has exacted my compliance, she urges me to join my friends, before moving back to her husband. I watch her running a hand along his back, his arm going instinctively around to draw her in close.

Patrick stands with his hands behind his back, the elderly couple he is chatting to beaming up at him. He looks every inch the respected head boy, the responsible older son. Rachel is doing her duty, too, although she appears less committed. Her eyes keep sliding away, as though seeking out someone else in the room. Niall is here as well, with his new girlfriend, an Asian beauty with a swathe of inky-black hair. He makes a point of introducing Thea to Rachel, an event which passes off innocuously enough, neither girl betraying any envy of or interest in the other.

I find Marcus in front of a portrait of himself. He looks baffled and amused.

'I can't believe he included it,' he tells me, one hand in his pocket, sipping a glass of white wine.

We stand side by side, considering the black-and-white image of Marcus standing under the arch leading to the stables, taken with the sun behind him so that his shadow and that of the walls appear long and sharp – angular.

'It's good,' I say, a remark which elicits a pointed look from him.

'Do you think so?'

'Do you not?'

He looks back at the picture.

'It seems a bit, I dunno, derivative. Like I've seen it before. It's like something you'd see hanging in the waiting room of a dentist's surgery, you know? With some kind of affirmation quote beneath it.' He makes a little noise of impatience or dissatisfaction, and then says: 'Also, it's a bit cheeky, don't you think? I mean, he didn't even ask me if it was okay to include it. And I know that my face is in shadow so you might not easily recognize me, but I kind of feel like he used me.'

'Used you?'

He takes his hand from his pocket and scratches at the back of his neck. Like Patrick, he is dressed in his school blazer. His hair has been freshly dyed, and the artificial blackness lends a new pallor to his face.

'You know I want to do architecture after finishing school, right? Well, I'd had this conversation with him about it. I suppose I got a bit carried away, telling him how I loved modernist structures, going on a bit about Walter Gropius.' With this admission, he shakes his head. 'And look at the picture he takes of me – all those hard lines and sharp angles. And me in the middle of it all. It's like he's taking the piss.'

'I think you're overreacting.'

'Maybe I am. It's just . . . I wish he'd asked me about it first. At least shown it to me. Did he show you yours?'

'Mine?'

He drinks again from his glass. 'Oh, you're here, too. We all are.'

There are so many people that it is hard to get a good look at each photograph. Strange to see Thornbury represented in this way. These black-and-white shots of the house, enlarged and framed, look otherworldly, rarified. Perhaps it's because they are, for the most part, unpeopled, and that lends the house a deserted look. Even when the pictures do contain a human being – Rachel or Patrick, Heather, even one of the dogs – they are captured from afar. The house is all.

It is only as the evening wears on and the crowd thins that I find my picture. People are beginning to leave. A woman with a coat over her arm stops briefly beside me, saying: 'Lovely picture of you.' She puts out her hand as she speaks and gives my arm a quick squeeze before moving past me to the door. It is disconcerting.

And there I am. Hung to one side of the chimney-breast in the second room. It is a small enough image – smaller than most of the others here – but what is striking about it is the proportion of space given over to the human subject. I am so much larger than the others in their pictures. There is something raw and defenceless in the way I am gazing directly out. The surfaces of the room look cold around me – the flagstones beneath my bare feet, the hard stone counter above which the rabbits hang. But it is my own face that captivates me. It almost doesn't look like me. The unsmiling mouth, the wide-eyed stare with something at the back of it – suspicion? Fear? I can hardly draw my gaze away from it.

When Hilary comes up behind me, I am engrossed.

'When was it taken?' she asks, startling me.

'A few weeks back,' I answer.

She doesn't say anything to that. There is a fine line running along her brow, one of concentration or tired-ness. A sprinkling of acne mars the skin of her chin. Her face is pale and she appears sullen.

'Is that the only time he's photographed you?' she asks, still staring at the picture, frowning in concentration.

'I think so.'

'You think so? You'd know if it wasn't. You'd know it all right.'

I can hear a sneer in her words. I don't know what she is getting at, but I feel like I am being called out for something – lying or being disingenuous. I watch her little piggy eyes drilling the picture with their stare and I experience a strong and immediate wave of dislike.

'What's the matter?' I ask her. 'Don't you like it?'

'I couldn't care less,' she says coldly.

'I don't know why you've come if you're going to be so bloody grumpy about everything. God, I'm so sick of you moping around all the time, this thing you've got against Rachel. We're all sick of it. Is it because she's friends with me now, is it? Are you jealous? Because if you are, then that's pathetic.'

She waits a beat before saying tightly, 'Not in the least.' Just before she turns away, I see the film of tears in her eyes. I don't call her back. As she makes her way towards the cloakroom, I am glad to see her go.

It is after ten. We have been warned to be back at school by half past. Patrick reminds us of this, and Rachel frowns, still wanting to hang on, even though most of the crowd has left and those that remain are making plans to wander up to Toners for a drink.

In the Ladies, we change back into our uniforms and wipe the lipstick from our mouths. The others are waiting for us at the door. And even as we leave, I see Rachel's eyes darting around the room one last time, as if still trying to catch a glimpse of the person who has not come.

15

I slept then. A fitful, narrow sleep. Fully clothed on top of the bedcovers, face down, limbs splayed like I'd just been shot in the back. I woke alone to a sticky mouth, a muddle of thoughts and a body that felt wrung out rather than rested. The light was coming brightly through the window, and I could tell by the whiteness of it that morning was already well advanced. I sat up, tired and disoriented, a hollow feeling inside me like I hadn't eaten for days.

I stared at my face in the mirror of the wardrobe door and felt the breath catch in my throat. The injury was grotesque. My eyelid, swollen and purple, sucked away the colour from the rest of my face, and there was a bulge above my brow. The wound had become the focal point, the rest of my face fanning out weirdly from it. It frightened me how unfamiliar I looked to myself.

From somewhere outside in the garden, I could hear Jinny barking. Turning from the insult of my own reflection, I looked out the window at the grass shimmering brightly under the sun. Two figures walked slowly from the stables towards the house, and I recognized the broad-shouldered figure of Patrick, and Marcus's long, lean shape. Suddenly, Patrick made a gesture, a quick wave of his hand that seemed to suggest impatience, and his pace quickened.

I was aware that I was staring, but couldn't bring myself to look away. Marcus, who had been holding himself stiffly throughout the exchange, seemed to become agitated. Catching up with Patrick now, he gave a quick shake of his head, before pointing to the house, an emphatic, stabbing gesture, and making some final remark before overtaking his friend, his pace increasing. Then Patrick reached forward and grabbed the other man's arm. With alarming swiftness, he drew Marcus back and slammed him against the wall, pinning him with one hand, the other hand pointing in his face.

Across the wall, the creep of ivy seemed black and heavy. I held myself still as Patrick stepped away from his friend, releasing him, and started back towards the house, grim and purposeful, but my eyes stayed on Marcus. His hand went to the top of his head. He held his body very still, and I had the sense he was trying to calm himself. Patrick would be entering at the kitchen door, to get the guns for the shoot. Perhaps, trying to steady himself, too, over whatever had passed between them.

The gong sounded from downstairs in the hall. Catching myself, I realized how closely pressed I was to the window, how intent I had been in my watching. Just as I was stepping away, I noticed something small and gilded on the windowsill. Bending to pick it up, I found it was the ashtray I remembered from the days when Heather Bagenal slept in this room. A little brass dish in the shape of an upturned turtle-shell. I thought again of the shadowy figure in my bedroom window, the glowing embers of a cigarette briefly flaring, then disappearing. The gong sounded again, resonating up through the floorboards.

'Fuck,' I said aloud, hastily returning the ashtray to where I had found it.

I dressed quickly, hurriedly combing my hair. As I turned to the door, I heard something falling to the floor. It was the little ashtray. I must have left it balancing precariously. The hard, chill sound of it meeting the floorboards stayed with me as I closed the door on the room and made my way downstairs.

We gathered on the lawn, all eyes fixed on Patrick as he talked us through how to conduct ourselves on the shoot. Behind him, the stone figure of the Earl of Baldonnell lay on it's side, silently communicating reproach. The statue seemed to have become more embedded in the gravel overnight, an immovable blockade, lying close to the threshold.

'The shotgun must remain broken until you stop, ready to shoot,' Patrick explained. 'This is mainly for your own protection. The trigger is fairly sensitive, and you'd be surprised how easily it could happen – you're climbing over a hedge and accidentally drop the gun and bang! You've blown your head off.'

There was a small ripple of laughter among the group, but it was nervous laughter and I wondered how many of the others were also thinking of Peter Bagenal. Patrick's manner seemed brisk and businesslike, most of his attention focused on Liv, who was the only one among us who had no experience of shooting. For his part, Marcus seemed pensive, standing a little apart from the rest of us.

'When you're ready to shoot, make sure there's no one in your line of fire, and no one about to walk across you. Close the gun, like this.' Patrick demonstrated, snapping it into place. 'And don't take the safety off until literally just when the gun is up and you're ready to shoot the trigger. Now, Liv. Take this.'

He handed her the gun, which she accepted with an air of misgiving. 'Is it loaded?'

'No. Those are blanks.'

He instructed her on how to hold the gun, bringing it up so the stock was against her shoulder.

'It needs to be right in against your cheek also,' he said.

'I'm a little nervous of it,' Liv said, her giggle invading my memory.

'No need to be nervous,' Patrick said. 'Just be cautious.'

I was hit by a sudden blast of déjà vu. My own first time shooting, uttering those very same words: 'I'm nervous.' Peter Bagenal's retort – *If you're afraid, then don't come shooting* – coming instantly to my ear. He existed only in my memory, and yet his curious blend of gruffness and affection had been the centre of this house – the beating heart of it. Somehow, I had assumed I would feel more of a sense of him this weekend. Surprising, then, to find it was Heather I felt more. The ghostly scent of her cigarettes and perfume, the languid movement in the air as if she had just passed; the way she stood waiting and watchful at the window. I turned quickly to look back at the house, as if expecting to catch her there at my window – *her* window – but there was nothing, only the windows gazing blankly back, opaque with the reflection of the sun.

'Keep both eyes open while you're taking aim,' Patrick went on. 'It's important that you don't shut off your peripheral vision. When you see a crow rise in front of you, take aim, fire, follow through, then fire again.'

'Not wanting to split hairs, Patrick,' Hilary said, 'but are you sure it's crows we're shooting? They looked more like rooks to me.' She held a gun under her arm, having rowed back on her assertion of the previous day that she would refuse to take part.

'Well, technically, you're right. Although "crow" is also commonly used as the collective term for the genus which includes rooks,' he said, leading us over the lawn towards the trees, and we followed in a loose grouping, the dog, Jinny, trotting alongside us, the sun rising in the sky, beating down on the backs of our necks. Ahead of us the trees rustled with the promise of relief and, as we headed towards them, Hilary asked if we would be shooting the birds where they roosted.

'No. In the fields,' Patrick said, to my surprise, and pointed to a spot beyond the woodland where the agricultural land began. 'They'll be in the wheat by now, and that's just where I want to clear them out from, before they decimate the crop.'

I thought of the early morning in April when I had come back to Thornbury, and how we had stood in the avenue together, Patrick and I, staring up into the trees bristling with hundreds of crows. Something jarred about it now, and I said to him:

'I thought you wanted to clear them from their roosts in the trees? I thought they were driving you mad – the noise of them?'

'Well, yes. Up to a point. But the main reason is to protect the crops from them,' he said, busying himself with checking the pockets of his gilet for cartridges.

He didn't look at me while he spoke, not even a quick glance, and I couldn't help but feel slighted.

'Let's get moving,' he said, hastening towards the trees, while the rest of us traipsed along in his wake.

'Someone got out of bed on the wrong side this morning,' Niall remarked softly, and Hilary said:

'Well, Lindsey? Did he?' And she sniggered, Niall guffawing next to her.

When I didn't respond, Niall said: 'Ah, sorry, Lins. Don't get the hump.'

'I'm not,' I replied, smiling resolutely at him.

His eyes flickered over my face, and he winced. 'That's quite the shiner you've got.'

'Yes. Thanks for that.'

'Here, tell you what, you can take a swing at me.' He pulled off his wraparound shades and offered his face to me, grinning. 'Come on. Go for it.'

'Don't think I'm not tempted.'

'Go on,' he encouraged, laughter bubbling to the surface, and Hilary said: 'Don't, Lins. He'd only enjoy it,' and then the laughter spilled over, the two of them creasing up at a joke that wasn't particularly funny. They were both unusually animated this morning – particularly Niall, who had brought his own gun with him. A William & Son Sidelock, he told us all, after Hilary noticed the particularly fine scroll engraving on the panelling of the stock.

'They only produce twelve guns a year,' he announced proudly.

'It must have cost a fair whack,' Hilary said.

'You buy cheap, you get tat,' he retorted.

'You're not shooting?' Rachel asked, coming up behind me. She looked pale and somewhat bored by the whole endeavour.

'Just my camera,' I said, and she remarked that it was just as well, all things considered. It was impossible to read her expression accurately, her eyes hidden behind a pair of shades.

I let them all walk on, hanging back for a moment

on the pretence of changing the lens on my camera. I fiddled with lens caps and apertures, my camera bag lying open on the ground at my feet, mulling over Patrick's moodiness. I couldn't help but feel hurt by his lack of enquiry about the injury to my eye, which had grown more visible and glaring overnight. But more than anything, I was troubled by what I had seen between him and Marcus – baffled as to what could inspire that violent reaction from him.

I put my camera to my right eye, closing the left, and through the viewfinder, I watched the others. They were all similarly attired, in jeans, T-shirts and boots. Some wore peaked hats to keep off the sun. Only Niall was distinguished, in a pair of khaki fatigues, the pockets bulging with cartridges. Marcus and Patrick wore shooting vests, their cartridges more neatly stowed. Even though my shooting eye was undamaged, I felt the strangeness of swelling in the left as I closed it to focus. Somehow, this new thickening about my face affected my ability to focus, unbalancing it. The camera felt wrong next to my face, unfamiliar.

I passed Niall and Hilary, who continued their banter, while Liv looked on. Marcus and Rachel were walking together. I caught a snippet of their conversation as I passed.

'I just couldn't sleep,' she was saying. 'I kept hearing this noise. It sounded like crying.'

'Probably foxes,' he remarked.

'It sounded so human, though.'

'They often do.'

'But it was coming from inside the house.' His comments about the acoustics of the place were lost to me as I caught up with Patrick.

'Hey,' I said, and he glanced at me, before offering a quick smile in a way that offered encouragement to keep up as he quickened his pace. We had broken away from the group a little, the others lagging behind in twos and threes, the hum of their conversation punctuated with the occasional shout of laughter.

'Is everything okay?' I asked.

'Everything's fine. Why?'

'You seem a little tense.'

'Not really. The others might joke around, but I'm responsible for everyone, and for the guns. Some one has to be the grown-up.' His manner remained somewhat aloof. His open affection of the previous day had disappeared. I couldn't imagine him taking my hand now, or slinging an arm around my shoulders.

'I'm sorry I left before you woke,' I said, lowering my tone, lest the others hear, although they were some distance behind us. 'I had forgotten my medication. It was back in my room,' I explained.

We were coming to a clearing in the woods, the path widening to reveal a swathe of open land bathed in sunlight. Jinny had bounded on ahead, the swish of her red tail disappearing into the long yellow grass. Soon we would reach the shooting point and the others would gather. But before that happened, I wanted to share with him what I had seen the night before.

'Someone at the window?' he repeated, his brow furrowed in thought.

'Yes. They were smoking. I could see the ash glowing through the darkness.'

'Are you sure?'

'Pretty sure.'

'It must have been Rachel,' he said.

'Rachel? But why would she have been in my bedroom?'

'I didn't mean that. Your bedrooms are alongside each other. You must have mistaken her window for yours.'

'I don't think so—'

'The smoking is the giveaway,' he went on. 'She's a terror for sitting up half the night, smoking her head off. Has been since we were teenagers.'

'Really?'

'She's an insomniac. Just like our mother.'

'I never knew that.'

My mind went to the small brass ashtray in her room – the upturned turtle. I tried to picture Heather sitting by her window, staring wretchedly out into the endless night, wondering which would come first – sleep or dawn? And I remembered again the scent in my room, and the sensation of someone sitting on the edge of the bed.

'I was sure I saw a person in my room.'

'It would be an easy mistake to make. Especially seeing how unreliable your vision has become lately.'

I thought about the tumour lodged fast against my optic nerve, pressing against the tail of my eye, and about all the tremblings and jumps in my peripheral vision. Was this the ocular flutter the doctor had talked about? Was it possible that I had been mistaken?

The coldness with which Patrick said it came as a surprise. To hear him state it so baldly, so matter-of-fact, made something rear up within me, a little burst of angry defiance.

'Well, someone was in my room, because they left something there that wasn't there before.'

'What?'

'An old photograph of me. One of your father's.'

He stopped abruptly and fixed me with a sharp look of enquiry.

'What photograph?' he snapped.

'The one from his exhibition. With the dead rabbits,' I explained, keeping my voice low and steady. His vehemence had taken me back. 'It was on the floor by the window, leaning against the wall.'

'It was probably there already. You just didn't notice.'

'It wasn't,' I said, softly but firmly. 'Patrick, what's the matter?'

I could see him struggling to decide whether or not he should tell me. But then Niall shouted: 'Are we ever going to shoot these fucking guns or what?' and his face cleared of indecision, taking on a harder, more determined look.

'This way!' he shouted back, turning from me and leading us out into the field.

The air held a dry heat among the wheat. My head full of confusion, deeply dissatisfied with Patrick's coldness, his irritation, I held the camera up to my face and looked through the viewfinder, seeing the darkness of the trees beyond, hearing voices approach. The camera still felt strange, but as I stood there framing and clicking, framing and clicking, I felt myself grow calm. Jinny had found me and thrown herself down by my feet, her long tongue hanging out, her mouth open as though grinning. Beyond me, the field lay on a slight incline and a gentle breeze came up and ruffled the long stalks, grain budding at the ends, before dying away. Stillness came over the land as I watched everyone walk down through it. The crows could be heard deep within the field – a sort of muffled cawing, as if their beaks were already full, their concentration fixed on the act of filling their bellies, making their calls muted, half-hearted.

At some point, someone's phone beeped. Then another, and another. It was as if we had crossed a threshold into the world of modern communication, and for a few minutes the entire group was consumed by the act of checking messages, responding to emails, listening to voicemails.

The phones put away, the shooters spread out across

the land, Patrick at the centre, leading the way. When he stopped and raised his hand, they all drew to a halt and waited. Etiquette demanded that the host take the first shot, and we all watched as Patrick loaded the gun, snapped the barrel into the lock and brought the stock to his shoulder. A hush fell over us, waiting for that first bird to break ground cover and rise up into the air.

A shot rang out. A crow fell to the ground with a heavy thud and, instantly, the sky was full of them. Flapping and black, calling out with startled indignation, feathers flying, a riot of avian fury. A flurry of shots fired at random; birds falling from the sky.

The hunters advanced through the field, taking aim and firing. Gunfire sounded over the land, and echoed in the silence after. It amplified the sense that we were in the middle of nowhere, far from the city.

I stopped every now and then, and scanned the vista before me in the hope of a good shot. From my position, I tried to capture them: Marcus, poised and deliberate, holding his fire until he was sure of his aim. Hilary, standing with her arms crossed, looking faintly disgusted by the proceedings. Niall, I observed, was a reasonably good shot. He picked his prey, followed the arc of the bird's flight with the barrel of his gun as he fired, then fired again, Liv behind him, conscientiously leaning down to pluck the spent cartridges from the earth where they fell.

'Would you look at him,' Hilary said, nodding with scornful amusement in Niall's direction. I followed her gaze to where Niall stood with a cigarette clamped between his lips, the gun held to his hip rather than his shoulder as he fired up into the sky.

'He thinks he's Clint Eastwood,' she remarked.

Behind Niall, Liv stood with her hands over her ears, her shoulders high and tense, looking as if she might bolt for the house at any moment.

'You'd think he'd give Liv a shot,' I offered.

'Not a chance! Even if she wanted a go, which I suspect she doesn't, I can't see him relinquishing the gun. Not for a second.'

We watched his cowboy stance, the way he threw back his head and hooted whenever his shot hit the mark.

'He seems a little hyped up,' I remarked. 'Is he always like this?'

She kept her gaze fixed on Niall, a smile coming to her face. 'He's got a bit of gunpowder in his system.'

'Gunpowder?'

'Fun powder.'

'Are you serious?' I asked, as she giggled. Her own eyes appeared a little glassy, the pupils wide. 'Cocaine and shotguns? Do you really think that's a good idea?'

'You're not going to tell on us now, are you, officer?'

'Of course not,' I muttered, looking down at my camera and changing the filter on the lens.

The sun had risen high above us as noon approached and the birds moved on. The field had emptied and, in the distance above the copse of trees that lined the perimeter, they appeared as a floating black cloud, the murder of crows escaping to safer ground. Marcus suggested we sit in the shade of the trees to cool down. His own face appeared flushed, and I could see that Niall's forehead was sunburned. But no one made any move to get out of the field.

'How many did you get?' Niall shouted over to Marcus.

'Three or four maybe,' was the reply.

'Is that all? I got seven.'

'Why does it always have to descend to bragging rights?' Hilary remarked.

'Can we take a break?' Rachel called, running a hand over her brow. 'I'm sweltering.'

Marcus agreed, but Niall started to protest. 'We should follow them!' he shouted, waving towards a field further down the valley where the crows were resettling. Liv had broken away from his side, and approached me and Hilary with a rueful smile.

'I think I've had enough shooting for one day,' she said. 'Do you suppose we could find somewhere to sit over in those woods?'

'The folly must be quite near here,' I remarked, following her gaze.

'The folly?'

'We used to go there sometimes, to put on little plays,' I explained. 'It was all very silly really, but it was fun. Remember, Hilary?'

She kept her eyes fixed on the field.

'Remember that play we put on? What was it called again? Persephone's Descent?'

'I don't remember,' she said.

'You do. What was it? Dido's Lament or something like that.'

She shrugged her skinny shoulders again.

'Come on, you must remember. You tore your costume just before we were supposed to start. Surely you haven't forgotten that.'

She took a step away from me, and said in a tight little voice, 'I'm sorry, Lindsey. I don't know what you're talking about. It must have been someone else.'

I stared after her as she moved away into the field, where Niall was pressing on through the wheat towards the perimeter.

Later on, I would be asked to return to this moment again and again, and to give a faithful and accurate account of the positioning of the hunters across the field, who among them had their guns locked and ready, who had guns broken.

I would remember the sway of grasses, golden in the sunlight, everyone spaced apart at irregular intervals, the stillness that came over them. I would remember the shiver of leaves amid the tangle of low branches in the copse of trees off to one side. A deer, tawny brown, elegantly lowering her head, came into the clearing. I would remember lifting my camera to my face.

The air, having fallen silent, exploded with sound.

As if the hammer hitting the cartridge echoed in my own head, I felt it pounding against my eardrum. I put my hand up instinctively, and saw a flash of white – the flanks of the deer, her rear legs kicking out as she turned and ran. The dog came roaring out from the grasses, tearing after the deer, which had disappeared into the trees.

We were all moving in that direction now. Except for Liv, who was charging off to one side, a kind of frenzy to her run, down the incline of the field, until she stopped suddenly, and dropped to the ground, only her head visible above the dry grass, her hand going to her mouth.

Niall, I thought. It must be Niall. But then I heard him shouting from the periphery of the field: 'Hey! What's going on?' He was looking in her direction, his gun broken and slung over his shoulder, light glaring off the dark lenses of his shades. She didn't answer, leaning forward now to examine something close to the ground.

I heard breathing at my shoulder, Hilary coming up close, her eyes intent on the space where Liv was kneeling. The realization came to her before me. 'Marcus,' she said, then hastened past me, dropping her gun as her pace quickened to a run. We were all running now, dust and insects rising as our feet beat paths to that spot in the field where a shrill cry was rising, Liv getting to her feet. I saw the bloodstain on her T-shirt before I saw Marcus, my ears ringing as her screams tore through the deep silence of the meadow.

PART TWO

16

2017

The blood spread through the cotton of Marcus's shirt. It appeared luridly red under the warm sunshine beating down hard on the field. I had shouldered through the crush of the others, ordering the rest of them to stand back as I bent over him, my professional instincts kicking in. He had been shot in the back and was lying face down with his arms pinned beneath him, his gun having fallen away to one side. There was something pitiful in the way his two feet were splayed inwards, facing each other toe to toe, like a small boy asleep with his boots on. Drawing back the collar of his shirt, I felt for a pulse at his neck.

'He's alive,' Liv told me. Having regained her composure, she was squatting at his side.

The pulse beneath his hot flesh was faint, and when I put my ear close to his chest I could hear breathing, shallow and laboured.

'Someone call an ambulance,' I said, adding: 'The guards, too.'

'There's no fucking reception!' Niall barked. The irritation in his voice wavered on the cusp of hysteria.

He waved his phone around in the air to no avail, before rushing off back in the direction from which we had come, shouting over his shoulder that he'd return once he had made contact with the emergency services.

'Marcus,' I called loudly, looking to get some sort of reaction from him, but there was nothing, and when I leaned in to listen to his chest again, the breathing sounded wet and more laboured, a faint gurgle in each exhalation.

'Shouldn't we turn him over?' Hilary asked, her voice coming shrill and taut from close behind me. 'In case he needs mouth to mouth, or something?'

I needed to be sure his airways were clear, even if it meant risking further injury. Instructing Liv to hold his head carefully and to turn it at my instruction, I put my hands beneath his shoulders and tried to ease him away from the ground. His body was a dead weight, despite his leanness and Liv's assistance, and by the time we had turned him over on to his back, the sweat was breaking out on my face and seeping through my clothes.

'Oh, Christ,' Patrick said, hunkering down at my side, his shadow thrown across the glare of crimson ballooning from Marcus's chest. Patrick's hand advanced towards the wound, then drew back suddenly. 'Where the fuck is Niall?' His hand was shaking, and he made a fist of it and pressed it to his mouth. He was visibly trembling.

All of this registered dimly in the background as I peeled the drenched shirt up over Marcus's belly and chest. There the exit wound gaped and spurted, blood cascading over his belly, which appeared shockingly white, a line of russet, curling hairs running from his sternum down over his navel, disappearing under the band of his jeans. Without thinking, I pulled my own sweatshirt over my head, and pressed it hard against the wound. I needed to staunch the bleeding.

'Marcus! *Marcus!*' Liv called, her voice coming out stern and insistent, but she couldn't rouse him.

His eyes were half open, unseeing, his jaw slack and splattered with blood, as was his neck above the collar. My hand grew wet as the warm blood gushed up through the fabric compress, making it slick and greasy. I pushed down harder, willing Niall to come back.

'What happened?' Rachel asked. 'What the hell happened?' Her voice sounded breathy and dazed, but none of us answered.

Liv had her head down close to Marcus's ear, and she had started talking to him in hushed tones, making noises of reassurance: 'You're all right, Marcus. Help is coming. It's on its way. Hang on in there. Listen to my voice. Focus on that. Just keep listening.'

Of all of us, she seemed the calmest. Hilary had started crying. Rachel was white and rigid with shock. Patrick was on his feet now, straining anxiously after Niall and berating himself for not being the one to fetch the emergency services. 'I know this land better than anyone!' he kept exclaiming, convinced Niall had gotten lost.

As for me, I was concentrating on keeping the pressure on the wound, trying to halt the relentless drain of blood from Marcus's body, and while on the surface I might have appeared calm, focused, in control, underneath my heart was pounding, beating out its own frightened rhythm. The clarity I had come to rely upon in situations like this – the deep calm that came over me when confronted by a crime scene, a trauma, a burst of shocking violence – seemed to have abandoned me. I couldn't think straight. An air of unreality hung over the scene. I didn't quite believe it. The whole thing held a dreamlike quality, as if I was witnessing something that had a thin veil drawn over it. All the time I was leaning over him, pressing my two hands hard into his chest, I could feel the throb of blood at the back of my own eyeball, a mounting pressure there that acted as a distraction, an annoyance I couldn't shake off.

'There he is!' Patrick cried, and Hilary broke off, sobbing, saying: 'Oh, thank God!' Then Niall was upon us, breathless and panting, announcing it might be twenty minutes before the ambulance got here.

'Twenty minutes?' Hilary repeated, in her new shrill voice. 'He could be dead by then!' And it was true that the beat of blood in his neck when I leaned forward to check it again had grown weaker.

'Someone should go to the gates,' I said. 'The ambulance will need directions to the field.'

'I'll go,' Patrick said. And before anyone else could volunteer he had set off, beating his way in long strides down the desire path bisecting the field.

An ache had started in my arms and across the back of my neck. In my head, I was rapidly running over the course of events while at the same time counting down the minutes until help came. Time seemed to stretch out before us, horrible and immense.

'This is a nightmare,' Hilary said. 'A fucking nightmare. If only we had taken a break, like Rachel suggested. If only we had listened to her, instead of charging on after those bloody crows.'

'Oh, it's my fault, is it?' Niall asked, his voice becoming indignant.

'Well, you were the one who insisted we keep going with the shoot. Everyone else wanted to rest, to take shelter from the sun.'

'I don't know why you're taking the moral high ground, Hilary. I'm not the one who shot him.'

Hilary had moved away, but now turned back. 'What the hell is that supposed to mean?'

'I was there,' he said, pointing back towards the edge of the field. 'Right out in front of all the rest of you. I had a clean shot. You lot were all behind me – including Marcus. So, it couldn't have been me who shot him, could it?'

'Well, it wasn't me,' Hilary retorted, angry tears standing in her eyes.

'Then, if it wasn't you, it was Rachel. Or Patrick.'

'This isn't helping,' I snapped. 'Now, for God's sake, give it a rest.'

My thoughts were scrambling all over the place. I lifted the sweatshirt compress, and still the blood came, but more thinly this time, not with the same force. I balled up one of the sleeves and pushed the dry fabric against the wound.

'His hand is cold,' Liv told me, shooting a meaningful look in my direction. She was kneeling, cradling his head, holding on to one of his hands and kneading it, silent now, having broken off the stream of her forceful whispering.

A hush had fallen over us. Everyone stood close and still and watchful. I could hear distant birdsong, a murmur of insects nearby, nature's industry continuing, oblivious to the calamity in the field. Beneath the stillness came the wet, raw gurgle of Marcus's jagged breathing.

Suddenly, charging through the wheat, came Jinny, the dog, barking frantically and leaping excitedly about Marcus.

'Get that fucking dog out of here!' Niall bellowed.

Rachel brought the dog to heel, grasped her collar and said, 'I'll bring her back to the house,' and marched off briskly, her gun lodged beneath her arm.

'Where are they?' Hilary asked, her voice strained with exasperation. 'How long's it been?'

Niall glanced down at his watch. 'They should be here by now.'

Liv started up her low, one-sided communication to Marcus again, while Niall began pacing down through the field, checking his phone for reception. That dreamy underwater feeling was upon me again, my thoughts murky and unclear. It was only when I noticed Hilary stooping to pick up the gun she had dropped from the prickly earth that something snapped inside me.

'No, don't,' I told her sharply. 'Don't touch it. Don't touch anything.' She stared at me, nonplussed. 'We must leave the scene intact. You can't move anything.'

'What? Why not?'

'The integrity of the scene must be preserved.'

'But it was an accident,' Niall exclaimed, picking up on the thread of our conversation. 'It's not a crime scene.'

'He's been shot,' I explained. 'The guards will need to investigate it.'

'Hang on a second. Marcus stepped into the line of fire. There was negligence, maybe, but it's hardly grievous bodily harm. Is it?'

'Everything must be left where it is. The guns, the spent cartridges, everything.'

'What about Rachel's gun?' Hilary asked, and it was only then that I realized I had allowed her to march back to the house with her gun in hand.

I felt a burn of frustration with myself for allowing the situation to slip out of my control, my instincts blurred and confused.

There wasn't time to dwell on it. An ambulance appeared from behind the copse of trees lower in the valley. It was a relief to remove my hands from the wound, and to step back from the situation, allowing the ambulance crew to take control. I realized how exhausted I was, my arms hanging limply by my sides, as I answered their questions as best I could and watched while they swarmed over him, tearing packaging from surgical pads, inserting lines into fluid-filled bags.

Any relief I felt fled when I saw the way Marcus's body sagged as they lifted him on to the stretcher. He didn't look alive. I could no longer make out the sounds of his liquid breathing. I caught sight of Liv, standing now, her T-shirt covered in bloodstains, a smear of it across her face and neck. I realized that I, too, was covered in gore, my fingers rust-coloured and smelling strongly metallic. My blood-soaked sweatshirt lay discarded on the grass as I followed the stretcher to the open doors of the ambulance.

I found myself inside the rear of it, almost without being aware of having got in. Perched on the little seat opposite Marcus, who was strapped and buckled on to the stretcher, it occurred to me that it should be Patrick in here, or Niall. They were his friends. They knew him better. But that half-hour spent with my hands pressed into his wound seemed to bind me to him and him to me in a way that went deeper than friendship. Distantly, I heard another engine, and presently came the sound of a car door slamming, followed by another, voices of authority calling out. Beyond the doors of the ambulance, I saw the faces of the others turn to these newcomers, Niall heaving in his breath, his hands on his hips, as if steadying himself. And then the doors closed on the yellow brightness of the field, replaced now by the blue-white artificiality of the fluorescent strip lighting, as the ambulance pulled away over the bumpy field, only speeding up when the tyres met the asphalt surface of the road beyond Thornbury.

It was an accident. An accident. This is what I told myself as the ambulance screamed along the M9 towards Kilkenny. I said it to myself and to everyone else who asked: the ambulance crew, the nurses and doctors in Accident & Emergency, the receptionist, as I gave Marcus's details. Later that day, I would say it to Marcus's boyfriend, Carl, when he arrived, pale-faced and shocked. *It was an accident. A horrible accident.* The words turned over and over in my mind like a mantra, along with those others: *Please don't die. Don't let him die.* An incantation or a prayer. For most of the day, my mind swung like a pendulum between these two thoughts.

I felt calmer now that I was away from Thornbury, away from the others and their obvious distress. The relief of surrendering responsibility to the medical professionals was tempered by my fear for Marcus's life. No sooner had I rushed into the hospital after him, answering some cursory questions, than he was whisked away to surgery in a flurry of blue scrubs and squeaky wheels, and I was left alone to wait.

Unsure of what to do with myself, I collapsed in a chair by the nurse's station, exhausted and confused. I gave no thought to my own appearance. It was only when a nurse approached me, offering a blue medical smock and suggesting kindly that I might like to get cleaned up, that I realized how distressing I must have appeared to any passer-by.

In the ladies' toilets, I stared, aghast, at my own reflection. Not only was there blood on my clothes but a good deal of my arms was stained brown from my exertions, and there were marks along my ear and the side of my face where I had leaned in to listen to Marcus's chest. I thought again of that gurgle in his breathing and imagined the pink bubbles in his throat. The thought frightened me and I shook it away.

Stripping off my T-shirt, I stood at the sink in my bra, working pink liquid soap from the dispenser into a weak lather and scrubbing myself as best I could. Most of it came away, but try as I might, I could not rid myself of the shadow stains clinging to the skin of my hands. I threw my T-shirt into the flip-lid bin and pulled the blue scrubs over my torso. Examining myself in the mirror, I looked a fright. My face rubbed raw and free of make-up, the livid bruising around my eye appeared more brutal under the harsh industrial lighting. The surrounding skin looked yellowish, jaundiced, deep purple grooves beneath my eyes.

Emerging back out into the bustling corridor, I was struck by how cold I felt. Hunger announced itself, and realizing I hadn't eaten all day and it was now almost three, I felt in my jeans pocket for change. In the chaos of my leaving, I had neglected to bring a bag or a wallet. I had only my phone and three euros in coins. Having received assurances from the nurse that they would call me once there was news, I slipped out of the hospital, crossing the road to the Eurospar on the corner.

It was like stepping out into a different day, a different season. Gone was the bright sunlight of our morning excursion, replaced now by iron-grey clouds hanging low in the sky, a biting wind cutting through the flimsy blue scrubs to my flesh. How odd it was to be in that shop among the Mars bars and Kettle Chips, the Insomnia Coffee and *Daily Mail*s, after all that had happened, all that I had been through. I felt disoriented, dazed by the glare of all that packaging, the once-familiar branding of chocolate bars and sweets now utterly strange. I took a Twix and an apple, the guy at the till looking at me strangely as I paid, but I didn't care how I looked. Still in the shop, I ripped open the bar, ravenous, and began to eat.

My phone rang as I stepped outside. The hospital, I thought, a wave of panic rising inside as I scrabbled madly to answer. But the name that showed up on the screen read *Thornbury* and, when I answered, it was Hilary's voice I heard at the other end.

'How is he?' she asked urgently, and when I told her

there was no news, that Marcus was still in surgery, she blew out a breath and said, 'My God, Lindsey. What are we going to do?'

The chocolate sat heavily in my stomach, the sugar cloying in my mouth, and I felt the rush of it to my brain, too fast, making me dizzy. Here on the street traffic was racing past, and I turned away from it into the shelter of the Eurospar, one finger pressed to my ear the better to hear Hilary. A stream of words had been released within her, and her account of what happened after the ambulance left came out in a sort of mad torrent. How the police had wanted to know from each of them what had happened, the confusion when it came to remembering whereabouts everyone had stood when the shot was fired, who had guns, how many shots were fired, who was experienced and who was not. The police had them there for hours, she told me in exaggerated tones, before continuing their questioning back at the house.

'They wanted to know if any of us had been drinking,' she went on breathlessly. 'Whether we'd had a little snifter of brandy or something. And of course, we hadn't, but I kept thinking of Niall, and whether he'd told them about the coke. It was me who gave it to him, you see, and if the guards found out about that—'

'Where are they now?' I cut across her.

'Oh, they're gone back to the station. Has anyone spoken to you?'

'Not yet.' Although it could only be imminent.

Again, I felt that rising panic. Where was the clarity I had come to rely on? Why were my thoughts and perceptions so blurry and opaque? 'What about the others?' I asked, thinking surely one of them would come to the hospital. If I could only see Patrick, I thought, then I could get my mind in order. Once I could consider his face, feel his arms about me, I could draw strength and clarity from him. I would know what to say, what to think.

'They're not here. They've left me on my own. And now some woman has just arrived who says she's here to prepare the meal for tonight, and I haven't a clue what to tell her—'

'Where has everyone gone?'

'Liv said she couldn't spend another night in this house and insisted Niall drive her to the train station. So, they left.'

'What about Patrick? And Rachel?'

'They're at the Garda station.'

I felt her hesitation, read her fear in it. I spoke sharply.

'What is it, Hilary? What's happened?'

She answered reluctantly, her voice dropping. 'It was Patrick who did it, Lindsey. He was the one who shot Marcus.'

'But it was an accident. Right?'

'Well, of course it was! But Patrick said it was his gun that had fired. He took the blame himself.'

'No,' I said again, but I said it so quietly that she might not have heard.

'They took him down to the station. Rachel followed in the car. That was over an hour ago. I've tried calling, but neither of them is answering. I rang the station, but they wouldn't tell me anything. Can you try calling, Lindsey? They might listen to you – another member of the force, and all that. What do you think?'

Her words were flying past me. All I could think of was Patrick foolishly taking ownership of the blame.

I said a curt goodbye to Hilary and hung up. Then I threw the remainder of my chocolate bar in the bin. Its sweetness left me cold. The only flavour that seemed to stay in my mouth was bitter.

17

1992

Most of the students at St Alban's have gone home. *The weekenders*, as those who stay are known, are a sorry lot. At least, that's the received wisdom of the place. But I don't mind being here this weekend. I'm here on the pretext that my mother is sick but, really, I've stayed because of Rachel.

'There's trouble brewing at home,' she'd said earlier in the week. Lying on her side, stretched out on the bed opposite me, half-heartedly reading *The Great Gatsby*, she'd announced her plans to stay on at school for the weekend rather than facing the pyrotechnics at home. It had been several weeks since I'd been to Thornbury – not since before Christmas, in fact. Secretly, I had been hoping for an invitation this weekend. I realized, with a pang, how much I missed it.

'Why? What's happened?' I'd asked, surprised.

'Heather's having one of her episodes,' she'd explained in a bored tone.

'Episodes?'

Putting down her book, she'd flung herself back on to the pillow as if it was all enormously tedious. 'She takes to her room for days, drinks far too much, and weeps constantly.'

'God! That's awful, Rach.'

She snorted. 'It's quite the performance, believe me.'

I was surprised by the lack of compassion in her tone, but didn't press her on it.

Rising from her bed, she crossed to the wardrobe to examine her reflection in the narrow mirror. She tugged at her hair with dissatisfaction, saying, 'I need to do something with myself. I swear, I look about twelve.'

'What does your father think?' I asked. 'He must be worried.'

'I doubt it. It's probably his fault she's gone to pieces.'

'Oh?'

'He must have done something to set her off. That's normally what happens. Anyway,' she went on, brightening, 'it will pass. It always does.'

Every weekender feels cast off. But we make up for it. That's what Rachel tells me when she finds me slouched in our room. It's Friday afternoon and the high-octane hysteria of the departures has just passed, dying away as the last of the pupils are picked up. In the quiet that follows, the atmosphere shifts from a code of rules and regulations to something more relaxed.

'Let's go to the shops,' she suggests. 'Get some munchies for the movie later.'

It is a grey day in early February, and little flurries of

wind come biting around our necks and knees as we hurry down the treeless avenue towards the school gates. Wrapped up in our school coats and scarves, we cling to each other while Rachel lists off all the things we will do that weekend: there is the movie after dinner tonight in the students' lounge, then tomorrow she has negotiated two passes for us to go into town for the afternoon. 'I'm going to get my hair cut,' she says, with an air of determination. 'Something dramatic. I need to change my look.'

I wonder if perhaps I should do the same, but I don't want her to think that I am slavishly copying her. We are best friends, but for all our closeness, I still feel that her friendship is a tentative thing she might snatch away at any moment to bestow on someone else.

In the little corner shop, we load up on goodies for the weekend – cans of Coke, Dime bars, Rancheros – things that are normally prohibited, the rules relaxed over the weekend.

I am filling a bag of pick'nmix when the bell over the door rings and Mr Ridgeway, or Ridge, as we call him, walks in. He teaches science and is the weekend residential assistant this term. He doesn't see us, or at least he pretends not to. He goes to the newspaper rack and surveys the papers. I return my attention to the bag of sweets I'm filling and hear Rachel's voice, except it does not sound like her voice, being lower, and more syrupy.

'Hello, Mr Ridgeway, sir,' she says.

'Hello, Rachel.' The flatness of his tone suggests his disinterest. He clearly doesn't hear what I hear in her voice or, if he does, he's chosen not to react.

'Are you going to watch the movie with us tonight?' she asks.

'I doubt it.'

'It's *Pretty Woman*,' she persists. 'Have you seen it?'

'I haven't, no.'

My back is to them, but above the pick'n'mix counter there is a round convex mirror – an anti-theft device – and looking up now I can just about make him out: his corduroy jacket and brown floppy hair, a newspaper in his hands. Ridge is one of the younger staff members. There was a great fuss, apparently, when St Alban's got him. Before he'd turned to teaching, he'd been part of a prize-winning research team at one of the big university hospitals. Whenever we play 'Which teacher would you snog if you had to?' he frequently comes out in front.

'It's supposed to be good, sir,' Rachel goes on. 'A sort of modern retelling of the Cinderella story.'

'Is that so?'

'Only instead of glass slippers, she wears thigh-high boots.'

His laugh emerges suddenly, like a gasp. Then he steps past her to pay for his newspaper. A brief nod in her direction and he goes to leave.

'So, will we see you later?' she asks, drawing him back for a moment as he stands at the door.

'Well—'

'I'm quite surprised we're allowed to watch it, actually,' she goes on in a rush. 'It's very raunchy, you know. Prostitutes and everything.'

'Imagine that,' he says, deadpan, but I have turned to look and can see the faint glimmer of amusement in his face.

She reflects the amusement back at him, a slow smile creeping over her face. 'Surely we will need a responsible adult in the room. A moral authority . . .'

He looks at her now, openly bemused, but there is something else behind his expression – as if he is seeing her in a new light.

'Well, maybe I will . . .'

The bell rings out above the door again after he leaves, and we go to the counter, where Mrs Fox behind the till casts disparaging looks our way as she rings it all up.

'What was all that about?' I ask Rachel, once outside on the street.

'What?'

I pucker my lips and do an exaggerated imitation of Rachel's seductive tones. *'It's very raunchy, you know. Prostitutes and everything.'*

'I don't know. Just messing with him.'

'I heard he made Dave Fogarty sit in the fume cupboard at the back of the lab.'

'Ridge did? Whatever for?' Rachel asks.

'He forgot his homework.'

Rachel's laughter is infectious. What I have told her is not that funny, but she can't stop laughing, giggling the whole way back to school.

Over breakfast the next morning, while the other girls discuss Julia Robert's glorious tresses, Rachel is dismissive. She plans to get her own hair cut into a short bob. Her style icon, she declares, is Daisy Buchanan, not Vivian Ward, and when we get the bus into town that afternoon, just the two of us, she heads straight for Peter Mark on George's Street and does just that.

'What do you think?' she asks, as we stand together on the blustery street corner, the wind lifting her newly shorn locks.

'You look older,' I tell her, and it is true. The haircut is that of an older woman, not a sixteen-year-old girl.

My comment sparks excitement within her and she grabs my arm and says, 'Come on,' and we hurry towards Grafton Street, where the crowds grow thicker.

'Where are we going?' I ask, but she just laughs and says:

'Wait and see!'

She leads me to Brown Thomas, an upmarket department store that I find faintly intimidating. Rachel nods to the doorman and marches in like she's a regular. At one of the make-up counters, she eyes up lipstick, passing her finger along a row of coloured tubes with a considered air. The one she chooses is brick-red. She eases it over her full lips, then pouts in front of the mirror. I can tell she is happy with the transformation and, while I make lots of complimentary noises, deep down this change in her appearance unsettles me. We go to McDonald's and eat cheeseburgers at the window, and I can see the looks she gets. All of a sudden, she has morphed into this older, sophisticated creature. Next to her, I feel mousey and colourless.

'Let's go to Penney's,' I suggest. 'I want to buy a new top.'

Rachel frowns and looks at her watch. 'Tell you what – why don't we split up and meet back here in an hour? We could go to the cinema then – what do you think? *Point Break* is playing in the Screen.'

Our plans made, we go our separate ways. I spend some of my money on a new top, then go to the Body Shop and buy a sticky pink lip-gloss. I am the first one back at the meeting place, and jiggle my weight from one foot to the other as the cold wind whisks down Grafton Street. When Rachel doesn't come, I look inside McDonald's. But she's not in the queues, or at the tables, or even in the Ladies when I check. I grow confused about our plan. Perhaps she meant we should meet at the cinema? I hurry to Hawkins Street and hang around the lobby for a while, before eventually buying a ticket and going in by myself. I spend a miserable couple of hours in the darkness, half absorbed by Patrick Swayze's onscreen presence while fretting over Rachel and where she might be.

It's dark when I leave – almost nine o'clock. I have to

run to catch the bus so that I'll be back at school before curfew. The dorm mistress asks me where Rachel is, and I tell her we got separated. When she quizzes me about it, I lie and say Rachel was at the cinema with me but, when we were running to catch the bus, she fell behind and missed it. The lie comes out easily enough but afterwards, in my room, I worry about the consequences of it being discovered. I get into bed and wait in the darkness, my emotions pitching between anxiety in case something has happened to her and the angry suspicion that she abandoned me on purpose. For I know enough of Rachel's nature to understand how bewitched she will be by her own physical transformation. Rather than hanging out with me, the temptation to test the new power of her appearance might have been too great.

It is almost eleven when she gets in. Instantly, I sit bolt upright and hiss: 'What happened to you? Where have you been?'

She puts a finger to her lips, her eyes flaring with a bemused warning.

'Sorry,' she says, shrugging off her coat and stepping out of her shoes. 'What did you tell Meara?'

When I explain the lie I've told on her behalf, she comes to my bed and throws her arms around me in a brief hug. She smells of cigarette smoke and cold air. Drawing back, she beams at me, 'You're a star.'

The lipstick is all gone from her lips, and her face is changed – like a light's been turned on inside her.

When I press her again on where she's been, she tells me she forgot the time and turned up at our meeting place too late.

'What did you do? Where did you go?'

'Nowhere, really. Just wandered around.'

'For, like, six hours?'

'I guess.'

She hurriedly changes, and when she gets into bed and turns out the light I hear her give a sigh of contentment. Soon her breathing grows soft and even, so I know she is no longer awake. It is a long time before I close my eyes, a long time before I sleep.

18

2017

People hate police stations. Not the bright, anodyne area of the front desk, but the rooms hidden away behind it, the cells and the interview rooms, the places where the real wheels of justice turn. They feel the same way about police stations as they do about hospitals. And just as there is fear and awe inspired by the surgeon, the same is true of the detective. They both, at some point or another, have to deal with death.

It turned out I knew the detective in charge of this case. When the door to the interview room opened, admitting Savage – the weary-looking sergeant I had met some months back – I was surprised. He was not.

'It's yourself,' he sniffed, dropping a thin file on the Formica-topped table and taking a seat opposite me. He eyed me with an air of mild disapproval. In fact, his whole demeanour was that of a man unimpressed by everything life threw up. 'So, you're back to us.'

'Couldn't stay away,' I replied.

I felt calm again. Perhaps it was the setting, which was familiar to me on so many levels. I had been more than happy to leave the hospital when the uniformed guard showed up and asked me to accompany him to the station. Marcus's boyfriend, Carl, had arrived by then – a young man with brown skin and bluish-black hair, a bewildered look on his thin face as I explained to him what had happened. An accident, I had told him. A horrible accident. I couldn't bear the thought of having to sit with him and Marcus's parents, waiting in baffled silence as the surgeon worked and the hours ticked by.

A good deal of my working life had been spent in police stations. I was well acquainted with the faded pistachio-green wall-paint and the brown nylon carpets of those places. I could make myself feel comfortable in those cheap plastic chairs. The thin Styrofoam cup of piss-poor coffee felt right in my hand. Added to that was the parochial charm of the place, the midlands inflections in the accents, the generally flat air, as if nothing truly bad could happen here – as if evil only lurked in big cities. I could have been back in my father's pub, so familiar did it feel.

'You warm enough?' Savage asked, looking askance at the scrubs top, my bare arms. And even though I was cold, I said I was fine. When he offered to grab something for me from Lost Property, I shook my head, repeating my assertion that I was okay.

He nodded his chin in the direction of my injured eye, softly asking, 'What happened there?'

'Oh, nothing. I walked into an elbow.'

A slight quiver of movement about his eyebrows. 'Care to elaborate?'

'Not really. It's unrelated.'

Unrelated to the shooting I meant, and he made a quick face as if to say, *Suit yourself.* He flipped open his file and unclipped the pen from his shirt pocket, and said sternly, 'Right, then. What the hell happened out there today?'

'It was an accident,' I said, surprising myself with my vehemence. Savage's expression showed he had noted it, too, and he asked:

'Do you think so?'

'Of course! It was a horrible accident. The deer appeared out of nowhere, Patrick reacted. Marcus, unfortunately, stepped into the line of fire.'

'He's a pretty experienced gunman, this Bagenal fellow,' Savage said. 'If I understand correctly. More experienced, certainly, than anyone else at the shoot. Why do you think he made such a mistake? It seems unlikely, don't you think?'

I remembered, with a pang, Patrick's instructions to us earlier that morning as we stood on the lawn. How careful he had been to point out the safety rules, his words of warning spoken with gravity and precision.

'It was the deer. It took us all by surprise. It was supposed to be a simple crow shoot, you see? None of us expected the deer. It startled us all, and I suppose he got carried away. Just as Niall did.' I was thinking as I spoke, trying to work it all out. 'Look, are you sure it really was Patrick? I mean, there were several shots fired. Patrick and Niall weren't the only ones shooting. I'm fairly sure the girls did, too.'

'Girls?' Savage said. 'Hardly girls, now, are they?'

I was taken aback by the derision in his comment. 'You know what I mean,' I answered. 'No need to be a dick about it.'

His mouth drew back fractionally into the faintest of smiles, and I felt somehow that he had elicited the reaction he'd wanted.

'School friends of yours, is that right? Some kind of reunion, was it?'

'You could say that.'

He asked me some questions about the nature of our friendships, who got on with whom, was there any tension, were there any disagreements, grasping at straws. I batted his questions away. 'You're barking up the wrong tree,' I told him.

'Mr Bagenal tells me he's selling the house,' he said. 'Getting a fair price for it, wouldn't you say?'

'I really couldn't tell you.'

'Why not? You're his girlfriend, aren't you?'

'That doesn't mean he shares the details of his personal finances with me. It's not like we're married.'

'Not that close, eh?'

'How is that relevant, Savage?'

'Just trying to get a picture of things. You know how it works.'

He changed tack then, started asking me where I was standing in the field in relation to the others. I was still smarting from his little skirmish into the realm of my romantic affairs, my mind tracking off down the avenue of Patrick and me. How was it that, when we were alone together in Dublin, what we shared felt solid and safe, untouchable. But barely twenty-four hours back at Thornbury, and we were all at sea. I hadn't asked Savage about Patrick yet, whether or not he had been charged, and I wondered if he was somewhere close by, possibly in an adjacent interview room, waiting for the detective sergeant to glean from me what he could and then return. Savage's change of tack took me off guard.

'I don't remember exactly,' I said carefully. 'I suppose we were about halfway down the field. Niall was a little in front of the rest of us. He had a better view of the deer when it came into sight.'

'So, you were back from him. What – nine or ten metres or so?'

'About that.'

'And who was near you?'

'Hilary. And Liv. We had been talking.'

'And the victim, we know, was off to your left. He was some distance to the side of the rest of you, I understand.'

'Yes,' I said, shrinking a little from the word 'victim'.

'And Ms Bagenal, where was she?'

'Rachel? I'm not sure. I think she was further back than the rest of us.'

'So that just leaves Mr Bagenal. You had your back to him. I understand.'

'That's right.'

'And would you say he was standing close behind you?'

The question was thrown out matter-of-factly, in the same manner and tone in which he asked the others. But I knew we had come to the crux of it. All day, I had been turning it over in the back of my mind, returning again and again to the scene, trying to isolate it in my memory, trying to see through the vagueness, to find that elusive clarity. I held his gaze, kept my body still, said:

'The shots I heard came from some distance to my left.'

'You're sure about that?'

'Positive.'

My voice was calm and firm.

'Did you turn to look in the direction of the shot?'

'My eyes were on the deer, I'm afraid. And then Liv, when she started running.'

'So how can you be sure—?'

'If he had been standing directly behind me, then I would be the one in hospital right now, not Marcus,' I said, allowing some impatience to slip into my voice. 'Look, are you charging Patrick with something or not?'

He raised his hands from the table, palms up in a gesture of maybe-we-will-maybe-we-won't, and said, 'It's early days. We've some more questions to ask.'

'Is he here? Can I see him?'

Savage gave me a benign but pitying look. 'Come on, now. You know I can't.'

'He's just trying to do the honourable thing,' I blurted out. 'As if it's somehow his duty to take the blame because it happened on his land with his guns.'

'Any animosity, or jealousy between them that you know about? Any disagreement—'

'Christ, no! They've been best friends since forever.'

He held my gaze, and I felt interrogated by it, as if somehow he could worm his way into my thoughts and see what I had seen: that moment in the garden this morning, Patrick slamming Marcus against the wall. Patrick's words from all those months ago coming back to me now and tunnelling in like an earworm: *All of you have a kind of freedom that I don't have. Every time I talk to Marcus, he's just come back from Amsterdam or New York or Madrid.* Was Savage right? Could Patrick be harbouring feelings of jealousy? No, it was ridiculous. The whole thing was absurd.

'How long are you going to keep him?'

'That depends,' Savage said, 'on how cooperative he is.'

'His sister . . .'

'Ah, yes. We had the pleasure of her company a short while ago. Lording it over the lads at the front desk, getting all riled up about police brutality.' He chuckled to himself.

'Is she still here?'

'No. Had her little scene, then stormed off.'

I could picture it, Rachel throwing her scorn around, taking no prisoners, then marching off in high dudgeon.

'What more do you want from me?' I asked, tired now of it all. The room was starting to feel unwelcoming, the familiar surroundings retreating into cold indifference.

'I think that's it for now.' He clicked his pen and flipped the folder closed. 'Where'll you be if we need to talk to you?'

'I don't suppose there's any point in waiting around for Patrick?'

'Ah, no. We'll hang on to him for another while yet.'

I took out my phone. There were no messages. No news from the hospital. I needed to eat, to shower and change. 'Then I'll guess I'll head back to Thornbury,' I said. 'Do me a favour? Give me the number of a local cab?'

'I'll do better than that,' he said, opening the door for me with a flourish. 'I'll drop you out there myself.'

The rain was falling heavily as Savage guided the car along the wet roads. I watched the sweep of the windscreen wipers, feeling cold to the bone. The bright morning was a distant memory. At first, he drove in silence, concentrating on the road, but as the minutes passed, he seemed to relax into my company and began asking me about work, mentioning some friend of his who had recently transferred to Special Branch and was dealing directly with Forensics. I didn't know the man and said as much. Then, aware of Savage's expectant silence, I told him that I was on desk duty now, having been taken off the field.

'Oh?' Savage asked. 'How come?'

'Medical reasons.'

I didn't elaborate, and he didn't press me on it. I could feel him making his own quiet assumptions. Breakdown, he probably thought. It happens often enough in a job like mine, with its own unique stresses. Or perhaps an alcohol or drug dependency.

He glanced across at me, a quick, searching look.

'Did you get that shiner up at Thornbury?'

'I did.'

'Not quite the reunion you'd all been hoping for?'

'I suppose not.'

He picked up on the glum note in my voice, the low ebb of my spirits, and his tone softened.

'They're a bad idea, I've always thought. Reunions. Trying to revisit your youth. It never works. People have too much to prove. Old scores to settle.'

I mulled over what he'd said in silence. Was he right? Was this weekend about settling old scores? I thought of Hilary, her dramatic transformation from dumpy, sullen schoolgirl to a waif-like beauty, all gaiety and frivolity. And Niall with his flashy car, his money, the gun – *They only make a dozen of them a year.* Even Marcus with his stern but expensive uniform of clothes, his immaculate grooming, casting his disapproval over the

216

house. I remembered suddenly the warmth of his blood under my palms and gazed down at my hands, a wave of nausea rising and falling away.

'Patrick has no old scores to settle,' I said quietly. 'He just wanted us to come and see the house one last time before he lets it go.'

We were drawing close to Thornbury now. The perimeter wall rose up to one side of the road, partially obscured by a canopy of leaves from the overhanging branches of the ancient trees beyond.

'Most of these big houses were burned to the ground during the War of Independence,' Savage remarked. 'In a way, it's miraculous that Thornbury has survived this long.'

'I suppose.'

'It'll change the area, of course,' he said, on a rising note. 'Good to open the place up a bit. Put the land to good use.' He talked a bit about the plans to build new homes, bringing the commuter belt to the locality. 'Inject a bit of life into the town,' Savage said. 'God knows, the place could do with it.'

We had reached the entrance, and he turned the car through the granite pillars, slowing as he began the journey up the overgrown, bumpy avenue, the rain pooling in long, muddy puddles along the track.

'I wouldn't like it myself, living here,' he said with a shudder. 'Whatever about the days, could you imagine what it would be like up there on cold, wintry nights? It'd give you the creeps just thinking about it.'

'I didn't think you'd scare so easily, Savage.'

'Yes, well . . .' His voice trailed off, and he spoke again in a different tone. 'I was called up here one night a few years back. A car had been mashed into a tree.' His car was travelling slowly past the rhododendron, and in the murkiness of the wet evening, I couldn't see the tree itself of which he spoke, the scarred trunk where the car had struck. 'A bitter cold night it was. I remember the hands were freezing off me as I stood there, trying to take a statement from the son. The mother, God love her, was wavering in and out of consciousness. Poor fella was in a dreadful state, blaming himself for what had happened.'

'Yes, he told me,' I said.

'Although if she had wanted to kill herself, there was little he could have done to stop her, short of hiding her car keys or locking her in the house.'

'You think it was a suicide attempt?'

'Perhaps. Perhaps not. Either way, it didn't kill her.'

'She had a brain tumour,' I told him. 'It was making her behaviour erratic.'

He nodded his head in understanding, but now that the words were out of my mouth I began to consider my own behaviour, my own tumour. Was it possible that it was making my own behaviour erratic? My judgement questionable? Could it be that my decision to come back here, far from being the considered, reasonable response to Patrick's invitation, was instead a dangerous choice, the product of an unsound mind?

I sat in confused silence, thinking of what I'd said back in the interview room, the answer I'd given when Savage asked about our positions in the field, where we had all been standing when that shot rang out, and when I thought about my answer now I felt a push of fear. I realized that I was afraid of what I had said, what I had done.

The car reached the top of the avenue, leaving behind the tangle of bushes and trees. The house rose up in front of us, grey and forbidding as the rain pelted at the brickwork, the windowpanes, the slate roof high above. The statue lying across the doorway seemed even more forlorn as little runnels of rainwater travelled over its weathered limbs. The front door was slightly ajar and beyond I could make out a dim light in the hall, although all the windows remained dark.

'You're sure you want to go back in there?' Savage asked, and I heard scepticism in his voice, but a note of kindness, too.

'I'll be fine,' I told him, unstrapping my seatbelt and reaching for the door.

I had to run across the gravel, the rain hitting my head and arms, penetrating my flimsy clothing. In the doorway, I stopped and looked back at Savage's car as it pulled away. And as I watched the red tail lights wending through the trees, I felt a sort of pang like a flash of intuition, an urge to shout after him, *No! Wait — stop!* But I didn't. I stood where I was, with one hand on the heavy door, until the tail lights disappeared and the only sound was that of the rain and, beyond it, the rustle and call of the birds in the trees.

19

1992

The next time I see Heather and Peter Bagenal is when they are summoned to the school to discuss their daughter's recent behaviour. Missing her curfew that Saturday night was just the start. Throughout February, there have been other incidents: unexplained absences from class, leaving the school grounds without permission, insolence towards the teachers. Her schoolwork has deteriorated, with little sign that she cares. When she was told that her parents had been invited to meet with the headmaster, her response was to roll her eyes, but little more.

'Aren't you worried?' I ask her, my voice betraying my own concern. I have it in mind that perhaps Rachel might be expelled. Or that her parents may decide for themselves to remove her from St Alban's.

'Why should I be worried?'

'What if you're expelled?'

She laughs, and mocks me for worrying over nothing. 'Look, they'll probably just give me a big lecture on applying myself and adhering to the school rules. I'll sit there and listen, all contrite. I'll probably even cry a little – the headmaster loves it when he makes you cry in front of your parents. I'll make a little speech on how I've let everybody down, most of all myself, and how I promise I'll do better. And that will be that. Don't sweat it, Lins.'

She has it all worked out. But despite her confidence – her cynicism – I can't help feeling a niggle of doubt. And when the Bagenals' Nissan Bluebird drives up the avenue and I see Peter and Heather get out, I feel a catch in my chest.

We have just left our form room, the corridor thronged as we hurry towards the labs for biology, when we see them through the window. Peter parks the car outside the guest entrance, then gets out, shutting the door behind him before buttoning his camel coat. The day is grey and blustery and, when Heather emerges, her blonde hair is buffeted about, and she reaches up with a gloved hand to tuck it back in place. She is wearing large, squarish sunglasses, even though the sun is well hidden today, and her clothes are black, funereal, patent shoes with stiletto heels on her feet. Several girls stop to watch her from the windows – the casual chic of her clothes, the regal manner with which she carries herself. I think of what Rachel has told me about her mother's lapses – 'Heather's episodes', as she calls them – and the image she has conjured of a woman falling to pieces seems so at odds with the cool, sophisticated creature we are all watching now that, for just a moment, I doubt the truth of Rachel's account.

Peter puts his hand on the small of his wife's back and guides her gently towards the door. Then Rachel says, 'Wish me luck,' and there's a tremor in her voice – the first show of nerves I've seen in her.

I hug her quickly, whisper, 'Good luck,' into her hair, and watch as she walks unhurriedly past the others, who are rushing to get to class, smoothing down her hair with both hands as she goes.

In biology, Ridge takes us through the reproductive system of a plant, but it is difficult to concentrate. The heating is on full blast in the labs and, with all the windows shut, it feels stifling, condensation misting the windows. Around me, I see my classmates wilting, one or two of them making nests of their arms and resting their heads down. Ridge doesn't seem to notice, too intent on the chalk diagram he has drawn on the board and is busy labelling as he talks. His voice becomes a background noise to my own clamouring thoughts. In my head, I am down in the headmaster's office with Rachel and her parents. The more I think about it, the more nervous I become.

Over the months that I've been here at St Alban's, I've come to rely on her. More than that, I felt the bond of our friendship growing stronger and tighter. For the first time in my life, I have a soulmate. We are kindred spirits – that's what Rachel tells me. But lately, I have felt a drift in her attention. She does not want to talk as much as she used to. Often, when we are in conversation, her mind appears to be on other things, an absence entering her gaze. She doesn't joke about as much as before.

A sudden stinging pain on my knee brings my attention sharply into focus. The boy to my right has pinched me hard.

'Sit still, for fuck's sake,' he hisses, and it is only then that I realize my leg has been jigging with nerves.

As soon as the bell rings, we spill out into the corridor, and I look out the window and see the Nissan Bluebird still there. Peter Bagenal is leaning against it, his hands in his pockets, staring up at the building with an unreadable expression. There is no sign of Heather or Rachel, and I am suddenly convinced that he is waiting for them to pack up Rachel's belongings and take her away from St Alban's for good. While the rest of my classmates file downstairs to the canteen, I race up to the dorms, flinging wide the door, only to find the room empty. Rachel's things are as she left them, and I feel the panic subside a little. Still, I can't help feeling anxious at the outcome of the meeting, and so I leave my books and grab my coat, flying down the stairs and outside into the wind and weather to where Peter Bagenal awaits.

He raises a hand in greeting as I emerge on to the courtyard, beckons to me to come forward, while he tamps down the tobacco in the bowl of his pipe and goes through the ritual of lighting it. There is something comforting in the smell of it.

'Where is Rachel?' I ask, breathless, and his jaw moves, smoke emerging fatly from his mouth.

223

'Inside with her mother. Thompson has invited them to take tea with him in his little parlour.' He says this with a slight push of sarcasm. His eyes meet mine and there's a hint of wickedness in them, and I feel a rush of relief.

'It went well, then?'

'Depends on your perspective. We didn't come to blows, so that's a plus.'

'And Rachel?'

'Oh, Rachel's fine. My daughter is quite the little actress. Managed to squeeze out a few tears, declared her intentions to mend her ways. It was quite affecting, really.' His tone is ironic, but he doesn't seem angry.

'What an ugly building this is,' he declares, casting his gaze over it with distaste. 'It looks more like an orphanage than a school. I can't stand these Victorian institutional designs. So unforgiving, don't you think?'

'I suppose.'

I sound unconvinced, but he doesn't appear to notice, saying, 'Shall we take a little stroll around the grounds? My ladies will be conducting their charm offensive on Thompson for a while yet.'

'All right,' I say, and wait while he fetches his camera from the car – it is the Leica that I remember – and then we walk around the side of the building towards the hockey pitches.

'My wife went to this school, you know,' he tells me. 'It was her idea to send Patrick and Rachel here. I wanted them to go to the local parish school, the way I did, but Heather had different notions.'

'It's a good school,' I say, and he sniffs at that.

'It's not the worst. That Thompson is a bit of a pompous prick, though.'

I'm not sure how to react to that, so I say nothing, just walk with my hands in the pockets of my coat, my eyes on the ground in front of me.

We round a grotto where a statue of Our Lady stands on a plinth surrounded by bursts of heather. He pauses to look at it and I think he might take a photograph, but the Leica remains slung over his shoulder and, after a moment, we move on.

'Tell me,' he says. 'Do you know what's gotten into her this term?'

'No, sir.'

'You don't have to call me sir – I'm not one of your teachers,' he says, not unkindly, before continuing: 'Has she become distracted over some boy?'

'Not that I know of,' I answer, thinking it isn't exactly a lie.

'I don't suppose you'd tell me if she was,' he declares, but he says it breezily, then adds: 'You're a loyal friend, Lindsey. Rachel is lucky to have met you.'

His words make me shy, and I mutter something about how I am lucky to have met her, too.

'Of course, the big question is how should I discipline her,' he remarks. 'Thompson has his own system of torture devised for her, but I feel I need to do something to shake her up a bit. Shout at her, perhaps. Rant and rave a bit. Lay down the law. What do you think, hmm? Is that what your father would do?'

I come from a family where raised voices are reserved for sporting fixtures or clearing the bar. Both my parents employ passive aggression as the chief weapons in their arsenal, resolving disagreement through stubborn refusals to engage.

'My parents prefer to steer clear of confrontation,' I tell him. '"Ignore it, it will go away," is their motto.'

'Ha!' He looks across at me, and it feels like the first time in our conversation that he has really seen me. 'What about you? How are you getting on at school?'

I shrug, and say, 'All right.'

'More than all right, I'd guess,' he says. 'Your father must be pleased with you.'

'I suppose.'

'You suppose?' he queries.

'He doesn't really say much.'

'No?'

I must have allowed some petulance to leak into my voice, for he eyes me with curiosity.

'Close to him, are you?'

'Not really.'

'That's unfortunate.'

He allows a silence to slip into our conversation, and this silence feels like an invitation of some sort. I recall, months ago, Rachel encouraging me to confide in

Heather about what had happened to me. Her words return to me now: '*You could tell her if you wanted, you know. She's very understanding.*' How surprising it is that, instead of turning to Heather, it's Peter I confide in.

'I used to worship him,' I say of my father. 'Really revered him. But then I started being bullied by this girl in school, and it kept going on and on, getting worse and worse, and my father did nothing about it. Even though he knew. He'd seen the scars. It took a cigarette burn on my neck before he actually did something about it, but rather than confronting the issue, he just moved me here, to get me out of the way.' I hear my voice, the emotion that has crept into it, despite my efforts to sound calm. Peter has stopped walking and stands now with his hands behind his back, a slightly military stance, concentrating on what I'm telling him.

'He must have had his reasons,' he says tentatively, watchful for my reaction. 'I'm sure he did what he thought was best for you.'

'Or what was easiest for him,' I say, and he catches the trace of bitterness in my voice, and his expression softens.

'Being a parent is difficult, Lindsey. Try not to be too hard on your old man.'

I feel the creep of emotions crawling up my throat and recognize with some alarm that I am on the verge of tears.

'We should go back,' he says, and we walk in silence back around the building, and by the time we near the courtyard, Rachel and Heather have emerged. We see them standing by the car, surrounded by a group of girls from our class. Rachel sees us coming and waves, a bright smile on her face. Whatever dressing-down she endured in Thompson's office, she looks untouched and unmoved now.

'You never took any photographs,' I say, as we reach the others.

He looks down at his camera. 'No. Too busy talking.' Then he thinks for a minute, before taking the leather strap from over his shoulder and holding out the camera to me.

'Here,' he says gently. 'Why don't you keep it this time?'

'Oh no, I couldn't,' I say quickly, conscious of the others watching and listening.

'Go on,' he urges. 'I hardly use it myself any more. I don't know why I thought to bring it today.'

'It's too much, really.'

'Please. I should like you to have it. And the next time you're at Thornbury, I will show you how to use the darkroom.'

I take the camera in my hands, feel the enormity of the gesture. 'Thank you, Peter,' I say softly, and when I look up he is smiling, and I know it's because, finally, I have called him by his Christian name.

'Sometimes I feel as if you are the daughter I should have had,' he says fondly, and I am too startled by the admission to answer.

He turns to go, and within minutes the car is kicking up dust as it travels back down towards the gates.

'How did it go?' I ask Rachel, hugging the camera to my chest.

'Just as I thought,' she tells me. 'No sweat.'

But the look she gives me is cold. It lasts just a second or two, before she pulls her coat tight about her and hurries back indoors.

20

2017

By now it was evening. The house felt different. The grey damp outside seemed to permeate through to the interior, a dank smell undercutting the sweet scent of lilies amassed in a display on the hall table. The doors giving on to the main reception rooms were open, and I saw that the rooms were empty and chilly, no fires lit in the grates, the lamps not yet switched on. Silence filled the spaces, and I wondered where the others had got to – Hilary and Niall and Rachel.

In the corridor behind the staircase, I heard a sudden clatter coming from the kitchen. Following it, I found Jinny lying on the rug in front of the Aga. She lifted her long russet head briefly as I came in, then seeing it was me and not her master, she dropped her muzzle back on to her front paws with a mournful air, exhaling through her wet black nose in a little disappointed puff. I bent down to rub at the back of her ears and, as I did, a woman I didn't know came in from the scullery with a basin full of muddy-looking vegetables and a peeling knife.

'What a mess,' the woman declared, before introducing

herself as I straightened up. Her name was Felicia. Patrick had mentioned her to me, a local woman who came in to help him out from time to time. She had the settled appearance of a country wife, but I imagined she was no older than I was, blonde hair drawn back into a short ponytail. 'No one seems able to tell me what I should do,' she declared with an air of mild harassment. 'I've laid out the dining room for seven, but now it looks like there'll just be four of you. Will you even go ahead if Patrick's not here? And I've my niece coming out from Borris in an hour to wait on the table. Should I call her and tell her not to bother? It hardly seems worth it, does it?'

'I don't know,' I said miserably. 'Do you know where the others are?'

'Haven't the faintest,' she replied, unimpressed. 'Rachel was moping around here for a while. I don't know where she went after that.'

She crossed to the sink and dumped the vegetables into the basin of water that sat within it, then began to peel them briskly. We passed a strained few minutes in silence. I had the impression she wished me to leave so she could get on with her preparations – fruitless or not. It was only as I began to retreat that she glanced up at me and took in my bedraggled state of dress. 'You've been up at the hospital, then,' she said, then gave a tutting noise, adding: 'That poor young man. Fighting for his life. Shot, imagine? For something like that to happen here, in this house . . . Well. It brings back bad memories.'

'Yes. It's terrible.'

'This house,' she said, going at a carrot with renewed aggression. 'It gives me the creeps now same as it did then. Best thing they could do, if you ask me, is put a match to the place.'

She surprised me with her fierceness, but I said nothing. Too tired, too wrung out by the day's events. My hunger had abated, but the cold had settled into the marrow of my bones. My skin reeked of the hospital hand-sanitizer. An agitation had started inside me at her mention of Peter. Even though she hadn't said his name out loud. Still he was there, and I felt the memory of what happened to him drumming away inside me all the way back up the stairs through the silent house.

The shower was one of those old-fashioned jobs with a hose hooked up to the taps, the water falling into the bathtub – an ancient roll-topped affair with claw feet and greenish streaks where the water hit the enamel. I stepped in and drew across the mildewed curtain, the rings singing along the rail above. Even after turning the hot tap to full, and waiting for a few moments, the temperature remained warm but not hot. The pressure was weak, a pitiful sprinkling coming from the shower-head, barely enough to lather up some shampoo, and I turned my shoulders this way and that, letting the water run over my limbs. My arms continued to ache, even though it was hours now since I had leaned over Marcus, pressing against the flow of his blood. My thoughts went to the hospital, imagined him now in Intensive Care, tubes and pumps and blinking machines tethering him to life. And like the pendulum swing of my earlier thoughts, so now my mind swung from Marcus to Patrick. How long would they detain him? What would the charges be? I imagined Savage, his snarky disregard for Patrick's essential decency, looking to dredge up some kind of dirt to bring a little colour to his dreary day.

I scrubbed myself clean and ran a razor over my underarms and legs. It was only as I dipped my head under the water to rinse out the shampoo that I heard a strange gurgling noise in the plumbing overhead, and the water thinned to a trickle.

'For fuck's sake,' I declared to the empty room.

With the water slowing now to an unsteady run of drips, the air felt suddenly cool and I twisted at the taps, trying to get some kind of flow going, even if that meant a cold stream of water. I just wanted to rinse the shampoo from my hair and get out. But nothing emerged, no matter which way I turned the taps. I thought perhaps Felicia was running water into the sink in the kitchen and that the ancient plumbing of the house couldn't cope with both, so if I just waited a moment the warm water would return. I closed both taps off, wiped the soap from my face and ran my fingers through my hair, counting down a moment or two before I would try the taps again.

It was as I waited that I heard a noise from above, a low rumble followed by a clanking sound. It seemed to come from the attics beyond. My gaze went to the ceiling, following the direction of the noise. I saw the spiderweb of cracks in the paintwork, the spots of mould at the corners, and a brownish stain spreading above the shower-head. The rumble had gone, and the clanking diminished, petering away to a tinny, tapping noise. For no reason at all, the maids in the attic sprang to mind. Rachel's ghost story. *Just the one bed between them. She would have woken up in the morning to find her friend stone cold dead next to her.* I blinked upwards, waiting, listening.

Nothing. And then a loud wrenching noise, and water burst from above. It came from the shower-head but in a blistering torrent that hit me full in the face. I screamed, a gurgling cry as the boil of water filled my mouth and I jumped out of its scalding stream, slipping in the process, my hip impacting with the side of the bath, my hand catching at the razor lying face up on the enamel floor. Crouching to one side, shaking and scalded, I fumbled for the taps, twisting them one way and then another as the steam rose around me, and the jets kept catching at my arms in little biting sprays. Blood from my cut hand clouded the water swishing around my feet, and the water lacerated my back until eventually I turned it off and clambered, shaken, out of the tub.

Kneeling naked on the bathroom floor, I felt the frightened beat of my heart, my shaking limbs. Using toilet paper to staunch the cut on my hand, I wound it round and round, the blood seeping slowly through. It took me some moments to calm myself. I strained to hear any further noises from the attics, but there was only the slow drip of water from the shower-head.

By the time I'd rubbed myself dry with a towel, I had managed to convince myself it was nothing. Putting it down to a fault in the Victorian plumbing, I dressed quickly in jeans and a woollen pullover, and returned to my room, towel-drying my hair as I went. On the dressing table, I found my camera. Someone – Hilary, perhaps – must have retrieved it from where it had lain in the field. I picked it up and turned it over in my hands, amazed at how little thought I had given to it all day, surprising myself at the lack of regard I showed as to whether I ever found it again. Now, something else strange happened.

Standing there in front of the mirror, I opened up the viewer and went to the last image I had taken – it was of Niall in the field, his gun resting against his shoulder, peering out into the distance. It was the last in a series, and as I flicked back through the images I had taken that morning, a low pulse of remorse started within me every time Marcus appeared. His countenance seemed pale and his expression tight and guarded in every photo. It was almost as if he had some instinct of impending danger, but perhaps that was a fanciful thought. He was not the only one who appeared tired or apprehensive. Rachel, too, I noticed, seemed thin-lipped and unsmiling, her usual grace and carriage replaced by tension in her shoulders, a stiffness to her poise. Patrick appeared preoccupied, and Hilary barely featured. Every time I had tried to capture her likeness she had turned aside or stepped away. 'I hate having my picture taken,' I remembered her saying. Of all of them, only Niall and Liv appeared sunny and relaxed.

All the time I was going through the photographs, I was half aware of a dark form hanging from the wardrobe and reflected in the mirror. I looked up at that point, saw my reflection in the mirror, and behind me I saw my evening gown on a hanger that was hooked over the rim of the wardrobe door. It caught my attention because I had no recollection of putting it there. Hilary must have taken it from the wardrobe and hung it out for me, although I couldn't think why, and this incursion into my privacy irritated me.

I put down my camera and turned. I had only taken a couple of steps towards it when the dress slithered off the hanger and fell heavily to the floor. Despite myself, I felt a little kick of fright. Coming so soon after the incident in the shower, the oddness of it struck me. But again, I tried to rationalize it. The dress was of a heavy material and I had foolishly hung it off a wire hanger with downward-sloping shoulders. My movement across the floorboards must have somehow reverberated through to the wardrobe, causing the dress to fall.

I crossed the room with purposeful strides, bending to pick up the dress, and as I crouched on the floor there was a loud bang behind me and, this time, I really did jump. A loud thud followed by a cracking sound, and it was only as I stood, clutching my dress to my chest, that I saw what had happened. On the floor near the wide skirting board lay the framed picture of my teenage self – the one Peter Bagenal had taken of me underneath the shot rabbits. The picture, which I had left leaning face in to the wall, must have slipped down as I passed. Turning it over, I saw that the glazing had cracked, a seam shooting up through the glass, cutting my image in two. It seemed strangely malevolent, and I was surprised to find tears coming to my eyes. I had the thought that there was something in the room with me – some shadowy threat. I knew it was probably something to do with the tumour, and the side effects of the medication I was taking, but that knowledge did not dispel the sense of menace I experienced in that room.

'Just leave me the fuck alone!' I said aloud to the empty space, then shook my head and angrily swiped at my eyes with the back of my hands, furious at myself for feeling this way.

A figure crossing the garden outside caught my eye through the window. Hilary, in wellingtons and a rain-coat, walking purposefully across the grass away from the house. In that moment, spooked as I was by what had happened, I didn't want to be alone. I pulled on my boots and grabbed my coat, leaving my dress on the bed. I listened to the creak of the steps underfoot, the steadiness of it fighting against the whoosh of blood in my veins as my frightened heart pumped quickly and urgently all the way downstairs and out into the rain.

I caught up with Hilary in the copse of trees. She was walking briskly, her hands thrust into the pockets of her raincoat, which flared over her bare legs.

'I had to get out of that house,' she said, by way of explanation, as I fell into step beside her, the grass clinging to my boots. 'I felt like the walls were closing in.'

'Me, too,' I said. Needing to take the sting out of what had just happened, I explained to her about the shower and the dress, the picture falling to the floor.

'Jesus. It must be Heather coming back to haunt you!' she said, and to my surprise she began to laugh. 'Do you suppose she pushed the statue off the roof as well?'

Her response made me feel a little foolish, but it also had the effect of taking me out of myself. I began to calm down, and almost to enjoy the walk out in the buffeting wind. The rain pattered away gently on the leaves of the beeches and sycamores that sheltered us from the worst of it and we talked for a while about Marcus and what had happened, about Patrick still helping the guards with their enquiries, about whether or not the dinner would go ahead.

'It would be obscene, don't you think?' Hilary said. 'Poor Marcus fighting for his life while we're wining and dining? And who knows when Patrick will be back. Or Niall.'

'Niall's not back yet?'

She shook her head. 'He rang a while ago. He planned to go straight to the hospital after dropping Liv off at the station.'

'And?'

'No news. Marcus is still critical.'

'What did you tell the guards?' I asked her. 'About the shooting?'

'Not a lot, to be honest. 'They made a big fuss over where everyone was standing, who was shooting – trying to work out precisely if it was Patrick, I suppose.'

'And what do you think?'

'If he says it was him, then it was him. Why would he lie? Anyhow, I told the police I didn't really know where he was standing and I certainly couldn't say for sure if it was him who fired the shot. Why? What did you tell them?'

'Oh, something similar.' I tried to make my voice sound light and breezy, but I felt the weight of the lie I had told Savage sitting heavily inside me.

'We shouldn't have come back,' Hilary said then, a wistfulness in her tone. 'Don't you think?' When I didn't answer, she continued: 'Why did you?'

'Because Patrick wanted it, I suppose.'

'Yes, although I'm beginning to wonder why now.'

Without discussing it, we had automatically set off in the direction of the fields where the crows had wreaked their havoc to disastrous effect. We were almost there, and up ahead I could see a thin glow of light through a break in the wet canopy of leaves.

'What about you, Hilary? Why did you come back?'

'Because of all the horrible things that happened here,' she answered immediately, with a firmness that was surprising. 'I know – you'd think that would be the very reason to stay away. But I wanted to feel that what had happened here that night was put to rest. For once and for all. I needed to feel like this place had been cleansed of the bad memories, and I believed, somehow, that if we all came back here just once, and if we filled the place with cheer and celebration and happiness, that it would dispel the bad memories. Put the ghosts to rest.'

'That kind of makes sense, I suppose.'

'Well, it did,' she said crossly, 'until it all went tits-up. Oh God, Lins, what if Marcus dies?'

I linked my arm through hers, and we walked along together in silence, each of us considering the consequences of that.

'Do you think,' Hilary said, picking up on an earlier thread, 'that ghosts come back to haunt a place because they were unhappy there? Or is it because they loved the place so much they can't stay away, even in death?'

'I don't believe in ghosts,' I answered.

'Even so. Do you think Heather was happy here?'

'I don't know. I used to think she was, most of the time. But now, when I remember her, it doesn't seem that way.'

We had come to the edge of the clearing, and stood now at the top of the field, both of us hesitant to leave the shelter of the trees and make our way back down through the wheat. In the distance, I could make out the yellow and black of the Garda tape as it flickered in the rain, cordoning off the area of the field where Marcus fell.

'Peter was very fond of you,' she said then. 'I remember he said you were the daughter he should have had. I always thought that was mean of him – to say that, in front of Rachel. It made me wonder if it was the reason the two of you fell out so spectacularly.' She gave me a searching look, and I answered:

'He was kind to me at a time when things were difficult between me and my dad. That's all.'

'I see,' she said, before continuing: 'It must have been hard for Rachel, though. She wanted so desperately to please her father – to be his favourite.'

We were still linking arms, and now her arm around mine felt hot, her grip too tight. A throbbing was starting behind my eye.

'I never meant to come between them.'

'Oh my God,' she said slowly, and at first I misunderstood, thinking her words were a reaction to mine. But then I saw her eyes were fixed on something behind me, her expression changing to one of horror, and as I turned around and looked into the trees behind me, I saw what it was that held her fascination.

It was a crow. A dead crow – larger than the ones we had seen in the field that morning. Someone had nailed it to a tree.

'It's like voodoo,' Hilary said, her tone flat and unreadable as she crept closer to it.

The feathers on the wings of the bird gleamed with the black iridescence of decay and gave a sheen of petrol blue. I had a fleeting thought of regret – regret that I had left my camera back at the house. Immediately, I felt ashamed of the impulse.

'It must be an old farmhand trick to scare off the other crows,' I ventured.

'It's a little eccentric, don't you think? Not to mention macabre.'

I didn't answer. I just kept looking at the bird. It looked like a king of crows, it was so big, or perhaps that's just how it felt because I was tired and distraught. Its wings were spread wide open, its head dropped and tilted to the side, its body shriven and crucified against the trunk of the old tree.

21

1992

Before we break up for the Easter holidays, Thompson announces an impromptu school social. Notice is given on a Wednesday – a celebration to mark the senior girls' hockey team win in the Leinster League – and on Thursday afternoon a sweep is done of all the dorms in search of hidden alcohol. Only the very green or very stupid hide their contraband under beds or in wardrobes. Such matters require skill and cunning. Whispers go around of coke bottles full of peach schnapps hidden in the grass beyond the basketball court. Other rumours circulate of vodka in the labs and cider filling the squeezy bottles in the boys' locker room. Rachel has filled an old shampoo bottle with vodka and 7Up and we take turns swigging from it while getting ready in the girls' bathroom.

'Oh God, it tastes like poison!' Hilary shrieks as she passes it to me, still wincing when she leans into the mirror to dab at her eyelashes with mascara.

She's right, and as I put the Timotei bottle to my mouth I have to fight the instinct to gag and force it down. The whole room feels chemical. Perfume and deodorant and hairspray fumes fill the air, the mirrors steamed from the incessant showering, a half-dozen girls elbowing for space to examine their reflections. From deep within the building comes the squeal and thump of the sound system being set up. It sends a frisson of excitement through the room and sparks off a good deal of chatter about who fancies whom, which of the boys we hope to dance with, which of them we wouldn't be seen dead with. Only Rachel is quiet. Leaning into the mirror, she pulls her eyelid taut while tracing a black kohl line thinly over it. Her concentration is intense, her hand steady despite all the jostling and high-pitched excitement that surrounds her. Unlike the rest of us, who are all squeezed into mini-dresses of different hues, Rachel is wearing black jeans and a Rolling Stones T-shirt which she has cropped to show off her flat belly and her brand-new navel piercing – a bold move in itself, for the school is strict about body-art.

'You look great,' I tell her, and it's true. Despite the casual clothes and her airy detachment, there is no doubting her appeal. The rest of us, it feels, look trussed up and overdone in comparison. She smiles and says, 'Thanks,' but doesn't look at me, keeping her eyes on her own reflection, so that the smile seems self-satisfied. I wait for her to say something complimentary in return, but she just reaches for the door handle, and says over her shoulder: 'Are you coming?' I feel the faintest push of dislike as I follow her down the corridor, watching her hand fluffing up her hair.

The music grows louder as we near the school gymnasium. Inside, the curtains are drawn and the lighting has been lowered. A stage has been set up towards the front with a drum kit and microphones waiting, the school banner slung low overhead. As the space fills up, Niall and Patrick take to the stage, along with another sixth-year student. A recent experiment, they are unveiling their new band tonight to the home crowd. Cheers erupt as Patrick and Niall pick up their electric guitars, looping the straps over their necks, while the third boy seats himself behind the drums.

'Look,' I say, elbowing Rachel and nodding in Niall's direction as he takes centre stage, holding his hand up in greeting to the crowd, before leaning into the mic, his voice coming out gravelly and low:

'What's up, people?'

The crowd whoop with delight, everyone screaming it seems, except for Rachel. She stands there watching, but her attention seems elsewhere.

Niall, grinning and soaking up the adulation, says: 'We are The Gin Freaks, and this is "Come Together".'

Patrick's head moves with the beat of his rhythm guitar, his expression earnest and concentrated, as is the drummer's, but it is obvious to everyone in the room that The Gin Freaks are all about Niall. His hoarse and urgent whispering of lyrics close into the mic is both odd and strangely compelling, and strikes a chord within all of us.

'He's good!' I shout to Rachel, and when she doesn't answer I turn to see her walking away from me through the crowd.

Once, I might have followed her, but something holds me back. The quiet self-containment of hers has been growing for some time. It makes me unsure of myself whenever I'm around her. Since the day her parents came to the school I have noticed a cooling between us, a withdrawal of her confidences in me. On the surface, she is as pleasant and friendly as she has always been, but she does not share her secrets with me any more. I reason with myself that it will pass, once she grows tired of whoever she is secretly seeing, then she'll come back to me and we will be as before. Still, the insecurity bores through me as I watch her now, edging closer to the teachers and members of the parents committee who line the walls of the gym, watching with detached amusement as the student body lets loose.

The Gin Freaks run through their repertoire – a set which encompasses a broad spectrum from glam-rock to electro-pop. When they start covering A-ha's "Take On Me", I see Marcus folding his arms, his face contorting into a mask of disgust.

Once the band has finished, a DJ takes over, and Hilary grabs my arm and swings me around as the B-52's sing 'Love Shack'. We scream and laugh, and I feel the vodka now racing through my veins and am able to forget about Rachel's coldness for a while, the crush of bodies keeping me buoyant. When The Cure's 'Love Cats' starts up, Marcus whoops with delight and dashes out into the middle of us all, taking ownership of the song, his eyes closed and his limbs and head swinging to his own internal delirium. His unmasked joy is contagious, and I dance along beside him, carefree and uninhibited.

The tempo changes then, the music slows, and when Sinéad O'Connor sings 'Nothing Compares 2 U' there is a fractional pause, during which time decisions are made. Partners identify each other, coming together in loosely bound pairings, while those unchosen depart the dance floor. I see Patrick take the hand of a fifth-year named Erica, and feel my good humour falter.

'Hey,' someone says, and I feel a hand on my shoulder and turn to find Marcus looking at me kindly, a thin sheen of sweat on his face. 'Do you want to go outside?' he asks. 'Get some fresh air?'

His suggestion is surprising but welcome, and I follow him through the crowd and out into the cold air, where the night sky throws up thousands of stars above the thin clouds of our warm breath. I had not thought I was drunk but, out here by the tennis courts, I feel my mind swoop and lurch from one thought to another.

The bench we sit on feels damp and cold, but Marcus is unperturbed as he opens a pouch of tobacco. He looks different tonight without his glasses – less serious, I suppose. The memory of his loose-limbed joy dancing to The Cure glows brightly in my mind. So, too, does his kindness – his unspoken understanding at my dismay. I push all thoughts of Patrick and Erica to the back of my mind, and focus instead on what this means – this gesture Marcus has made. He's a nice boy, I think, and not as remote as I had previously thought. Perhaps I have misjudged him.

He drops a pinch of tobacco on a sliver of cigarette paper.

'Now for the secret ingredient,' he says, reaching into his pocket. He takes out a packet of Disprin, unpacks one of the tablets and breaks it up, sprinkling the grains over the tobacco before licking the side of the paper and rolling it up.

'You're going to smoke that?' I ask.

'We are,' he replies, without looking up.

I've never done anything like this before. I say as much to Marcus, and he replies: 'I'm sure there's a lot you haven't done, Lins.'

I ask him what he means as he hands me the cigarette, or joint, or whatever it is, and he answers: 'You're only sixteen. That's all I mean. There's lots of things we both haven't done yet.'

It's a nice thought. A thought that brings me closer to him. A thought that warms me as I toke hard and struggle to suppress the cough that rises in my throat.

Marcus laughs and slaps my back a little. My breathing comes under control and I pull more gently on the roll-up this time. Everything seems soft around me – the low hum of traffic beyond the school walls, the night sky looming above us, even the distant beat of music from the gym. I didn't think the school and its grounds could look so beautiful in the moonlight. I know it's the vodka and the tobacco blurring the edges of everything around me, but still I feel a tug of warmth for Marcus as I pass back the cigarette. I lean into him a little and grin, and he grins too, for we are complicit in something. He has a nice smile, I think – it warms his features. I had not noticed that about him before. His arm hangs loosely off the back of the bench behind me, and it feels like I am tucked up against him, a perfect fit. And in that moment, it strikes me that we *are* a perfect fit for each other. Both of us are quiet, both of us hold back and observe rather than being the centre of attention. We are outsiders, the two of us – why shouldn't we gravitate to one another? It strikes me as oddly appropriate that Marcus would recognize it before I did. His act of chivalry – inviting me out here – now takes on a different, more meaningful colour. He removes the cigarette from his lips and exhales with satisfaction, and when he turns to me again, I lean in and my mouth finds his. I feel his dry, tobacco-ey lips against mine, feel the coldness of his chin and the brief hesitation of his arm half raised above my shoulders as he moves to embrace me. At least, that is what I think he will do.

But then his hand, rather than drawing me in, presses against my shoulder and pushes me away, and as our faces part I catch a glimpse of his fleeting expression – it is an awful mixture of horror and panic.

'Lindsey,' he says, and I can hear the shock and embarrassment in his voice, and feel myself shrink from it. 'I didn't mean—'

My laughter cuts him off. High-pitched and false to my ears, still I make myself do it. It's the only thing that can obliterate the awful humiliation flushing through me. 'I'm sorry, Marcus! I just couldn't resist! God, I'm so drunk, aren't you?'

I grin crazily at him, and an uncertain smile comes to his face.

'Actually, I should get back,' I tell him, getting to my feet, and for a moment, I really do feel woozy, lending weight to my performance with an awkward turn on my heel. 'I feel a little queasy.'

I leave him there on the bench, not looking back as I totter away through the darkness, burning with humiliation, my step quickening to a run as I near the school building. Already, I am reliving the expression of horror coming over his face – it burns into my brain, leaving a scorched image I fear will be there for ever.

I need to be alone. The drumbeat of the hall repels me, and already I know that the dorms will be racked with shrieks of laughter as girls run back to top up their alcohol levels and swap notes about various conquests. I cannot cope with any of that right now. I want to find a dark hole that I can climb into where no one can see me, no one can come near.

The classrooms are all empty. In darkness, I go quietly along the passageway, keeping close to the walls, listening out for voices, for footsteps, but there are none. I try door after door, but each one is locked. Rounding the corner, the music from the hall grows more distant and I feel myself becoming calmer. By the time I reach the labs, the burn in my brain has eased, the compulsion to weep has ebbed.

I put my hand to the door and am about to open it when I hear a laugh coming from inside the room. Softly now, I lean into the door, pressing my ear against the wood panelling.

'Come on now, Rach,' he says. 'We agreed. Just one cigarette.'

'Five more minutes,' she says, in her coy, syrupy voice, and it is this that alerts me to her companion. I remembered this voice, the seduction in it.

'We could get caught. It's too dangerous. I could get fired.'

'We won't get caught. No one's here but us.' Her voice is so low, so whispery, I have to strain to hear it. My heart is hammering away in my chest, the pieces of it all fitting dizzyingly into place.

'Rach,' he says, but the warning in his voice is fading, changing now as he succumbs to her.

'Please, sir,' she tells him, and I can tell how much she enjoys calling him that. 'You know you want me.'

I stand still, as quiet as I can, listening, although there are no words now, only the shuffle of clothing, the sudden groan of moving furniture, and then nothing. Just the blood pounding in my own ears, the sour plunge in my stomach as I hold my body still outside the door. But my mind crosses the divide. It is there with them in the shadows, listening alongside them, watchful of every touch and thrust, each sharply taken breath, every little scream.

22

2017

Patrick returned not long after eight. We were all in the drawing room at the time. Niall, who had come back from the hospital not long before, had fixed us drinks, and the rest of us were sitting around, despondent, each of us unsure of what to say, or how we should proceed. No one said it, but I think we were all on tenterhooks, waiting for the phone to ring. Niall, shaken by his experience at the hospital – the fear and shock of Marcus's relatives, the uncertainty as to whether he would survive – wouldn't sit down, a nervous energy twitching inside him as he paced from the fireplace to the window and back again, until Hilary snapped at him to for God's sake keep still, he was driving her mad. He looked at her coldly, but acquiesced to her demand, taking a seat on the couch next to Rachel, who the most part remained silent, keeping her thoughts to herself. With her legs folded up underneath her and her upper body swathed in a hooded woollen cardigan, her beauty seemed particularly severe. The couch had been pulled up to the hearth, where a crackling fire was burning in the grate, and some of the lamps had been switched on, but the room still couldn't shake off its air of gloom. Draughts crept beneath the door and through the windows, and the shadows lingered in the corners.

I was sitting at the window-seat when I saw the car approach. The rain had stopped falling, but darkness was coming on, and the tyres sloshed over the wet gravel before drawing to a stop beyond the fallen statue, Patrick's pinched face in the passenger-seat window swimming into view. Apprehension and relief jumped at once in my throat.

Patrick looked subdued, exhausted, his face and body wispy as a ghost's as he got out of the car. Stepping past us into the hall, he raised a hand that seemed to ward off the clamour of our questions: was he all right? What had happened? Was he being charged?

'Just give me a second, will you?' he asked, then, turning from all of us, he disappeared into the study. Rachel, ignoring his request, followed him, closing the study door behind them.

'Has he been charged?' I asked Savage, who had come from the car and crossed the threshold now, an anorak over his clothes, hands in his trousers pockets. I couldn't tell anything from his expression, except for the fact that he seemed to be waiting for something.

'Not yet. We'll have more questions for him once the guys from Ballistics get back to us. Poor fucker,' Savage added. 'Bawled his eyes out in the interview room — begged me to pin the blame on him. I didn't know whether to charge him or hug him. Anyway, there's no point rushing things,' he continued. 'I prefer to wait.'

He sounded amiable enough, but it was all surface. Underneath, he was watchful and grave. Taking a couple of steps further into the hall, he bent down to examine a glass case containing a dead stoat, stuffed and beady-eyed, arranged with a small bird caught between her jaws, a gang of pups cowering around her, awaiting their share of the kill.

Straightening up, he gave me a wolfish smile, jangling the coins in his pocket.

'So I was having a look back through the records, and your name cropped up,' he said casually.

'Oh?'

'You gave a statement on the night of Peter Bagenal's death.'

'We all did.'

'You never told me you were there.'

'You never asked.'

'You didn't think it was worth mentioning?'

My heart kicked out uncertainly. 'It didn't occur to me. I try not to think about it, to be honest.'

'It's a bit weird, though. Don't you think?' he asked, walking back to the door, leisurely, taking his time. 'Taking up with the son after that?'

'It happened years ago, Savage. It's not so odd, surely, for the paths of two old friends to cross again?'

'I suppose not,' he conceded, before adding: 'Who can account for the ways of the heart, eh?'

But there was something mean in his tone, and I felt that he was judging me. 'Here you are, Sergeant,' Patrick said, crossing the hall with his arm outstretched, a sheaf of documents in his hand.

Savage looked through them for a moment – gun licences and a passport – before folding them over and stuffing them into the pocket of his anorak. The uniformed guards, who were here earlier, had already taken away the guns.

'We'll be in touch in the morning,' Savage said, and catching my eye as he left, he gave me a fractional nod.

Patrick stood at the door until the tail lights had disappeared, and then he seemed to wilt. Pushing the door closed, he turned to me and we went into each other's arms, clinging to each other for a moment, feeling the silence of the hall around us.

'I can't believe this is happening again,' he said, drawing free of my embrace and shaking his head in disbelief. 'All those questions. Guards. Witness statements. It's just like Dad's death.'

'What did you tell them?' I asked, and then listened while he explained that he had been aiming for the deer when Marcus had stepped into his line of vision. That he had been too slow to react.

'If only I had been quicker. If only I had seen what was going to happen—'

'But how could you? It all happened so fast.'

'We shouldn't even have been firing at the fucking animal!' he went on, not listening. 'We had shotguns, not rifles. It was stupid of me.'

By now, the others had come back out into the hallway, and Niall urged Patrick to come inside and have a drink. Wearily, he did as was suggested, collapsing into the armchair, his legs stretched out in front of him, eyes closed, until Niall put a large whiskey in his hands and said: 'Here. Get that down you.'

He was disinclined to talk, and all of us hung back, watchful as he drank and seemed to recover himself a little. The colour came back into his cheeks, the glassiness left his gaze. Once he'd drained the glass, he pushed himself to his feet. 'I'm going to have a bath. Then we should eat.'

We all stared at him.

'You can't be suggesting we go ahead with the dinner?' Hilary asked, her voice querulous.

'Why not? The dinner is cooked. It would be a shame to waste it.' He said this with a deadened air, as if he was too far gone to think about it.

'But what about Marcus?' Hilary asked.

'Well,' Patrick began, before saying quietly: 'We'll save him a plate.'

I stared at him, shocked. 'Patrick!' Hilary cried, horrified.

Patrick blinked, as if disbelieving he had actually said those words. Confusion crossed his face, then anguish, before Rachel stepped in. 'We're all tired and upset. Some food would do us good. And Patrick is right – it would be a shame to waste it.'

'To tell the truth, I'm famished,' Niall admitted.

'Maybe a quick freshen up,' Hilary suggested, with a doubtful air. 'Or should we just eat as we are?'

Patrick had already made his way to the door, and left the room without waiting to hear the answer. In his absence, Rachel lowered her voice, saying: 'Let's meet back down here in half an hour. Wear what you want, for God's sake.'

We all retreated to our rooms and, as I closed the shutters on my window, and listened to the gurgling of the pipes as Patrick filled his bath, I felt disappointment. Not just at Patrick's distance – I had hoped there might be an opportunity for us to talk before dinner – but about how the weekend itself had turned out. Looking at my evening gown stretched out on the bed, I recalled my apprehension when buying it, my fear and doubt at the prospect of what the night might hold. The occasion had become fraught with anxiety and uncertainty, and the realization that I had been right to have my doubts gave me no satisfaction. I hung the gown back inside the wardrobe – there would be no need for it now – and lay down on my bed. From downstairs came the clatter of kitchen activity, and I could hear Niall's voice in the hall. He was on the phone and, from his low tone and the ripple of irritation in it, I guessed he was talking to his wife.

'Of course I didn't,' he was saying, 'No, you listen,

Claire . . . What the hell difference does that make? . . . No, she isn't here, actually, not that it's any of your business . . .'

I heard the bathroom door creak, footsteps on the stairs, and when I came out into the corridor, I saw light coming from underneath the door to the old nursery. This was Marcus's room, and it struck me as odd that the light should be on, so I went down the corridor and pushed open the dark wood door.

The room, lit by the overhead light, was empty. A dinner jacket on a hanger was spread over one side of the narrow bed. The walls were covered in vintage paper with a jaunty hunting print – the same paper I imagined had lined the nursery when Peter Bagenal passed his infancy here. In one corner of the room, a large strip of it had come away from the wall, and an ugly brown stain of damp mushroomed from the corner. On the floor, a number of photograph frames lay face down and partially dismantled, the backings pushed to one side. It was as though someone had begun framing photographs but had been interrupted.

'First Rachel, now you,' Hilary said, and I swung around to see her standing in the corridor.

'I saw a light on,' I explained.

'Rachel must have left it on earlier,' she surmised, peering past me, explaining: 'While you were at the hospital, I found her in here. She was pretty upset – well, we all were. She said she heard something that sounded like a child, or a baby.'

I remembered the snippet of conversation I had overheard that morning as we walked out to the fields. *'I kept hearing this noise,'* Rachel had said. *'It sounded like crying,'* and Marcus had guessed it was foxes. Had she said something then about the noise coming from inside the house? I couldn't remember.

'It seems wrong to be in his room,' Hilary remarked, and she took a step backwards towards the stairs. 'Like we're trespassing or something. Come on,' she urged, and I did as she asked and switched off the light. Because of the lateness of the hour, we had decided to forego pre-dinner drinks and gathered instead in the dining room, where the table had been laid with fine porcelain, with an oriental pattern in blue that seemed brighter against the white damask tablecloth. I recognized the ancient family silver, the scalloped heavy handles of the cutlery, each one embossed with the Bagenal crest. There were candles lit on the table and on the mantelpiece beyond, as well as a fire crackling in the grate. Someone – Felicia, perhaps – had gone to some trouble to arrange flowers in posies dotted along the table. Daisies and forget-me-nots, small twists of wild and humble nature marooned among the heirloom crockery and family silver.

Patrick and Rachel were seated at opposite ends of the long table, in the places I remembered their parents once occupying. Niall and Hilary sat next to each other, while I took my seat at Patrick's side, the empty place next to me a reminder of Marcus.

'Like Banquo at the feast,' Hilary remarked, catching my eye.

'He's not dead yet,' Niall said, picking up the bottle of wine in front of him. It was clear he was still furious about the phone call with his wife. I glanced at Patrick, but there was nothing in his expression – apart from a slight concentration in his brow – to suggest he was pained by the comment.

'Here's some advice for you all,' Niall said, pouring a glass for himself and then passing the bottle to Hilary. 'Avoid the married state. You can have that for free, gratis.'

'Thanks,' Hilary replied flatly, while Patrick encouraged us all to tuck into our starters – a carpaccio of salmon on a bed of lamb's lettuce.

'I second Niall's opinion,' Rachel said. She gave a tight little smile before spearing some salmon with her fork. Despite her composure, there was something beneath the exterior that suggested unease: her doughy complexion set off by the pale diaphanous fabric of her gown, or perhaps the way her eyes kept flickering across the table towards her brother. She was the only one of us who had opted to change into formalwear. I was surprised by her decision, made uneasy by it. It seemed disrespectful, as if she hadn't fully taken in the seriousness of the situation. Somehow, the grandeur of her dress set her apart from the rest of us still wearing jeans and sweaters.

'What about you?' Niall asked, tilting his chin in my direction. 'Ever tempted?'

'Not really,' I said, then laughed to cover my embarrassment, relieved when he dropped the topic of conversation and we all fell silent.

The truth was my only significant long-term relationship had lasted a little over eighteen months and had taken place almost a decade ago. It's hard to explain to someone like Niall how you can watch the months and years roll past as you constantly try to gain purchase on another human being to call your partner, your love, your life's companion, only to find that your hold is slippery and nothing will stick. And even though you battle to understand the reasons for your aloneness, and you strive to change, it feels as if a pattern is being etched into your life over which you have no control.

Once the starters were finished, Patrick got to his feet and began clearing away our plates while Felicia carried in the next course – a roast leg of lamb with all the trimmings. It seemed she had chosen not to have her niece come out after all, and had to rely on the host himself to help serve the guests. For his part, Patrick seemed nervy. There was a strain in his voice and tension in his shoulders, as if braced for a blow. As he carved the meat and Felicia passed around the plates, I could see the whites of his knuckles showing in the hand that held the knife, and the pull of muscles in his jaw and neck. With Marcus fighting for his life in hospital, there was little that could be done to dispel the air of disaster.

Niall picked up the bottle of wine that Patrick had opened and examined the label. 'A 1961 Margaux,' he observed. 'Where did you find this?'

'It was in the cellar. I chose it especially for this dinner.' He spoke in a quiet, regretful way, and I had a sudden glimpse of how excited he must have been, making all the preparations for tonight, and how all of that had been dashed now, replaced by remorse and self-reproach.

'That would set you back a few bob, I'd say, if you had to pony up for it in the off-licence.'

'More than a few bob. About a grand, I would imagine.'

Niall, having just taken a swig, swallowed quickly, his face curling with distaste or horror. 'A grand? You've got to be kidding me!'

'My father fancied himself a bit of a collector. He put a few good ones down, and I thought it only fitting we lash into the best of it tonight.'

'Quite right. Let's drink our inheritance. Why not?' Rachel said, in her quiet, stony voice.

'I think paying that sort of money just for a bottle of wine is obscene,' Hilary remarked softly. She was eyeing her glass with uncertainty, and she retained an aura of unhappiness. Her discomfort at being present at the dinner while Marcus was in hospital fighting for his life persisted throughout the night.

'Nothing wrong with it if you can afford it,' Niall maintained.

'Does it really taste a hundred times better than a ten-euro Bordeaux from Tesco?'

Niall was unconvinced by her argument. 'You buy cheap, you get tat.'

Annoyance flashed across Hilary's face, and she looked at him now with real distaste. 'Why do you keep saying that?'

'What?'

'That phrase. That's the second time you've trotted it out today.'

'So what? It's my mantra,' he stated proudly.

'It's not *your* mantra. It's Peter Bagenal's,' she murmured.

'I borrowed it from him. So what?' He laughed, looking around the table at the rest of us, uncomfortable with the slide of the conversation.

'I'm sure he wouldn't have minded,' Patrick said kindly.

'Do you remember his trick with the champagne bottle?' Niall asked. 'Taking the top off with a knife?' He proceeded to recall Peter's party trick – a dramatic swift 'beheading' of a champagne bottle, slicing the glass neck off the bottle, cork and all, before pouring from the brimming and spurting bottle, not a fragment of glass in the champagne. 'It was a clean cut,' Niall said, before adding in a tone of near-wistfulness: 'It takes a steady hand and a sure head to do that. Did you ever master that trick, Patrick?'

'Afraid not,' was the reply, and I heard Rachel adding softly:

'Of course not.'

We all looked at her, surprised by the meanness of her words. The expression on Patrick's face registered how conflicted he must have felt: indecision over whether to confront her, battling against his desire to smooth things over and rescue the mood.

Niall came to his aid. 'Funny, isn't it? Being back here, all these little memories triggered,' he remarked. 'Like the crow shoot this morning – I wasn't thinking of the times we all went out with shotguns as teenagers. Instead, I was remembering the odd occasion where Peter would take a pop at them with his pistol. Did you ever see him doing that?' he asked me, and I nodded. I remembered.

He laughed abruptly at the memory, recalling the madness of it – Patrick's old man, attempting to concentrate on some paperwork, when the raucous cawing of crows outside would cause something inside him to snap. It was then that he'd snatch up his gun and start firing out the window, aiming indiscriminately up at the trees.

Finished with the recollection, Niall gave a sad shake of his head, and we could all see the pain it caused him. Rachel reached across and put her hand over his, her expression softening. 'You loved him, didn't you?'

'I was fond of him, yeah. I really looked up to him.

And I suppose it's true that I've tried to emulate him in some way. If I can be as good a father to my kids as he was to you guys—'

'I would have liked to have children,' Patrick said then, and we all looked at him. 'It's a peculiar sort of failing, isn't it? The failure to breed.'

'You've still got time, man. No need to give up yet. Eh, Lindsey?' And Niall winked at me across the table. We had all grown uncomfortable with the turn the conversation had taken.

'I really couldn't comment,' I said, trying to meet his levity, but underneath it I felt a thread of doubt. It was one of the things that worried me about the course of treatment I would be embarking on. Would chemotherapy harm my chances of one day having a baby of my own?

'I've had some of my eggs frozen,' Hilary announced, and then giggled at our startled silence. 'Just in case.'

Niall gave his head a slight shake of amazement, then turned his attention to Rachel. 'What about you, Rach? Got some of your eggs in the freezer?'

Meeting his gaze coolly, she said: 'No point. They wouldn't be able to do anything with them. I have Asherman's Syndrome, you see? My uterus, it turns out, is an inhospitable place.' Her tone was light, seamless, and yet the charge in her words made us all fall silent.

Hilary was the first to react. 'Jesus, Rach. That's awful.'

'Forgive my ignorance,' Niall began, 'but what is Asherman's . . .?'

'Scarring or adhesions in the womb,' Rachel went on, in her falsely bright tone. 'Typically caused by a D&C after a miscarriage or a delivery. Or, in my case, a termination.'

She sipped from her glass, then put it down, a sort of primness in her manner that gave away her brittle discomfort.

'You had an abortion?' Hilary asked quietly.

'Yes. When we were at school. Didn't you know? Well!' She laughed her false, tinkly laugh. 'That was one thing we managed to keep quiet! Still, I suppose you could say that, as a family, we are quite adept at hushing things up.'

Her lashes fluttered as she looked around the table. Niall had lowered his head, and Hilary held her napkin to her mouth; both looked somewhat shocked by the admission. As for Patrick, he met his sister's gaze with disapproval, and was about to say something, I'm sure, when the door opened and Felicia's head appeared around it, saying: 'If you don't mind, Patrick, I'll be off now.'

She issued some instructions about dessert, although none of us seemed inclined to eat anything further.

Patrick got up to see Felicia out, and even though the rest of us remained seated, waiting in silence for his return, it seemed apparent to all of us that the dinner was beyond recovery.

23

1992

'Can you keep a secret?' Rachel asks.

By now it is May and, even though Rachel doesn't know it, I have been carrying the burden of her secret for some weeks. Keeping my distance, I have observed her dreamy introspection, knowing full well what thoughts fill her head. I have struggled with myself, wondering how to broach the matter without betraying what I was a witness to, what I overheard that night. But every hint that I have dropped has been met with a self-satisfied silence, every opening I have created has been ignored. Her romance with Ridge is something best nursed in secret, and I have felt rebuffed by it, excluded, pushed out.

It is not until I am back at Thornbury for the first time in months that she chooses to tell me. We are lying in a pool of sunlight under the sycamore tree. Spring has burgeoned in the trees and fields beyond. The sun coming through the branches turns the leaves acid-green. We have hauled the rug out here on to the grass, idly reading our books after lunch, but Rachel – an avid reader – seems too distracted to read. I can feel it in her – the tug towards him – and I know that it is only here, at a distance from her lover, that she can open up about him. As if by telling me about him, she can conjure him up with her account of their great romance.

'I'm in love,' she tells me, and I almost laugh out loud at the word.

Instead, I put down my book and play dumb. 'With who?' I ask, and she bites her lip, half afraid, half thrilled at the bombshell she's about to drop.

'Promise you won't tell?' she says again, and it is only when I swear on my life that she acquiesces. 'It's Ridge,' she says, her eyes widening with a challenge and then darting all over my face for my reaction.

I feign surprise. 'Mr Ridgeway?' I say, and she nods vigorously.

'Are you shocked?'

When I admit that I am, she leans forward so that she is lying on her stomach, peering up at me, and she says with urgency: 'Oh, Lindsey, you can't tell anyone, do you hear? Tim would kill me if he knew I was even telling you.'

'Tim? Is that what you call him?'

'Of course! You can't expect me to call him Ridge, can you?'

'I dunno. It's odd, that's all. Hearing you call him that.'

She giggles, then turns over on her back and closes her eyes, momentarily losing herself in some private trance.

'Isn't he a bit old for you?' I ask.

'He's only thirty-one. That's younger than my father was when he fell in love with Heather.'

'But Ridge is our teacher. Don't you see how weird that is? And kind of creepy?'

'You make it sound like he's some kind of perv.'

'Some people might see it that way.'

'I couldn't care less about people like that. The fact is Tim and I were both drawn to each other. It's not like he was some predatory male and I was an innocent, unwilling victim. I wanted it as much as he did!' Her eyes are open now, and she has rolled back on to her front to face me.

'How long has it been going on?'

She shrugs. 'A while. Three, four months maybe.'

'Is it serious?'

'Yes.' Her eyes lock on mine in a challenging way. 'We're in love.'

'Are you sure?'

'Of course!'

'Have you had sex with him?'

She blushes, which surprises me, and lowers her eyes. 'Yes.'

'Oh my God – Rachel? That's illegal!'

She looks up quickly. 'Oh, but you can't tell anyone! You swore on your life!'

'I know, but what if something happens? What if you get caught?'

'We won't.'

'How can you be sure?'

'We are . . .' she begins, then, glancing around to make sure no one is listening, she lowers her voice and says: 'discreet.'

I draw back from her, undone by a sudden visual confrontation with their intimacies. And yet, inside, I find myself leaning forward, curious, wanting a better look.

'Where do you do it?' I ask tentatively, and she picks at a blade of grass and sighs.

'It's, like, really difficult finding places to be alone. Mostly in his car – there's this place we go. A couple of times in school.' Her eyes flare with mischief. 'That was really nervy. Tim kept looking around, convinced someone was going to walk in on us. I swear, it was hardly worth it!' She giggles again, and I find that my curiosity, rather than being slaked, is only further aroused.

'What's it like?' I ask softly, my heart beating inexplicably loud.

'Sex?'

'Yes.'

Her gaze grows distant and that look comes over her face – knowing and secretive. It's a look that pushes me further from her rather than drawing me in, reminding me that I am uninitiated, and she has left me behind.

After a pause, she says: 'Spectacular,' then presses her lips together. It's not enough, though.

'But the first time,' I persist. 'Did it hurt?'

She laughs then, leaning back to rest her weight on her elbows. 'My first time with Tim wasn't my first time.' She sees the surprise on my face, and shakes her head in mock-exasperation. 'Oh God, Lins – surely you must have known that? Niall and I did it ages ago.'

'*What?*'

'You remember the night of our play last summer?'

'The night in the folly? You did it *then*?'

'Uh-huh.' She closes her eyes and shakes out her hair. It's a preening gesture that makes me suddenly angry. How have I been so blind? And why didn't she tell me until now? It further exacerbates the distance I see opening up between us. Cowed by the wealth of her sexual experience, I feel my own meagre forays into that field hanging limply about me.

'Wouldn't you prefer to be with Niall than Ridge?' I ask.

'God, no!' she scoffs.

'At least he's closer to you in age.'

'Niall is ridiculously immature.'

'Someone else, then. Marcus or—'

'Marcus?' she squeals. 'He's gay!'

The word hits me like a slap in the face. For the second time in a few short minutes I feel winded by information so obvious and yet, somehow, I have been blind to it. How have I been so naïve?

She is back talking about Ridgeway again now. 'Tim is going to leave St Alban's. He might even go back into research. His old colleagues at the hospital are always on at him to come back . . .'

I imagine the two of them together, like the night of the disco, and ask her: 'What about pregnancy?'

'It wouldn't be so bad.'

I look at her in shock – something in the way she says it makes me feel funny inside.

'It would be a disaster,' I tell her.

'I don't think so. I think it would be nice to have his baby. We'd be a proper couple then.'

She is smiling at me. I ask her if she is out of her mind, and she just places her hand on her belly.

She could be playing a trick on me, I think, but she lowers her head and her hand remains where it is.

'I'm late,' she says softly, and I feel a twinge of panic. 'How late?'

'Enough for me to know I'm going to keep it.'

I cannot believe it. Her serenity in the face of her predicament is baffling – maddeningly so.

'What about your parents?' I splutter.

'They don't know.'

'You have to tell them. I mean, it's not like they're not going to notice.'

'Oh, I'll tell them all right. But not yet. Not until enough time has passed.'

Her steadiness amazes me.

'If they found out now, they would make me have an abortion. But if I wait until after Patrick's birthday, then it will be too late for that.' A secret smile comes to her lips, and it appears to me superior and self-satisfied. She wants me to be happy for her, but instead I feel angry and confused.

'Your parents will kill you,' I tell her. 'And him.'

'That will be their initial reaction, yes. But they'll come round. Besides,' she adds, 'it's not like they were paragons of virtue when they were my age. Did you know that Heather got pregnant when she was seventeen?'

I didn't know, and the shock must briefly register on my face.

'Oh, yes. It was quite the scandal,' she tells me, enjoying herself. 'A shotgun wedding ensued. Seventeen. Only a year older than I am now. So you see, they hardly have a leg to stand on, do they?'

I am dumbfounded by her scheming, as well as the revelations about her parents' marriage. And then a thought occurs to me. 'Does he know? Ridge. Does he know about the baby?'

This wipes the smug look off her face.

'Not yet. I'm waiting for the right moment to tell him. But I know he'll be happy. I know this is what he wants.'

'Do you?'

'Of course,' she says, but I hear the quiver of uncertainty in her voice. 'I can trust you, can't I? You're not to tell anyone. Ever. You have to swear on your life to say nothing, do you hear?'

I do as she asks. I swear the words, but they sound

hollow and flimsy, like promises extracted over silly childish things, when we have moved well beyond that. Her face relaxes. She leans back, closing her eyes to the sun. But now I am burdened by her secret, and it weighs on me, and I feel more clouded and miserable than ever.

My dispirited feelings continue through that day and into the next, although Rachel doesn't seem to notice. She doesn't notice anything beyond her own moods these days. Love has made her selfish. When she asks me the next morning if I mind being alone for a couple of hours – Heather wants her to help out at the local church fete – I am content to let her go. Some time alone is welcome and, once the others leave, I go out into the gardens around the house – slick with recent rainfall – and take some photographs using the Leica Peter has given me. He has stayed home, too, and when I have tired of traipsing through the damp grass, I decide to seek him out. Reminded of his promise to show me how to use the dark room, I knock on the door of his studio then push the door open.

He looks up, startled, and something crosses his face – an expression I can't pin down, but it makes me wish I had waited for him to call out before entering the room. There is a large book open on the desk in front of him, and I have the impression that he has hastily slipped something between the pages in the instant that I opened the door.

'I'm sorry. I shouldn't have disturbed you,' I say, confused by that flash of guilt on his face.

'No, that's quite all right,' he counters, then arranges his face into a more benign expression. Holding out his hand and gesturing to the chair in front of him, he urges me to come forward. 'They've left you all alone,' he remarks, as I close the door behind me.

I come forward, the camera in my hand, feeling bashful now that I am in front of him. I try to recall that sense of closeness I felt the last time I saw him – that windy afternoon in February – remembering his words to me: *Sometimes I think you're the daughter I should have had.*

'I've been taking photographs,' I say hesitantly.

'Ah.'

'I was hoping you might show me how to develop them,' I try, but I catch the faintest hint of reluctance in his face, and stammer, 'But you're busy. I'll leave you.'

I start to back away and I see it flash across his face again – a beat of indecision – before he puts up a hand to hold me there and says, 'No. Wait.'

He looks down at the book on his desk, and opens it to where a small bundle of additional pages are amassed.

'Come and look at these,' he suggests, and as I step closer I see that they are photographs. Black and white or sepia-tinted, and I can tell, even from a distance, that they are old. The thickness of the paper they are printed on, along with the dog-eared corners and the glossy shine, point to their age. From the form and composition, I think they must be portraits. It is not until I am standing there at the desk and he pushes one and then another towards me, that I see that the subjects are all naked. The whiteness of the flesh seems to loom large in the midst of the shadows, and I try not to gape or show my horror at the expanse of flesh before me. Victorian life models, he calls them, but I barely hear him. Blood is thundering in my ears as I look on these nude women standing stoutly with fabric draped over their bulky arms, leaving their breasts swinging. One model sits on a stool with her back to the camera, her buttocks spread over the velvet cushioning. Another has hair in ringlets, her hand resting against her thigh, a pastoral scene painted on a screen behind her as she gazes dreamily into the distance as if unaware she is being captured so fully in the flesh.

'It's my little hobby,' he says softly, a trace of awkwardness in his tone. 'You could say I'm a bit of a collector. I can see that you're shocked.'

'No,' I say, but my voice catches, and I put my fingertips on the desk to steady them. My mind is catapulting in all directions, confronted by this strange mosaic laid out in front of me.

'All through the ages, man has captured the human form through art. And even though photography is a relatively new art form, it has made huge strides in that area.'

He talks some more about the history of the presentation of the human body through art and, even though some of it makes sense, I can't help but feel aware of my own flesh beneath my clothes. I am embarrassed by these images, while at the same time indignant. These photographs feel in some ways like violations. Is it right that these women, long dead, should have their breasts, their privates, their buttocks, exposed in this manner to generations to come? There is something faintly sinister about them and, when his voice penetrates my thoughts, and I hear him say: 'Well, Lindsey? What do you think?' what I answer is this:

'They remind me of the animals in the hall. The taxidermied ones.'

And he stares at me for a moment, and then lets out a brief, uncertain laugh, and says: 'I think I see what you mean. The way they are frozen in time.'

Imprisoned by it, is what I think. But I don't say that to him. Instead, I pull the images closer, allowing myself to be drawn in. I'm so confused by how I feel – bombarded by these images, unsettled by his possession of them, just as I was thrown by Rachel's revelations.

But there is something else. Something in the way that he has allowed me to see them. He has drawn me into his confidence. He has respected my opinion enough to show me his collection.

'These are not like the topless models you see splashed across page three of the *Sun*,' he explains patiently. 'There is beauty here. Sensuality. And history. You do see that, Lindsey, don't you?'

'Yes,' I say. 'Yes, I see that.' And my voice has recovered from nerves and comes out clearly, with confidence, and this makes him smile.

'I knew you'd understand,' he tells me. 'I knew you'd see it the way I see it.'

And I feel it again – that thing passing between us – that thing I cannot put a name to.

'To understand these pictures is to understand the perception and appreciation of the human form,' he tells me. 'Sometimes, when I look at these images, I wonder what it must have been like – both for the photographer and his model. Think of the length of time involved in each exposure?'

He describes it tenderly, in a way that suggests intimacy. And it's also true that it feels intimate and special, the way he is involving me, allowing me access to his thoughts in this way.

'Of course, there are those who would look oddly on these pictures – on my interest in and possession of these images.'

'Yes.'

'So perhaps it would be best if you didn't mention these to anyone.' I look up and our eyes meet. 'Let's keep it as our little secret, hmm?'

I pause for just a second. If it seems strange for him to ask me this, it's no stranger than the fact of him showing the pictures to me in the first place.

'That's the second time this weekend I've been asked to keep a secret.'

It slips out, and I see the glimmer of curiosity in his eye and feel a sudden lurch of panic that he is going to ask me about it. But instead he reaches out with his hand, touches me gently on the chin.

'Lindsey. Keeper of Secrets,' is all he says.

24

2017

'I have a surprise for you,' Patrick told us when he came back into the dining room.

There it was again – that straining within him to ameliorate the situation, to somehow compensate for the air of muted despair that had fallen over us.

'Come into the drawing room,' he urged, telling us we would have our desserts in a while.

Rachel was the first to follow him, followed by Hilary, who cast a questioning glance back at me and Niall. Each of us taking our wine glasses and Niall carrying the bottle, our heels clacked across the old wooden boards, but there was no lightness of step, no gaiety, and when I came into the drawing room, after the chilly shadows of the hall, I was momentarily dazzled by the light. The chandelier was blazing overhead, along with various lamps dotted around the room. Added to this was a small army of pillar candles of varying heights and thickness, their little flames flickering from the mantelpiece, from the console tables and windowsills, a host of them blazing from the hearth itself, forming a semicircle around the grate where a fire burned brightly.

'Sit yourselves down,' Patrick said, clapping his hands together, trying to rouse some excitement within us as we took our places on the couch and wing-back chairs. 'Back in a sec,' he added, before leaving the room.

'Rach,' Niall said slowly, a troubled look on his face. He was the last to enter the room and, closing the door behind Patrick, he ran a hand along his jaw and said hesitantly: 'What you told us back there . . . Well, you and I messed around a bit when we were in school. It wasn't me, was it? Who got you . . . you know . . .'

'Pregnant?' She said the word for him, amusement in her voice. 'No, it wasn't you, darling. In the matter of my infertility, your conscience is clear.'

I heard the push on the word *your* and, even though she didn't look in my direction, I knew it was meant for me. I found myself recalling in a most uncomfortable way the single moment of confrontation all those years ago. '*Traitor.*' The word was echoing in my head now, causing something to drop violently within me, and I had to look away, seized as I was by the vividness of the memory.

I was saved by Patrick, who flung wide the door and came in, pushing a trolley with a television and a video player, an untidy nest of cables and plugs amassed on top.

'Oh God,' Hilary groaned with a mock-dramatic air. 'Not home movies, please!'

He grinned at her then, before bending to find the right plug, reminding us all of his promise to take us on a trip down memory lane. Niall, who remained standing, sidled up and looked askance at his friend's activities, but from his silence I could tell that he was still bothered by what Rachel had admitted. And when the phone rang in the hallway, startling us all, and Rachel got up to answer it, he watched her leave the room with an expression of concern on his face. Perhaps his concern was for Marcus – for that was the conclusion we all jumped to: the hospital – but I couldn't help but remember how it had been between them as teenagers. For all his braggadocio, his mockery and machismo, he had felt something for her once.

From outside in the hall, we could hear Rachel's voice. 'Yes? I see. Yes, thank you. I understand. I'll tell them. Thank you for letting me know.' We were all straining for news. Patrick, I saw, had paused in his negotiations with the somewhat antiquated and clumsy technology. And even though his back was to the rest of us, I could read his tension in the taut pull of the muscles in the back of his neck.

Presently, Rachel returned, and Patrick said, rather sharply: 'Well?'

'No change,' she told us.

'Was that the hospital?' Niall asked. 'What did they say? Is he still critical?'

She hesitated, then said, 'Yes, I'm afraid so,' and stepped past me to take her seat at the far end of the couch.

'Oh God, it's so awful,' Hilary said. 'I can't stop thinking about it. If only we hadn't gone shooting—'

'Please, Hils. Can you stop going on about that?' Niall pleaded, and it was clear his earlier annoyance over this line of argument had turned to weariness, maybe even regret.

'Sorry.'

'They'll keep us informed of any changes to his situation,' Rachel assured us. Then, lifting her tone, she asked: 'So, are we going to watch this movie or what?'

Despite her best efforts, I was struck by the rigid manner in which she sat, and also the slight tapering-off in her voice. She seemed unsettled by the phone call, unnerved.

'Right. Lights, please,' Patrick said, and Niall began switching off the lamps around the room, the chandelier overhead, until there was only the flickering glow of the candles and the smoking fire, and then the glare of the television as the movie began.

It opened with a shot of the side of the house. The camera seemed to wobble before steadying itself, taking a long, slow look at what appeared to be the west side of the house. The brickwork of the front façade changed to grey at this side and, in the grainy image, the window frames seemed warm in what appeared to be evening sunshine, the French doors of the kitchen open to the little patio beyond, long net curtains billowing slightly in a soft breeze.

'Where did you find this, Patrick?' Hilary asked in a hushed voice, her eyes on the screen.

'Dad had dozens of these – hundreds, even,' he told her. 'All squirrelled away in his darkroom. I found them when I started clearing out the place in the last few weeks.'

He was the only one of us not sitting, choosing instead to stand off to the side by the fireplace, his arms crossed over his chest, watching the moving images closely.

I was aware of the sound of breathing coming from the speakers, the soft exhalations of the cameraman and, as a figure emerged on to the patio, a soft huff of laughter was audible.

'Oh my God. Is that you, Niall?' Hilary asked with delight, and Niall groaned good-naturedly as he watched his teenage self appear onscreen, wearing Bermuda shorts and some kind of singlet. 'Look at your hair!' she cried, and it was true that his hair was thicker and curlier than I remembered, reddish-blond – a sort of Irish Afro. In his hands he held some kind of sword, curved like a sabre, which he wielded with authority, swishing it through the air.

'*Very good. Very good,*' we heard Peter say, chuckling with amusement, and it was shocking to hear his voice again, so close, so immediate. Rachel shifted a little in her place, and I saw Niall lean forward. We all felt it – his presence in the room.

'Here I come now,' Patrick informed us, rubbing a finger along his upper lip, as if to suppress the smile that surfaced as the teenage Patrick stepped out on to the patio, fussing over a long brocade coat he was wearing. How skinny and gawkish he looked then – how shockingly young! I felt a warm tug of endearment for him as we all watched the boy tying and re-tying the belt of his costume.

Rachel appeared next, a delicate, feminine entrance, holding her skirts in one hand, her hair held back by the other, stepping out cautiously, careful not to trip, and Niall turned to her and said something, and the two of them stepped off to one side, the camera focusing now on Patrick, who had started pacing, talking as if to himself, and I realized he was running through his lines.

'When was this?' Hilary asked, a shiver of caution in her tone.

'Wait. You'll see,' he told her.

Another voice onscreen – a woman's voice – it sounded distant. *'Peter, darling, I'm taking everyone down. Are you coming?'* And then the camera swung towards Heather, her hand held up to shield her eyes from the evening sun, a brilliant smile visible beneath the shadow of her hand, and despite myself, I felt a waver of uncertainty. Seeing her there onscreen, as I remembered her, vibrant, graceful, beautiful, acted as a sharp relief to the image of Heather that had been growing in my mind – older, troubled, dessicated and withdrawn.

She stepped out of the camera's view, which then moved towards the house, getting closer to the players as they assembled themselves, and I felt my own heart give out a startled beat as I recognized myself lingering behind the others, looking abashed and lost in my heavy gown, my hair plaited and twisted around my head. Amid all that commotion and fussing, the nervous laughter and the giddiness, I saw my own face turn towards the camera. It was held there for a lingering moment in its serene, untroubled entirety, something bold in the way I stared right back, before the screen blurred, cutting away, and Niall asked:

'Is that it, then?' before Patrick hushed him, saying:

'No, wait. There's more.'

'Do we have to?' Hilary asked in a quiet voice, but Niall shushed her, hunching forward again as the screen came to life once more.

The footage, now, appeared to have been taken later in the evening. The quality of the light had dimmed, and there were shadows and occasional bright flashes of flickering candlelight as the camera followed the troop of actors down towards the folly.

'*Stop it!*' we heard Rachel say, in her girlish, bossy voice, and then Niall's low laughter, Patrick telling them to get a move on.

'Look. There's Marcus,' I said, and I heard Hilary draw in her breath, silence falling over us as we watched our friend, his pale face and dyed black hair. How skinny he looked, glancing back at the camera, the flash of his glasses catching the light, his grave face giving way to a sudden impish smile.

'I don't think I can sit through this,' Hilary said, and Rachel told her to be quiet and watch, the command issued softly yet firmly. It was the only thing she said during the whole interlude.

The camera shook as the cluster of plinths and columns that circled our stage came into view, and there was cheering from the adults, the sound of a woman's laughter and then the single word '*Shit!*' said in a girlish squeak. A corona of reddish curls swam into view, and then Hilary's face, round and pale as a full moon, her heavily made-up eyes looking anguished before the camera cut away and swung down to her ripped costume.

All the time we were watching, I could feel Hilary there by my knee. With her back to me, I could barely make out the shadow of her jaw, lit by the flickering candles. There seemed to be something rigid and intent about the way she was watching, and now, as we heard Peter Bagenal behind the camera saying: '*One of my dress shirts ought to do just as well. Come along, young lady,*' I saw the adult Hilary turn her face to Patrick with an implacable stare, saying:

'Please, Patrick. I don't want to watch any more.'

He affected not to hear, and the screen went blank anyhow, before coming to life again, and this time, we were all amassed on the stage some time later, a stuttering applause dying out at Patrick stepped forward to introduce the play, the camera staying on his face, before swinging outwards to the rest of us.

We watched it all – the whole performance – which in the end proved shorter than in memory. It was only when it reached the conclusion, when we all stepped up in a line to take a bow, and the camera panned from one end, where Marcus stood, down to Hilary at the other end, hovering over her for a moment with her head down, refusing to look up, that Hilary jumped to her feet beside me, rushed over to the television, and switched it off.

'That's fucking enough!' she cried.

'What the hell . . .?' Niall said, his voice rising, and Patrick took a step towards her, a look of dismay on his face.

'Don't you see?' Hilary said, turning on him now. 'Can't you understand how upsetting this is?'

He said her name softly and put his hands out to her, but she shrugged away from his touch, not wanting to be placated or comforted, something fierce welling up inside her. Niall had stood up and moved to the door, switching on the overhead light, and the sudden illumination seemed brutal in the way it caught Hilary's face, crumpled with fury, tears streaming over her cheeks.

'Why did you show us that?' she demanded.

'I don't know. So we could remember what it was like.'

'I don't *want* to remember that night,' she said vehemently. 'I've spent the past twenty years trying to *forget* it.'

Wordlessly, Rachel got up from the sofa and went to the console table, where the drinks were laid out. She poured a generous measure of whiskey and held it out to her cousin, saying: 'Here, take this.'

But Hilary crossed her arms and turned away, mutinous, saying: 'No. I've already drunk too much.'

Some of the power had leaked from her voice, but the brittleness of her mood was there in the line of tension across her shoulders. Rachel, keeping the whiskey for herself, said in a taut voice: 'It's been a long day, Hilary. We're all tired and upset,' trying to defuse the situation, but it felt like there was a warning in there, too – a subtle pressure not to unleash what seemed to be building. And even though I could guess what was coming, I felt myself shrinking from the knowledge, a wave of panic rising inside me at the thought of what would come out.

'Can someone tell me what the fuck is going on?' Niall asked, looking from one face to the other. 'What the hell happened that night that was so awful, Hilary?'

'Peter Bagenal,' Hilary said softly. 'Your precious mentor, Niall.' She broke off and shook her head, while he stared at her, nonplussed. Then she seemed to gather herself, taking a breath and pushing her shoulders back, she turned to the room and addressed us all, her voice gaining strength as she let it all out. How her costume had ripped. How he had taken her back to the house and upstairs to his bedroom. How she had stood in the doorway while he selected a shirt for her to wear.

How he had handed it to her and walked past her to the doorway. How she heard the door shut.

'I thought I was alone,' she said, her voice dipping. 'I thought he had left so I could change. It was only when I stepped further into the room and started unbuttoning my costume that I saw his reflection in the mirror. He was standing right there at the door. He had his camera.' Her voice shook.

Rachel muttered: 'Oh, for God's sake,' and walked over to the fireplace, putting out a steadying hand to the mantle. For all her annoyance, I could tell she was rattled. The filmy layers of her dress quivered as she took a swig of whiskey. My own heart was beating away madly.

'So what happened?' Niall asked. His question came out harshly, and I could tell from his intent stare, the frown above it, that there were furious calculations going on behind his eyes. His revered mentor recast in this shabby way? He couldn't comprehend it.

'He told me to take my clothes off and, when I protested, he just kept on telling me to do it. I went to step past him, but he blocked the door and I couldn't get out. He told me there was no point shouting or screaming. Everyone was down at the folly, you see? He had let the cook go home. So there were only the two of us in the house.'

She stopped and put a hand to her throat, momentarily closing her eyes.

'It's all right,' I said quietly, even though I knew it wasn't. A dreadful unease filled my chest, frightened at what Hilary might say next.

Her dry lips parted, and she went on: 'He said it would only take a minute. That the sooner I got on with it, the sooner it would be over. I couldn't believe it, you know? The words coming out of his mouth – and the way he was saying them! He was a stranger to me then. A complete stranger.'

'This is ridiculous,' Rachel murmured from the fireplace, but Patrick didn't say a word.

'It's not ridiculous,' Hilary retorted, more controlled now. 'He photographed me.' A hard note came into her voice, and her eyes momentarily closed, as if she was steeling herself against the memory. When she opened them again, there was a dull look to them. The effort of telling her story was taking its toll, wearing her down. 'I had to stand there while he kept clicking and clicking and never saying a word, except to tell me to put my hands down by my sides, or to look at the camera. He got me to turn around so that he could take photographs from behind. And I was so ashamed of my body then! I was only fifteen, and so unhappy with the changes happening to me. And there he was, staring at all of me with his camera – recording it – and I just wanted to die.' She swallowed hard then gave a thin laugh. 'Perhaps I should have taken that drink, Rach.'

But Rachel didn't respond. She stood quietly by the

fire, locked in her own thoughts. Her silence, and Patrick's, made me wonder how much they already knew.

'He warned me not to tell anyone – said they wouldn't believe me anyway, because why on earth would anyone want to photograph me?'

She could have been making it up. But I didn't challenge her. Of all of us, Niall was the most shocked. He had remained standing throughout her account, watching intently, but now he sat down heavily and sank his face into his cupped hands as if defeated by the revelations.

Memories from all those years ago came back at me then, each one making sense where they hadn't before. I thought of how Hilary had abruptly stopped coming to this house after the night of our play. I thought of her question to me at Peter's photography exhibition: '*Is that the only time he's photographed you?*' And when I'd said that I thought it was, her strange reply: '*You'd know if it wasn't. You'd know it all right.*' I thought of how she had worked assiduously to transform her body, and the way she turned from the camera as if repelled by it, protesting not to like having her photograph taken. All of these things went through my mind as the shocking truth sank in.

'Did Marcus know?' I asked then.

I don't know what prompted me to ask this question – some instinct announcing itself – and even though Hilary answered, 'No,' I saw the way Patrick turned around, I saw the sharpness of his glance, his eyes wide, fear evident within him and something else: guilt. His eyes were boring through me, and I saw the distress in them – distress that, somehow, I had found him out.

All this time, the candles had continued to flicker and glow, their waxy scent wending through the stifled air in the room. Now, distantly, I became aware of an acrid smell of burning. But it was only when Niall lunged forward from his seat that my attention was tugged away from Patrick and I became aware of what was happening. It all happened so fast. A sudden whoosh of air, a burst of light. Rachel, who had been standing by the hearth, now staggered away, fire ripping through the filmy layers of her gown, licking up along the side of her body, her face above it a mask of horror.

Violently, Niall fell upon her and, for a moment, they rolled around on the ground like frenzied lovers, Niall kicking and beating at the vicious tongues of fire until he had tamped each one of them out. For a moment then, they lay side by side in what looked like post-coital exhaustion, both panting, and out of breath. I realized that I hadn't moved, that I had remained rooted to the spot, paralysed with horror. Hilary stood with her hands covering her mouth, her eyes round with disbelief.

Patrick rushed to his sister's aid, reaching for her hands and dragging her to her feet, while Niall sat up slowly.

'Are you all right?' Patrick asked. 'What the hell happened? Are you burnt?'

'I'm all right,' she said, in a small, shocked voice. I could see her doughy pallor looked whiter than ever.

'Are you sure? Let me see.'

But she pulled away from him. Her composure seemed restored, but there was a dazed quality to it, a glassiness to her gaze.

'Sit down. Let me get you a glass of water,' he urged, but she moved past him, unhearing. 'Rachel?' he said after her, but she didn't turn her head, didn't respond. Without casting a glance back at any of us, she bunched up the skirts of her ruined dress with one hand, and silently left the room.

25

Rachel stares out the window as the train rocks from side to side. Her book lies on the seat next to her, unread. It's just the two of us for the weekend. Patrick and the others have stayed in school. Extra study classes have been put on for the sixth-years as their Leaving Certificate exams approach.

The day outside is brightening, and she frowns against the sunlight. It catches her pale face, making purple shadows under her eyes. Something about her manner tells me she doesn't want to talk and, before long, she closes her eyes and slips into an uneasy sleep.

Peter meets us at the station with the car. He raises his hand in greeting, and I wave back. Rachel hands him her bag and says, 'Hi, Dad,' in a tired voice, then gets in the back. He turns to me with a question in his face, but I just shrug and smile. Peter has brought the dog with him for the journey, and Rachel has him across her lap on the back seat. I sit up front with Peter, making up for Rachel's silence by chatting the whole way to Thornbury.

Something has happened with Ridge. Rachel doesn't

say it, but I have my suspicions. Her silences, her moods, the permanent set of her downturned mouth – all of it points to a falling-out. A parting. I have seen her in the school corridor trying to catch his attention as he walks past, and noted the deliberate manner in which he refuses to meet her eyes. I have seen the dismay in her face as she stares after him. Part of me feels for her in her heartache and longs for her to confide in me, but it is an unspoken rule with Rachel – she must be the one to initiate any conversation about Ridge. She has made it known how tiresome she finds my questions about him and their relationship. When I tell her I'm concerned, she accuses me of nagging. And so I bide my time.

Her sullenness continues through dinner; she barely offers a civil response to any of the questions her parents put to her. She slouches at the table, pushing her food around her plate, before Heather laughs her tinkly laugh and says: 'Goodness, how gloomy you are, Rachel!' But the look she gives her daughter is pointed and anxious.

Rachel declares that she's tired and slopes off to bed. I have little choice but to follow her. She spends a long time in the bathroom, before it is my turn, and when I return to the bedroom I find her crouched in front of the fireplace, hastily drawing her hand back out of the opening. She pulls down the sleeve of her pyjamas and casts a cross look in my direction. I look at the hearth and then back at her. There is something furtive about her, something underhand.

'Are you all right?' I ask, concerned, but she just mutters:

'Why does everyone keep asking me that?'

We lie together in the darkness and, despite her claims of tiredness, for a long time I feel her fidgeting along the margin of the bed, before eventually I close my eyes and sleep.

The next morning, Rachel shows no inclination to get up, so I eat breakfast downstairs on my own, then throw a stick for the dog outside on the lawn. It's one of those surprising May days that feel like high summer, the air already hot although it's well before noon. I think of Patrick and Niall and the others cooped up in the classrooms at St Alban's and feel sorry for them, having to resist the lure of sunshine on spring grass beyond the locked windows.

The house is quiet today. Heather remains in her room, and Peter is in his studio out in the stables. He has promised to let me use the darkroom this morning, and when I return to the bedroom to get the camera I find the room empty, clothes scattered about. Plumbing noises in the attic tell me that Rachel is in the bathroom. I have a few minutes alone. Quickly, I go to the hearth, crouching in front of it as I had seen Rachel do the night before. I peer inside, and there is only darkness, but when I reach my hand in, my arm disappearing upwards, I feel about and find a sloping ledge at the back where the chimney flue starts, and on this ledge there is a hard object. It's large enough to require both my hands to draw it out. A biscuit tin blackened with soot. The lid comes off easily. I have but a moment to look inside, to find the note and read it, before the bathroom door opens down the hall. I hastily shove the tin back to its hiding place.

When Rachel enters the room, I am standing by the window with my back to her so she can't see me rubbing the soot from my hands.

'I've nothing to wear,' she announces, her voice punched with irritation.

She throws a balled-up shirt on the ground, and I turn to see her in her dressing-gown, a dark look on her face.

'What about this?' I ask, picking up a soft lemon-coloured top that Heather has just bought for her.

'God, no,' she says dismissively. Then, taking it from my hands, she pulls at the stretchy material, and says in a quiet voice: 'I hate all my clothes.'

'Rachel,' I say, softly admonishing, but she just drops the T-shirt on the ground with all the others and goes and flops on the bed. There is a dangerous edge to her this morning. Sleep, rather than easing her, seems to have made her more unsettled.

'It's a beautiful morning,' I tell her. 'We could go for a walk, if you like?'

She takes her cigarettes from the dressing table and proceeds to draw one out. 'No, thanks.'

'It would help take your mind off things.'

Her eyes narrow as she lights the cigarette. But even after she has inhaled and drawn it away from her lips, the narrow look remains.

'Take my mind off what?' she asks coldly.

I sit down tentatively on the side of the bed. Softly, carefully, I say: 'You're beginning to show, aren't you?'

She draws on the cigarette again, but when she doesn't answer, I go on:

'You can't keep hiding this. You're going to have to tell your parents.'

'No way,' she says, with a hint of aggression.

'Has something happened between you and Ridge?'

'Tim,' she says in a hard voice. 'His name is Tim.'

There is a challenge in the way she stares at me and in the frosty manner of her speech, but I push forward, nonetheless. 'Have you told him about the baby? You can talk to me, Rach. If something has happened, you can confide in me.'

She makes a sharp little noise of amusement, but offers nothing more.

'I've seen the way he avoids you in the corridor. Has he broken it off with you?'

She pushes herself down further in the bed, leaning back against the pillow so that she is staring at the ceiling rather than holding eye contact with me.

'I've been standing by, not wanting to say anything, knowing how much you care about him. But I can't stand seeing you this unhappy.' Tentatively, I reach out my hand and touch her ankle. My voice growing in confidence, I go on: 'You must have known it would come to this, Rach? He's so much older than you. There was never any real future in it. Tell your parents. Please. It's still not too late . . .'

Her ankle slithers out from under my grasp and she kicks out, sending me flying off the bed. Stunned by this sudden violence, I look up at her from the floor. She is sitting up, her hair askew, wildness in her eyes.

'What would you know about it?' she hisses. 'What the hell would you know about anything? Don't you dare lecture me, you little virgin!' Her face contorts into an ugly sneer, and I feel the lancing pain of the word. 'For weeks now I've had to put up with your sanctimonious bullshit, your prudish disapproval. God, do you even listen to yourself? *He's so much older than you, Rachel. There was never any real future in it,*' she mocks, making a prissy face, before snarling: 'You're worse than some spinster aunt the way you go on, and deep down you know you're just jealous!'

'Jealous?'

'That's right! Jealous because men are interested in me. Because they desire me. Jealous because I'm not some flat-chested, sad sap like you who's so witless and naïve she'll even try to snog a gay guy!'

The words cause a plunge in my tummy. I stare at her, aghast.

'Who told you?' I ask, my voice shaking.

'What does it matter? Everyone knows.'

'Everyone?'

'You're pathetic, Lindsey – you know that? I'm fucking sick of you hanging around me all the time. You're a leech. Here' – and she plucks my nightdress from where it is folded neatly on my pillow and fires it at me, 'you can sleep in the spare room. I can't stand the fucking sight of you!'

I drop the nightdress on the ground and flee the room, thundering down the stairs and charging across the hall. Too shocked to cry, I feel like I can't breathe, and bursting outside into the sunshine, I take lungfuls of green spring air, sucking it in, my hands on my hips, shaking.

Her savagery is astounding. The way she had lashed out with no provocation at all – I can't take it in. Her words keep circling around and around in my brain – the spitefulness of them, the loathing on her face. A part of me whispers that she is just taking her anger out on me, that Ridgeway is the real target of her ire. But the words cut deep, the venomous flash in her eyes as she'd ripped into me over Marcus. *Everyone knows*. The words wash over me like vinegar, making me want to scuttle into the shadows, into a dark hole where no one can ever find me. I start to walk quickly, feeling the words taunting me, chasing me. *Virgin. Virgin.* Pins sticking into my flesh.

Past the sycamore and over the lawn, I head for the shadows of the trees, the protection of the stone wall. The courtyard is empty and quiet, the door to the studio open.

'Hello, there,' Peter says, glancing up but not really looking at me. 'Come to use the darkroom, have you?'

He is intent on his work, cleaning the lenses of his cameras, and only looks up properly when I don't say anything, then puts his head to one side when he sees my face.

'Lindsey? Are you all right?'

I won't cry. I refuse to cry. Instead, I walk into the room, and past him to the wall. Hanging from the beam that crosses the ceiling is a canvas backdrop. There are several of them hooked up there, and the one that's unfurled is painted with a bucolic scene of rolling fields, fencing, sheep grazing on the meadow. I feel him waiting for me to say something, but there are so many things swelling inside me – confusion, hurt, anxiety, self-doubt, anger. I want so badly to change myself, to not be this innocent, naïve child. *Virgin*. The scornful, pitying look she gave me. It's chased by the memory of Marcus – the horror on his face, his stammering voice: *'Lindsey, I didn't mean that . . .'* The pins keep on pricking. *Everyone knows.* My skin feels tight over my body. How much I hate myself! How much I want to shrug off my flesh! The desire fills out inside me like it could burst through my skin.

'Those pictures you showed me,' I say, and his face darkens a little. 'Can I see one of them?'

He sees how worked up I am, how shaken, and hesitates. But it's only for a moment. Without saying a word, he goes to the desk at the far wall and opens a drawer.

He handles it carefully – the picture he removes – like it is precious to him. And when he puts it in my hands I am careful, too.

Flesh and more flesh. Nipples like copper coins riding on sloping breasts. Curls of dark hair between legs. I have no idea what age this woman is. Twenty? Forty? A cloud of hair arranged in an artful pile on top of her head, her face looking to the side.

'Do you think she's beautiful?' I ask, and he answers:

'Yes.' But nothing more. The last time, he had lectured me on art and the human form. Today, he is wary of me, watchful, alert to something new and alive inside me.

I look at her body, the folds of fat and dimpled flesh, the paunch of her belly, her rounded shoulders. Her face betrays no emotion. But even though she is unsmiling, I do not see fear. Nor is there shame. Instead, there is ease, confidence. A secret pleasure hidden behind her eyes. And I know why I have come here. I know what it is I want.

'Will you take my picture?' I ask him, and he nods and turns back to the desk for his camera.

'Perhaps outside,' he suggests, glancing past the doorframe to the sky beyond. 'The light is good—'

'No. No, not like that,' I say. My heart is thudding in my chest. I feel it bursting out of me. I hold the photograph up to him. 'Like her.'

His mouth opens fractionally, his eyes move from her to me. 'Lindsey,' he says.

'Please, Peter. I want you to.' Despite the boil of emotions inside me, my voice is resolute, firm. 'I need you to.'

A pained expression clouds his face, his chin sinks to his chest and he stands very still. Then he looks at the lens in his hand, then back at me. He moves now to the door and closes it, flicking the bolt in place. The studio instantly darkens, and darkens further when he goes to close the window shutters. With his back to me, he instructs me to go behind the screen to get ready, and while I am back there he turns on the lights. As I pull my T-shirt over my head and unhook my bra, I can hear him hauling furniture across the floor. Dropping my jeans on the wooden boards, and pushing down my underwear, I hear the snap of fabric. Blood burns through my veins, a fire of excitement in my belly. I cannot believe my own audacity! And when I walk out from behind the screen, I feel myself stepping across a breach. I am leaving myself behind, and with it all the hurt, the slights, the unseen cuts and scars of my adolescence. I am stepping across to a place where Rachel's words cannot hurt me.

He has set out a chair for me, draped it in some kind of plush-velvet cloth. The lights are stark, blinding, so that I can only see his silhouette. He is standing very still, watching me. I cannot make out his features. The lights hum. A hush has come into the room between us, and it feels like the morning beyond – the trees, the birds, the grass and sky – has fled somewhere far, far away.

'Sit,' he says, and I do as he asks.

The muscle of my heart must be visible through my skin, so hard is it pumping. The air is cool, drawing goosebumps to the surface of my skin, making the tips of my breasts hard. His instructions are short, mono-syllabic, intense. He must feel it, too – the charge in the air between us. And when he stands behind the tripod and puts his face to the camera, I feel myself filling the frame, alive to this new sensation. The thrill as the shutter clicks is immediate and intense. My body is an object that wants to be possessed. I feel myself surren-dering to the camera.

We do not talk – not then. But unspoken words swirl within. *Look at me now, Rachel*, they say, sensation pour-ing through my body like a flood of colour, a glow of heat. I tilt my chin up higher, the shadow of a smile on my lips. The words harden inside me. *Look at me now*, they say.

26

There was a moment of silence. Then Patrick walked swiftly over to the television, where the screen still retained granular fragments of light. He stabbed at one of the buttons to eject the cassette, hastily snatching it out, and in one swift movement, he turned and threw the cassette on to the fire. The tape was alight instantly, a burst of flame licking at the plastic, and the four of us watched as the tape wrinkled and shrank in upon itself, the chemical odour of burning celluloid meeting our nostrils.

'For God's sake, Patrick,' Hilary said, quietly angry, and he turned on her.

'What?' he snapped. 'Isn't that what you want me to do? Erase the past? Pretend like it never happened?'

A look of dismay came over her face, and she dropped down on to the ottoman, while Niall advanced towards Patrick with his palms raised, saying: 'Let's all calm down, why don't we?'

But Patrick didn't look like he was about to calm down. A high colour had come into his cheeks and an agitation had entered his limbs. I could tell that he was flailing around inside, trying to regain some kind of equilibrium, and in that moment he looked so reckless and miserable that my heart went out to him. I said his name, taking a step towards him as I did, but it wasn't until I put my hand to his arm that he registered my presence. He jumped at my touch as though scalded, drawing his arm violently away from me, and when he looked at me, there was a wildness in his eyes that alarmed me.

'And you!' he said. 'You're just as bad!'

'What?'

'You know what!' he countered, his voice coming out in a shriek, and shocked as I was by his scouring attack, I was more shocked to see the tears springing in his eyes.

He held me there in his gaze, and it was a searching look full of boiling emotion. Deep inside me, something turned over. I began to feel afraid.

'Patrick,' I said again, but he turned from me, shaking his head furiously, and marched out of the room.

I went to follow, but Hilary stopped me.

'Give him a few minutes to calm down first,' she advised, and even though there was wisdom in her words, I could feel the blood thumping in my ears, alive to a new threat.

'I don't know what the fuck is going on,' Niall said, turning back to the drinks press, 'but I need a serious drink.'

'Me, too,' Hilary agreed.

The pounding in my head alerted me to the fact that I was due my medication. More than that, I needed to be alone, to compose myself. Patrick's reaction had dangerously unnerved me. Explaining quietly that I needed to go to my room for a painkiller, I left them to their drinks, closing the door softly behind me.

The hall was empty. Jinny had gone after Patrick, and from the back of the house came sounds of her whining. I decided not to follow – not because of Hilary's advice. More because of the fear that had jumped alive inside me from the way Patrick had looked at me – the fierce accusation in his stare. I felt it again, that cool unease as I stepped across the hall. Something caught my attention as I mounted the first step. It was the telephone on the hall table. I noticed that the receiver had been set to one side, as if someone had left it off the hook.

Going over to the phone now, I lifted the receiver to my ear and said, 'Hello?' But there was no answering voice. Nothing, only the insistent bleeping of an empty line. I replaced the receiver on the cradle, somewhat disturbed by why the telephone had been left that way while we were all anxiously awaiting news of Marcus.

This thought was barely in my head when I heard footfall on the stairs and turned to look. For a moment, I couldn't speak. It was like the blood stopped in my veins, the breath paused in my chest. The only movement was the words running through my head, saying: *No, it couldn't be.* For there was Heather Bagenal, coming down the stairs at me.

A trick of the eye – the tumour toying with me.

She paused where she was, about halfway down, and the fluttering continued in my chest, even when I realized that it was not Heather, but Rachel. She was wearing her mother's outfit – the same one Heather had worn on the night of her son's party, the night her husband had died: a gold lamé dress, long-sleeved and ruched at the centre so that all the folds of glittering fabric seemed to burst from a point between her breasts. Rachel was also wearing Heather's white turban with the diamante broach pinning it closed, and with her dark hair tucked up inside it and invisible to view, the resemblance to her mother was startling. Their features were strikingly similar – from the heavy-lidded, sensual eyes to the broad, full-lipped mouth. Rachel still held the dazed expression that had come over her face in the aftermath of her scorching, and the glassiness of her gaze made her look even more like her mother – the same vagueness in her eyes that had frequently possessed Heather Bagenal.

'Rachel,' I said, recovering myself a little, but I could still hear the quaver in my own voice, 'you gave me a fright. I thought I was seeing a ghost.'

She gave the faintest smile, and proceeded down the stairs. There was a brittleness to her movements that was suggestive of some kind of chemical change in her, as if she were drifting down in a drug-induced miasma. And when she reached the bottom step and paused close to me – close enough for me to smell the alcohol on her breath – she spoke in a silent, sinuous way:

'My mother always said there were no such things as ghosts. That what people mistook for spirits were actually the manifestations of their own guilty consciences. Don't you think there's some truth in that, Lindsey?'

'I don't know,' I answered softly.

She held my gaze for a few seconds before a wrinkle came to her brow, and her eyes grew misty with some private recollection.

'Ever since I came back to this house,' she began, 'I keep thinking I can hear a baby crying somewhere. Upstairs in the bedrooms. At times, in the attics. Even though there's nothing there.' Her eyes lit on mine, and they appeared sharper now, more alert. 'Do you suppose that is my guilty conscience over the baby I had killed?'

'I don't know,' I said unsteadily, uncomfortable with how close she was standing to me, with the turn our conversation had taken. In my head crept the images of all I had experienced over the past twenty-four hours: the malevolent presence in the bathroom, the dress slithering to the ground, the shattered picture.

She smiled at me in a knowing way, her face looming close, her eyes locked on mine. Her voice when she spoke was barely above a whisper:

'Tell me, Lindsey. What is it that's weighing so heavily on your conscience?'

Her lips remained parted, and I could see a smear of red lipstick on her teeth, and I recalled, with astonishing clarity, her mother leaning in close in the same way, the pupils of her eyes like pinpricks, her breath sour, her rasping voice: *'Tell me, Lindsey – what is it you want? Is it my daughter or my son? Or my husband?'*

I pushed myself away from Rachel now, scoured by the memory, and felt her gaze following me as I ran, that glassy-eyed stare fixed on my back, all the way up to the landing, my heart drumming like a madman. It was not until I was in my bedroom, the door slammed shut behind me, that I felt released from the grip of her gaze.

Hurrying to the dressing-table, I found my pills and, with shaking hands, I emptied two of them on to my palm before tossing them into my mouth. Trembling, I took a swig of water, felt the sharpness of the pills going down my throat. I thought it would soothe me, but the agitation continued in my chest. Downstairs, someone had turned on the stereo. Music drifted up through the floorboards, a vague resonance at first, the song indistinguishable, before the volume was turned right up and I heard the strained chords of Marc Almond singing 'Tainted Love'. A wave of nostalgia came with it, a remembered past of vibrating dance floors, sweaty teenagers dressed in black with bad hairstyles, angst and desire beating their own rhythm along with the drumbeats. But I was sick of nostalgia – made frightened by what it was dredging up. As I paced around my room, I felt a nervous skitter travelling through my body.

My camera has always made me calm. With almost talismanic properties, it has kept me safe from the demons of my past, and I went to it now, picking it up, hopeful that it might quell the fear that had sprung to life inside me. I opened the viewer and began flicking back through the photographs I had taken that day, attempting to look at them with a critical eye, trying to zone in on the framing of each shot, the focus and movement captured within each picture. My attention was fretful, and I found it hard to concentrate, my mind scuttling off in all directions as I tried to haul it back. It was not until I reached a photograph of Niall with a cigarette dangling from his lips, his gun slung over one shoulder, adopting a gung-ho pose, that I felt my attention caught.

In the picture, he was bathed in sunlight – it reflected sharply off the lenses of his shades. It was this bright light that brought into relief the dark shadows behind him of the woods and trees, a pair of slender figures in the background. I zoomed in and to the side, focusing in on these two shadowy forms, growing clearer now as they became magnified. Rachel and Marcus. They were too distant for their expressions to be distinctly made out, but I was caught by the body language between them. They were facing each other, standing quite close. Marcus had his hands in his pockets, but he was leaning slightly towards her, his chin thrust forward fractionally – a pose that appeared at once birdlike while also vaguely threatening. Whatever it was he was telling her, she appeared shocked by it; one hand had gone up to cover her mouth while her gaze remained locked with his.

Perhaps I was peering too closely, too intently, but I felt a burst behind my eyeball, like a sudden release of pressure, stars rushing at me even after I closed my eyes, even after I dropped the camera on to the dressing table and pressed the heels of my hands against my eyeballs.

In my head, I began counting – a method I had been employing whenever the tumour made this happen – to try and calm the panic that inevitably surged at times like this. When I reached twenty, I forced my eyes open. The stars had faded, but shadowy flecks remained, troubling the field of my vision, objects appearing blurry and indistinct. My legs weakened by the episode, I sat down on the bed, waiting for it to pass. A strange kind of routine had been formed around these incidents, and I found myself now seeking out a focus on the floor, something to fix my gaze on until my vision regained clarity and normalcy. The point I found was the skirting board, and immediately my gaze travelled to the picture still half within its frame, the glazing sheared through the middle, lying where I had left it on the floor near the window.

As I gazed at it now, it triggered something in my head, and my mind went instantly to Marcus's room. The pictures on the floor, partially dismantled, just as this one was. As the weirdness of the coincidence caught up with me, I saw now what I hadn't seen before. Getting up from my bed, I crossed to where it lay and, crouching down, I could see that the picture had slipped in the frame, revealing another picture hidden behind it. I could just about make out the corner of it, but there was definitely something there.

Carefully, I turned it over, picking free the tiny brass hinges that held the whole thing together. The backing came away, and there behind the larger photo lay a smaller one. It was square, like a Polaroid, and I felt my breathing slow as I turned it over, knowing, somehow, what I would find.

It could have been someone else – another adolescent girl with small breasts, a sparse clutch of hair at her pubis. It could have been someone else entirely, so unfamiliar to me was this version of myself. I looked at the pallor of my teenage skin, the slight flare of my hips, the upward tilt of my chin – a kind of wilful defiance in the pose, except for the fact that I was smiling. What I felt, looking at it down the dim corridor of all the years gone by, was a mingling of sadness and regret. Regret for the folly of allowing that photograph to be taken in the first place – for *wanting* it to be taken – but regret, too, for all that had passed me by. Twenty years elapsed and, with them, the hopes and dreams and expectations I had held as a teenager, each one put to rest, abandoned, or simply let go.

I wondered why he had hidden it here? Had it given him some kind of additional wicked pleasure to know it was there, buried in plain sight? That when others peered closely at the image of my clothed self beneath those dead and hanging rabbits, the image of my unclothed self lurked behind? And just as I wondered this, I thought of Hilary's account of her own shame, and then I thought of the pictures on the floor in Marcus's room.

Downstairs, the music was blaring. As I emerged quietly from my room, I could hear Depeche Mode on the stereo, 'Personal Jesus' thumping through the house with a beat of doom. Apart from the music, the house was still, no evidence of the others as I hurried across the landing, keeping close to the walls, turning down the corridor to Marcus's room.

It was as I had left it – the light still on, the pictures spread out on the floor, dismantled from their frames. With haste, I bent over them, picking up one after another, searching beneath the exterior shots for the forbidden pictures secreted behind. I did so with a thudding heart, half dreading what I might find. I knew there were other pictures taken of me, just as I knew now that there were private photographs of Hilary, too. One after another, as I lifted the staid and safe images of Thornbury and its environs, I was disappointed – or perhaps relieved – to find nothing there. But I knew I had stumbled upon an essential truth. I picked from its frame a photograph I remembered from all those years ago – a black-and-white image of the teenage Marcus standing under the arch by the stables, the sun behind him casting a long and angular shadow. The photograph Marcus had scorned as derivative. Intuition crept over me.

I felt it in my blood, which was growing calmer, the beats slowing as I felt the clarity begin to come. That sharpening of senses, that sense of peace, of clear vision and understanding that came to me whenever I was there in the midst of a crime scene. So it came over me now.

Marcus. Clever, thoughtful Marcus. He must have seen the picture hanging on the wall of his room and felt the old irritation come alive – enough for him to take the picture from the wall, to push aside those same brass fittings and remove the backing. What he intended to do with his portrait, I can only imagine – burn it, perhaps. But before he had a chance, he must have found the illicit pictures. I was certain they existed. He must have pieced it together. I recalled the scene I had witnessed between him and Patrick in the garden that morning – the sudden violence of Patrick's reaction. I remembered, too, how withdrawn Marcus had been at the shoot, the curious look he had given me when he'd caught me looking, a penetrative stare, as if he was trying to communicate something urgent, and it was only now that I understood. He had seen the photographs. The private ones Peter had taken.

I recalled the photograph of earlier today, capturing Marcus and Rachel unawares. I thought back to their body language – how shocked she had appeared – and realized now that he must have told her what he had discovered.

'*First Rachel, now you,*' Hilary had said when she had

316

come upon me in here earlier. *'While you were at the hospital, I found her in here.'*

I had a flash of Rachel hurrying back across the fields to the house, holding Jinny by the collar, her gun under her arm. The rest of us were gathered around ailing Marcus, staring helplessly after her.

She must have come in here for the photographs. I tried to make myself still, to feel the beat of intuition pass through me. I closed my eyes and tried to be patient, to allow the deep clarity to sweep through me, to do its work. The house shuddered and thumped with the raging soundtrack of our teenage years relentlessly pounding through the speakers downstairs, but here, in the stillness of the room, it came to me. Of course. Rachel's place. Her secret place.

As I crept back along the corridor, my blood began to stir again. Nerves announced themselves in my cautious movements, the squeak and groan of floorboards sending shockwaves of doubt up through me. I arrived at her door and listened against it. Hearing nothing, I knocked gently. After a brief interval, I reached for the handle and let myself in.

It had been years since I had stood in that room, yet still it reached out to grasp me with its familiarity. I felt it in the tang of nail polish mingling with the stale scent of cigarettes. The walls remained a bright ochre made lurid by the overhead light which I had switched on. The room was in disarray, much as it had always been, only now the clothes thrown over the bed and dropped upon the floor were more sedate, more expensive. The pieces of jewellery discarded upon the dressing table were studded with genuine precious gems, not plastic resin imitations. The smells of the room were undercut by the dying odour of burning, and I saw that the ruined, charred dress had been flung upon the window-seat. Outside, the night bore on, dark and moonless, but my business here was not outside. It was within the walls of the house, within the very fabric of those walls.

Carefully now, I knelt in front of the fireplace, the thread of my heartbeat counting time as I felt my hand guided by memory – the memory of finding Rachel's secret box, where she stored the keepsakes of her clandestine love affair. And just as it did all those years ago, my fingers now alighted on the hard surface of a tin box. An old biscuit tin, still bearing the faded image of biscuits and the letters 'USA' embossed on the surface.

I held it on my lap for a moment, steadying myself, and then I opened the lid and put my hand inside. The scratchy edges of photographs, some curling over, others folded and creased, all containing variations of the young female form. Different faces, different body shapes. Some half dressed, others not dressed at all. Some facing the camera and others turned away, either out of shyness or shame. Very few facing the photographer head on. And only one with a smile of satisfaction on her face – of pleasure.

I looked at this picture of myself, and I imagined Marcus holding it in his hand, staring in horror. I imagined Rachel, too, the shock of finding not just this one, but all of them, a tidal wave of horrors coming over her. And I thought then of the phone call from the hospital earlier that evening, Rachel's pinched face and tight voice when she re-entered the room. I knew, somehow, that Marcus was dead. Just as I knew she had lied to us about it. For a moment, I was back there in that field in those diminishing seconds between the deer coming into sight and the shots ringing out. I was back there again, and Rachel was behind me. In my mind's eye, I could see her watching everyone else on the cusp of reaction, I could see her gaze turning to Marcus, I could see her lifting her gun.

I saw it clearly. And then the bulb that had been shining in this yellow bedroom flickered, there was a loud bang beneath me, and the music which had been blaring was suddenly cut and the light went out. At first, I just sat there, overcome with fright, blinking, my eyes trying to adjust to the blackout. The suddenness of the silence felt like a kind of violence, and I dropped the pictures on to the ground. Straining for a sound, for a chink of light, I got to my feet. I put my hands out in front of me, edged cautiously in the direction of the door. I couldn't see a thing. Coming up hard against the bed, I cried out involuntarily. The dark was thick around me. And then I heard the door opening, a foot-step on the threshold. 'Rachel?' I asked, squinting to see. 'Is that you?' Urgency in my voice. A swift move-ment through the air and fear loomed in my heart. I stumbled backwards but the blow came anyway – I felt the hard crack of it, heat exploding through my face, my eye, and then the murkiness and silence flooded through me, taking me down, down, sucking me into darkness.

27

1992

I arrive back at school alone. When asked about Rachel, I say that she is sick. Throughout Monday and Tuesday, I answer this question over and over again.

'What's wrong with her?' Hilary asks.

I shrug and say: 'Tummy bug,' then quickly look away.

The questions have petered out by Wednesday, interest moved elsewhere.

The following week, when Mrs Meara, our form mistress, interrupts class to announce that one of the students – Rachel Bagenal – will be absent for the rest of term, whispers ripple through the classroom, heads turning in my direction.

'What happened?' Hilary hisses, but I shake my head and tell her I don't know.

As soon as class is over, I race back to our room to find Rachel's bed stripped of its sheets, her belongings packed up and spirited away. It has all been done so swiftly, every trace of her removed while I was sitting through a geography lesson. Her side of the room is bare like a wound, and when I sit on my bed and stare at it, for the first time I feel the gravity of the situation. My heart kicks with fear.

Patrick remains in school, and his answers to any queries about his sister are distant and laconic. She's been sick, he says, some kind of gastric flu that's wiped her out. Their parents have decided to get a private tutor for the rest of term to help her catch up while recuperating at home. After a while, he grows sick of having to talk about it, withdrawing into mulish silence. I don't ask him about Rachel. It feels like we are both keeping our distance.

Rumour is rife throughout the school, but I close my ears to it. When Ridgeway is replaced by another teacher just weeks before final exams, the whispers become a cacophony. I am worried about Rachel. Wracked with guilt about the ugly row we had, I ring Thornbury, in the hope of speaking to her. But every time I call, Heather tells me Rachel is resting or studying and cannot be disturbed. She promises to let Rachel know that I called, but her voice is cool and I'm not sure I believe her. Several times, I sit at my desk and begin writing a letter, but the words look wrong on the page and I cannot express myself clearly. I put down my pen and sit back in my chair. I am losing her, I think.

The room feels large and empty without her. Sometimes when I lie awake at night I am seized by anger. She pushed me away, I think to myself. This is all her fault, not mine. Indignation boils in my veins. I close my eyes and I am back in Peter's studio, in the eye of the camera, being seen the way I have never been seen before. I hear the echo sound of the shutter click and feel that jolt of electricity go through me. Again and again I return to it, the memory a welcome distraction to my troubled conscience. And then, a reprieve. Just before term ends, I receive an invitation to Patrick's eighteenth birthday party. It is to be held in Thornbury on Midsummer's Eve. All the sixth-years have been invited but only Hilary and I have been chosen from the lower years. I am surprised and secretly delighted. I think, for the first time, that the coldness I felt emanating from the Bagenals has all been imagined. When I meet Patrick in the corridor, it feels like months since we've talked, both of us made shy by the time that has passed.

'Thanks for inviting me,' I say, and he shrugs like it's no big deal.

'Will you come?'

'Yes,' I answer, and I cannot suppress the smile of joy that comes over my face.

School breaks up at the start of June, and I spend the rest of the month at home with my parents, earning some money helping out behind the bar.

'You seem chirpy,' my father comments, observing my happy manner with the punters, whereas before I was always sullen, slightly resentful of having to lend a hand clearing tables or serving drinks.

Hilary and I have arranged to go to the party together and, when the day arrives, my father picks her up from her home in Kilkenny and drives the two of us the short distance to the house. We sit in the back seat in our gauzy gowns – the invitation issued a formal dress code – as the car turns through the granite pillars and begins to drive up the avenue. It is only now that I start to feel nervous.

This is the first time my father has been to Thornbury, and I can feel the hushed awe emanating from him as the car rounds the final bend and the house comes into view. In the early-evening sunlight, it appears at its best. The wisteria drapes its way over the arched entrance in lazy elegance and the stone walls appear warm in the sun. High overhead, the statues that line the rooftop's perimeter have been rigged out in yellow bunting. Their stone faces blankly oversee the lawn below, where men and women in uniform carry trays between the house and a large, striped marquee pegged to the grass. A horseshoe of trestle tables around the sycamore tree shimmers with glassware catching the light.

'Look,' Hilary says, pointing to a stage that has been set up outside, massive speakers hanging like ballast around it. 'The Gin Freaks must be playing.'

She giggles next to me, and I can feel the excitement trembling through her.

Neither one of us has seen or spoken to Rachel in weeks, and as my dad leaves us outside the house and drives off slowly, I look up to the window of her bedroom, watchful for a face looking down, but the glass, opaque in the sunlight, glares blankly back at me. Then Hilary tucks her arm in mine and starts marching me to the house, our stiletto heels sinking into the gravel. We are the first to arrive, and I feel uncomfortably conspicuous in my pale blue dress, tight around my body as a bandage is to a wound. My mother had cast a disapproving eye over it, but she had let me wear it anyway. As we reach the front door and cross the threshold, I wonder how it will be between Rachel and me, and grow suddenly fearful of the reunion. Braced for confrontation, I step into the house, trailed by a wistful thought that I am no longer a favoured guest here. No longer Rachel's special friend. For the first time, my invitation does not extend to staying the night. I am one of a crowd, that's all. But then voices from the kitchen corridor grow louder as they near the bend and I see Peter walking towards me in conversation with a friend of his – a man of similar age and bearing – both of them dressed in tuxedos, and when he sees me his face lights up and he holds his hands aloft and cries: 'Lindsey!'

My heart moves in my chest. He opens his arms to me and we hug warmly, and all the while I am thinking: *this man has seen me with my clothes off. He has looked on me in a way no other person on this earth has done.* Hilary stands off to one side, her hands clasping her purse in front of her, silently observing.

He pulls back, holds me at arm's length, his eyes running over my face as if alert for changes in me the way that I am in him. *Is he thinking about it?* I wonder. *Is he thinking about what we did together?* Then, remembering his friend, he introduces us, and the friend – Steven – shakes my hand, his brow wrinkling as if he knows me from somewhere and is trying to place me.

'How is Rachel?' I ask, and Peter waves his hand in the direction of the staircase.

'She's up there somewhere, getting ready. Why don't you go up to her?' Already he is steering Steven into the library and, when the door closes behind them, I find myself alone. Hilary has disappeared. From behind the closed door comes a low rumble of male laughter.

Tentatively, I start up the stairs. Outside, I can hear tyres crunching over the gravel as the guests start to arrive. Voices rise in greeting – I think I hear Patrick's among them. My heart is still recovering from my reunion with Peter. Perhaps it is the tuxedo and bow tie, but he looks older than I remembered. I have grown used to his louche presence in jeans and rolled-up shirtsleeves, a flap of hair hanging rakishly over his brow. Strange to see him oiled and shaved and buttoned up.

I am halfway up the stairs when a shadow falls across my face.

'Well. Look who it is,' Heather says.

I don't say anything, too startled by her appearance for words to form. A woman who has always been stylish, she has pushed the boat out tonight. A statuesque vision of gold lamé worn with old-style Hollywood glamour – the white turban around her head is pure Marlene Dietrich, as are the carved lips painted crimson, old diamonds gripping her earlobes and knotted at her throat. She towers above me, staring down under dense black lashes, and I feel small and insubstantial beneath her gaze.

'You look amazing,' I say, and she smiles. But the smile doesn't reach her eyes. Pupils like pinpricks, they flicker over me, and she remarks:

'You look different. There is something changed about you.' I'm pinned by her examination of me. Scanning my body, she asks: 'Have you grown since I last saw you?'

'I don't think so.'

My answer dissatisfies her, like she cannot tell what it is about me that's different and it irritates her.

'I was just going up to see Rachel,' I venture, but she stops me:

'No. No, don't do that.' Softening her voice a little, she adds: 'She will come down when she's ready.'

She waits on the step. Dutifully, I turn around and go back down the stairs beneath her watchful gaze. She has been perfectly polite, but there was a shard of glass in her voice, something rigid about her stance that suggests to me I am not welcome here. I cannot help but feel that the party has barely started and already I have overstepped a mark, crossed some invisible line.

By the time darkness falls, the party is in full swing. The night pounds with noise. The Gin Freaks, having played their set and departed the stage, are replaced by a DJ playing Soft Cell, INXS, U2 and The Cure. There is laughter and screaming, the loud hum of voices. The marquee is lit up like a luminous jellyfish. There are people I know here from school – all sixth-years – as well as adults I understand to be friends of Peter and Heather. Generations mingle with ease and, at the bar, no one asks for ID or quizzes you on your date of birth. There are kegs of beer and bottles of wine, and it's all free until it runs out, Niall informs us. He's pretty wasted already. We all are.

'He was drinking brandy and smoking cigars with Peter,' Marcus says with amused contempt. 'You should have seen him. Five minutes out of school and he's acting like he's forty.'

'Have you seen Rachel?' Hilary asks, shouting to be heard above the throng, but Marcus shakes his head.

'She hasn't come down yet, I don't think.'

'What's keeping her?' Hilary wants to know. She is eager to see her cousin, driven by curiosity. I see her hungry eyes roaming the crowd and know she is desperate to discover whether the rumours about Rachel are true. I feel it again – that creep of guilt; nerves making themselves felt in my tummy at the thought of her reaction to me. I knock back the dregs of my glass and look around for a refill.

Rachel doesn't appear during the dancing. Not even

when the music stops and Peter takes to the stage to raise a toast to his son.

'It's an important birthday,' he tells us all. 'It's the birthday which really ushers one into adulthood, into a life of responsibility. To know where one has come from, and to honour that place, and one's past, is a privilege. It's one I believe Patrick will uphold with dignity, and with integrity.'

While the crowd listens, then erupts into applause, I scan the faces for Rachel's. I barely hear Peter's speech, or Patrick's, so intent am I upon finding her. Surely she is here somewhere?

Patrick makes his way through the crowd to join us. He is red-faced and delighted, his mood soaring as the party reels around him. He puts his arm about my shoulders and leaves it there while Niall and Hilary slag him over the speech he made, his lame joke about having to sell the family silver to pay for the party. It feels nice having his arm about me, like I am once again being marked out as special. Hilary sees it and raises her eyebrows at me, grins into her wine. Something is happening between Patrick and me. I haven't felt it for months, but it's back now, warming me against the night air, making everything fizz and sparkle. The anxieties of the past few weeks seem to dissipate and fade. I am welcome here. I am happy. I feel Patrick's arm around me and think: I belong here.

'Dad!' Patrick calls out, as Peter moves past us back towards the house. He turns and sees his son, and comes towards us. I think he notices the way Patrick has me held against him, but he doesn't comment, doesn't look directly at me.

'How are we all doing? Not too drunk, I hope?'

Niall makes a sozzled face, his knees buckling, and we all laugh.

'Are you going to hit the dance floor with us?' Patrick asks, but Peter holds his hands up in a halting gesture and says:

'Count me out. That's a younger man's game.'

'Sloping off to bed with your cocoa already?' Niall teases him, and Peter laughs.

'Not to bed, but I think I'll slope off to my study,' he says, then his eyes slide to mine and he adds: 'Or to my studio. Leave the party to you youngsters.'

He smiles all around, slaps Niall on the back, and departs through the crowd.

Patrick's arm is still around me, but it feels different now. Leaden. For the past few minutes, my mind has been racing on ahead. I have been imagining weekends at Thornbury as Patrick's girlfriend now, rather than as Rachel's best friend. I have seen in my mind's eye the two of us taking walks in the woods hand in hand, or snuggling up together on the sofa in front of the fire. I have imagined Patrick sneaking me into his room at night and then, in the morning, the two of us at the breakfast table, pretending that nothing has happened, bound by our silent complicity. I have imagined all these riches, but with that one glance Peter has kicked it all away, shattering the illusion. How can I ever sit down at a breakfast table with Patrick and his father, knowing what I have done? For the first time since it happened, I feel a wave of regret so strong it throws me.

'I'll be back in a minute,' I tell Patrick, and slip out from under his arm. Heat has come into my face, a loosening deep in my guts. I need the bathroom and hasten towards the house. Inside, the hallway is thronged, and it is clear that most of the older set have taken refuge indoors, leaving the garden to the younger folk. Music is replaced by a cloud of conversation and laughter, and I hurry through it. Finding the bathroom, I lock the door behind me and lean against the sink. The room whirls about me, alcohol scrambling my thoughts.

After a few moments, I feel calm again. I wash my hands, fix my dress, reapply lipstick and go back out. But the door has barely closed behind me when I feel the grasp of someone's hand about my upper arm. Looking down, I see red nail polish, a claw-like grip. Heather's eyes are rheumy and cold, and however drunk I am, I can see she is worse.

'Tell me, Lindsey – what is it you want?' she asks, sibilance becoming a slur.

'I don't want anything,' I say, shrinking from her. The grip around my arm is uncomfortable, but what frightens me is the anger in her eyes, the white-hot rage.

'Is it my daughter or my son?' she persists, and as I tug my arm from her grasp, she adds: 'Or my husband?'

I'm too shocked to answer. *She knows*, I think, a sour taste coming to my mouth, fear contracting inside me.

Her face changes. Her eyelids grow heavy. She seems to slump inwardly.

'You shouldn't have come back,' she says, then turns away.

Outside, the air feels too warm. Dry-mouthed, I rush to the bar table and grab the first thing I reach – a glass of red wine. I fill my mouth and swallow, then fill it again. I see the back of Hilary's head, the auburn frizz of her hair, and hurry towards her. I need company. I need to be among friends, so that the shrivelled feeling inside me can inflate to their familiar laughter. I don't want to think about what I've done. I shrink from the possibility that Heather has seen those pictures. My head fills with the image of her mouth curling with disgust.

There is a burst of noise overhead – a loud explosion followed by screams and shouts and applause as the night sky is studded with fireworks. The crowd separates and parts as people move to get a better view and, as they do, I see Hilary turn, and there beside her is Rachel. I stop where I am and stare.

The change that has occurred in her is remarkable. She has grown thin, emaciated even. It looks like she's been starving herself for weeks. Arms like sticks emerge from a grey chiffon dress that hangs loosely from boney shoulders. The dress stops above her knees, which seem bulbous and swollen compared to the narrow, fleshless calves. Everything about her seems sinewy and brittle. Her hand clutches a glass of red wine to her chest, and it seems amazing that she has the strength to hold it, to stand up. But the biggest change is in her face. It has shrunk back to the bone, shadows lurking around her eye sockets and underneath her cheeks. Her eyes are black, liquid pools, dead eyes in a sunken face. Those eyes are on me now while everyone else stares up at the pyrotechnics. I gather my courage and move towards her, making myself smile as I do. But she doesn't smile back. It's like she's looking through me. Even when I'm right up close to her, her eyes seem unfocused, glassy and lifeless.

'Hello, Rachel,' I say.

Her empty gaze rests on me for a moment. Then she flings the contents of her glass at my chest. Gasping, I feel the cool splash coming through the fabric to my skin and, looking down, I see the purple stain spreading across my breast like a gunshot. I am breathless with shock, but she is cool, and unmoved. She leans in close – close enough for me to feel the heat of her breath.

'Traitor,' she says, clearly and distinctly.

28

2017

'You must be Lindsey,' Peter says through the darkness, and takes me by the hand. I turn to smile, and there is Ridgeway's hand clasped around Rachel's calf, rubbing. He has worked her sock down to her ankle. 'You can keep a secret, can't you?' he asks.

'It's a taxidermist's dream!' Hilary exclaims, and I follow the sweep of her hand to the glass cases holding stuffed animals in varying poses. As we pass, I see they are not animals, but women, fleshy and lumpen, coarse hair matted to their heads and to their naked bodies, glass beads for eyes twinkling in the light. 'It's my little hobby,' Peter explains. 'You could say I'm a bit of a collector.' Mr Thompson frowns and says that is not the St Alban's way. And my father goes on polishing glasses behind the bar.

The ghostly maids dance in the attic, and Marcus says: 'Rooms must be lived in or they will start to die.' In the scullery, the rabbits on their hooks drip blood on to newspaper, and Peter says, 'That's not the kind of picture I'm after.' Heather thinks it's disgusting, and rips the creatures down from their hooks, stuffing them away into a biscuit tin. Marcus says: 'There's lots of things you haven't done yet, Lins,' and the crows stir in the trees outside and, somewhere, a baby cries, while the statues maintain their lidless stares.

Fireworks burst through the night sky. Peter says, 'There's only so much you can do with light and shadows,' and all the men laugh.

'Oh, Christ!' Patrick shouts, and puts his hands into the wound, the wheat bending to the breeze around him. Somewhere in the distance, Jinny is barking and a door opens. 'You shouldn't have come back here,' Heather says, as she sits on the bed. There is the smell of cigarettes, and the dusty odour of clothes too long packed away in airless closets. She puts her hand to my forehead, and it is a dead weight, heavy as a stone pressing against my temples.

'You shouldn't have come back here,' she says again, and I try to open my eyes, but something stops me, a hardening crust over my eyelid.

'It was a mistake, letting you back in.' I feel her close to me, the heat of her breath on my cheek, her voice throaty and urgent and kept very low. 'You're like poison to this house.'

Her image is blurry in the darkness. It slowly swims into vision: the white turban, blood-red lips, the jewels at her throat. In the shadows around us, silhouettes reveal themselves as a wardrobe, a marble fireplace. The bed takes shape beneath me. And as the dream recedes, pain rushes in. Hot and molten, it fills the socket and my hand goes instantly to it. The blood hardening at the point of the blow scares me and, taking my hand away, I find my vision off balance. When I close my good eye there is only blackness, and I panic.

'I need help. I can't see.' I try to sit up, but a hand goes to my chest, holding me there.

'Lie back. Rest.' Her tone is gentle, coaxing, but there is emotion in her voice, and as I blink through the darkness and her face looms into vision, I see that it is wet with tears.

'Rachel?'

'You shouldn't have come back,' she whispers again, and the tone of her voice is not bitter but regretful, sorrowing, and without having to think, I know something terrible has happened.

'Where is Patrick?' I ask. 'Where are the others?'

'The party's over, Lins. Everything is finished.'

I try to sit up again quickly, but the blood swarms in my head and I'm afraid to lift it. Already I am fearful that the tumour has been dislodged. Blinded in that eye, I am nervous of movement, frightened of doing more damage.

'We used to share this bed. Do you remember?' she asks, her tone growing wistful. 'When you first started coming here. We were close, then. Weren't we?'

'Best friends,' I say carefully, and a watery smile comes over her face as she repeats the words.

'We shared so much. I think I was closer to you than I have been to any other friend before or since. That's why it hurt so much – your betrayal.'

The word is spoken softly, but it cuts through the air between us, nonetheless.

'Rachel, I need to get up,' I tell her quietly. 'My eye is bleeding. I need to get to a hospital.'

'What for, Lindsey? So they can poke around inside you? Scrape away all the bad bits?' She says it to me, but it feels like her own private recollection. And when I don't answer, she goes on: 'Do you know, they didn't even tell me I was having an abortion? My parents, I mean. They just packed me into the car one morning and drove to the ferry terminal. I kept asking them where we were going, why wasn't I in school? But Heather was in one of her moods and Peter just kept answering, "Wait and see." I didn't even think they knew about me and Tim! Can you imagine? Not one word did they speak of him, or of what they'd found out. It was only when we were at the clinic and I had to sign all these forms that I realized. "What is this?" I asked them. "What are we doing here?" Heather just gave me this cold stare and said, "Fixing your mistake." Peter wouldn't even look at me. He never really did look at me again, not properly. It was like I disgusted him, that just the sight of me made him sick.'

She delivers her account in a deadened tone. It has the feel of a story revisited over and over. A memory made threadbare from her relentless re-examination of it.

'I kept asking them how they knew,' she goes on, and through the blur of my vision, I can see her eyes return to me. 'They never said. But I knew it was you.

337

It was the only explanation. You promised you would keep it a secret – don't you remember? Did you think you were doing me a favour? Or were you trying to usurp me?'

'I don't know what you mean.'

'You were the daughter he should have had!' she declares, falsely bright. 'Isn't that what he said?'

The venom in her tone is unmistakeable. She moves on the bed, edging closer, and I feel our bodies brought towards each other through the depression in the mattress.

'You were so desperate to be like us,' she tells me. 'To be one of us. I wonder, had you had any idea what we were really like – our family – would you have been so eager?'

'I don't know what you're talking about.'

'Don't you? I mean the family flaw. Surely you know about that by now? Remember all the episodes Heather used to have? When she'd take to her bed and cry for days – drunk, of course. Sodden and morose. I used to hate her for it. But now,' she paused, then began again: 'Now that I have had my own episodes, I begin to understand her. Don't you think it's odd, though? That she was the depressive one, and yet it was my father who committed suicide?'

There's a lightness to her tone, but I sense how dangerously on edge she is. Her question cuts through me. I feel the accusation in it and wonder again how much does she really know? In the poorly lit room, with my

338

blurred vision, she seems more like Heather Bagenal than ever. And it's not just the clothes. It's in the way she holds herself, the manner of her address, her regal bearing that you can tell is only surface. Scratch the skin and insecurity bleeds through.

'Didn't it frighten you?' she asks me now. 'Getting involved with my brother, knowing the weakness that runs through our family? Or didn't you think he was affected by it?'

The house is quiet. There is a pervasive stillness. I have been so distracted by Rachel and by my own physical pain that it is only now that I take in the enormity of the silence that surrounds us.

'Rachel,' I say slowly. 'Where is Patrick?'

She gets to her feet and goes to the window. Beyond her, the sky is a granular black against her darker silhouette.

'One time,' she tells me, 'when we were children, and Heather was having one of her episodes – a bad one – she bundled us into the car, put me and Patrick in the back seat, and started driving like a madwoman, roaring at us that she'd had enough. She couldn't face it any more. She told us she was going to drive us all off a cliff, put an end to all our suffering. Patrick and I were screaming – she was driving so fast!'

I'm sitting up a little now, although my limbs feel swamped and heavy, as if my body is underwater. The deep silence of the house frightens me. 'Where is Patrick?' I ask again.

'They'll be here soon,' she says in a dreamy voice, staring out the window. 'Niall ran down the avenue to call them. We don't have much time.'

'Who'll be here?'

'The police,' she says lightly, then draws in her breath.

'Rachel,' I say quietly. 'What have you done?'

I cannot see her face. All I can read is the tightness about her body as she holds herself still. She reaches out a hand to the window, traces a line down through the condensation.

'I have spent so much time in this room. I feel like I know it intimately. Strange to think it will soon be no more.'

I hear her in the darkness, stepping towards me.

'Patrick didn't think I would care too much if he sold Thornbury,' she goes on. 'Presumed that just because my life had been in London, I wouldn't give a damn what happened to this place. But everyone needs a home they can go back to, don't they?'

Still there is that manic edge to her that keeps me pinned to the bed. 'Especially when everything goes wrong. He certainly chose his moment! Although he can't be blamed, I suppose. How was he supposed to know that my marriage had just ended? Graham couldn't take it any more – the endless cycles of fertility treatment. And when the final diagnosis came through – the scarring to my womb, fatal to any chance of a pregnancy – he decided to call it a day. With the marriage, too. I thought of you then, Lindsey – how you betrayed me. If you hadn't told my secret, I might have had a child. My womb might not have been scarred beyond all use. After it was all done – the marriage, our lives together – I came home to Thornbury to lick my wounds. Took to my bed, much the way my mother had done. Stewed in vodka and self-pity for a while. But then,' and here her voice dropped low, ice crept into her tone, chasing out any jot of strained humour: 'Then one morning, Patrick lightly drops it into conversation that he is seeing someone. Someone up in Dublin, adding that it's serious. That he thinks it's love. And then he tells me it's you.'

There is a snarl in the curl of her voice. I hear it plainly, feel the threat alive in the room between us.

'I didn't say anything. Didn't express approval or disapproval. I acted like I was not fussed one way or the other and then watched him moon around the place, disappearing into the fields to find bloody mobile coverage so he could phone you. I waved him off on Friday afternoons for his weekend delights, and endured his big, sloppy grins when he came home. All that time I never said a word but, inside, I seethed!' I cannot see them, but I can feel her eyes burning in the darkness. 'That he had fallen in love with the author of my misery! With the very person who had betrayed me and destroyed my chance of happiness! I had endured it once, the disgusting way you insinuated yourself with my father, and now I was being asked to watch you repeat the performance, only this time with my brother? It was too much! I couldn't bear it! All the time, Patrick was going on and on about selling the house and most of the estate, ploughing the money into swanning around the world with you. Worse, that he meant to bring you back here, have the two of you set up home together right there, next to where my father took his own life! Did you really think I would accept that, Lindsey? Did you?'

Her voice trembles, and I can feel the waves of her hate coming at me. She quivers with indignation and fury. My head is throbbing, and my mind is anxiously clawing in all directions, but I know I must remain calm. She has the upper hand here. And she is dangerous.

'What did you do?'

'I suggested to him that he should have a party. A sort of reunion. Gather the old crew around for one last hurrah.'

'It was your idea?'

'Oh, yes. Poor Patrick was never any good at that sort of thing. Yes, it was my idea.'

She sounds so proud of herself that for a moment my fear is nudged aside, my anger rising.

'So, what? You planned to get us all down here? Plotting some kind of revenge?'

'Not revenge. Not as such,' she answers calmly. 'Don't you see? All the foundations of my life were collapsing. I had come home to try and mend myself, to recuperate, and all I keep hearing is a baby crying. Just like I did in the weeks after the termination. Everything is leaving me, Lindsey. Soon there will be nothing left. What I want is an ending. A proper ending – for all of us. For Thornbury.'

'Is that why you shot Marcus?'

A pained silence comes over her. She takes a step towards the fireplace. She knows this room so much better than I do, and I have the hindrance of my blighted sight, my weakened body.

'He found those pictures,' she says quietly. 'Got himself worked up into a state. He even threatened to say something. Scared the hell out of poor Patrick.'

My mind flicks to the argument I witnessed in the garden – Patrick's violent reaction, so out of character.

'You shot him to shut him up?'

'People have killed for lesser reasons, don't you think?' she asks quietly, and I feel her nudging at something, a current of suspicion underneath her words.

'Did you know about the photographs?' I ask, tentative because we are edging close to dangerous territory for me, and her mood is precarious, unstable. If I could only lift my head . . .

'Not overtly. There were rumours over the years, various girls coming forward to squeeze us for money – even though Peter was long dead. We paid them off, of course – that's the Bagenal way. Keep everything hush hush. But I never really believed it. Not even in the last years of my mother's life, when she began alluding to a deviance in my father, and how it had killed him in the

343

end – still I couldn't give credence to it. She used to send me these long, rambling letters with veiled references to his proclivities. I thought it was just her way of trying to win me back. I wouldn't speak to her after he died, you see? And as soon as I was old enough, I left this house and swore I wouldn't return. And I didn't – not while Heather was alive anyway.'

'You blamed her for your father's death,' I say.

'Oh, yes,' she acknowledges freely. 'Isn't it what the police always think? That the spouse is the number-one suspect? She was the one who found his body, after all. And while I realize that shock makes people behave strangely, there was something about Heather that night – in her reaction to his death. It seemed almost furtive. Guilty. I knew she was hiding something. They were all or nothing, my parents. Either falling into one another's arms or ripping out each other's throats. Yes, I believed she'd had a hand in his killing.' She pauses, and there is something faltering about her confidence. Doubt creeps in at the edges. 'She died without my ever having spoken to her again. But still, those letters got to me. The way she kept going on about photographs hidden away somewhere in the house.' She gives a mirthless laugh and plucks something from the mantelpiece. When she strikes a match, the sudden flare of light causes me to jump.

'And all along, they were hanging on the walls. Peter's little joke.' But she doesn't sound amused, and I can tell how much it wounds her.

She puts the match to the wick of a candle, and soon the glow of light expands. It illuminates her face — wretched and drawn, luridly made up with red lips and heavy lashes. But with the play of mixed emotions there and the shadows reflected cruelly, her face appears a grotesque mask of her mother. It's as if she has lost herself in the fitful confusion of trying to be someone else.

'I wonder now whether I was wrong about her. Whether what I read as her guilt was something else. Perhaps she was trying to protect us.'

She takes the candle and bends down, and I have to painfully turn my head to see what she is doing. A small pile of kindling had been set into the grate — she must have put it there in the time I had passed out — and now she sets it alight. The smell of smoke greets my nostrils, and I hear the little whoosh and crackle as the fire takes.

'Why did you hit me?' I ask, watchful as she opens the tin box at her side.

'Curiosity killed the cat,' she says, taking the photographs and peering at them mournfully. 'I should have known you'd come snooping.' She feeds the first picture to the flame. It shrivels over on itself, shrinking and burning, sending a chemical odour out into the room. One by one, she burns the pictures. There is nothing savage in her movements. It's resignation more than anything.

'Taking care of family business,' she says slowly. 'Someone has to.'

There has been something niggling at the back of

my mind like an irritation. And now, it comes, strikingly, to the fore.

'Why did Niall have to call the police?' I ask.

She smiles, but does not answer.

'Why did he leave the house,' I persist, 'and not just use the phone downstairs?'

'I cut the phone line, of course.'

Again, that sour plunge happens inside me. She is not looking at me, intent on her task, but I feel the menace in the room.

'I have no quarrel with Niall,' she says lightly. 'I let him go.'

The silence of the house is screaming now.

'Where are the others? Patrick? Hilary? What have you done?'

She pauses in her task, and her mask seems to wobble. For the first time, I see fear in her face – fear over what she has done.

'I told them. I told them that Marcus is dead.'

I had guessed it already, but still the fear rises in me. He is dead, and his killer is in the room.

'Poor Patrick. He couldn't take it.'

'What do you mean, he couldn't take it?'

'He blamed himself, even though he knew I was the one who pulled the trigger. He was always like that. Blaming himself for everything. Perhaps my father put too much pressure on him to accept the mantle of patriarch. He wasn't able for it, but he tried. And he failed, and that failure fed his desire to compensate.

346

Assuming the blame was like a safety blanket for him. Like he never really grew up; he used it again and again. My mother's car crash, her subsequent death, my father's suicide – Patrick felt like he was in some way responsible for it all. He suffers from that malady. It's a twisted logic, but I understand it.'

As she talks, I fear the worst.

'He takes the blame when it's not his to take, when it's none of his business to. He's lost his mother, his father, he thinks he's going to lose me, his sister, because I shot Marcus. He doesn't want to lose me. We may have been a strange family in our own way, but we were a close family, and blood runs thick. Patrick was the fall guy to the last, when he should never have been, when he had no right to be, but he loved me the way a brother can, and Lindsey, believe it or not, that's real, that's true. It's more than he could ever have felt or done for you.'

'Rachel, where is Patrick?'

'He was an honourable man, I'll say that of my brother. Things weighed heavily on his conscience – too heavily – but in the end he couldn't live with it.'

I struggle to sit up – panic, fear, dread all battling inside me. I scramble against the pain and lean over. She watches me carefully as she tells me how her brother had silently left the room, and then, a few minutes later, they had heard the sharp crack of the gun, and all three had raced into the library to find Patrick sprawled across the desk.

'No,' I say, my voice tiny. My heart is beating quietly in my chest, but I feel the pain seeping into the muscle, like it is too tired for any of this. Too tired to go on.

'He always wanted to emulate our father,' she tells me. 'And now, in the end, he has.'

I turn my face away from her, tears leaking from the corner of my eye, only half listening to what she is telling me now. How Niall ran down the avenue to call for help. How Hilary remained bent over Patrick, trying to staunch the bleeding. How it seemed so simple – clean and honest, as she put it. To wipe the slate. To finish things, once and for all. An act of purification. It was time for all that grubby talk to die. Put a match to the scandal, watch it wither and fade.

'Just like these photographs.'

I know that Hilary is dead. Killed for her confession – her pointed finger. Killed for what she knew. Made a victim all over again. It seems so pointless and futile. Distantly, I hear the sound of feet pounding across gravel. My eyes flicker to the window, and I see the panes of glass briefly glow blue. For a moment, Rachel does not notice it, too intent on the photograph in her hand. It is the last one, and she pauses to gaze on it.

'Look at you,' she says softly. 'So young. But not innocent. You look, in fact, like you're enjoying it.'

She holds it in her hand while the flame licks at the corners, waits for it to burn down before dropping it into the grate, where it mingles with the ashes of the others.

The blue light at the window intensifies, and I can hear the car engine approaching through the trees. She hears it, too, and picks something up off the floor before standing.

'It is time,' she tells me. The floorboards creak as she approaches. My good eye travels down her arm and, even though my vision is blurred, I see the shine of the gun.

'No,' I say, scrambling to retreat, desperate to get away from her, as she draws close.

'Hush,' she whispers, and I feel her cloying breath, the weight of her body as she leans in. Outside, a car door slams. 'It's all over now,' she tells me, my temple pressed by the nose of the gun. 'You'll hardly feel a thing.'

29

1992

I run. Through the crowd of people, past the tables of booze, the sycamore tree strung with lights – I run to the shadows, to where the garden grows tangled along the periphery, nettles and dandelions springing up around me. I run until I reach the wall, shining blue in the moonlight, reaching out a hand to the old stone to steady myself. Breathless and panicky, I stumble along, desperate to get away from the clamour of the crowd and Rachel's needling presence. More than anything, desperate to get away from my guilt. It looms over me, like an angry god, as I flounder along the asphalt path that leads to the stables.

The lights are on in the studio. They draw me like a beacon. Through the sickening confusion of my thoughts, one thing stands out – the need for refuge. I can't go back to the house, not now, not ever. But this place – this one room – holds something unnamable for me, the site of a deep, meaningful act. The light shines through the darkness, soupy with nocturnal insects and the sulphuric smell of spent fireworks. It calls out to me as a safe place. I need to see him. To hear his voice. To have him explain to me in his quiet tones that what we did together was not shameful or smutty but beautiful. A thing of art. How the camera had caressed me, not exploited me. That what I had done for him was an act of empowerment, not victimhood.

I pull open the door and lurch inside, but the emptiness echoes back at me, the only sound my own footsteps loud on the wooden boards. I lean against the wall for a moment, feeling the welcome coolness of it seep through my dress to my body. Drenched in sweat, I look down at the ruined fabric, darkly stained. Chalky marks from the wall cling to the bodice and skirt, my shoes are scuffed and torn. I catch sight of my own reflection in the windowpane, the dark night pressing up against it, and see my bewildered expression, the wildness of my hair.

The room is as I remembered it. The canvas backdrops hanging from the beam, cutting the space in two. The bulk of the old roll-topped desk set back against a wall, locked tight and neat. The side lamps are set up but switched off, the only light coming from a bare bulb swinging on a flex wrapped around the beam. And the camera – sitting on the tripod, the lens cap firmly in place. I fancy that it is sleeping, waiting to be called to life and put to its task once more. The only thing that's different is the couch that has been placed in front of the backdrop. A green leather, buttoned thing, it squats in the middle of the floor, beckoning. I realize how exhausted I am the moment I sit down. Alcohol has dulled my senses and, as the adrenaline hangover kicks in, my limbs start to quiver and shake.

The room is different at night. Even though the door and the shutters had been closed against the light the last time I had been here, some quality of the morning had still managed to seep in. I close my eyes and remember it – the creak of the boards expanding in the sunlight, the plucking sounds of a bird walking on the roof, and among those gentler sounds the startlingly loud snap of my bra opening, the splat as my jeans dropped to the floor. I think of that moment, stepping out from behind the canvas cloth, unable to see his face in the shadows, but oh, the heavy weight of his gaze! The memory brings with it a rush of feeling. Remembering the liberation of being so completely exposed, unhidden – I had felt triumphant! Something of that triumph returns to me now, but it is almost immediately punctured by the word 'Traitor'. It had hit me like a bullet, and it comes whizzing through my memory now, again and again. Any feelings of pride or triumph begin to wilt and curl over on to themselves. *What have I done?* I think, as the triumph fades to disquiet. And then shrinks further into itself to become dread.

A noise outside. Footfall on the asphalt. A man's voice. Laughter. I jump up, panicked. There is no time to run outside, their voices growing louder, so instead I run behind the canvas backdrop, hold myself still with my hands to my mouth, as if that may stop the noise of breathing.

The bulb swings down on the other side of the canvas. Back here, it is darker, the light seeping in at gaps in the sides and punctuating small holes in the heavy material. I put my eye to one of these now and watch as the door opens and Peter enters the room, followed by two other men.

'Close the door there, will you?' Peter instructs, and the third man does so. I recognize this man as the friend I'd been introduced to earlier in the evening. Steven, his name is. He is tall and white-haired above a darkly tanned face. All three men are wearing tuxedos, but the third man has neglected to wear a bow tie. Smaller than the other two, he circles the room, hands in his pockets, occasionally sniffing as he inspects the place.

'Quite the little set-up you have here, Peter,' he remarks, and Peter swirls the drink in his glass and nods but says nothing. 'It's not what I expected.'

'What did you expect, for God's sake?' Steven asks, mildly exasperated.

'I dunno. Something flashier. Less . . .' He searches about for the word before alighting on it. 'Less rustic.'

'Ha!' Steven laughs, and Peter looks down at his shoes, and the third man walks right up to the canvas backdrop behind which I am standing, and stares at it.

'Where'd you get this antique? Looks like it came from some Victorian music-hall,' he remarks with disgust.

He is so close to me, I can smell him. Booze and

cigars, undercut with a vaguely fungal odour. I wonder can he smell me, too?

He takes another step closer, leaning in to examine the paintwork, perhaps, and I can see clearly the shaving rash along his cheek and the bristles of his moustache, reddish-brown turning to white. His eyes move quickly. My heart is hammering so hard I feel sure he must hear it.

'Well, get on with it, Peter, and show us these pictures,' Steven says, unwittingly rescuing me. The small man turns away.

Peter extracts a key from his trouser pocket, goes to the desk and unlocks it, rolling back the top. There is a desk lamp on the upper shelf and he switches this on, light pooling over the surface before him. The other two men join him. With their backs turned to me, I cannot see what they are looking at, nor can I hear them as distinctly. Peter stands in the middle, flanked by the other two, and from the movement of his shoulders I can tell that he is laying the photographs out flat along the desk, in the same way he had done for me all those months ago. But unlike me, these men's reactions betray no shock. In lowered voices, they murmur their approval.

'That one's good,' the small one remarks, and Steven responds:

'Oh, yes. I agree, Mike. Very fine.'

Mike points out a few more 'beauties', as he calls them, then turns to Peter and asks: 'You been into this long?'

'Three or four years now, it would be. You?'

Mike sniffs. "'Bout the same.'

'I particularly like this one,' Steven says in his prim manner, and they talk for a while about the play of light and the distinctive style, the use of drapery and props, the varying compositions. I am only mildly shocked at their shared interest in Victorian nudes. More pressing than their fetish is the pain I feel in the backs of my knees and the base of my spine, aching from the effort of keeping still. I peer down at the stiletto heels on my feet and bitterly regret not kicking them off when I had opportunity to do so.

'How many of these are your own?' Mike asks, and Steven answers for his friend:

'Oh, these are all Peter's.'

'Seriously?' Mike sounds impressed.

'That's right,' Peter admits modestly.

'I thought I recognized the backdrop.'

'The backdrop?' Steven laughs. 'Earlier this evening, we met the model! Didn't we, Peter?'

Instantly, I forget the pain in my legs.

'Back in the hall,' he goes on. 'Girl in a blue dress. I didn't recognize her with her clothes on, did I, Peter?' He laughs and takes a swig of his whiskey. Bile surges up my throat. I see Peter rubbing the side of his face, a slight tremble along his back and shoulders, and I realize with horror that he is laughing, too.

'Seriously? This one?' Mike says, stabbing a finger at the picture on the desk. 'Where'd you find her? Where'd you find any of them, for that matter?'

'Most of them are local girls,' Peter explains, 'but this one is a friend of my daughter's.'

Mike whistles through his teeth. 'Bit risky, don't you think?'

Peter's voice when he speaks sounds suave, unfazed. 'She wanted it.'

My hands are crushed against my face. I am scream-ing inside – *no, no, no!*

The others laugh, and Mike murmurs: 'Dirty girl,' Steven reaching around to give the smaller man a dig.

'Just your type, eh, Mike?' he sniggers.

'Sweet little buds,' he jokes, and drops his heavy weight on to the captain's chair that has been pushed to one side of the desk. He swings it around so I can see his face – red-cheeked, overfed, pompous. I hate this man. I have never felt such visceral hatred in all my life. It floods my limbs. I am heavy with it.

'Here, what's this?' Mike asks, reaching for some-thing in the back of the desk, something squirrelled away in a cubby-hole.

'Don't touch that,' Peter says, but Mike ignores him, and I can see the gun in his hand. A small pistol, ornate and neat, like something a lady might have kept in her handbag generations ago.

After a surprised instant, Steven lets out a honk of laughter, and says: 'Is that how you get the ladies to undress? Point a gun at them?'

'Give that here,' Peter says, taking the gun with

irritation and returning it to its place. 'It's just a prop,' he adds, and Mike eyes him carefully.

'Looks real to me.'

'So are you interested in making a purchase or not,' Peter says testily. The incident with the gun has left him flustered.

I remember stories Rachel has told about how her father, driven to distraction by the raucous noise of crows outside in the trees, has been known to throw open the window and start firing indiscriminately at the branches with a pistol. I know that it is not a prop.

'How much are you looking for?' Mike asks, and the horse-trading begins.

Behind the shelter of the canvas, I listen to them haggle, and something hardens within me. Humiliation is too small a word for what I feel. I am swamped in shame. I am torn apart by it.

'Are these the only copies?' Mike asks. He seems to be the only one buying. Steven is the middle-man in this shady triumvirate.

'There are others.'

'How many?'

'I've made three copies of most. These ones here are for sale. My own I keep up at the house.'

'Got them framed and hanging on the walls?' Mike asks, and Steven sniggers.

'Not exactly,' Peter replies, smooth and polite.

'I take my hat off to you, Peter. If I could bottle your

charm and sell it, I'd be a rich man. Well, a richer man,' Steven says.

They reach their agreement, and Steven hauls his weight out of the chair and comes to examine which of the pictures Mike has chosen – what lucky few get to occupy his lustful gaze. He murmurs his approval and, while Peter shuffles the photographs into neat groups, I hear Steven say to Mike:

'You didn't go for Peter's little friend, then, eh?' and he laughs, and so does Mike, but when Peter doesn't join in, Steven elbows him. 'What's this? I think I've touched a nerve! Steal your heart, did she?'

My breath catches in my chest. My heart thuds madly.

The answer when it comes is crushing. 'Not at all,' he says, in a manner that suggests boredom. 'If anything, she was a disappointment.'

'Do tell!'

Airily, he says: 'Girls of that age – you know what they're like. Dying to shrug off the remnants of childhood, eager to be transformed into sexual beings. This one, God love her, was the inexperienced type. Interested in sex but terrified of it, too. A prudish streak. But they're always the ones who are the most eager and willing once they've shed their qualms. She marched in here one day, had worked herself up into a state, practically shaking, that's how desperate she was to declare herself a woman – an object of desire. Asks me to photograph her. Then out she struts, head held high – regal. Like the Queen of Sheba.'

'And you?'

'Well, my heart kind of sank. I mean there's only so much you can do with light and shadows. I humoured her, of course. Gave her the full session. Told her a lot of guff about beauty and art and revering the naked human form.'

'And she bought it?' Mike sounds faintly disgusted. Behind the canvas, I am fighting waves of nausea and shame.

'Young girls,' Peter says, then adds with finality: 'If it's what they want to hear, they'll buy anything.'

Grief, shame, anger – it all comes at me in bilious waves. What a stupid little fool I have been! To think he liked me – to think he cared about me! That we understood each other. That we shared something precious that has now been cheapened and coarsened beyond all hope of repair.

'Peter!' a voice calls from outside – a female voice.

They all jump at the sound, as if jolted by electricity. I, too, feel panicked, here in my hiding place.

'Oh, God,' Steven says.

Peter shuffles the pictures into a pile, saying: 'Quick.'

The door opens, and I can see the white turban, the gold dress.

'There you are! I've been looking for you everywhere!' Heather exclaims. She remains outside, leaning into the doorframe. 'Come back to the house. The Hadleys are leaving.'

She waits in the doorway, and all three file out,

taking their drinks with them. I hear the door close, the lock turn, the crunch of feet over the ground outside. Then, silence.

It takes a few minutes for my breathing to return to normal, for the stiffening in my limbs to ease off enough for me to move. I creep out from my hiding place, cast my gaze around the room, changed now for ever – cheapened by all I've heard. In their haste to leave without Heather interfering, they have left the desk lamp on, the roll-top pulled back, and I feel myself drawn towards it. I can't not look. Not now. Not with all I know.

One by one, I spread them out on the desk in front of me. Teenage girls, young women, different shapes and sizes, different-coloured hair. I find my picture among them, just another collection of flesh and features jumbled together into a silly pose. I thought I was special. I thought I was making a bold statement. Now all I see is the enormity of my folly. I look at my image in the photograph. How ridiculous I look. How ridiculous I am. Too ridiculous to live, to carry on. My thoughts narrow to a tunnel. Already, the emotion is flattening out inside me, steadied by the knowledge of what I must do. It is the only thing I can do now. I reach into the cubby-hole, and feel my fingers wrap around the gun.

Strange the way it happens. I seem to be floating outside my body, like my spirit has flown out of me, already parting with my corporeal form. I am a bird perched high up on the rafters, looking down at Lindsey as she crosses the room. I watch her as she lies down on the sofa, pushed beyond all endurance, a strange sound coming from her – strangled sobs heaving in her chest, a pained noise emanating from deep within. She lies there, quivering in her blue dress with the rust-coloured bloom across the bodice. 'I am nothing,' she whispers to the room. 'Nothing.' She puts the pistol to her head. The liquid sobs and the unendurable pain mingle, rise in volume. She can take no more. That is the only thought that occupies her head. She doesn't see the door opening, she doesn't see him come in.

Her finger is wrapped around the trigger, poised to pull, when he finds her.

'Wait!' he cries out. 'What the hell are you doing?'

She opens her eyes, and what she sees is his face full of irritation and impatience, what she hears is his voice, cross and scolding. There is no love there, no affection or tenderness. He has brought her to this. He has ruined her.

He comes for the gun, but it flashes across her brain so clearly what she must do. What is real and what is imaginary? She feels like she has slipped into a dreamworld, but the gun is solid in her hand. When she pulls the trigger, the angry snapping sound of the hammer hitting the bullet is real to her ear, as is the sharp recoil of the gun in her hand. Real, like the smell of burning inhaled by her nose. Real, like the spray of blood on the white wall, small rivulets starting to run down over the chalky surface. Real, like the dull thud of his body hitting the ground. The dream-world melts away. She sits up, surveys the room. Blood pools around his head where it lies on the floor. But she does not scream or panic. She feels no fear. Instead, her body is growing calm, and still. The alcohol has all seeped away, and her head is clear. Her vision feels sharper than she has ever known it, like every detail of the room is imprinting itself on her mind, getting locked firmly into memory. She is consumed with a sense of deep calm and stillness, of perfect clarity. She feels safe. She feels alive in the world.

It is the first time she has felt this way. It will not be the last.

30

2017

On a clear, fresh September morning, I stand on the corner of Adelaide Road and wait. The silver birches behind me shiver in the breeze, and I look up to see their autumn leaves, brilliant yellow against a brittle blue sky, and feel a small lurch inside. Funny how colour affects me these days. I have difficulty with shapes, the blurred edges of things, but on a morning like this one, colour jumps out at me, vivid and assailing.

The traffic is loud coming over the bridge, but I don't have long to wait, and soon enough a white Range Rover pulls over to the kerb, causing a storm of honking. Opening the door and climbing in, I find Niall, smiling warmly.

'How's the eye?' he asks.

'On the mend,' I reply. For months now, I have worn a patch. It's a small price to pay, and I know I have been lucky.

'Good,' he says, and we shoot the breeze while he drives. I ask him does he see anything of Liv now, and he shakes his head, no. I had wondered if he might reconcile with Claire, his wife, but instead he cheerfully announces that he's back on Tinder. I tease him about repetitive strain injury to his thumb and we bat mild insults back and forth at each other, but underneath the levity lies a strained air. He is as nervous about going back there as I am.

A couple of weeks ago, Niall had called me out of the blue. He had heard from a contact in the construction industry that Thornbury was about to be demolished. 'Any chance you want to wander back there for one last look around?'

His tone had been speculative, but I was touched by his thoughtfulness – uncharacteristic for Niall, it has to be said – that he would hear the news and think of me. I think I said yes because of that, more than any desire to relive the past, or lay old ghosts to rest. Also, it offered a break from the tedious business of treatment and recovery.

In the days following that awful night, I had undergone surgery to remove the tumour. Another operation in recent weeks sought to repair the damage done to the optic nerve. My vision still hangs in the balance, although Professor Puri is quietly confident. In the meantime, as I wait, I occupy a sort of limbo. Not an invalid, I am nonetheless unable to work. I cannot drive a car or take a photograph. I cannot read a book, and even television can be exhausting. I spend a lot of my time sleeping. With half my vision gone, it feels like my equilibrium has been dangerously upset. I am neither here nor there but, as we leave the city and hit the

M50, none of that seems to matter. I have an unsettling sense of déjà vu, and remember with a pang that, the last time I took this journey, it was Marcus at the wheel.

'I rang Hilary,' Niall tells me. 'Asked her if she wanted to come with us.'

I turn my head to look at him with my good eye. 'And?'

He makes a face and shakes his head, no. 'Said she'd rather stick hot needles in her eyes than go back there. Said the best thing they could do is torch the place and she only wished someone had done so sooner.'

'I suppose it's understandable that she feels like that.'

'She's doing all right, under the circumstances.'

The circumstances being surviving a bullet to the neck. An inch to the side and she'd have been paralysed. A couple of inches higher and she'd have been dead. 'As it is,' she had told me, bravely making a joke of it in the aftermath of surgery, 'I'll just have to wear polo-necks for the rest of my life.'

'She's got a new boyfriend,' Niall informs me. 'Some New Ager she met at a healing event.' He can barely hide his scorn.

'Sounds like Hilary's type,' I say, but Niall snorts.

'She'll probably have to be de-programmed in a few months' time.'

Underneath his tone, I sense relief. Relief that she has survived. There are only three of us left. The others are gone to their separate places of rest. Fifty-fifty, we have been cleaved down the middle.

Is it chance that separated us – those who survived? I feel that it is. When my thoughts return, as they often do, to that moment with the gun to my temple, and Rachel's breath hot on my face, I am convinced by the notion that it was luck that saved me. Luck that stayed her hand for just that small fragment of time, enough for me to summon a last reserve of strength and grab her wrist. When the gun went off, and I heard the loud crack of it, and felt the startling splatter of blood in my face, I was sure in that moment that it was me who had been hit. Darkness can be merciful, and I was glad of it then – glad that I didn't see her face when the bullet hit, relieved I didn't have to look in her eyes as the light faded from them. Chance was all it was that allowed me to stagger out of her bedroom that night, while she was left behind.

Niall exits the ring road on to the M7, where the traffic is lighter, and he can press down the accelerator. Our conversation has petered out, both of us lost in our own private contemplations, and I wonder is he returning to thoughts of that night, too?

Twice I have cheated death, and both those times were at Thornbury. Most recently, my struggle against Rachel, but there was the first time, all those years ago, when I came so close to taking my own life. Outside the car window, wispy clouds float suspended in an azure sky but, inside my head, storm clouds gather. I think about those moments after the gun went off, those intense moments of clarity when Peter lay sprawled on the ground, blood spilling from his head and seeping into the floorboards. I knew he was dead, and that I had killed him. I also knew what I had to do to survive. I wiped the gun clean on my dress, and then I bent to put it in his hand, still warm as I wrapped the fingers around the weapon. I almost expected them to twitch. I made it look like a suicide, and I thought there was a certain irony in that, for it had almost been a suicide – *my* suicide. But why should I let what he had done kill me? Instead, I chose to kill him and save myself.

Even now, when I look back on it, I am amazed at my own sangfroid. How calm I was when I put the gun in his hand! The stillness inside me as I turned to the desk and shuffled through the photographs until I found those of me, plucked them from the collection, and tucked them into the bodice of my dress. The only moment I had of panicked indecision was when it came to the remaining photographs, whether to leave them scattered there upon the desk for whoever found the body, or to take them, too, destroy them along with the pictures bearing my own image? And then an idea came to me. Among the various detritus littering the desk was a large blank envelope. I scooped up the photographs and dropped them into this envelope, sealed it, and picking up a pen, I wrote the name *Heather* on the front, making my handwriting blocky and plain in the manner of Peter's own hand. It was as close as I could get to faking a suicide note – evidence of his perversion, as good a reason as any for taking his life, the shame involved. I slotted the envelope into a book, partially hidden, and imagined Heather coming upon it later when searching through the desk for some kind of note, an explanation. I imagined her tearing it open and all those pictures spilling out. The whole time I was doing this, he was lying on the floor, his lifeblood seeping out of him.

I knew I had to get out of there before anyone found me. At the door, I took one last look, and there was such perfect stillness in the room, the shape of his body on the wooden boards, the light catching in the darkening pool of his blood. I know I should have been frightened by it, repulsed even. But instead I found a kind of beauty there. Later, when the body was discovered, I knew people would come pouring into the room, cluttering it with their physical presence and their raw emotions, and the whole business of medics and police investigations would kick in. But for just that moment, the room held the light and stillness with a soft, forgiving air. I had the most unexpected longing to preserve the image – to photograph him.

Was it a perversion? Was it, in its own way, akin in its depravity to Peter's dark desires for capturing on celluloid the young female body? Whatever you might call it, it was not enough to keep me there. I went out into the night, back to where the party was still swinging. I picked up a half-full glass of wine that someone had abandoned, and walked out on to the lawn feeling extraordinarily contained and clear in my thoughts. I laughed and drank and danced with the others, and when the screaming started, like the others, I turned to look. I followed the shouting along with everyone else. I stood among that gathering of people around the stables as the sirens came screaming up the avenue and the whispers of rumours rippled through the crowd, knowing in my heart what had happened. And when the news was imparted to me in tones of hushed disbelief, I acted like I didn't believe it either. I feigned shock, then distress. I think in those hours as night segued to dawn, I managed to convince myself that I was just like everyone else there, another guest dismayed and horrified by the sudden death of our host. The word *suicide* was mentioned and I latched on to it, ready to believe in it, just like everyone else. For those few hours, I managed to convince myself that I had not been there in the room with him, that I had not watched him die.

There was no mention of photographs found – not that night, or any other time. But I have often wondered what Heather did when she discovered them. Did she share them with the police as evidence – a reason behind her husband's suicide? Or did she keep them to herself, and in so doing did she unwittingly draw suspicion of her own possible involvement in his death? I have returned to this thought over and over again in the intervening years. More often than not, I reach the same conclusion: that she destroyed the photographs, burying the knowledge of them deep within her subconscious, protecting her children and preserving the family name. But in her last days, with the tumour gnawing through her brain, did the memory of those indecent pictures come bubbling to the surface? Might she have let slip, in among the ramblings of her troubled mind, some hint or clue as to the images that haunted her, and the knowledge of her beloved husband's depravity? And did she know that all those years there were replicas of the very same pictures she had destroyed hanging, hidden, on the walls of her house? Peter's little joke. In a way, he had the last laugh.

When we reach Thornbury, the granite pillars are no longer there. Replaced by iron-mesh gates, we can see beyond that the avenue has been widened – the foliage flanking the dirt road severely cut back, deep track-marks in the mud from the traffic of heavy machinery. The gates have been left open and, as Niall turns the car into the avenue, I hear him suck in his breath and feel my own body bracing itself. But before we are even within sight of the house, our car is stopped by a builder in a hard hat and yellow jacket. Niall rolls down the window.

'Can't let you through, I'm afraid,' he tells us.

'We're old friends of the family,' Niall explains. 'We just wanted to come and take one last look at the place.'

'Sorry, bud, only authorized personnel allowed on site.'

But Niall persists, adopting a genial, chummy tone, saying we won't take long, that we're not looking to gain access to the house.

'The house is gone, bud,' the builder says, and for a moment, neither of us can speak.

Niall recovers himself, but his voice sounds a little less confident.

'Already? I thought it wasn't due for demolition for another week.'

'No, no. They brought it down a few days ago.'

Niall gets out of the car, closing the door behind him, and the two of them talk. I can't hear what they're saying, I can just make out Niall's wheedling tone, and after a few minutes, he claps the builder on the shoulder, returns to the car, and the man waves us through.

'We've half an hour, tops,' Niall says.

Trees and rhododendrons have been cut away, uprooted, a clearing made for the machinery, and when the car emerges from the avenue, I find myself leaning forward, staring, astonished. The wide expanse of lawn is now completely overgrown. Ragwort and nettles have broken out in a patchy rash through the long yellow grass, the sycamore has been felled, and halfway up the lawn a hoarding has been erected. And there it is – the shocking absence. The complete erasure of the house. My good eye stares, fixed on the space, but I can hardly take it in. The hoarding snakes around the void, and I am assailed by the shock of it. Astonishing to be so confronted by a deep pocket of space, trees revealed in the distance. All that sky! There are warning signs on yellow placards alerting trespassers to the dangers present, along with signage advertising the construction companies at work here, and above it all, a giant crane rises, several diggers clawing at the rubble, a mound of it visible to one side. The noise of industry clamours in the air.

Niall stops the car, and we get out, walking the short distance up the driveway to the fence. Dust fills the air. The gravel sweep has been partially denuded by the frequent traffic of heavy vehicles and even though the place teems with noise and activity, there is an eeriness about it – the enormity of the void looming in front of us.

Niall looks dispirited.

'You'd swear no one had ever lived here,' he remarks.

'I know.'

His shoulders slump. With his hands in his pockets, he looks around him. 'So, what do you want to do?'

With no house, there are only the grounds to be walked, and we agree to split up and meet back in half an hour. Niall wants to return to the wheat fields, where Marcus fell, and I have the sense that he means it as a private, meditative act, a way of saying goodbye one last time to his friend, so I let him go alone. Besides, there is somewhere else I want to see.

The big house is gone, but the outbuildings – the stables and the studio, the little house where Patrick had intended to live – these remain. Even though they stand outside the perimeter fencing, there is an uninhabited, abandoned air to them, windows boarded up, heavy padlocks on the doors. The original plan had been to retain this part of the property along with some of the farmland, but now that there is no one left, the whole estate has been parcelled up and sold off.

The sunlight falls on the horseshoe of low buildings and I step up to the place where Peter's studio was. I have no camera with me today. It is months now since I have held a camera in my hand – not since the night of the killings. There was a time when the absence of my camera when visiting a place like this would have felt like a missing limb, but now I can imagine a future where I never take a photograph again.

The door to the studio is locked and, through a gap in the boards, I try to peer in with my good eye. Light filters through the crack, falling in a beam across the wooden floor. That is all I can see. I am reminded of the morning I went to him, when he closed the shutters and locked the door and I stepped out from behind the backdrop into that artificially lit space, feeling like I had shed a skin – as if I had willingly shrugged it off. I think back to that pocket of time when it was just the two of us together and, although he was a distance from me, behind the camera, although he never laid a finger on my body, it felt charged and intimate – the most erotic experience of my life.

And when it was over, when I again went behind the backdrop and put my clothes back on, when I came out to find he'd switched the light off and opened the shutters, the daylight streaming in, I thought that something of that intimacy would remain. That there would be a look or a smile, words spoken to recognize and maintain the charge between us.

He was sitting at his desk, his back to me, writing in his book. He turned to look at me, and gave me a rueful smile, not exactly regretful, but there was a kind of sadness in it that I felt related to my loss of innocence.

'You mustn't tell anyone what we did here today,' he said gently.

'I won't.'

'People wouldn't understand,' he reasoned softly.

'I would never tell . . . I promise.' And even though he was considerate in the way he spoke, I was nudged by the feeling that something had been taken from me, some promise exacted that I had not wished to make.

He smiled and got to his feet, holding his arms wide. I stepped into his embrace, the side of my face pressing into the warmth of his chest. And despite what had passed between us in this room, there was nothing sexual about the hug. More, it was a return to what we had once been, only it was stronger now. A bond not of blood but of mutual understanding. I was again the daughter he never had. He must have shared the thought for, as he drew back, still holding on to my upper arms, he looked deep into my eyes and said:

'You mean a great deal to me, Lindsey. You mean a great deal to this family. I hope you know that.'

I hardly knew what to say, embarrassed by the colour I felt rushing to my cheeks. I began to stammer a response, but the words were overtaken by a gust of emotion – a sudden squall brought to life by the sympathy he had shown.

'What is it?' he asked, concerned. 'What's happened?'

'We had a fight,' I said, the words coming out thick and wet.

'Who? You and Rachel?'

I nodded furiously, overwhelmed by the tears that wouldn't stop. All the hurt, the anger I had felt towards her, had faded to the background, replaced now by sadness. I felt it as a loss.

'She hates me—'

'No, she doesn't!' he protested, laughing at the vehemence of my statement.

'She does! She doesn't want me around any more. I don't think I'll ever be back here.' As soon as I said it, I realized that it was true, and with those words I understood the meaning of my loss.

'Look,' he said, adopting a patient, reasoning tone, 'so Rachel's got her knickers in a knot about something or other. She'll snap out of it, and then the two of you will be right as rain, and all of this silliness will be forgotten.'

I felt his amusement, his easy belief that things would be restored with little fuss, infuriating. He had no idea. No clue.

'You think it's all so easy, don't you?' I said, my voice cool, my emotions mastered. It made him look at me anew, this change in tone.

'Well, why ever would it not be? Friendships like yours are not easily broken.'

He spoke so softly, warmth and care in his voice. I could hardly bear it.

'It's not that simple. Things change.'

'What things? Tell me, Lindsey. Tell me what has happened.'

His voice – the velvety softness of it. I felt him pulling me towards it, luring me, almost as if he was the one guarding the secret while I was the one leaning in close, trying to glimpse it.

'She's pregnant.'

The word was released into the room. It softly detonated like a tiny powder bomb. His face registered dismay, his mouth dropping open slightly, but no noise escaped it. The room seemed eerily quiet.

I told him then about the secret box hidden in her bedroom. About the note from Ridgeway, along with a pregnancy test I had found. I told him how she planned to keep the baby. How intent she was upon keeping it. He listened to me, wordlessly taking everything in. And then, when it was finished, he closed his eyes and brought his hand up to briefly shield his face from my gaze. And in that gesture, I read his shock and his sadness, his dread at the path opening out before him, and just for a moment, I felt a wavering indecision.

'Thank you,' he said softly.

And I retreated from the room, leaving him there alone, like a wounded bear, to nurse his injury.

And then I walked away. I don't think I felt bad about it. Not then. He deserved my honesty – that is what I believed. And Rachel, too, would thank me for it, in the long run. I didn't recognize it as a betrayal, too wrapped up in the deluge of emotions inside me as I strode back to the house.

It was not until later that evening, when I sat alone on the train, looking out the windows at the fields flying past, a tunnel rearing up abruptly so that all at once my own face was reflected back at me, that it hit me. My hand instantly went to my mouth. *My God*, I thought. *What have I done?*

A shadow of that feeling comes to me now – the creep of conscience over an old betrayal – and I push myself away from the building, walking fast as if to shake the feeling off, anxious to put distance between me and what I have done.

Niall is waiting for me in the car. In his hands is a glossy brochure and, as I sit in next to him, he passes it to me. There are pictures of brand-new houses, brick and rendered facades, zinc-clad bay windows, cobble-locked driveways. The houses are all named after trees – Oak, Maple, Sycamore – and there are tasteful descriptions in the syrupy language employed by estate agents to sell these units.

'How many houses do you think they'll build?' I ask.

Niall stares back at the building site. 'Eighty? A hundred? Who knows, maybe more. Why? Interested in buying one?'

'No.'

He gives a shiver. 'Don't see how anyone's going to

buy, once they learn of what happened here.' He puts the key in the ignition.

'What? Scared the land is haunted?' I tease, but he shoots me a look, closed and bullish.

'You're the one that kept hearing noises.'

And all at once, I hear Rachel in my head. Her sinuous voice, her glassy stare: *There are no such things as ghosts, Lindsey. It's just your own guilty conscience.*

'I don't believe in ghosts,' I say quietly.

But this is not strictly true. For while I don't believe in spirits roaming houses, I know now that the voices of the dead can haunt you. Their whisperings echo inside my head.

I don't say this to Niall. I can't read his expression, his eyes lost behind reflective shades, his jaw set. Whatever business he's had here is done.

'Ready?' he asks, taking a last glance at the bright space where the house had stood. But there is nothing of it left – no earthly reminder of the people who had lived here and how they had met their fate – and perhaps, I think, that is a good thing.

'Ready,' I tell him, gripping the seat beneath me with both hands, refusing to look back, as we take off in a roar of grit and gravel.

Acknowledgements

This book has been a team effort in many ways, and we are deeply grateful to the following: Jonathan Lloyd, and everyone at Curtis Brown, in particular Lucia Walker, Melissa Pimentel and Luke Speed; Maxine Hitchcock and Clare Bowron, and the team at Penguin UK / Michael Joseph; thanks too to our dear friend, Tana French, for her advice and support; finally Aoife Ni Dhornain and Conor Sweeney whose patience, love and humour kept us going throughout the writing of the novel.